William Rufus Chetwood, William Johnson

The Voyages, Dangerous Adventures and Imminent Escapes of Capt. Richard Falconer

Intermixed with the voyages and adventures of Thomas Randal. Sixth Edition

William Rufus Chetwood, William Johnson

The Voyages, Dangerous Adventures and Imminent Escapes of Capt. Richard Falconer
Intermixed with the voyages and adventures of Thomas Randal. Sixth Edition

ISBN/EAN: 9783337343583

The Author revenges the Death of his Indian Wife, by killing Two of the Three Indians that attack'd them P. 208.

THE

VOYAGES,

DANGEROUS

ADVENTURES,

AND IMMINENT

ESCAPES,

OF

Capt. RICHARD FALCONER.

CONTAINING

The Laws, Cuſtoms, and Manners of the *In-dians* in *America*; his Shipwrecks; his marrying an *Indian* Wife; his remarkable Eſcape from the Iſland of *Dominico*, &c.

Intermixed with

The VOYAGES and ADVENTURES of *THOMAS RANDAL*. of *Cork*, Pilot; with his Shipwreck in the *Baltick*, being the only Man that eſcaped; his being taken by the *Indians* of *Virginia*, &c. and an Account of his Death.

Bold were the Men who on the Ocean firſt
Spread their new Sails, when Shipwreck was the worſt.
More Danger now from Man alone we find,
Than from the Rocks, the Billows, or the Wind.
WALLER.

The SIXTH EDITION, Correcƭed.

To which is added, A Great DELIVERANCE at *SEA*, by *W. Johnſon*, D. D. Chaplain to his Majeſty.

LONDON:

Printed for G. KEITH in *Gracechurch-ſtreet*, and F. BLYTH, No. 87. *Cornhill.* 1769.

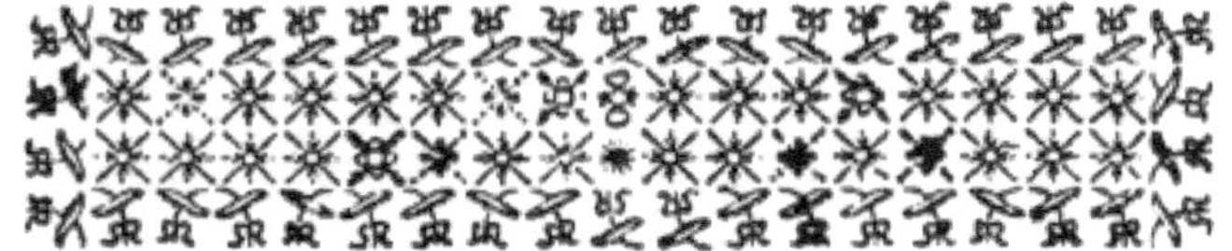

THE

PREFACE

To the Fourth EDITION.

'TIS in Compliance with Sir *Roger L'Estrange*'s Maxim, " That a " Man had as good go to Court " without a Cravat, as appear in Print without a Preface;" that I give the gentle Reader any Interruption of this Kind; for to be plain with him, the Book itfelf, as full of Misfortunes as it is, is but a Preface to the Misfortunes I have met with fince its firft Publication, which I muft freely confefs are wholly owing to the Bent of my own head-ftrong Inclination, in not taking my Father's Advice at my firft fetting out into the World.

This

This fourth Appearance indeed, is, I can't help owning, a Pleasure to me, tho' it is much more owing to the Candour of the Public, than the Merit of the Performance.

The Age of Gallantry I observe, seems to roll round again, for certainly Plays, Novels and Romances, were never more in Vogue that at this Juncture. And as to those who have a more refined Taste for Masquerades, Operas, and Grotesque Entertainments, this good Town is fully convinced, that Dr. *Fauſtus* from *Germany*, now vies with our Countryman Mrs. *Robinſon* at the *Haymarket*; that Mr. *Leveridge*, as a Devil, has more Admirers than Signiora *Cuzzoni*; and that *Heydegger* has a much greater Number of Pollers, than the laudable Society established for Reformation of Manners. These latter Gentlemen are, if Dr. *South* may be credited, arrant Hypocrites; for that learned Divine honestly tells us, That instead of making Godlineſs a Gain, they make a Gain of Godlineſs: So much for Politeneſs.

nefs. But at the fame Time it muſt be confeſſed, that it is very rueful to behold the
Quill-drivers of the prefent Age, fo egre-
giouſly triumphant over thoſe of the laſt;
for now *Shakeſpear* and *Ben Johnſon*, muſt
give way to *Robinſon Cruſoe*, and Colonel
Jack; as well as *Dryden* and *Otway* to
Moll Flanders, and *Sally Saliſbury*: And I
myſelf am terribly afraid, that the Voyages
and Adventures of Captain *Richard Falconer*, muſt in a ſhort Period of Time, ſtrike
to Sir *John Mandeville*'s lying Travels, and
Mademoiſelle *Beleau*'s unheard of Intri-
gues. Tho' I have ſtill fome Confolation
in my Hopes, that this fourth Edition,
wherein many Errors of the Preſs that eſcaped in the former, are correĉted, will
come to a fifth, and fo on.

To conclude, if Mr. *Dennis*, or any
other Critick of Renown, ſhall think fit
to fall foul on me, to fuch I ſhall only reply, in the Words of the fame Gentleman
with whom I began this Preface: " Thoſe
" that don't like my Book may let it
" alone, and there's no Harm done. "

V A L E.

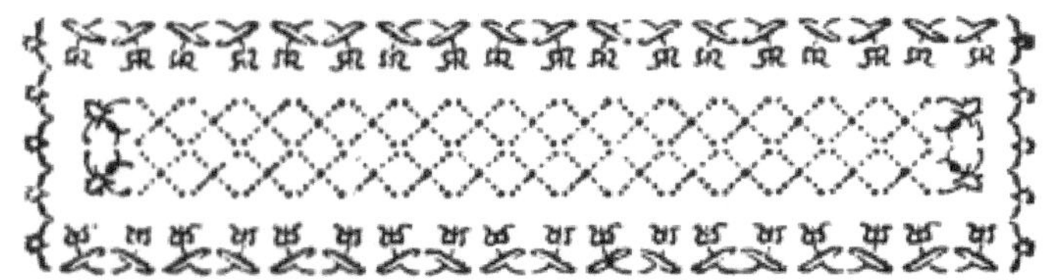

THE

VOYAGES

AND

ADVENTURES

OF

Captain Richard Falconer.

I WAS born at *Bruton*, a Market Town in *Somersetshire*, of Parents tolerably well to pass in the World; my Mother died when I was very young: my Father, *Richard Falconer*, had been a great Traveller in his Youth, and frequently repeating his Adventures abroad, made me have a great Desire to follow his Steps: I often begged he would let me go

to Sea with fome Captain of his Acquaintance; but
he would reply, *Dick*, ftay where you are, you
know not the Hazards and Dangers that attend a ma-
ritime Life: You fhall have a good Trade in your
Belly, and that will keep you from a Defire of ram-
bling; therefore tell me what Calling you like beft,
that I may immediately put you out in Order to your
living hereafter: You know, continued he, that my
Fortune is but fmall, and I living to the Extent of
it, it will not be poffible for me to leave you wherewithal to fupport you without fome Employment.
Therefore, (replied I,) as you have a Daughter, you
may leave your Subftance to her, fhe muft be provided for; as for our Sex, we can beft take Care
for ourfelves; and if you pleafe but to fit me out
to Sea, even in what Station you think convenient, it fhall be all I will defire. Son, (faid my
Father) think no more of going to Sea, for I'll not
have it fo; I know it is only a Defire of Youth
prone to change: If I fhould give you Leave, I am
affured one Week's Voyage would make you wifh to
be at Home again. I ufed all the Arguments my
young Senfe prompted me with, but all to no Purpofe, my Father was not to be moved; and thus I
lived two Years longer with him in Expeétation of
his Mind altering. At laft an Accident happened
that furthered my Defires, and tho' it was the Ruin
of our Family, I muft confefs, I was not much
concerned.

My Father was Supervifor of a Tax laid upon the
Burning of Pipes, and he having gathered a Sum of

Money,

Money, amounting to 3800*l.* in Order to pay in to the Government for the King's Use, was, by an under Excise-man robbed of the whole Sum, who made his Escape. My Father used all possible Means to apprehend him without Noise, but all his Endeavours were fruitless: So finding his Affairs in a desperate Condition, resolved to retire to some Part of the World where he might be safe from the griping Hands of the Law. One Morning, just before his voluntary Exile, he called me to him: *Dick*, (said he) you have been often desirous of going to Sea, and I have always used Arguments to dissuade you from it; but now, since what has happened, it being impossible for me to continue upon the Place of my Birth, the Patrimony of my Ancestors, I must even recommend that Way of Life to you which I should never have chose, but that the Exigency of my Affairs will not permit me to provide any other Way for you. Here (continued he) take this 100*l.* which I can ill spare out of my little Fortune, but since it is all I can do for you, take it, and may Heaven prosper thy Undertakings; may the Blessing of a Father always live with you, whose Prayers shall ever be sent to our Almighty Creator for thy Welfare. Here (added he) is a Letter of Recommendation for you to Captain *Pultney* of *Bristol*, whose Friendship I am sure will be of Service to you. With that, he embraced me with Tears in his Eyes, gave me his Blessing, kissed me, and took his Leave for ever, for never have my Eyes beheld him since.

B 2

This

This Parting, I think, was the greateſt Grief my Thoughts had ever known till then; (for nothing could be fonder, or ſhew more paternal Affection, than my dear Father at his laſt Farewell) but the Joy of my being at Liberty to follow my own Deſires, ſoon drowned my Sorrow for parting with ſo good a Parent.

I had now nothing more to do, but to provide my little Equipage in order to go to *Briſtol*, to my Father's Friend; I packed up my Things in a Portmanteau, and gave them to an old Servant of my Father's, who would ſee me as far as *Briſtol* for his Sake. We ſet out in the Morning, and reached it by Noon: I enquired for Captain *Pultney*, and ſoon found him out. I acquainted him who I was, and gave him my Father's Letter. He read it, and received me very kindly. It was to this Effect:

Dear Pultney,

" **I** Hope you'll forgive this Trouble of your
" Friend. I have ſent my Son to you, in order
" to get him ſome Poſt by Sea, I know it is in
" your Power to do it: Something has happened that
" hinders my providing for him as I ought, I
" would have waited on you in Perſon, but a Gap
" has happened in my Affairs that I ſhall never
" cloſe again. *Dick* will tell you all. Let me
" conjure you by our old Friendſhip to take all
" the Care you can of him; and whenever he
" comes to *England*, let him come to you, for as
" yet I know not where to lead my wretched Life;

"   " ſo

" fo that I fhall confide in you, and let you know
" by a Letter, or Meffenger, as foon as poffible,
" where I fhall fettle.

Your moft faithful

Friend and Servant.

R. FALCONER.

Falconer, (faid the Captain) I am heartily
forry for your Father's Misfortunes, which he tells
me in his Letter you will inform me of. After I
had related to him every Circumftance, he told me
he would provide for me as foon as poffible, and till
then I fhould be as welcome to him as his own
Son: In the mean Time, faid he, I would have you
verfe yourfelf in the Mathematicks, which may be
of Ufe to you: I'll take Care to provide you a
Mafter, and Inftruments, which accordingly he
did; and as I had a great Defire to be abroad, and
had fome fmall Knowledge of it which I learned at
School, apart from my other Studies, I foon at-
tained to the Theory of it.

After I had run through the whole Courfe, and
the Captain was informed I was capable, he got me
to be Mate (or rather Affiftant) on Board the *Albion*
Frigate, Captain *Wafe* Commander: and on the fecond of *May,* 1699, we fet fail, (bound for *Jamaica*)
with a fair Wind. As foon as we loft Sight of Land,
I began to be extremely fea-fick, and bore the Jefts
of the Sailors but indifferently, who cryed, There's

an excellent Master's Mate, he'll hit *Jamaica* to a
Hair, if the Island were no bigger than the Bung-
hole of a Cask.   I must confess, I believe myself to
be the only Person who ever set out on his first
Voyage as Master's Mate, without having seen a
River that was navigable.   But in a Day or two I
was perfectly well, and was never troubled with
any Sickness afterwards.

We had nothing material happen'd to us till we
enter'd the Bay of *Biscay*, where we were encounter'd with a dreadful Storm ; the Billows ran Mountains high, and our Vessel seem'd to be the Sport
of the Waves : A Ship that overtook us the Day before, and accompany'd us, tho' it were not at half
a Furlong Distance, was sometimes lost, by Reason
of the Height of the Waves. The Storm continued
with this Violence three Days, and at last abated
something of its Fierceness, but still blew very hard.
The other Vessel, by firing a Gun, and making a
Signal, made it appear she was in Distress, but the
Sea ran so high it was impossible to give them any
Assistance, yet we bore down to them (being to
Windward) as nigh as we could without Danger to
ourselves; we enquir'd into the Matter, and found
she had sprung a Leak; they had all Hands to
pump by Turns, but yet the Water gain'd on them.
They begg'd of us to hoist out our Boat (their own
being stav'd) to give them Succour upon Occasion :
Accordingly we put out our Long-Boat, with two
of our Men in it, but the Rope that held her to the
Ship, broke by the Violence of the Waves, and
drove

drove away with the two unfortunate Men in her, and what became of them we could never learn; but undoubtedly they perish'd by the Sea, or Hunger, we being twenty Leagues from any Shore. The Ship, after prodigious Labour of the Sailors, and in less than ten Minutes, funk to the Bottom; out of fifty-feven Men, but four were fav'd, and they, by good Fortune, laid hold on Ropes we threw out for that Purpofe; but it had not been poffible to fave any, if we had not bore down to Leeward when we faw them in the laft Extremity. And here we ought to admire at Providence; for this very Veffel was a Pyrate, one Captain *Jones*, Commander, who in an open large Boat fet out from *Dover*, and, near *Oftend*, ftole upon a *French* Veffel in the Night, murdered the Captain and fome others, and fet all the Sailors afhore that would not embrace their Defigns, and had refolv'd to attack us as foon as the Storm was over. The four Men that were fav'd, were three *Englifhmen* and one *Frenchman*, who faid they were forc'd, with feveral others, by the above-mention'd Captain *Jones*, to take to that Courfe of Life; but whether true or falfe, I can't tell; indeed they behav'd themfelves very well with us all the Voyage, and were entered into our Books as four of the Ship's Crew, inftead of two we left on Shore, who were not to be found when we fet fail, and the two poor Wretches that were loft in the Boat. The Storm ftill continued, but the Wind fair, fo we ran it away with a riv'd Forefail all Night, and the next Morning we had a violent

Storm of Rain, and some Thunder, but about Noon
the Sky cleared up, the Rain ceased, and the Tempest
was laid; the Wind however continuing fair, with
a middling Gale.

May the 28th, we discovered the *Canaries*, and
the Peak of *Teneriff*, and passed this Island, or rather Rock, of a prodigious Height. At Night the
Wind rose again, and continued to blow very hard
for two Days. As I was walking on the Deck one
Morning, my Chops were saluted with a Fish which
dropped down; I took it up, panting at the Gills
for Life; it proved to be a flying Fish, pursued (as
I suppose) by some Dolphin, or Albacore; the Manner of these Fishes avoiding their Enemies, is jumping out of the Water, and flying till their Wings are
dry, then fall down again into the Sea. The Dolphin that chases them, is one of the finest coloured
Fishes that swims. I have observed our Painters
draw them bending like a Bow, but I think it is
as strait a Fish as any in the Sea. We caught one of
them with a Fizgig, an Instrument made of several
Rows of Iron Spikes, bearded like Hooks, and
a Staff four or five Feet long to it; to this they tie a
Cord of a great Length, and dart it with all their
Strength; the wounded Fish immediately flounces
downward many Fathoms, and up again, which the
Darter observes, giving him Rope and Play till his
Weakness makes him more tame: then they draw
him up the Ship's Side, and cut him in Pieces. The
first we caught in this Manner was about six Feet
long, which we dressed, and Part of it served the
whole Ship's Company for Dinner; as soon as it

was

was caught, it loſt that beautiful Colour it had in the Water; as for my own Part, notwithſtanding their praiſing it, I had rather eat a Herring or a Mackrel than this rare Fiſh.   I don't know whether theſe Fiſh can hear, or love Muſick, but this I am ſure of, we had an excellent Trumpet on Board, which diverted us in good Weather, and I have obſerved, that at the Sound of it, the Number of theſe Dolphins ſeemed to increaſe, and ſwim within two Feet of our Veſſel, but that may be pure Accident; yet I fancy there's ſomething in it, that occaſioned the Fable of *Amphion* and the Dolphin.   Sharks are taken as we take common Fiſh, only the Hook is about two Feet long, and an Iron Chain above that about four Feet long, and a long Rope to that; they generally bait the Hook with a Piece of Beef of three or four Pounds, which the voracious Fiſh ſwallows immediately, Hook and all; then they give him Play a while, and when he is pretty well ſpent, they draw him in with a Tackle: There's always one ſtands ready with an Axe to make a Divorce between his Tail and his Body, otherwiſe he would give ſuch large Thumps with it that might do the Ship Damage: I myſelf was thrown down but with a Touch of it.   This that we took, had in its Paunch the Collar-bone of a Man and a Boatſwain's Silver Whiſtle, with a red Ribbon in it, intire, not ſo much as bruiſed, which was given to me as a Preſent, to make me Amends for the Fall I received; it may be ſeen at my Bookſeller's, if any one has the Curioſity to aſk for it; as to the Collar-bone, not any one would accept of it, fo I return'd it to the watry Element again.

We paffed the *Tropick*, attended by the *Tropick-*Birds, a Fowl fomething bigger than a Pidgeon; but one would think, as it flies, it had an unlighted Candle fix'd in its Tail. I cannot let go the Ceremony of paffing this *Tropick*: When you are in the Latitude, the old Sailors afk the reft of the Ship's Crew, Whether they were ever that Way before? If not they muft either pay a Bottle and Pound, (as they call it) or be duck'd: They that don't pay, are fix'd to a Rope at the Main-Yard-Arm, and duck'd three Times in the Sea; at which the reft of the Crew Huzza! and fire a Volley of fmall Shot.

When Admiral *Bembow* went with his Squadron of Men of War, the whole Fleet duck'd, but the Admiral gave them Notice, by firft firing a Gun, which was immediately follow'd with a Volley of Muflets, and Huzzaing, by every Ship in the Fleet. A Day or two before our Account is out, we fend a Man to the Topmaft-Head, in order to difcover Land, where he ftays an Hour, and looks about him: He that difcovers it firft, is rewarded with a Bottle and Pound: that is, a Bottle of Rum and a Pound of Sugar, which is demanded as foon as the Anchor is caft in a Place where fuch Commodities are to be had. Now the Bottles and Pounds that accrue from the People that are not willing to be duck'd, in paffing the *Tropick*, are referv'd by the old Sailors for a merry Bout, when fafe in Harbour,

bour, which muſt not be touch'd by the freſh Men, as they call 'em.

July the third, our Man at the Topmaſt-Head, inſtead of crying Land, (as we expected) called out a Sail! a Sail! which, in a Quarter of an Hour, we diſcovered plainly upon Deck. We did not know what to think of it, we knew we were near Land, and conſequently in Fear of thoſe Pyrates, or Buccaniers, that infeſt thoſe Coaſts : Our Captain called all Hands aloft, and told us, Gentlemen, 'Tis One to one, but this Veſſel we ſee may be a Pyrate, if ſo, how muſt we behave ourſelves ? If you are reſolved to ſtand it, I'll ſtand it to the laſt ; if not, we'll ſurrender without firing a Gun, which may induce them to be civil to us. The Sailors cried, Let's fight 'em, let's fight 'em. With that we put our Cheſts into the Hold, and brought up our Hammocks, to place them in the Netting on the Quarter-Deck; we cleared our Guns, which were twelve, and muſtered our Men, which amounted to Thirty Eight, Paſſengers and all, who were as willing to fight as any of us, they having ſomething on Board that was valuable ; and ſome of them perhaps all their Fortune. We kept our Way, and the Ship bore up to us with all the Sail ſhe could make. Night coming upon us, our Man at the Topmaſt-Head diſcovered Land, and another Ship to the Windward of us. With that, we called another Council, and perſiſted in our firſt Opinion of fighting ; but yet to uſe all Means poſſible of making to Shore, (which was *Barbadoes*) : But for all our En-

B 6

deavours,

deavours, the firſt Ship got up with us, and about
Twelve o'Clock at Night hailed us, and commanded
us to hoiſt out our Boat, and to come on Board him,
with our Captain.   We anſwered, We had never a
Boat, (as indeed we had not) but we told him, if
he would ſtay 'till Morning, ſomething might be
done.   At laſt he threatened to ſink us, if we would
not ſend our Captain on Board immediately ; and
thereupon fir'd a Gun, which ſtruck our Veſſel on
her Quarter.   With that we fir'd our Broadſide
upon him, accompany'd with ſome ſmall Arms ;
which, they little expecting, I believe, did ſome
Damage, and put them in Confuſion.   Whereupon
we tack'd about, and with our ſix Guns rak'd her
fore and aft ; but was immediately ſeconded with
a Broad-ſide from them, which kill'd us two Men,
and wounded a third.   Upon which, with loud
Huzza's and Firing, they immediately boarded us on
our Starboard-Quarter, and poured into us at leaſt
fourſcore Men : We reſiſted them with all the Force
we had, but all to no purpoſe ; they drove us into
the Fore-caſtle, where, by good Chance, we made
ſhift to barricade ourſelves ; but they threaten'd to
turn our own Guns upon us, if we did not ſurrender immediately : But our Captain being reſolute, order'd us to fire upon them with our ſmall
Arms. Now we had under the Gratings, cloſe to
our Steerage, a large Ciſtern, lin'd with Tin,
where we had unwittingly plac'd ſeveral Carriages
of Powder, but happily for us, whether it was our
firing, or in the Buſtle ſome Match dropt in, I
know

know not, but the Powder took Fire, blew up the Gratings, with some Part of the Quarter-Deck, and Thirty of the Enemy, at least, into the Air. Upon that we sally'd out, and drove the rest, with our Cutlasses, into their own Vessel again, with the Loss of several. But this signified little, for with the Fall and Breach of our Quarter-Deck, the Powder-Room was intirely stopp'd up; nor could we, without great Difficulty, clear it from the Lumber, so that we had not any Powder, but what was in the Mens Cartouches, for their Muskets: However, we fir'd briskly with them; yet nevertheless they prepar'd to board us again, with all the Menaces imaginable. This Fight continued at least four Hours, and the Dawn began to break upon us, which discover'd to us the other Ship we saw over Night, and we distinguish'd *English* Colours; with that we gave a great Shout, and fir'd our small Arms again. The Enemy no sooner saw the Ship with *English* Colours, but they cut off their Grappling-Irons, and did their Endeavour to make off, but their Rigging was so shatter'd, that their Sails could not be hoisted. In the mean Time the other Ship came up to us, and, without hailing, pour'd a Broad-side into the Pyrate, and there follow'd a desperate Fight between them. As for our Ship, it was of little Use, so we steer'd off, and clear'd our Gun-Room, and in half an Hour (the Fight continuing all that while) we had charg'd our great Guns, and returned to the Fight; but upon the Instant we saw the Pyrate sinking; the

English

English Ship had tore a Hole between Wind and Water, that she sunk in a Moment, and but eight Men sav'd, who told us their Captain was a Pyrate from *Guadalupe*; that when they were sinking, they had not above twenty Men left, out of an hundred and sixty; and most of them wounded. The Ship that gave us this Reasonable rescue, was the *Guernsey* Frigate, whose Station was *Barbadoes*. We lay by for an Hour or two, to repair our Rigging, &c. and hail'd her, desiring them to send a Boat on Board for our Captain, because we were without one, which accordingly they did. Captain *Wase* and I went immediately on Board, to pay our Respects to their Commander, who receiv'd us with all imaginable Civility. We had on Board our Ship seven Sailors and two Passengers kill'd: the one *Joseph Ridge* of *Barbadoes*, and the other *Daniel Thompson* of *Mevis*, Merchant; and four wounded. The *Guernsey* had sixteen Men kill'd, and three wounded; among which was the Lieutenant, who died the same Day of a Wound he receiv'd in his Thigh, with a Musket Ball chew'd, which made the Wound mortal. The Captain invited us to dine with him, which we did; where we were treated with a new Dish, (at least to me) a *Pollo*, that is, Fowls boil'd with Rice and salt Pork; which was very palatable. We took our Leave of the Captain, and went on Board of our own Vessel, and at five o'Clock in the Evening (*July* the 4th), after saluting the Town, cast Anchor in *Carlisle* Bay.

Barbadoes,

Barbadoes, for its Bigneſs, is the richeſt and beſt peopled Iſland in all *America*; it is ſeated in thirteen Degrees, twenty Minutes ; in Length, twenty-four meaſur'd Miles, and in the broadeſt Part about ſixteen : It reſembles a Leg of Mutton, with the Knuckle off. The North and Eaſt Sides are fortify'd by Nature, from any Harm from Ships of War, by Reaſon there is no Anchoring Place. On the South-Eaſt and Weſterly Part, are four excellent, commodious, well-fortify'd Harbours. The chief is that where we now ride, which will contain a thouſand Sail of Ships, free from the Danger of any Winds. At the Bottom of this Harbour ſtands the Capital of the Iſland, call'd St. *Michael*'s ; with a Fort at each End, and a Platform in the Middle ; which makes it of Strength ſufficient to oppoſe a royal Navy : 'Tis a neat large Town, with two Churches, one with a handſome Organ : For Largeneſs, I think this Town may compare with our City of *Saliſbury*, but better inhabited. As for the other three, which are, 1. *Charles Town*. 2. *James's Town*. 3. *Little Briſtol* in *Spright's Bay*, I can give no Manner of Account of : But for my Reader's Satisfaction, if he will conſult *Legon's Hiſtory of Barbadoes*, he may come to the beſt Knowledge of the whole Iſland. They are govern'd by the ſame Laws as we in *England*. A Native of *Barbadoes* told me, the whole Iſland contain'd at leaſt 12000 Inhabitants, Slaves included.

July the 20th, (after our Captain had left his Paſſengers, and Part of his Cargo) we ſet Sail for *Jamaica :*

maica: Here you muft Note, that from *Barbadoes* to *Jamaica*, you always have the Wind in your Stern. We pafs'd *Martinico*, *Dominica*, *Guadalupe*, and *Antigua*, and the firft of *Auguft* anchor'd at *Nevis*, where we had immediately the Friends of Mr. *Daniel Thompfon*, Merchant, on Board us, to unlade the Goods; for they had heard of his Death, by a Veffel from *Barbadoes* a Week before.

Mevis, or *Nevis*, lies in feven Degrees, nineteen Minutes; it is fix Leagues in Circumference: There is but one Harbour in the whole Ifland, which fome call *Mevis* Harbour, or *Bath* Bay, where lies the Town, under the former Denomination. It is pretty well fecured with a Fort and Platform of great Guns. I was inform'd by one of the Inhabitants, that there is a Mineral Water, very good to bathe in, which cures the fame Diftempers with our *Bath* in *Somerfetfhire*.

The *Englifh* fettled here *Anno Dom.* 1628, and have increafed from one hundred and forty, to five thoufand and upward. They fend abroad as much Sugar, Ginger, Cotton, and Tobacco, as any Ifland of its Bignefs in the *Caribbees*. They are very regular in their Government here; they neither allow Drunkennefs, nor Whoring, (I mean in common, as in *Barbadoes*, *Jamaica*, *&c.*) Here I was firft faluted with a little Fly, call'd a *Mufketo*; and tho' it is fmall, yet it has a devilifh fharp Sting with it. They get into our Stockings, and are fo very troublefome to new Comers, that there's hardly any Bearing of them. If you fcratch the

Places.

Places stung by them till the Blood comes, it may prove dangerous; I myself kept a sore Leg three Months upon that Account. I was also inform'd there was a Flea they call *Chigoe*, which breed in Dust, or Ashes; and of all the Insects in the *Caribbees*, this is the most dangerous: they get into the Nails of the Toes imperceptibly, and from thence run over all the Body; tho' they chiefly fix themselves in the Bottom of the Feet: Which occasions an Itching, follow'd with Holes in the Skin. They make Blisters as big as Peas in the Flesh, where their young ones breeding, cause Ulcers and rotten Flesh, which there is no Remedy for, but to eat away the Parts affected with *Aqua-fortis* and burnt Alum. While we lay here, there was a Sword-Fish ran himself ashore, (which was suppos'd to be done in eagerly chasing some other Fish:) It had no Scales, but a dusky Skin, and a white Belly, rough like a Smith's File, a flat head, two Fins on each Side, two on the Back, and one instead of a Tail. It is a Fish of prodigious Swiftness: The Sword (which is fix'd in the Head) is six, seven, and sometimes eight Feet long: Near his Eyes are two Nostrils out of which he throws the Water a great Height into the Air. This Fish often encounters with the Whale, and proves too hard for him; for with his Sword he rips up the Whale. I bought one of these Swords of a poor Inhabitant, for four Bottles of *English* Beer, (which is a great Rarity with them) that he got in a Piece

of

of Wreck, but thruſt in ſo far, that the End in getting out, was broke three Inches.

Next to *Mevis*, lies St. *Chriſtopher*'s (or, as we generally call it St. *Kit*'s) in ſeventeen Degrees, and twenty-five Minutes, *Northward* of the Equinoctial. It is twenty five Leagues in Circumference, the Soil light and ſandy, and produces Fruit common with us in *England*. In the Middle of this Iſland riſes a high Mountain, from which run Streams of freſh Water, that ſometimes ſwell ſo high with ſudden Rains, that they drown all the Country near them. This Iſland is inhabited by both *Engliſh* and *French*, who even in the Time of War live very friendly together. There was formerly diſcover'd a Silver Mine here, which the *Engliſh* and *French* claim an equal Title to; but neither make any Uſe of it, by Reaſon of the Want of Miners. The *Engliſh* Liberties are better peopled than the *French*, but the *French* have more Conveniences, and better fortify'd Places than the *Engliſh*. An *Engliſh* Fryar belonging to the *French* Jeſuits, (who gave me this Deſcription) told me that the *French*, had built a Town, call'd *Baſſe Terre*, (in a Harbour of the ſame Name, and Chief in the Iſland) full as big as *Graveſend*, with very handſome Houſes, for the Merchants, and Trades People, which are many; where there is alſo an Hoſpital to maintain their indigent Sick, together with a handſome Free School, with large Endowments, for the Children of the Iſland. But what they moſtly brag of is, their Caſtle, which is built about a Furlong from the Sea, at the Foot of a

high

high Mountain, fhadow'd with great Trees. In the Way thither, ftand the Houfes of the Governor, and other Officers, for more Security; feated in a Walk of Orange and Lemon Trees, from the Brow of the Sea up to the Caftle; which is three Story high, built with Freeftone and Brick: The Halls and Chambers are very lightfome and high, and the Walls are adorn'd with Cedar; On the Top is a flat Terrace, which yields a delightful Profpect all over the Country. The Winds which blow from the Hills, fo temper the Heat, that it makes it more pleafant than any other Ifland of the *Caribbees*. As to the *Englifh* Plantations, they are not much inferior to the *French*; they have fix Churches, and two Chapels, for Divine Service. This Ifland was planted jointly by *Englifh* and *French*, in 1625. Captain *Thomas Warner*, for the *Englifh*, and one *Defnambuc* for the *French*. The Natives made a vigorous Refiftance, but to little Purpofe. With this Succefs they return'd back to their feveral Countries, and went again and fettled there; but the *Englifh* having more Supplies from *London*, daily encreafed; when on the contrary, the Merchants at *Paris* grew weary, feeing no Return for all the Charges they had been at. But whilft this Bufinefs feem'd to go on with Succefs, an Accident happen'd, which ruin'd all at once. The King of *Spain* fet out a Fleet the fame Year, of thirty one Galloons, three Galleafes, and four Pinnaces, with four Thoufand Men, under the Command and Direction of *Frederick de Toledo*, from *Cadiz*, *Antonia*, *Nunnes*, *Barrico*, *and Francifco de Almeida*, Commander of twenty Galleys, from *Portugal*;

gal; thefe join'd with the abovemention'd, with a
Refolution to drive the *Englifh*, *French*, and *Dutch*,
entirely out of the *American* Iflands. Coming before
Mevis, they took nine *Englifh* Veffels: After that they
fail'd to St. *Chriftopher's*, where Captain *Defnambuc*
(altho' not prepar'd for Defence, becaufe their Forti-
fications were not finifh'd) drew all his Forces near
the Shore, to hinder their landing: But Captain
Roffey, who commanded another Port, fuffer'd them
to land without the leaft Refiftance. Whereupon
young *Defnambuc*, Lieutenant of a Company under
Roffey, fally'd out, and fell valiantly on the firft Company of *Spaniards*, killing many of 'em, and put them
to the Rout; but the *Spaniards* being feconded by a-
nother Battalion, he was flain, after having made a
ftout Refiftance, and forfaken by all his Men. *Roffey*,
upon this, abandons his Intrenchments, and flies to
the Hills, and high Grounds: Whereupon the *Spaniards* became Mafters of the Forts, but durft not
follow *Roffey*, for Fear of an Ambufcade; which Fear
prov'd true: For *Defnambuc*, undermining the Fort,
retir'd on board fome Veffel prepar'd for that Purpofe,
and made off. In the mean Time, the Powder taking
Fire, blew up the Fort, and fix hundred *Spaniards*,
into the Air. The *Englifh* relying upon the League
between *Spain* and *England*, made no Refiftance, but
fent Agents to *Toledo*, *&c.* to put him in Mind of
the League between their Mafters: To which he reply'd, That St. *Chriftopher's*, being Part of the *Weftern*
World, was given by the Pope to his Mafter *Philip*.
Neverthelefs

Neverthelefs he gave them fix of the nine Veffels they took at *Nevis*, to imbark themfelves, on Condition they would fail immediately for *England*; which they agreed to; but the fix Veffels not holding all, the reft were left on the Ifland, for another Opportunity: No fooner was *Toledo* out of Sight, but the remaining Part of the *Englifh* Inhabitants took frefh Courage, and rebuilt feveral Forts, and made every thing ready for Defence, if Occafion fhould be. In the mean Time *Defnambuc* fuffered a great Deal of Hardfhip, through ill Weather, and Want of Provifion; having been at feveral Iflands, intending to fettle, with his little Company, but not liking any of them, and hearing that the Enemy were gone to the *Havana*, and the *Englifh* were bufy tilling their Ground, he return'd to his former Station, where they fuffered many Hardfhips; till fome Veffels from the *Netherlands* arrived, and furnifh'd them with Provifions, Ammunition, and Cloaths, upon Credit: But in a few Years they paid all, and grew rich, from their plentiful Stock of Tobacco, Sugars, Ginger, and Indico, till they brought it to the rich and flourifhing State it now remains in.

Having ended our Affairs, we fet Sail for *Jamaica*, the 21ft of *Auguft*, 1699; and, on the 7th of *September*, anchor'd fafe in *Port Royal* Harbour, in the great and flourifhing Ifland of Jamaica, without any Accident. This was our laft Station: Here we were to unlade the remaining Part of our Goods, and take in its Return, Rum, Sugar, and Spice.

This

This Island of *Jamaica* is the only Mart of all *America* for the *English*, who drive a large Trade here; but Wickedness is in its full Perfection; I remember Captain *Wase* afk'd one of our Men, that had fpent fome Money afhore, what was his Opinion of the Honefty of the Women of *Port Royal?* Why truly, fays *Tar*, very bluntly, if there's one honeft Woman fhould happen to tumble down, I believe there's never another to take her up. Provifion is prodigious dear here; two or three of us went on Shore to Dinner, one Day, at *Port Royal*, where we had only a roafted Turkey, wretchedly lean, and nothing nigh fo well tafted as our *English* Turkeys, and our Eating came to thirty Shillings; but then, to make amends, Money is plenty enough: We had a Sailor on Board, that had been a 'Taylor by Trade; this Fellow got Leave of the Captain to go on Shore for a Month, where he clear'd, by working Journey-Work, twelve Pounds for that Month: But then he had the Ship's Provifion carry'd on Shore to him two or three times a Week; had he been to have paid for his Diet, he had fav'd but a fmall Matter. I was mightily furpriz'd to fee a Market for Turtle, in the fame Manner as our Butchers. This is a Meat, or rather Fifh, of an odd Nature, but of an excellent Tafte; the Lean looks like the Flefh of Pork, but fomething of a deeper red; the Fat is a Sort of a light green, but very lufcious; this is the common Diet of the Slaves, or meaner Sort of People; but if Strangers eat too much of it, it is

apt

apt to give them the Bloody-Flux. This is a very reigning Diſtemper here, and carries off Abundance of new Comers. The Iſland of *Jamaica* lies ———— Leagues *North* from the *Southern* Continent of *America*, in the Sea call'd *Mare del Nor*; and *South* from the Iſle of *Cuba*, about twelve Leagues; and twenty *Weſt* from *Hiſpaniola*, in eighteen Degrees *Northern* Latitude; and beareth from *Rio de Hach*, *North Weſt*, an hundred and fifty Leagues; from *Santa Mertha*, N. N. W. an hundred and thirty five; from *Carthegena*, N. an hundred and fourteen; from *Portobello*, N. E. and by N. an hundred and ninety; from the *Iſthmus* of *Darien*, N. and by E. an hundred and ſeventy; and from the Bay of *Mexico*, an hundred and fifty. Its Form is almoſt oval; being in Length, from *Eaſt* to *Weſt*, about fifty-four Leagues; from *North* to *South*, in the broadeſt Part, twenty three Leagues, growing narrower toward each End, like a Rowling-Pin, (a good Compariſon.) In Circumference, one hundred and fifty Leagues. The Air of this Iſland is more temperate, and the Heat more tolerable, than any of the other Iſlands, by Reaſon of the cool Breezes which conſtantly blow from the *Eaſt*, with frequent Showers of Rain, and Dews that fall in the Night. Theſe Dews are very pernicious to careleſs drunken People, that lie expos'd all Night to them. This is alſo the only Iſle of the *Barloventi*, which is not ſubjeƈt to violent Storms, and Hurricanes, as the other Iſlands are. And the Diſeaſes that are predominant here, are only bred by Intemperance; as Surfeits, Bloody-flux, Fevers, and

Agues;

Agues; or occafioned by ill Diet, or Slothfulnefs. This Ifland is well water'd with Springs and Rivulets of frefh Water, (with many handfome Rivers ftored with feveral Sorts of Fifh;) and is all over (efpecially in the *Weftern* Parts) full of high Mountains and Hills: It is alfo well wooded; for the North and South Parts chiefly abound with large and tall Woods. Neither are there wanting Savana's, or Plains. The Commodities of this Ifland are very many; and firft, for Vegetables; the Sugars are fo good, that they now out-fell thofe of *Barbadoes* 5*s. per Cent*. Tobacco is fo excellent, that it is bought up fafter than the Planters can cure it: The Indigo is alfo here very good: The Cotton is much the beft of all the neighbouring Iflands. Tortoifefhell is very plenty here. Here are alfo great Variety of Dyewood, as *Frftick, Red-wood,* a kind of *Log-wood, Cedar, Ma'ogany, Lignum vitæ, Ebony, Cranadille,* and many others. Nay, there are many Mines, both of Silver, Copper, and Gold; but that the Inhabitants think it would be dangerous to break them up, for fear of drawing the *Spanifh* and *French* Buccaniers upon 'em. There are feveral Fifhermen who have found Pieces of Ambergreafe upon the Surface of the Water, near the Shore. Ginger grows better here than in any other Part of *America*; and Cod-Pepper very plentifully: And alfo, a certain Kind of Spice call'd, *Piemcte,* in Form of *Eaft-India* Pepper, of a very aromatical and curious Tafte, partaking, as it were, of feveral Spices together: It grows wild among the Mountains, and is highly

valu'd

valued among the Inhabitants. Of Medicinal Plants I have seen several, as *Guaiacum, China-root, Caffia Fiftula, Veuillard, Achiotes, Tamarines, Contrayerva, Ciperas, Adiantum-nigrum, Aloes, Cucumis, Agriftis, Sumach, Acacia, Miffelto,* with many other Drugs and Balfums. The ingenious Sir *Hans Sloan* has wrote an elaborate Book of the Plants of this Ifland. *Cochineal* is produc'd by a Plant that grows in this Country, but not brought to Perfection, without much Care and Induftry. This Ifland is alfo very well ftock'd with Cattle, as Horfes, Cows, and Affes; there have been many Mules, but the Inhabitants made fo little Ufe of 'em, that now there are but few. Sheep are large and tall, and their Meat indifferently good, but their Fleece worth nothing. *Goats* (or *Cabirates*) are without Number, being a Beaft peculiar to the Country. Hogs, both wild and tame in Abundance. I have been hunting the wild Hog in *Porto Morant* Bay, and it gives good Diverfion, tho' fometimes dangerous: You go with fome Ten or a Dozen in Company, arm'd with a Musket and a Cutlafs; as foon as ever (with your Dogs) you have found 'em out, you all take Aim, and fire as quick as you can, but if you don't kill them immediately with your Shot, they fet upon you open-mouth'd, fo that you muft either hew 'em down with your Cutlaffes, or club your Muskets. Generally as foon as you have 'em, you flay 'em, as you do Mutton, and *Barbicue* 'em, even in the very Place where you kill 'em; that is, you dig a fquare Hole in the Earth, then clap four Stakes at

C

each

each Corner; and on 'em put your Meat, fo make a
Fire under it, and when one Side is done enough,
you turn the other.   For tame Fowls, they have of
all the Kinds that we have in *England*; befides *Guinea* Hens, *Parrots, Parachetes, Machaws,* and *Boobies,*
(which are *Boobies,* indeed, for they will fit upon a
Tree, or Poft, till you come and take 'em.)   They
have three Crops a Year, in this Ifland, and the
Trees are always green.   They have three Sorts of
Bread, one of *Englifh* Corn, another of *Guinea*
Wheat, and the third of a Root they call *Cafavi,*
which is rank Poifon, till prefs'd and bak'd in an
Oven; 'tis very white, but taftelefs, and the Bread
made of it, the Size of our thin Oat-Cakes.   But
of all the Fruit this Ifland produces, the Pine-Ap-
ple is the beft, which grows very low, with Leaves
fomething like the *Indicus Ficus* that I have feen in
Gardens here in *England*; the Tafte is fo excellent,
that I know not what to compare it to, it having
the Relifh of all fine-flavour'd Fruits.   There's a
Fruit that grows upon a low Bufh, call'd the
Prickle-Pear, the Infide of which is red, and on
the Top is a little thorny Thing like a Star, which
if you do not take away before you eat it, may
prove pernicious.   If you eat but two of this
Fruit, it will make your Urine as red as Blood.
Plantains are very good Fruit, which is, when
bak'd in the Afhes, ufed by the Slaves inftead of
Bread: 'Tis a Fruit with a Skin on it, like our
Beans, which is taken off, and then the Fruit ap-
pears, about the Size of a *Bolognia* Saufage.   *Ban-*
nanas

nanas is another Fruit fomething of the fame Kind,
but fhorter, and more lufcious: Both thefe Fruits
are ripe all the Year, for when fome are fit to
gather, others are green, and fome in Bud. The
Oranges and Lemons, are neither of 'em good, in
my Opinion: But their Limes are wonderful; they
grow upon a Tree full of Thorns, where you muft
be fure to prick your Fingers, if you'll gather 'em.
Thefe, with Spring Water and Sugar, was the chief
of my Liquor, while we ftaid there. The Potatoes
are very fine here, exceeding, in my Opinion, even
thofe of *Ireland*. Then there's another Root call'd
Yams, fomething like a *Jerufalem* Artichoke, but larger and ftringy. The Onions of *Jamaica* are much
milder and better tafted that our *Englifh* Onions, and
very wholcfome: they ufed to make a great Addition to our Crogick Brewis; that is, Bifket foak'd in
fair Water, for fome Time, then the Water thrown
away, and the Bifket ftrew'd over with Salt, Oil,
and Lime-Juice, together with Onions; and fo eaten
as a dainty Difh. There is a fenfitive Plant in this
Ifland; the Stalk, furrounded with Leaves full of dark
red Spots, bears a fweet fmelling violet-colour'd
Flower; the Leaves, as foon as touch'd, clofe up together, and die; and accordingly as they are held in
the Hand a fhorter or longer Time, this Alteration
continues. Ginger grows plentiful here; the Male
Plant (for there are Sexes) hath generally bigger Leaves
than the Female: The Stalks, which are without
Knots, have more Leaves upwards than downwards,
and fpreads along the Earth, ftill taking Root anew.

C 2

When

When the Leaves wither, then the Ginger is commonly ripe, but it has not that Poignancy whilst green, as when dry'd.   The Cotton of this Place (of which the Cloaths and Hammocks are made, and vended in moſt Parts of the *Weſtern* World) grows on a Tree about the Height of a Peach-Tree, with a ſtrait Stem, or Body, out of which ſhoot Boughs of an equal Length, and at equal Diſtances: Between the Leaves, which are narrow and long, grow red Flowers, and from 'em, oval Cods, which, when ripe, incloſe the Cotton, and a Seed like Pepper.   Of hurtful Creatures, there is the Crocodile, or *Alligator*, which infeſts many Rivers and Ponds; this is a Creature of a monſtrous Size; I have ſeen one twenty-ſix Feet long; it moves ſwiftly and ſtrongly forward, but turns ſlow; they are impenetrable every where but in the Eye, or Belly; they have four Feet, or Fins, with which they go, or ſwim; their uſual Courſe of getting their Food is to lie on their Backs as dead, then with a ſudden Onſet they ſpring upon their Prey, whether Man or Beaſt: But 'tis eaſily avoided by a Man, by Reaſon of an aromatic Smell that comes from the Body, which may be ſmelt five hundred Yards; but if a Man has got a Cold, and can't ſmell, if he has Eyes they are eaſily avoided; for if they run right forward, it is but ſlipping on one Side, for they are as long in turning as a Coach. The Oil that's made from theſe Creatures, is good for ſeveral Diſtempers.   They lay their Eggs (about the Size of a Turkey's) and cover 'em with Sand, which heated by the Beams of the Sun, hatches the young ones,

who

who naturally creep into the Water.   One of these
Creatures swam after us fifty Yards in *Porto Morant*
Bay, and rais'd his Head upon the Edge of our
Long-Boat, which was deeply laden with Casks of
Water; our Carpenter, who had been felling of
Timber to wood the Ship, struck him a very great
Blow on the Nose with his Hatchet, that I am sure
hurt him, for he gave a Sort of Shriek, which no-
body ever heard before. *** him to Shore; where
I observ'd him to run his Head into the Mud, as if
it pain'd him, which makes me think that their
Heads are not invulnerable, as is reported.   The
Guana is another Creature amphibious as the *Alliga-
tor*, but nothing nigh so large: There's an Island
near *Jamaica*, call'd *Guana* Island, inhabited by nothing else; our Seamen eat these latter, but much
Good may it do 'em, for their Flesh looks like a
Piece of a *Black-a-moor*'s Arm; but how it tastes I
can't tell, neither do I ever design to try.   The *Co-
coa* Nut is a Fruit that is both Meat, Drink and
Cloathing to the Natives (I mean the Blacks):   the
Rind serves for weaving of Cloaths, nay and rigging
their Canoes, before they knew the *Europeans*; and
when you have taken off the Bark, you must be beholden to a Saw to cut off the Monkey's Face, which
is the Top, with three Marks that make it something resemble that Animal; then the Inside contains, first a liquid Substance, like Whey, but very
sweet; after you have taken out this Liquor, round
the Nut is a Substance a Quarter of an Inch thick,
which you cut out, and that's the Meat, which is

C 3   very

very delicious and grateful to the Taste, but not
wholesome, if eat of too much: There's another
Thing that's very remarkable, and that is the *Phy-
sick Nut*, much of the Taste of our Pig-Nuts, but
one or two of 'em will do your Business, upwards or
downwards, as well as Dr. *Anodyne Necklace*'s Sugar-
Plumbs. As I was going one Day to dine with
Captain *Kendal*, (a Gentleman Inhabitant within a
[illegible] by a Black
a Servant of his, I saw in the Hedge a fair [illegible]
growing on a Bush, which I readily gathered, and
was conveying to my Mouth, but prevented by the
Black's giving me a Blow on the Hand, which struck
it from me; I immediately drew my Sword in the
Scabbard, and fell to belabour the poor Fellow for his
Insolence, for I having been familiar with him,
and talked to him along the Road, thought he made
our *English* Proverb true, *if you give an Inch they'll
take an Ell*; but it seemed the Fellow saved my Life
by it, for this Fruit, which was called a *Manginel
Apple*, was rank Poison, but what I never had seen
or heard of before; I was so concerned for the Blows
I had given the poor Fellow that I gave him a Dollar to make him Amends. I remember I was afterwards washing myself at a River, in the same Bay,
and it raining very hard, I went under a Tree, to
save my Cloaths from being wet, and in placing
them together in a Cavity of the Shore the Drops of
Rain fell on a *Manginel* Tree, and so on my Back,
but in less than half an Hour my Flesh burned very hot,
and white Blisters appeared upon my Skin, insomuch
that

that I was in a high Fever; but a Native of the Place being with me, ran for salt Water and washed me all over, and afterwards got some Oil, and dipped my Shirt in it, and put it on my Back, which gave me Ease immediately; but the Spots remained upon my Skin several Years afterwards. One of our common Sailors by eating two or three of these Apples dyed in three Days raving mad. This Island was first discovered by *Columbus*, *Anno Dom.* 1499. After he had conquer'd the Natives, and built a City called *Sevilla*, (afterwards *St. Jago de le Vega)* consisting of about seventeen hundred Houses, two Churches, two Chapels, and an Abbey, he made his Son *Diego Columbus* Governor of the whole Island, for his Master *Ferdinand* King of *Spain.* The first Attempt made upon this Island by the *English*, was *A. D.* 1592, under the Command of Mr. *Anthony Shirley*, but after vanquishing the *Spaniards* they deserted it, as not thinking it worth their keeping, and returned home. The *Spaniards* again possessing it, remained unmolested, till *Anno Dom.* 1654, when *Oliver Cromwell*, then Lord Protector, fitted out a Fleet of Ships to make a Descent on *Hispaniola*, under the Command of Colonel *Kenable*; but being disappointed of their Hopes, and meeting with ill Success, steered away for *Jamaica*, and on the 10th of *May* (after a stout Resistance) made themselves Masters of it. The Island is supposed to contain two hundred and fifty thousand Inhabitants, Slaves included. The chief Towns are, 1*st*, *St. Jago*, about six Miles up the Country. 2*dly*, *Passage-Town*, six Miles from that. 3*dly*, (And indeed the largest, before

C 4

the

the Earthquake deſtroyed it) *Port Royal*; it contained a thouſand Houſes, many of them eminent Buildings; but as it is now built on a ſmall Neck of Land,
which forms the Harbour, I take it to be about the
Bigneſs of *Deptford*. At both Ends of the Town is
a large Fort, known by the Name of the ſquare and
round Fort: This ſquare Fort, or Caſtle, contains a
hundred Pieces of Ordnance, and the other about
thirty, beſides ſeveral Cannon on the Platform,
which reaches from one Fort to the other; ſo that,
without Treachery, they need not fear an Attack
either by Land or by Sea. About a Mile farther, is
another ſmall Fort, called *Landward* Fort, which
ſecures the Town from any Attempt by Land: Off
the Mouth of the Harbour, towards the Sea, lie ſeveral ſmall Iſlands, upon the moſt *Weſtern* of which
(lying within half a League of the Town, and by
which all the Veſſels muſt paſs) they have erected a
Fort which contains eight Guns. The chief Harbour, after *Port Royal*, is *Port St. Anthony*, on the
North; a very ſafe, commodious landlocked Harbour, only the coming in is ſomething difficult,
the Channel being narrowed by a little Iſland
that lies off the Mouth of the Port. 2*d. Porto Morant*,
a very capacious Harbour, where Ships do conveniently wood and water, and ride ſafe from all
Winds. 3*d*, On the *South* is *Port Gagway*, which is
much the largeſt of all that has been mentioned, it
being five Leagues over in ſome Places; it is landlocked by a Point of Land that runs S. *W*. from the
Main of the Iſland: The Road is ſo deep that a
Ship of a thouſand Tons may lay her Side to the

Shore

Shore of the Point, and lade or unlade at Pleasure, with Planks afloat.

Now finding our Affairs would detain us half a Year longer, I got Leave of the Captain to go in a Sloop, with some of my Acquaintance, to get Logwood, and on *September* the 25th we set Sail for the Bay of *Campeche*, with a fair Wind. The old Manner of getting this Wood is as follows; a Company of desperate Fellows get together in a Sloop, well armed, and land by Stealth, but in Case of any Resistance, the whole Crew attends on the Cutters, ready armed to defend them; indeed there's a Colony of *English* that fell this Logwood, but many chuse the other Way; all this was strange to me, for I knew nothing of the Matter, till we were out at Sea. There was one Fellow there that told me, that about ten Years before he went with a Vessel, and they took the same Method as usual, in getting it, and landed all their Men but six, that they left on Board to look after the Vessel; in the mean Time the *Spaniards* having Intelligence of their Descent, sent a hundred Men in several Canoes, to seize their Vessel; which accordingly they did, without any Resistance from the six Men on Board. After they had clapped these Men under Hatches, they searched and ransacked the Vessel, sending every Thing on Shore that was of any Value; then they prepared to trepan the Crew, as they came on Board, which happened the very next Night, when some of the Men coming on Board with a Load of Logwood, the *Spaniards*

C 5

caused

caufed the fix Men to ftand upon Deck, and on Pain of Death, not to difcover the Truth of the Matter, which happened as they defired, for the Men coming on Board carelefly without their Arms, were all feized immediately and clapped in Irons. The reft that were on Shore, wondering at the Stay of the Boat, fent a Canoe with fix Men, to know the Reafon of their Delay, which were likewife taken in the fame Trap with the former. The Man that told me this Story, was one of thefe laft fix, who found Means fecretly in the Middle of the Night to flip into the Water, and fwim afhore, tho' half a League off, where he happily inform'd the reft of the Crew (which were forty three) of the Misfortune that had happened to the reft of their Companions : Whereupon they confulted what they had beft to do; when it was unanimoufly agreed, to feize upon three large Canoes, that lay at the Bottom of the Bay, that belonged to fome *French* Hunters that were on Shore ; which was done accordingly : On Board they immediately got, well armed, and fteered away for their Sloop : But as they defigned to trick them the fame Way as the others had done their Companions, they confulted what to do if they fhould be difcovered before they could get on Board, which was probable enough. At length it was agreed to carry on the Plot in order to deceive them, and as foon as ever they could get over the Ship's Side, to affault the Ene-my with all the Vigour imaginable, appointing two or three to releafe their Companions, and put

Arms

Arms into their Hands, to be affiftant in recovering
their Liberties. Every Thing happen'd as was
fuggefted, for when they came within half a
Furlong of the Veffel, they were hail'd by fome of
their own Men, as it is ufual in fuch Cafes ; which
was anfwered by them in the Canoes, with fwearing
and curfing at 'em, for not coming afhore with
their Long-boat, as ordered, but to-force 'em to bring
their Wood aboard in Canoes. They afked from on
Board, how many were come with them ? All (anfwered they in the Boat) but three, that we left A-
fhore to look after our Arms, and a fmall Re-
mainder of Logwood, which you muft go and fetch
immediately with the Long-boat, (which they pretended could not go to them before, by Reafon fhe
had a Hole broke in her Bow, againft a Piece of
Rock, that gave them a great deal of Trouble in
getting her to the Veffel.) Our People fmiled to
themfelves to hear they had got their Leffon fo
ready. In afking and anfwering thefe Queftions
they had reached the Veffel, and getting nimbly up
the Side, they drew from under their Watch-Coats,
their Piftols and Cutlaffes, and firft fired upon the
Spaniards, who were running to feize them, half
unarmed, as not fufpecting any Refiftance : Thofe
whofe Office it was to releafe the Prifoners under
Hatches, did it immediately, by killing the two
Centinels that watched over them ; and then coming up with this frefh Recruit foon overcame the
Spaniards, and make them call for Quarter : Which
was not granted till they had thrown down their

C 6

Arms.

Arms. When they had furrendered, they chained them all under Hatches; and fo the Conquerors became Prifoners and the Prifoners Conquerors. After the Action was over, they looked after the Dead, which was found to be nine *Spaniards,* and one *Englifhman,* who was fuppofed to be killed by our own Men, in the firft Fire.

Upon this good Succefs, they having Notice that there lay a rich Ship in the Harbour before the Town of *Campeche,* they refolved to try their good Fortune farther, which they contrived as follows: They hoifted *Spanifh* Colours, and failed away immediately for the Port of *Campeche,* where they arrived by next Morning, faluted the Caftle and Town with feven Guns, as Friends, and were paid back the Complement. The Shore was filled with Numbers of People, to fee the *Englifhmen* brought afhore Prifoners; but they were miftaken. The Ship which they had a Defign upon lay about a League from the Town, as having arrived but two Days before, but was to put farther in that very Evening, before the Sea-Breeze failed; our Men boarded her on the Starboard Side, which lay from the Town, and took her, without firing a Gun, cut her Cables, and made out to Sea, before the Town knew what was the Matter: But as foon as ever they fmelt the Trick, a *Spanifh* Man of War of thirty Guns (being all that was in the Harbour) flipped her Cables, and crouded all the Sail fhe could, to come up with us; we finding fhe gained upon us, called a Council, and at laft refolved to bring up moft of our *Spanifh* Prifoners bound, and expofe them to the whole Fire of the Enemy.

Which

Which succeeded accordingly, for the Ship coming
close up to us without any firing on either Side, commanded us to strike. Upon that we ordered the
Spanish Captain to lay before them the Condition;
which profited little at first, but after many Intrea-
ties from them, and Threatnings from us, the
others were prevailed upon to steer off, and make
towards the Town, while we made the best of our
Way. But the *Spaniards* making up to the Town
again, was met by several armed Boats, with the
Governor himself in one of them, who gave a strict
Command not to regard any Thing, but use all
possible Means to retake the Ship, and the Pyrates
(as they termed us.) When we perceived the Boats
making up to the Ship, and observed her tack about
to give us Chace, we guessed at the Matter, and
finding she gained upon us, we put ourselves into a
Posture of Defence, and proposed to engage her in
the Prize we took last, which carried 20 Guns: We
mustered our Men, and found we had 71, but then
we had 200 *Spanish* Prisoners, who, we feared, if by
any Accident they should get loose, might prove our
Ruin; whereupon a Consultation was immediately
held to put most of them to Death. Upon which
the Captain of the first Prize stood up, and said (in
pretty good *English)* Gentlemen, you have taken us
fairly, and done no more than we ourselves did to
you; now seeing that Ship which pursues us, and
gains upon us every Moment, is coming in order to
fight you, we shall run a more certain Danger by
it, by being your Prisoners, if you expose us to the
Fire of their Cannon, as you did before; and if they

do

do really Fire, I may as well take them for an Ene‑
my, as you, since we are sure to receive the most
Damage.   But to make the Matter short, being the
Time is so, I propose to you that if the Vessel fires
at you, we may reasonably conclude, they have no
Manner of Regard for us, so we shall not have any for
them, and, if you'll give us that Liberty, we will
freely fight under your Command, and endeavour,
as far as in us lies, to defend your Vessel, as much
as if it was our own.   This Speech of the Captain's
was approved of by the rest of the Prisoners ;
so that at last we agreed to set sixty of them at
Liberty, and the rest fast bound under Hatch‑
es, where we put two Centinels, with two Patér‑
reroes fixed, charged with small Shot, with Orders
that if there seemed to be any Thing like Distur‑
bance, to fire in upon them.   The sixty we chose
out to be assistant to us, were ordered to the great
Guns, so that we still had the Command over them,
because they had no Arms.   After we had settled
every Thing, we lay by, (seeing it impossible to es‑
cape without fighting) in order for their coming up
to us, which they did in a short Time, and coming
within Hail, they ordered us to strike immediately,
and make no Resistance, or else they would have
no Regard to their Friends on Board our Ship, but
sink or take us, and put every Man of us to Death.
Upon which the *Spanish* Captain that was our Priso‑
ner, made Answer, That if they offered to fire a
Gun, every *Spaniard* on Board resolved to fight against
them as Enemies : Which was answered, They must
obey the Governor's Orders, who had just left them,

and

and was returned on Shore.   Upon this they fired a
Broadside upon us, but we returned it immediately
with our small Arms, and great Guns, which were
well plyed by our *Spanish* Prisoners. The Fight continued half an Hour with all the Fiercenefs imaginable ; at laft the *Spaniard* prepared to board us with
his Boats at the fame Time, but were received fo
brifkly, and fo damaged by our Hand-granadoes,
that they were obliged to make to the Ship with
great Lofs. The Hand-granadoes, ftood us in great
Stead, for we difpatched three or four of our Men
into the Main-Top, who from thence difcharged
feveral Granadoes, that by their own Report killed
and wounded above thirty Men. They attempted
to board us once again, and came on brifkly with
firing and loud Shouts, to terrify us ; but we returned them their Shouts and Firing with Intereft, for
with a lucky Shot we drove away their Main-Maft,
which put them into ftrange Confufion : This Accident (if we could have laid hold on't) might have
given us an Opportunity of out-failing them ; but
that was not once thought of, for Defire of Revenge
made us fight like Furies. The next Broadfide we
gave them, ftruck away their Rudder, which rendered them incapable of fteering their Veffel, or
tacking about : Upon which we perceiving what had
happened, tacked about, and with a Broadfide that
raking her fore and aft, killed them, by their own
Confeffion, fixteen Men, for it fplit two of their
Guns, whofe Splinters did moft of the Execution.
Now what we call to *Rake Fore and Aft*, is to lay
the Side of our Ship againft the Enemy's Head or
                                                    Stern,

Stern, and fire into them, fo that every Shot goes
from one End of the Ship to the other, inftead of
going acrofs, fo that of Confequence one Shot that
Way will do more Damage than ten directly Side
to Side. The Heat of the *Spaniard* now began to
abate, but yet he hectored as much as ever; at laft
a lucky Shot entered her Powder Room, and blew
up her Main-Deck, with feveral *Spaniards*, into the
Air; upon which were heard fuch Groans and Yel-
ling, from wounded and dying Men, that were
enough to frighten Men lefs inured to fuch Encounters: With this Succefs we prepared, in the Confufion, to board them in our Turn, but was prevented, by feeing their Veffel finking; whereupon they
ftruck down their Colours, and afked for Quarter
and Help; underftanding their Diftrefs, we immediately gave them Affiftance, by putting out our
Boats, and faved all the Men they had left, which
were ninety-five, out of four hundred and odd.

This Succefs flufhed us mightily with Hopes of
fucceeding in any Enterprize. We loft out of our
Spaniards twenty-fix, and of *Englifh* nine killed, and
two wounded, who died the next Day. The *Spaniards*
were of fignal Service to us, and fought bravely, even
to Defperation; well knowing, if they fhould be
taken (after fighting on our Side) they muft all inevitably fuffer Death: which proved happy for us;
for it had been impoffible to have efcaped them, even
if all the *Spaniards* on Board us had ftood neuter.

After

After we had cleared our Vessel of the Blood and dead Men and refreshed ourselves, we called up our *Spanish* Prisoners, that they might refresh themselves likewise, and returned the others (who had fought so bravely in our Defence) our hearty Thanks; and the *Spanish* Captain expressed himself so handsomely, that our Master freely offered him our Sloop, victualled and ready fitted up, to do what he thought fit with.   Upon this kind Offer the Captain smiled, and told him he would not take it without buying: And as for Money, I have not a single Dollar, (pursued he) but if you'll listen to a Stratagem of mine, I'll engage to furnish you with Money for your Vessel, and something over and above.   With that he proposed to take six of the *Spaniards* that had fought for us, and in our Long-Boat to go on Shore to the Governor, and demand a Ransom for the Prisoners we had taken; which was agreed to: Accordingly they went ashore, and told the Governor, If he did not immediately send fifty Dollars a Man, for two hundred and twenty, they would be every Soul tied Back to Back, and thrown into the Sea.   Upon which there was a Gathering made through the Town, and the Money raised immediately, and in twelve Hours the Captain returned with 11000 Dollars, gave our Captain 5000, distributed 3000 among the Sailors, and kept the rest for himself. The next Day we set the *Spaniards* that were saved from the Man of War on Shore, and as many more that were willing, out of the other Ship, and of our own Sloop; so that Captain *Fernando*, our friendly

Spaniard,

took his Leave of us, with eighty of his Countrymen, with Intention for the *South-Sea*; and we steered our Course, in our rich Prize, for *Jamaica*, where we shared it: Every common Sailor had to his Share 800*l.* Moreover the Captain ordered me in particular 200*l.* more, for the Service I did in swimming ashore unperceived, to give them Notice.

After ending his Story, I asked him how he had improved his Money from that Time? Psha (said he) that, and five Times as much, is gone since then. And this is no Wonder, for Sailors are such Fools, that what they get with the utmost Danger, they spend as the meanest Trifles. We sailed before the Wind six Days together, towards the Bay, but on the seventh, the Clouds darkened, and the Welkin seemed all on Fire, by Times, with Lightning, and the Thunder roared louder than ever I heard it in my Life; in short, a dreadful Hurricane approached, which was suspected by a deceitful Calm, and Showers of Rain, described by the inimitable *Shakespeare*, thus:

> *We often see against some Storm*
> *A Silence in the Heav'ns, the Rack stand still;*
> *The bold Winds speechless, and the Orb below*
> *As hush as Death.*

The Sailors had furled their Sails, and lowered their Top-masts, waiting for it under a double-reefed Fore-sail: Which at last came with most extreme Violence.

Either

Either Tropick now
'Gan thunder : At both Ends of Heav'n the Clouds
From many a horrid Rift abortive pour'd
Fierce Rain with Lightning mix'd, Water with Fire,
In Ruin reconcil'd.   Dreadful was the Rack,
As Earth and Sky wou'd mingle.   Milton.

In vain the Master issues out Commands,
In vain the trembling Sailors ply their Hands,
The giddy Ship, between the Winds and Tides,
Now backwards and forwards, in a Circle rides,
Stunn'd with the different Blows; then shoots amain,
Till counterbuff'd, she stops, and sleeps again.
The Face of Things a frightful Image bear,
And present Death in various Forms appear.
                                    Dryden.

The Storm lasted with all its Violence three Hours,
and at last insensibly abated, till it was stark Calm,
and not one Breath of Wind was stirring, nor any
Sign of one, but a little Froth on the Surface.

The Tempest is o'erblown, the Skies are clear,
And the Sea charm'd into a Calm so still,
That not a Wrinkle ruffles her smooth Face.

                                    Dryden.

After the Storm was over, we loosened our Sails,
in Expectation of the Wind, which in half an Hour
stole out again, as frightened at the violent Storm.
                                    or,

or, (if you'll grant me to make a Simile) like a poor Debtor that steals out of his Lurking-place, when the blustering Bailiffs are gone out of Sight. About six in the Evening, we saw a Water-Spout: this is an aerial Engine, or Limbeck, that draws up the salt Water of the Sea, and distills it into fresh Showers of Rain: This Cloud comes down in Form of a Pipe of Lead of a vast Thickness, and by the Force of the Sun sucks up a great Quantity of Water. I stood an Hour to observe it; after it had continued about half an Hour in the Water, it drew up insensibly, by Degrees, till it was lost in the Clouds; but in the ceasing of the same, it shut out some of the Water, which fell into the Sea again, with a Noise like that of Thunder, and occasioned a Smoke in the Water that lasted for a considerable Time. The Sailors informed me, that these Water-spouts sometimes did great Damage to Ships that by Calms were too near them when they fell. One Fellow told me, that he saw a Bark of sixty Tons sucked out of the Sea by one of them, which caused the Breaking of the Spout, and sunk the Vessel with the Fall of the Waters, In the *Streights*, when Ships approach these airy Engines, they fire off a Gun, and that breaks them before they come too near. The Person told me that at the Fall of the Water, the Sea was curled as much as if you had thrown a large Stone into a standing Pond of Water. We have sometimes at a Distance seen fourteen or fifteen at a Time at Work, but I never saw one so large as this.

In

In the Evening we caught a small Shark, with two sucking Fishes that stuck close to her till laid on the Deck, and then dropped down of their own Accord. This is allowed the *Remora* of the Ancients. It is about the Bigness of a Mackrel, with a flat Head, and is of a grisly Substance. These stick to the Sides of Vessels very frequently, and sometimes swim upon the Surface of the Water, and are even caught with a naked Hook. I have sometimes seen these Fishes sticking to a Log of Wood, in the Water. When we hogged our Ship, (a Hog is an Instrument of six Feet square, something like a Harrow, and Stumps of old Brooms fixed close in the middle Part; this is put to the Bottom of the Ship, with a Rope before and another aft, fixed to the Capstand, which cleans the Vessel from all Sorts of Filth) I have seen many of them in the Hog together, with Barnicles and Oysters, and several other Shell-fish.

October the 6th, we anchored at *Trist Island*, in the Bay of *Campeachy*, and sent our Men on Shore at *Logwood-Creek*, to seek for the Logwood-Cutters, who immediately came on Board. The Bargain was soon struck, and in Exchange for our Rum and Sugar, and a little Money, we got in our Lading in eight Days, and set Sail for *Jamaica* the 15th Day of *October*.

Now in getting up to *Jamaica* again, generally takes up two Months, because we are obliged to ply it all the Way to windward One Day it being stark calm, I went into the Water to wash myself, tho' I was dissuaded by all the Sailors, by Reason of that

Coast

Coaſt being infeſted with Sharks, which often aſſault People and bite off a Limb: But being there had not been any ſeen that Day, I would venture, yet tied a Rope about me, for Fear of any Accident that might happen, or the Wind ſtriking up of a ſudden. But I had not been long in the Water, before they cried from the Gunnel, A Shark! But I thinking they only bantered, as ſometimes they do, when any one is in the Water, did not mind them, till at laſt they pulled me by main Force, up the Side of the Ship; when looking into the Water, I ſaw a ſwinging large Shark, with his white Belly turned up in order to bite at me. Upon which I thanked God and good Friends that had prevented him, by ſwiftly pulling me up; though the Rope had rubbed off the Skin, and ſome Part of my Fleſh, with the Force. Now a Shark cannot get his Prey, without firſt turning himſelf upon his Back, becauſe their upper Jaw is much larger and longer than their under: Which often prevents Accidents.

I one Day went down into the Hold, to bottle off a ſmall Parcel of Wine that I had there, for Fear it would ſour, and not being a very cleanly Place, I was ſoon in a filthy Pickle: Coming upon Deck again, I wanted to clean myſelf, but did not care to go into the Water, as before, ſo went into the Boat a-ſtern, that we hoiſted overboard in the Morning to look after a Wreck that we diſcovered upon the Water: Being in the Boat, I began to waſh myſelf, and when I had dreſſed myſelf again, I pulled a Book out of my Pocket, and

ſate

fate reading in the Boat; when, before I was aware, a Storm began to rise, so that I could not get up the Ship's Side as usual, but called for the Ladder of Ropes, that hangs over the Ship's Quarter, in order to get up that Way; but whether it was not fastened above, or whether it broke thro' Rottenness, as being seldom used, I cannot tell, but down I fell into the Sea; and though the Ship (as they told me afterwards) tacked about to take me up, if it was possible, yet I lost Sight of them, through the Duskiness of the Evening, and the Storm together. Now I had the most dismal Fears that could ever possess any one in my Condition: I was forced to drive with the Wind, which fate (by good Fortune) with the Current, and having kept myself above Water, as near as I could guess in this Fright, four Hours, I felt my Feet every now and then touch Ground; and at last, by a great Wave, was thrown and left upon the Sand; yet it being dark, I knew not what to do; but I got up and walked, as well as my tired Limbs would let me; and every now and then was overtaken by the Waves, but not high enough to wash me away.

When I had got far enough, as I thought, to be out of Danger, I could not discover any Thing of Land, and I immediately conjectured that it was but some Bank of Sand, that the Sea would overflow at high Tide: Whereupon I fate down to rest my weary Limbs, and fit myself for Death, for that was all I could expect, in my own Opinion. Then all my Sins came flying in my Face, which I repented

pented of with all the Sincerity imaginable: I offered up my fervent Prayers to our Almighty Creator, not for my Safety (becauſe I did not expect any ſuch Thing) but for all my paſt Offences; and I may really ſay, I expected my Diſſolution with a Calmneſs that made me think I had made my Peace with Heaven. At laſt I fell aſleep, (tho' I tried all I could againſt it, by riſing up and walking, till I was obliged thro' Wearineſs to lie down again.) In the Morning when I awaked, I was amazed to find myſelf among four or five very low ſandy Iſlands, but all ſeparated half a Mile or more (as I gueſſed) by the Sea. With that I began to be a little chearful, and walked about to ſee if I could find any thing that was eatable, but to my great Grief I found nothing but a few Eggs, that I was obliged to eat raw; this laid my Condition before my Eyes in a moſt horrid Manner, and the Fear of ſtarving ſeemed to me to be worſe than that of drowning; and oft did I wiſh that the Sea had ſwallowed me, rather than thrown me on this deſolate iſland; for I could perceive by the Evenneſs of them, that they were not inhabited either by Man or Beaſt, or any Thing elſe but Rats, and ſeveral Sorts of Fowl.

Upon this Iſland there were ſome few Buſhes of a Wood they called *Burton* Wood, which uſed to be my Shelter at Night; but to compleat my Miſery, there was not to be found one Drop of freſh Water on the Iſland; ſo that I was forced to drink my own Urine for two or three Days together; which made

my

my Skin come off like the Peel of a boiled Codlin. At laft my Mifery fo increafed, that I was often in the Mind to put an End to my wretched Life, but defifted, on the Opinion that I had of fome Alligator, or other voracious Creature, coming to do it for me. Strange Circumftances indeed! to wifh to be devoured alive as the leffer Misfortune.

I had lived a Week here upon Eggs only, when, by good Fortune, upon a Bufh I difcovered a *Booby* fitting. I ran immediately, as faft as I could, and with a Stick knocked him down : I never confidered whether it was proper to eat or no, but I fucked the Blood, and eat the Flefh, with fuch a Pleafure as none can exprefs, but them that have felt the Pain of Hunger to the fame Degree as myfelf. After I had devoured this Banquet, I walked about, and difcovered many more of thefe Birds, which I flew.

Now my Stomach being pretty well appeafed, I began to confider whether I could not, with two Sticks, make a Fire, as I had feen *Blacks* in *Jamaica* : I tried with all the Wood I could get, and at laft happily did it. This done, I gathered fome more Sticks, and made a Fire, picked feveral of my *Boobies*, and broiled them as well as I could ; and now I refolved to come to an Allowance. This Bird is a Water Fowl, about the Bignefs of a large Crow, of a grey Colour ; it has a long ftrong Bill, and Feet like a Duck, and its Flefh feemed to me to tafte fomething like a Duck's, but ftronger, and

D   a little

a little fishy: And it is such a Booby, that it will not get out of your Way without beating.

At Night I and the rest of my Fellow-Inhabitants had a great Storm of Rain and Thunder, with the reddest Lightning I had ever seen, which well washed us all, I believe; as for myself, my Cloaths (which were only a Pair of thin Shoes and Thread Stockings, and a Cotton Waistcoat and Breeches) were soundly wet; but I had this Happiness, to find in the Morning several Cavities of Rain-Water, which put in my Head a Thought of making a deep Well, or hollow Place, that I might have Water continually by me, which I brought to Perfection in this Manner: I took a Piece of Wood I found on the Island, and pitched upon a Place under a *Burton* Tree, where with my Hands and the Stick together, I dug a Hole, or Well, big enough to contain a Hogshead of Water, then put in Stones and paved it, and got in and stamped them down hard all round, and with my Sticks beat the Sides close, so that I made it capable of holding Water for a long Time.

But now the Difficulty was, how to get the Water there, which at last I contrived very well, for with my Shirt I effected it, by soaking it in Water for some Time, and then afterwards it would bear it very well; so with this Holland Bucket I could carry two Gallons of Water at a Time, which would not leak out above a Pint, in two hundred Yards; so in two Days Time I had filled my Well.

Now

Now I began to think of Life again for a while, for I had ready broiled forty of thefe *Boobies*, defigning to allow myfelf half a one a Day. I alfo made myfelf a Cupboard of Earth, by mixing Water with it, which was four Feet in Length, three in Height, and two in Breadth, though it lafted but four Days, the Sun drying it fo faft, that it cracked, and afterwards fell in Pieces. What moft amazed me, and pleafed me together, was, that my *Boobies* continued fweet without the leaft Taint. I had a fmall *Ovid* printed by *Elzevir*, which I had by good Fortune put in my Breeches Pocket, when I was going up the Ladder of Ropes, and by being preffed clofe was not quite fpoiled, but only the Cover off, and ftained a little with the Wet. This was a great Mitigation of my Misfortunes, for I could entertain myfelf in this Book, under a *Burton* Bufh, till I fell afleep. I remained always in good Health, only a little troubled with the Head-Ach, for want of a Hat, which I loft in the Water, in falling down from the Ladder of Ropes. But I remedied this as well as I could, by gathering a Parcel of Chicken-Weed (which grows there in Plenty) and ftrewing it over the *Burton* Bufhes, under which I fate. Nay, at laft, finding my Time might be longer there than I expected, I tore off one of the Sleeves of my Shirt, and lined a Wooden Cap that I had made of green Sprigs, and twifted with the green Bark that I peeled off, fo that if I had been feen in this Figure, I fhould have appeared like

D 2

a Mad-

a Madman, with the Basket of a Cudgel upon his
Head.

One Day coming from washing myself (which
I used often to do to cool me) I heard a flouncing in
the Water, and turning my Head, to see from
whence the Noise came, I saw the oddest Fish, I
believe, that ever was known. It had (as I suppose) chased some other Fish very eagerly, and run
itself too far on the Sand, and the Tide being almost at the lowest, it had left it there. It was (as
near as I could guess) about fifteen Feet long; it
had a Head like a Horse, and out of the Mouth
came two Horns curled like a Ram's Horn, only
twice as large; it had but one Eye, and that was at
the Extremity of the Nose; it seemed, as it
flounced, to be something of a changeable Ash-
colour, with a Tail that tapered to the End in a
sharp Point: It looked so terrible to me, that I was
afraid to approach it; as it laboured it seemed to
groan; it lay in this Hole of Water half an Hour,
with its Body in, and its Tail out; and as soon as
the Tide came up to it, it shaked its Tail to and
fro, as a Dog does when he seems pleased, all the
while it felt the Water; it struggled but now and
then, and at last, when the Water was pretty high,
it turned its Head, and made a Noise something like
the Clucking of a Hen with Chickens, but louder;
and when it had Water enough to swim away, it
lay moving up and down a Quarter of an Hour, being as I suppose hurt with its struggling. But when
                                                    it

it had recovered itself, (as I imagined) it gave a Spring into deep Water, and I faw it no more.

I had been here now a Month by my Reckoning, and in that Time my Skin looked as if it had been rubbed over with Walnut-fhells. I had a Mind feveral Times to have fwam to one of the other Iflands; but as they looked only like Heaps of Sand, I thought I had got the beft Birth, fo contented myfelf with my own Station. Boobies I could get enough (who built on the Ground) and another Bird that lays the Eggs which I ufed to eat, but I never ventured to tafte them, though as their Eggs were good, we may fuppofe their Flefh was fo to : But however, I was fo well fatisfied with my Boobies, that I did not care to try Experiments.

This Ifland, which I was upon, feemed to me to be about two Miles in Circumference, and was almoft round, and on the *Weft* Side there is a good anchoring Place, for the Water is very deep, within two Fathoms of the Shore. God forgive me, but I often wifhed to have had Companions in my Misfortune, and hoped every Day either to have feen fome Veffel come that Way, or a Wreck, where perhaps I might have found fome Neceffaries which I wanted: But I would often check myfelf in thefe Cogitations, as not becoming a Chriftian, yet they would as often awake in my Mind, in fpite of all my Devotion and other good Thoughts; it being natural to defire Company. I ufed to fancy, that if I fhould be forced to ftay there long, I fhould forget my Speech; fo I ufed to talk aloud, afk my-

felf

self Questions, and answer them; but if any
Body had been by to have heard me, they would
certainly have thought me bewitched, I used to ask
myself such odd Questions.   All this while I could
not inform myself where I was, or how near any inhabited Place.

One Morning (which I took to be the 8th of *November*) a violent Storm arose, which continued till
Noon; when in the mean Time I observed a Bark labouring with the Waves for several Hours, and at
last with the Violence of the Tempest, was perfectly thrown out of the Water upon the Shore, within
a quarter of a Mile from the Place where I observed
them.   I ran to see if there was any Body I could be
assisting to, where I found four Men (being all that
were in the Vessel) busy about saving what they could
out of her: When I came up with them, and hailed
them in *English*, they seemed mightily surprized;
they asked me how I came there, and how long I
had been there? When I told them my Story, they
were all mightily concerned for themselves, as well
as for me, for they found there was no Possibility of
getting their Bark off the Sands, being the Wind had
forced her so far; With that we began to bemoan one
another's Misfortunes; but I must confess to you,
without lying, I was never more rejoiced in my
whole Life; for they had on Board Plenty of every
thing for a Twelvemonth, and not any thing spoiled.
Their Lading (which was Logwood) they had thrown
over-board to lighten the Ship; which was the Occasion of the Wind forcing her so far: Had they kept
in

in their Lading they would have bulged in the Sands
half a quarter of a Mile from the Place where they
did, and the Sea flying over them, would not only
have fpoiled their Provifions, but perhaps been the
Death of them all. By thefe Men I underftood
where we were, *viz.* upon one of the Ifles of *Alcranes*,
which are five Iflands, or rather large Banks of Sand;
(for there is not a Tree, nor Bufh upon any but that
where we were) they lie in the Latitude of Twenty-
two Degrees *North*, Twenty-five Leagues from *Jucatan*, and about Sixty from *Campechy* Town. We
worked as faft as we could, and got out every Thing
that would be ufeful to us before Night. We had
fix Barrels of falt Beef, three of Pork, two of Peafe,
and two of Flour, and eleven Barrels of Bifket; a
fmall Copper, and Iron Pot; feveral wearing Cloaths,
and a fpare Hat, which I wanted mightily; We
had befides feveral Kegs of Rum, and one of Brandy,
and a Cheft of Sugar, with many other Things of
Ufe; fome Gun-Powder, and one Fowling-Piece.
We took off the Sails from the Yards, and with fome
Pieces of Timber erected a Tent big enough to hold
twenty Men, under which we put their Beds,
that we got from the Bark. It is true, we had no
Shelter from the Weather, for the Trees were fo low
they were of no Ufe to us. I now thought myfelf in a
Palace, and was as merry as if I had been at *Jamaica*, or even at home in my own Country: I could joke
now and then, and tell a merry Tale. In fhort
when we had been there fome Time, we began to be
very eafy, and to wait contentedly, till Providence
fhould fetch us out of this Ifland. The Bark lay

D 4

upon

upon the Sands, fifty Yards from the Water when at the higheſt, ſo that I uſed to lie in her Cabin, by reaſon there were no more Beds aſhore, than were for my four Companions, *viz. Thomas Randal*, of *Cork* in *Ireland*, (whoſe Bed was largeſt, which he did me the Favour to ſpare a Part of now and then, when the Wind was high, and I did not care to lie on Board) *Richard White*, of *Port Royal*, *William Muſgrave*, of *Kingſton* in *Jamaica*, and *Ralph Middleton*, of *Cowes* in the *Iſle of Wight*. Theſe Men, with Eight others, ſet out of *Port-Royal* about a Month after us, bound for the ſame Place: But thoſe others lying aſhore, and wandering too far up in the Country, were met, as it is ſuppoſed, by ſome *Spaniards* and *Indians*, who ſet upon them: Yet by all Appearance they fought deſperately, for when Mr. *Randal* and Mr. *Middleton* went to ſeek for them, he found all the Eight dead, with fifteen *Indians*, and two *Spaniards*; all the *Engliſhmen* had ſeveral Cuts in their Heads, Arms, Breaſts, &c. that made it very plainly appear they had ſold their Lives dearly. They were too far up in the Country, to bring down their Dead; ſo they were obliged to dig a Hole in the Earth, and put them in as they lay in their Cloaths. As for the *Indians* and *Spaniards*, they ſtripped them, and left them above Ground as they found them, and made all the Haſte they could to embark, for fear of any other unlucky Accident that might happen. They ſet ſail as ſoon as ever they came on Board, and made the beſt of their Way for *Jamaica*, till they were overtaken by the Storm that

ſhipwrecked

fhipwrecked them on *Make Shift Ifland* (as I had named it.)   When I told them of the ftrange Fifh I had feen, there was not any of them, but Mr. *Muf-grave*, that had ever feen the like, and he told me when he was a Prifoner in *Mexico*, he had feen one there, and they called it the *Ram Fifh*; but he told me, I was miftaken concerning the Eyes, for they were on the Top of the Head, but very fmall, not bigger than a Mufket-Ball; and that which I took for an Eye, was a Hole that they fometimes fpouted Water through.   This that he faw at *Mexico* was carried about for a Shew in a Cart, but it was but eight Feet and a half in Length, and was by Order of the Viceroy fent two Leagues into the Bay, to be buried, for it ftunk fo intolerably they were afraid it would breed an Infection.

Now we had all manner of Fifhing-Tackle with us, but we wanted a Boat to go a little Way from Shore to catch Fifh, therefore we fet our Wits to work, in order to make fome Manner of Engine, and at laft we pitched upon this odd Project. We took fix Cafks, and tarred them all over, then ftopped up the Bungs with Cork, and nailed them clofe down with a Piece of tarred Canvas; thefe fix Cafks we tied together with fome of the Cords of the Veffel, and upon them we placed the Skuttles of the Deck, and fixed them, and made it fo ftrong, that two Men might eafily fet upon them; but for fear a Storm fhould happen, we tied to one End of her a Coil or two of fmall Rope, of five hundred Fathoms long, which we fixed to a Stake

D 5

on

on the Shore; then two of them went out, (as for my Part, I was no Fisherman) in order to see what Success they should have, but returned with only one *Nurse*, a Fish so called, about two Feet long, something like a Shark, only its Skin is very rough, and, when dry, will do the same Office as a Seal-skin. The same boiled in Lemon Juice, is the only Remedy in the World for the Scurvy, by applying some of the Skin to the Calves of your Legs, and rubbing your Body with some of the Liquor, once or twice. We sent out our Fishermen the next Day again, and they returned with two old *Wives* and a young *Shark*, about two Feet long; which we dressed for Dinner, and they proved excellent Eating. In the Morning following we killed a young *Seale*, with our Fowling-Piece, but first she was so kind as to give me a Blow on the Forehead, that cut the Skin, and bled very much, which was done with her Fins, for as they run towards the Water, they throw backwards the Gravel, as Horses do when they gallop hard; this we salted, and it eat very well, after lying two or three Days in the Brine.

We past our Time in this *Makeshift Island*, (for we had given it that Name) as well as we could; we invented several Games to divert ourselves; One Day, when we had been merry, Sorrow (as after Gaiety often happens) stole insensibly on us all. I, as being the youngest, began to reflect on my sad Condition, in spending my Youth on a barren Land, without Hopes of being ever redeemed.

Whereupon,

Whereupon, Mr. *Randal*, being the eldeſt, roſe up and made the following Speech, as nigh as I can remember.

Mr. *Falconer*, and my Fellow-Sufferers; but it is to you, (pointing at me) that I chiefly addreſs my Speech, being you ſeem to deſpair of a Redemption from this Place, more than any other. Is not the Providence of a Power Supreme ſhewn in every Accident in the Life of Man; even you yourſelf, how much better is your Condition now, than you could have imagined it would have been a Month ago? There is a Virtue in manly Suffering, and to repine ſeems to doubt of the All-ſeeing Power, which regulates our Actions. If you ſeem conſcious of your deſerving (as a Puniſhment for any Crime you have committed) what has happened to you, why do you not with a contrite Heart lift up your Voice to Heaven, and ſincerely aſk Forgiveneſs of all your paſt Offences, and that Way free yourſelf of thoſe groſs Errors that are crept into your weak Faith. Think you that the Divine Providence that caſt *Jonas* from the Bowels of the Whale, has not the ſame Power ſtill left, to aid and fetch us from this Place.

Here (purſued he) we have every thing that can be required to ſatisfy Nature; we have Beds to lie on, and a Covering from the Weather; we have Proviſions for a Twelvemonth, and if we ſhould continue here a longer Time, we need not fear ſtarving, the very Iſland producing wherewithal to ſupport Nature, as Eggs and Fowls; and tho' there.

D 6

is

is no Rivulet of fresh Water, yet it rains so frequently, we need not fear even that, being we have Vessels enough to save it in: You have the least Reason to spurn at Providence of any one here, that had only a Hole in the Earth to save your Water, which had not lasted two Days longer, before we (very happily for you) were thrown on Shore. Is there not a Providence in being thrown on Land, when you expected drowning before the Morning dawned, which happened otherwise? Is there not a Providence in getting Food, when you expected to starve? Is there not a Providence in getting Fire by rubbing two Sticks, which you know you could not effect since, though we have all endeavoured at it? Was it not a Providence, that your *Bodies* remained sweet, even till the Day that we came here? And was it not a Providence that we were thrown here, which brought you all Sorts of Provisions, (I mean all that is necessary) with Flint and Steel, and other Utensils? And can you then doubt of a farther Providence, that have had all these? Besides, even Company is some Allay to Sorrow; you were alone before, and had only yourself to talk to. Our Bark is strong and firm, and by Degrees, I do not doubt but with Time and much Labour to get her into the Water again. I have been on Board her this Morning when you were all asleep, and examined her carefully inside and out, and fancy our Liberty may soon be effected; I only wonder we have never thought before of clearing the Sand from our Vessel, which

once

once done, I believe we may launch her out into deep Water; we have all our Tackling, Sails, and Masts, entire, without Damage; I do not despair of the Mercy of God in working our Deliverance, whose Ways are past the Knowledge of us poor insignificant Mortals. I myself have more than once been in the same, or worse Condition.

In a Voyage I made twelve Years ago, I suffered Shipwreck, and not one Person saved but myself: I sat out from the City of *Cork* in *Ireland*, on Board a Bark bound for the *Beltick*; we passed the *Streights* of *Elsenore* and *Helsinburgh* without meeting any Thing material; when one Evening it began to thunder, lighten, and rain prodigiously; the Storm was so violent that we expected every Moment when we should be drove on Shore on the Coast of *Sweadland* or *Norway*, and be dashed to Pieces. The Storm continued so long, that all our Masts came by the Board, our Vessel sprung a Leak, and the Water gained upon us every Moment; at last it overpowered us so much, that we left Pumping, as believing it impossible to save ourselves, and recommended our Souls to the Mercy of the Lord. At last our Ship sunk downright, and most of our Men with it; but I and two more had the good Fortune to lay hold of the Main-Mast, (that had been cut above Deck, being it was sprung below, and thrown over-board to prevent any Danger) which was tangled in some of the Cordage; but the Ship sinking downright, with the Rope that was turned to the Main-Mast, gave it such a Tug, that pulled it under Water; but afterwards loosing

that

or flipping off by good Fortune, it rofe with two of us again, but the third was never feen after. The other that faved himfelf upon the Maft, was the Mafter, a Man about fixty Years old, who held pretty well for about an Hour, but at laft through Weaknefs and Age (recommending his Soul to God) fell off, but yet called for Help, and I being willing to give him what Affiftance I could, laid hold of him, which I had no fooner done, but he grafped at me, and laying faft hold of the Skirt of my Waiftcoat, (having never a Coat on) pulled me off the Maft ; but with his Weight, and fome Struggling I made to fave myfelf, my Skirt ripped off, and the Mafter funk to the Bottom, and I by good Fortune laid hold of the Rigging that hung to the Maft ; fo once more got on ftride it, but with little Hopes of Life ; yet doing my Endeavour to fave myfelf, but with a Refignation to the Will of Heaven.   At laft, after being toffed about for two or three Hours more, the End of the Maft rufhed with fuch Violence againft a Rock (as I fuppofed) that with the Shock I was thrown off ; but laid hold of fome of the Cordage again, and held faft till it fixed itfelf in fome of the craggy Clifts of the Rock.

By this Time the Tempeft was very much abated, and the Waves not dafhing fo often, nor fo fierce, I found that the Maft hung on the craggy Clifts of the Rock, which I climbed up as faft I could, left another Wave fhould dafh me againft it, and beat my Brains out.   After I had got as high as I could, and out of Danger of the Waves, I kneeled down
and

and returned Thanks to the Almighty for my wonderful Deliverance; which was wonderful indeed! For tho' the Mast beat so often against the Rock, yet I escaped without being so much as bruised. When I had poured out the Fulness of my Soul to the All-seeing Power, that had protected me from such an imminent Danger, I composed myself to Sleep, but with a Calmness wonderful, (even to myself) wonderful in every Circumstance, that the Almighty Providence should chuse me out of thirty poor Souls that perished in the stormy Deep, for a Monument of his Mercy. I slept, but yet my Dreams were troubled; I thought in my Sleep, I was cast on Shore upon a barren Rock, where there was not a Creature but myself, no Food, nor any Thing to sustain Nature; which proved too true. I was awaked by something that licked my Face, which in my Fright I laid hold on, but soon let it go again upon finding it hairy, which startled me very much; and tho' it was still dark, I could not get to Sleep again for the Concern I was in, for fear some devouring Creature should come and seize me. I listened, and observed the Storm was laid, and the Dawn approaching, I began to compose my Mind, and put my Trust in him, that had hitherto preserved me.

When it came to be light enough to perceive any Object, I rose up and began to view the Place; when, to my great Surprize, I found it to be only a large Rock, about half a Mile in Circumference, as near as I could guess; but the north Part so inaccessible acceffible, there was no getting to the Top of it: Looking about me, I faw coming fawning towards me a large Bitch, which was the Creature that awaked me by licking my Face. I muft confeſs I was furprifed and pleafed, and made much of my new Companion. I hoped from it I fhould find fome human Creatures; but fearching about, and not meeting with any, I was more grieved than before; yet ftill I refigned myfelf to the Will of him that fees all Things, and knew it was in his Power to fetch me out of Darknefs and the Shadow of Death. In walking up and down, in a little Cavity of the Rock, I met with feven young fucking Puppies, that I found belonged to the Bitch my Companion, for fhe gave them fuck, which I ftayed a little while to obferve. Then a Thought came into my Head, that this might be fome Refort for Fifhermen, and I fhould very fhortly fee fome that would take me from this defolate Place.

I began to fearch about for fomething to fuftain Nature, but could find nothing but fome *Perriwinkles*, and other little Shell-fifh, which I ventured to feed upon, for I now began to be very hungry. I wondered mightily at my poor Bitch, how fhe got Food to fupport herfelf, and her feven young ones. I obferved fhe ufed to leave me two or three Times a Day, but returned in a Quarter of an Hour. Once Day I had the Curiofity to watch her, but fhe went fo faft, that I could not come up to her, but ftill I followed, and at laft came to the Point of a Rock where fhe went down, and looking below, faw her

feeding

feeding upon a dead *Seal*; but how it came there I could not suppose, neither could I go down the Rock to see farther, it being so dangerous a Place : When she had eat her fill, she came up again, and went to give her young ones suck. I was mightily put to it for Water, though there were good Quantities in several Cavities of the Rock, but so hard to come at, that sometimes I ventured breaking my Neck to get it; besides, I could not expect that would always last, for the Sun was pretty warm, though not intolerable. I had in my Pocket a Knife and Fork and a Case of Lancets, but they were rusted by being wet, and of no Use to me, for I could get nothing to exercise them on ; indeed my Fork served me to twist out my *Perriwinkles.*

I had been here now fifteen Days, and nothing to feed on but these Sort of Shell-fish ; yet still my Strength and Health continued to a Miracle : I slept well, though my Bed was something hard; it was composed of Part of the Rigging that came on Shore with the Mast, which I had untwisted, and pulled into Okum, and laid it under a hollow Part of the Rock, where no Rain or Wind could hurt me, unless it blew hard South, which when it did, would force a little into my Bed-chamber.

Looking out one Day, I saw a Boat coming towards my rocky Island; the Sight raised my Spirits wonderfully; but observing her narrowly, I found she was only driven by the Wind and Tide, without any one in her : However, I got down my Rock, and waited for her coming on Shore, which she did

within

within twenty Yards of me; I immediately got in
her to rammage her, and, furprifing Providence!
found twenty dried Fifh, a Salt-box filled with Bifket, and about half a Pint of Brandy in a Bottle.
After giving God Thanks with great Sincerity of
Soul, I fell to, and eat heartily. There were two
Oars in the Boat, a Boat-hook, a fmall Fifhing-net,
and a Tinder-box, with a Grapling-iron and Rope
for a Cable : Upon this I began to be exceeding
eafy, and thought myfelf to be in a happy Condition : I brought my Fifh on Shore, and ftowed it in
my Bed-chamber, and over it (for fear of my Bitch)
put feveral Pieces of Ropes. I had a Tinder-Box,
and could ftrike a Light, but had no Candle to
burn, or any Provifion to drefs.

After I had fettled every thing as I would have
it, I refolved to take my Boat and go round the
Rock, to fee if I could difcover any Thing on the
other Side of the inacceffible Part. Whereupon I
took two of my dried Fifh, and half a dozen Bif-
kets, and put myfelf on board : But my poor Bitch
came to tne Shore Side, and took on fo mightily,
that I went and took her in. I rowed half round
(as near I could guefs) the firft Day ; but what
made me fo long was, that in fome Places I was
obliged to row half a League from the Shore, to
avoid fome Shallows which lay out towards the
north-eaft Side. I ventured to lie in my Boat all
Night, and the next Morning went onwards with
my Voyage, and at laft came to that Part of the
Rock that I could not get over when I was afhore.

Here

Here I found upon the Ground a Nest of Eggs, about the Bigness of a Duck-egg; yet I could not discover what Fowl owned them; but I took them all away, and ventured to suck one of them, which I found as pleasant as a new laid Hen-egg. Here the Bitch grew very uneasy, and by her whining and fruitless Endeavours to pass the Rock, (which was perpendicular) let me understand she wanted to be with her Puppies. Finding nothing here for my Benefit, but my Eggs, I got on Board, and endeavoured to go round, which I did, till I came to the Place where the *Seal* lay that my Bitch found, but it stunk abominably; yet she fell too, and after having eat, ran up the Rock, and so (as I suppose,) to her Puppies. I went on Board again; but there arose such a Fog on a sudden, that I could hardly see the Length of the Boat, so rather chose to go back again than venture farther out of my Knowledge, which I did in a little Time, the Sea being higher over the Sand, and arrived at my own Habitation.

I pulled up my Boat as high as I could, and went on Shore, and coming to visit my young Companions found the weakest dead for want of the Dam, which I immediately took, cut open and flayed off the Skin, when after being dried, I made me a Cap of, by cutting it in Form, and sewing it together with some fine Rope Yarn that I twisted on Purpose, and my Fork I used instead of a Needle. The Fat served me to make Candles in this Manner, by pulling to Pieces fine Rope Yarn and twisting it

hard;

hard; then I ftruck a Light, and with an Egg-
Shell heated my Fat, and drew the Rope Yarn
through it, fo I provided myfelf with a new
Sort of Candle. But then I had but a fmall
Piece of Match, and when that fhould be gone, I
fhould be at a ftrange Lofs how to light my Candle.

Finding my Provifion decreafe, I came to an Allowance of a Quarter of a Fifh a Day, and Half a
Bifket, and not to touch that if I could get any
Shell-Fifh, which began to be fcarce too, for fome
Days I could not find above ten or twelve, and
when I came firft there, I ufed to take them up
by Handfuls. Upon this I began to reflect, that
Winter was approaching, and confequently very
cold Weather; and then perhaps I fhould not get
any Food; I refolved within myfelf to venture in
my Boat, and fail which Way the the Wind fhould
direct me; but then I was put to it for a Sail, (for
we had cut off the Yards and Sails of the Main-
Maft, before we threw it over Board) but at laft I
thought of a White Dimity Waiftcoat that I wore,
which was lined with Linnen; this I unripped and
fowed together again, fo pieced the Lining to the
Outfides, and made me a tolerable Sail. But in
the mean Time the Wind blew fo high, that I durft
not venture out; and continued fo long, that my
Provifion was diminifhed to two Fifh, which almeft
put me to my Wit's End. Shell-Fifh were not to
be had. So at laft I refolved to kill one of my
Bitch's Whelps; which I did, made a Fire with
fome Boards I found at the Bottom of my Boat, and

roafted

roasted it; it was palatable, and eat wonderfully well, they being not two Months old.

I don't question but you'll laugh at me, when I shall tell you that it went very much against me to kill this harmless Creature; but my Necessity had no Law; besides, I had observed but two Days before, that the *Seal*, which was the Dam's Food, was gnawed to the Bones. n short, after some Strugglings with myself, I killed five of the six, and salted two of them; for after eating my Biskets out of the Salt Box, I found a Handful or two of Salt at the Bottom, which I made Use of in that Manner. The Entrails I boiled and gave to the Dam and t'other Puppy, who eat of it heartily, making no Scruple though their own Flesh and Blood. The sixth and last Puppy I resolved not to kill at all if I could help it, it being so like the Dam, and would always be with me if it could, when the others would only play about the Hole where they lay.

In short, I began to find the Weather cold, and so resolved to set Sail in my Boat, with my two Companions, my Bitch and Puppy; and on the 1st of *September*, after being on the Rock from *May* the 30th, I set Sail with the Wind about N. E. a middling Gale, and steering with my other Oar; for you must know my Boat-Hook was my Mast, and a Piece of slit Wood that I saved from the Fire was my Yard; so that I could make Shift to ply it to Windward upon Occasion, but was resolved to sail before the Wind till I discovered Land; for my

Boat

Boat being pretty large, and my Sail but small, I could not make my Way as I might have done with a Sail fitted to the Boat; so that I could not discover Land that Night, but sailed on till about Midnight; then I was so fatigued that in Spite of myself, I was obliged to lie along in the Boat, and fell asleep, and slept till I was awakened by a Fisherman in a Boat, whom I understood not, but found by his Dialect to be a *Dane.* I gave him to understand my Condition, by speaking and Sighs together, which he seemed to be sorry for by beating his Breast, and shaking his Head.

He carried me ashore to a Village, where they made very much of me, and gave me Cloaths; but I would not stir without my Dogs. My Boat was sold, and the Money given me for my own Use. After I had staid at the Village three Days, I was carried to *Copenhagen*, to Mr. *Bridgwater*, the Factor for several *English* Merchants, who made a Gathering for me, which amounted to twenty-seven Pounds in *English* Money. The King of *Denmark*, sent a Person to me, who understood English very well, and took down the Particulars of my Voyage in the *Danish* Language, that I saw afterwards printed there; but no one could ever fix upon the Rock that I lived on. One said it was such a One, another such a One; and some conjectured it to be a Part of the Main Land of *Sweden*, which I should have found if I had ventured when hindered by the Fog.

But I forgot to tell you, that by printing this Account, a Man came to demand his Boat, that he

said

said he had loft by the Carelessness of a Boy, to whom
he had given it in Charge, who neglecting to fasten
it on Shore, it drove out to Sea, and came where I
had the good Fortune to meet with it, or rather
guided by the Eye of Providence, to be the Means
or Instrument of saving my Life; which, but for
that, I muft have inevitably perished. The Fisherman that owned the Boat, had a new one given him
in the Room of it, and to the Value of five Pounds
for the Things it contained.

The Gentleman that was ordered to take the
Notes mentioned above, brought me a hundred *English* Guineas, collected from Merchants and Gentlemen of the City. The King likewife ordered me
a hundred more from his Privy Purfe; fo that on
November the 18th, I went on Board an *English* Ship,
called the *Happy*, Captain *John Gibfon*, Commander.
We immediately fet fail for *London*, and arrived at
Deptford, *December* the 25th, being *Chriftmas-Day*,
1688; but finding Things out of Order in *England*,
I thought it was no Place to fettle in. So *January*
the firft I took Horfe for *Briftol*, and from thence
embarked for *Cork*, where I had fome fmall Effects,
and happily arrived there *January* the 14th; where
I was welcomed from Death, by all my Friends.

But I forgot one Thing which happened to me at
Copenhagen. Dining with the Gentleman that fpoke
English very well, and feveral other *Danes*; I happened to drink to him in *English*, with, *Sir, my humble Service to you*, and afked him if he would *Pledge
me*: Upon which, he told me, I muft never mention
Pledging

Pledging among *Danes*; for, added he, it is the greateſt Affront you can put upon them. How ſo, Sir, ſaid I ? Why, ſaid he, I know it is your Cuſtom in *England,* but if you all knew the Meaning of it, you would ſurely aboliſh it. Whereupon, I preſſed him to tell me the Foundation of that Cuſtom according to his Notion. Why, ſaid he, when the *Danes* invaded *England,* and got the better of the Natives, they uſed often to eat and drink together; but ſtill allowing the *Danes* to be their Maſters : And very often, upon ſome Pique or Intereſt, they uſed even to ſtab them when they were lifting the Cup to their Mouths. Upon the *Engliſh* being frequently murdered in this Manner, they contrived at laſt when they were at Meals, or drinking with the *Danes,* to ſay to to their next Neighbour, *Here's to you* : Upon which, the other cryed, *I'll pledge you* : Which was as much as to ſay, he would be a Surety or Pledge, while the other drank ; and accordingly the other would guard him while he drank. When done, the other would drink ; and then he that drank before, was to ſtand his Pledge likewiſe. Nay, it came to be ſuch a Cuſtom at laſt, that when one *Engliſhman* came into the Company of ſeveral *Danes,* he would ſay in taking up his Cup, to his next Neighbour, Will you pledge me, with an Emphaſis ? upon the other's anſwering he would, he might drink without Fear.

After ſtaying the Winter at *Cork,* I deſigned to embark with Captain *Clark,* on Board the Ship *Gilliflower,* and accordingly we ſet out from *Cork, April*

the

the 23d, 1689, for *Boston* in *New-England*, and so for *Virginia*; we arrived at *Boston June* the 3d, having a quick Passage. After having done our Business there, we set sail for *Virginia*. We doubled *Cape-Cod* without any Danger: But one Night a Storm rose, that flung us on Shore upon the Main, within six Leagues of *Cape-Charles*, where our Men were all saved, but in a poor Condition. Our Ship lying upon the Sands a Furlong from Shore, fourteen out of twenty of our Men that could swim, went into the Long-Boat, and went on Board the Ship to get some Necessaries; as soon as they had got what they wanted, they came towards the Shore again; but the Boat being deeply laden, could not come nigh enough to Shore to unload, so that they resolved to go farther to seek for deeper Water, and bid us follow along the Shore, which we did; but they doubling a Point of Land we lost Sight of them: However we followed on still, when going over a little Swamp, we perceived several *Indians* in a Wood on our Right Hand. Whereupon we began to be in a desperate Fright, but still we marched on; when coming to the Skirt of the Wood, they let fly their Arrows at us, which killed one of our Companions, and wounded two more, one in the Arm, and the other in the Side of his Neck; as for my Part, I still remained unhurt, but had an Arrow sticking in the Sleeve of my Waistcoat. After the *Indians* had fired, they ran to us with incredible Swiftness, whereupon (having no Weapons) we kneeled down to them, and implored their Mercy. One among them spoke *English* pretty well, who

E   said

faid, You *Englifh* White Men, we will kill you
to be revenged of your Brothers at *Lameftown,*
who kill us many *Indians*; we will take you
to our *Werowance,* (i. e. *King,*) and he will order us
to burn you, where we will drink your Blood, and
feed upon your Flefh. They hurryed us along that
Night at leaft twenty the Miles up in Country, and
next Morning brought us to their Village, where
was their *Werowance,* fick in his Cabin; but hearing
of our coming, he rofe up, and with feveral of his
Officers (who are called *Cockeroofes*) came towards us.
After he had examined the *Indians* (as we fuppofe)
how we were taken, he ordered a great Fire to be
made, and had us all tyed to one Stake fixed in the
Earth; but we were no fooner tyed, and the Signal
giving for firing the Wood about us, but we were
untyed and brought back to the Tent, to ftay, as we
were informed, till the next Day, till more *Indians*
could come to be Spectators of our Tragedy. They
had ftripped us naked, and in my Breeches-Pocket
had found my Box of Inftruments, which they examined very narrowly, and afked which of us it belonged to? When they were informed it was mine,
I was immediately fent for before the *Werowance:*
who afked me, by his Interpreter, the Name and
Ufe of every Inftrument, which I informed him:
When he came to my Lancets, and being informed
they were to bleed, he afked in a great Paffion, If I
was the Murderer of the *Indians* that were taken by
the *Englifh?* But when I let him know it was to let
Blood in many Diftempers, for Eafe for the Body,
and that we were Strangers to thofe *Englifh* that kil-

led

led their *Indians*, he abated of his Anger, and asked me if I could shew how I let Blood? which I
told him I could, if any one wanted it, and was not
well. Whereupon the *Werowance* said he was not
very well; but he would have me try upon one of
my Companions, before he would let me bleed him.
I told his Interpreter that he should tell him I would
feel his Pulse, that I might know whether it was
proper to let him Blood or no; Feel his Pulse!
What's that? said the Interpreter, who thought I
meant something else; whereupon I took him by the
Hand, and showed him what I meant. When the
Interpreter had satisfyed him with what I said, he
beckoned me to him, and held out his Hand, which
I felt, and found he was in a high Fever. I told
the Interpreter that he must be let Blood, for his In-
disposition was a Fever, and explained his Distemper,
which he finding to agree with his Condition, seemed to be mightily pleased; but he would have me
bleed some other of my Companions before him. I
pitched upon one that it would not injure, and bled
him upon the Ground till he had bled enough, and
then tyed up his Arm. The *Werowance* and the rest
of the *Indians* were amazed to see him bleed such a
Quantity, and asked me if he must bleeds
much? I told them, yes, or rather more; but that
I would have something to save the Blood, because
I could make a better Judgment of the Cause of his
Distemper. Whereupon they brought me a *Calli-
bash*, which I supposed might hold a Quart; and
upon this I tyed up his Arm, and let him bleed
till I had taken about sixteen Ounces from him,

so tyed up his Arm again. When I had done, he wanted to go into his Hammock to Sleep; but I told him he muſt not go to Reſt till Night, which he complyed with. The next Day he was much better, and ſent for me again, from the Place where they had kept us walking all Night, by ſinging and dancing round us; and if any of us offered to ſleep, they would jogg us and hinder us. When I came to him I unbound his Arm, and he looked at the Orifice, and finding it cloſed, was more amazed than before; then he made his Interpreter aſk me concerning his Blood, which was corrupted; and when I told him if I had not bled him, he would ſoon have died, he got up, and made me ſit down upon a Mat which lay in his Cabin, and told me by his Interpreter, if I would ſtay with him, he would ſave both me and my Companions, if we would fight againſt the *Whites*, and marry *Indian* Women, that ſhould be allotted us. I told him I would aſk my Companions, who rejoiced at the Propoſals; and though all marryed before, yet they made no Scruple of having another Wife. As for myſelf, (though not marryed) I did not much care for ſuch a tawny Rib, therefore told the *Werowance*, none of our Profeſſion ever marryed: he being well ſatisfyed with this Anſwer, ſpared all our Lives. For my Part I had a Houſe allotted me to myſelf, that is a Place about the Height of one Story with us, and covered with the Barks of Trees; the Fire-Place is in the Middle of the Houſe, and all the Chimney is the Door. The Country is generally pretty even, and agrees very well with an *Engliſh* Conſtitution; I

need

need not defcribe the Climate, for I fuppofe you all know the Nature of it as well as I.   All the *Indians* that ever I faw, were well limbed, and near fix Feet high.

The Marriages were made the next Day without much Ceremony, they were only joined by their Priefts, without any Queftion on either Side, and fo carryed Home to their feveral Tents.   All the while I was here, they were making Preparations to go againft the *Englifh*.   One Day I was fent for and ordered to feel the Pulfe of the King; after I had done, he afked me if I could tell any Thing of the Affairs of the *Englifh* by feeling the Pulfe; but I told him, that was impoffible, without I was with them in Perfon.   Whereupon the King afked me if I would go to the *Englifh*, and come to him again, and give him a true Account of them ; but faid he, you muft leave your *Sagamore* (meaning your Box of Inftruments) behind you.   I told him I would make it my Bufinefs to inform myfelf in every Particular, but that I did not know the Way; he told me I fhould have a *Canoe* and four *Indians* that fhould car- ry me within a League of the *Englifh*.   I muft con- fefs I went with Joy and Sorrow ; with Joy to leave fuch a curfed Place, where Death threatened me every Day; with Sorrow to go without my Com- panions.   We went into our *Canoe*, which lay about fix Miles from the Place where the King lived, but took no Provifions with us, becaufe my *Indians* were to provide for me by catching of Fifh, in which they are very dexterous.   We went down the River that the *Indians* called *Kaftorra* River, till we came to

Chesapeack-Bay; then we rowed in our *Canoe* past *Ruffel's* Iflands, and made toward *Cape*, or *Point-Comfort*; but coming about a League or thereabouts near the Ifland, a Boat came down the River, and upon what Account I cannot tell, but they fired a Mufquet, which being heard by the *Indians*, they immediately jumped over-board, and fwam back again to Shore. I was not much concerned I muft own, for there was no Danger of their being drowned, for moft *Indians* fwim like Fifhes. I took the Paddles and made the beft of my Way to *Point-Comfort*, which I paffed, and entered *Pawhattan* River, (being directed by my *Indians* fo to do) and directed my Way to *Lameftown*, where I arrived very late, and was mightily rejoiced to find my Companions all well in Health, and ready to embark the next Day for *Bofton*, in a Veffel bound for that Place. After refrefhing myfelf, and felling my *Canoe*, I with the reft of the Company fet fail the next Day, and after various Adventures am arrived where you fee me.

Now think with yourfelf, Mr. *Falconer*, whether we need doubt the Providence of God in helping us from this Ifland? There is nothing here like the Hardfhips I have undergone, and yet have been happily freed from; and therefore you need not defpair. Defpair is the Frenzy of the Mind, and ought to be avoided, by having a true Notion of the Power we ferve. Upon this I happened to fmile, but was mightily checked by Mr. *Randal*, who afked me with a clouded Countenance, what I fmiled at? I

replied

replied his Story might have had the fame Effect upon fome old Women, (if it were in Print) that the Sufferings of our Saviour had upon a Perfon in Years. What mean you by that, faid Mr. *Randal?* Why, I'll tell you, but I would not have you angry at it, for I really believe every thing you have faid to me: But a Reverend Divine once at *Stamford* in *Lincolnfbire*, was preaching a Sermon upon Chrift's Paffion, where he expatiated on the many Sufferings, and what our Saviour underwent to redeem us Mortals from the Curfe that was laid upon us: An old Woman (one of the Auditors) took the Parfon by the Sleeve as he went out of the Church, and faid to him, Indeed, Sir, you have made a very feeling Sermon, which has moved me very much, and more efpecially to afk you a Queftion or two. Say on, good Woman, faid the Parfon. Pray then, Sir, (faid fhe) how long is it ago fince this Matter happened? Almoft feventeen Hundred Years ago. And how far off? (added the old Gentlewoman) A great Way off, fome three or four thoufand Miles from hence. Alack-aday! cried the old Woman, I'm glad on it; Why fo, faid the Parfon? Becaufe (added fhe) 'tis fo long ago, and fo far off, I hope in God it is not true. As to your own Belief, (Mr. *Falconer*, faid he,) I leave it to yourfelf, but I don't like jefting with facred Things; The old Woman's Ignorance was Compaffion; your Knowledge feems to be prophane.

I have known a great many airy young Fellows that have talked idly on fuch Things, to make

E 4   People

People have an Opinion of their Wit; but yet, I believe, even in the very Time of their Utterance, their Conscience told them, they were doing what was not pleasing to God or Man. I really took Mr. *Randel's* Way of expressing himself very kindly, and as I ought; for there appeared so much Sincerity and Candour in all that he said, that it would move any one that had a Sense of Heaven or human Nature. Therefore I begged his Pardon, and was heartily sorry if I had said ought that might any Ways offend him; which he freely forgave. After we had spent the Night in Reflection of what had passed, the next Morning we (after imploring the Assistance of the Almighty) went to work to clear the Sand from our Vessel, which we continued working on for sixteen Days together, resting only on *Sundays*, which at last we effected. We had thrown up the Sand on each Side, down from the Vessel, quite, to the Surface of the Water, when it was lowest. Now the next Thing we had to do, was to get Poles to put under our Vessel to launch her out; which we got from the *Burton* Wood, but with much Difficulty, for we were forced to cut a great many before we could get them that were fit for our Purpose. After we had done this, we returned God Thanks for our Success hitherto, and on the Day following resolved (God willing) to thrust off our Vessel into the Water, but were prevented by Mr. *Rahdal's* being taken ill of a Fever, occasioned (as we suppose) by his great Fatigue in working to free our Ship from the Sand, wherein

he

he fpared no Pains for to encourage us as much by
his Actions as his Words, even beyond his Strength.
The Concern we were all in upon this, occafioned
our Delay in not getting our Veffel out, befides one
Hand out of five was weakning our Strength.
Mr. *Randal* never thought of his Inftruments till
now, which he wanted to let himfelf Blood, but not
feeling them about his Cloaths, we fuppofed they
might have been overlooked in the Veffel, fo I ran
immediately to fee if I could find them ; and getting
up the Side, my very Weight pulled her down to
the Sand, which had certainly bruifed me to Death,
if I had not by the Appointment of divine Providence funk into the Hollow that we had made by
throwing the Sand from the Ship. I crept out in a
great Fright, and ran to my Companions, who with
much ado got her upright, and afterwards we fixed
fome fpare Oars on each Side, to keep her up from
falling again : For the Pieces of Wood that were
placed under her were greafed to facilitate her flipping
into the Water, and we had digged the Sand fo entirely from her, that fhe refted only on them, which
occafioned her leaning to one Side with my Weight
only, which had not happened, I believe, if I had
endeavoured to have got on Board on the other Side,
which was higheft, but chufing the loweft for my
more eafy Entrance was the Caufe of the Accident
that happened to me. When we were entered into
the Veffel, and found our Endeavours to find the
Box of Inftruments fruitlefs, we were all mightily
concerned, for we verily believed that bleeding

E 5

would

would have cured him; nay, even he himself said, that if he could be let Blood, he was certain his Fever would abate, and he should be easier; yet to see with what a perfect Resignation he submitted to the Will of Heaven, it would have inspired one with a true Knowledge of the Being good Men enjoy after a Dissolution from this painful Life. He was still worse and worse; but yet so patient in his Sufferings, that perfectly amazed us all. He continued in this Manner a whole Week, without tasting any Thing but Water-gruel ill made, for what little Oatmeal we had, was sour. When we saw by the Course of Nature, it was impossible he should last long, we all were very much grieved; as for my own Part, I could not forbear shedding Tears, for I had taken such an Affection to him, that almost equalled a Child's Love to a Parent. He seeing me weep, called me with a faint Voice towards him; and when I was near him, he made me sit down by him. "After several kind Expressions, which made my Tears flow more plentifully; he said to me, Mr. *Falconer,* If you grieve for me, dry your Tears I desire nothing but your Prayers. I am going to pay a Debt incumbent on me by Nature, and a Debt that must be paid, which was contracted at my Birth, and Death will not admit of any Evasion; all Mortals owe the same Acknowledgement, but some squander away that Substance which should be freely paid when called for. How happy are they that provide against such a Creditor, that may come at any Hour of Day or Night, and lawfully demand his Due?

Here

Here is no Shuffling as in worldly Matters, no putting off the important Vifitor; therefore as we are
fure he will call upon us, 'tis good to be always
provided againft the Time.   How happy are honeft
Minds, when they have provided to fatisfy their
worldly Creditors; they then live in a Contentment
of Mind, peculiar to an honeft Heart: But what
muft be faid for the laft Debt, upon which depends
the Welfare of the Soul, our doing well or ill hereafter, is it not of the utmoft Importance? Therefore as I am endeavouring to pay that Debt, whofe
utmoft Limit will foon expire, help me by your
Prayers to finifh what I hope I have well begun,
and, as a Friend's Advice, prepare to make up
your Accounts to Heaven, for you know not how
foon they may be called for; befides you will have
one lefs to eat of the Provifion that is left.   After
this, being tired with fpeaking fo much together,
he turned to reft himfelf, but his Fever was fo violent, he could take no Eafe in Body, though tran-
quil in Mind.   So finding we could not expect his
Life, we prayed for a fpeedy and painlefs Releafe
from it. After this we gave him fome Water (which
he often begged for in vain) to cool his Mouth.
When he had drank it, he faid he found himfelf a
little eafier, and the Pain and Burning fomething
abated, which we took as a Lightning before
Death, or as the Spirits collected together to make
their laft fruitlefs Efforts.

When he found himfelf juft upon the Point of
expiring, he made this fhort Prayer, which was fo

E 6

imprinted

imprinted in my Memory, that I shall never forget it : O Almighty Creator of Heaven and Earth, whose all-seeing Eye looks into the inmost Corner of the Heart ! Pardon my Offences, which I heartily repent of, and rely upon the infinite Grace of thy wonted Mercy to absolve me of all my past Crimes, through the Merits of my Lord and Saviour Jesus Christ. Then, lifting up his Hands and Eyes to Heaven, expired, with the Happiness of continuing in his right Senses in such a Fever, which is almost always attended with a Frenzy.

After our Sorrow for his Death was something abated, we consulted how to bury him. Mr. *Middleton* and Mr. *Musgrave* were for sewing him in his Hammock and throwing him into the Sea ; but Mr. *White* and myself were for burying him on the Land, which they agreed to ; so we digged the Hole which I designed for my Well, seven Feet long, and seven deep, and returned him to Earth from whence he came. Upon the Bark of the Tree that shaded his Grave, I wrote this Epitaph :

‘ Under this Tree lies the Body of *Thomas Ran-*
‘ *dal,* Gent. born in the City of *Cork, Anno Domini,*
‘ 1641. who was thrown ashore with *Richard White,*
‘ *William Musgrave,* and *Ralph Middleton,* all of
‘ *Jamaica,* to the Consolation of *Richard Falconer* of
‘ *Bruton* in *Somersetshire,* who was unfortunately cast
‘ on Shore before them on the 18th of *September*
‘ 1699, yet received from their Conversation a Mi-
‘ tigation of his own Misfortune. Whose Chance
‘ it is ever to read these Lines, pay a Tear to the
‘ Memory

‘ Memory of *Thomas Randal*, and endeavour to make
‘ as good an End as he did, who died a natural
‘ Death, on *Friday December* the 21ſt, 1699, in his
‘ perfeſt Mind, and a true Notion of the Power of
‘ God to pardon all his Faults, whoſe Failings were
‘ correſted by a ſincere Penitence, dying every Day
‘ he lived.’

This took me up a whole Tree. Mr. *Randal*
made no Will ; yet I claimed his Dog, being the
Whelp of the Bitch he found upon the Rock which
he was thrown upon in the *Baltick*, the Bitch being
dead ſome Years before. We were forced to tie
him up after we had buried Mr. *Randal*, for with
his Feet he would ſcrape Holes in the Grave two
Feet deep, and howl prodigiouſly.

After this we prepared once more to launch our
Veſſel ; but firſt we put on board what Proviſion we
had left, and all the Things that we took from
thence. Mr. *Randal*’s Death gave me (with the
others Permiſſion) a Title to a Bed, which I wanted
before. So that I took up the Cabin which was
allotted me, and laid on board every Night. And
now we bent our Thoughts entirely on our Veſſel,
and on *Monday* the 31ſt of *December* launched her out
into the Sea, and deſigned to ſet ſail the next Day.
After we had fixed her faſt with two Anchors and a
Halſer on Shore, we went on board to dine and
make ourſelves merry, which we did very heartily,
and to add to our Mirth, we made a large Can of
Punch, which we never attempted to do before, being we had but one Bottle of Lime-juice in all, and

what

what (indeed) we defigned for this Occafion; in fhort, the Punch ran down fo merrily, that we were all in a drunken Condition; but when it was all gone, we refolved to go to reft: But all I could do, could not perfuade them to lie on board that Night in their Cabins, (yet without a Bed;) but they would venture, though they were obliged to fwim a hundred Yards before they could wade to Shore; but however they got fafe, which I knew by their hallooing and rejoicing.

Having brought my Bed on-board, I went to reft very contentedly, which I did till next Morning; But oh! Horror! when I had dreffed myfelf, and going on Deck, to call my Companions to come on board to dine, which was intended over Night, and afterwards to go on Shore, and bring our Sails and Yards on board, and make to Sea as faft as we could, I could not fee any Land, which fo overcame me on the fudden, that I funk down on the Deck, without Senfe or Motion: How long I continued fo I can't tell, but I awaked full of the Senfe of my lamentable Condition, and ten thoufand Times (fpight of my Refolution to forbear) curfed my unhappy Stars, that had brought me to that deplorable State. O Wretch that I am! what will my unhappy Fate do with me; is any one's Condition equal to mine? (I would cry.) But 'tis a juft Punifhment, in not rendering to God the Tribute due for his Mercies, that we had hitherto known. Inftead of coming on board to be frolickfome and merry, we fhould have given Thanks to him, that

gave

gave us the Blessing of thinking we were no longer subject to such Hardships, that we might probably have undergone, if we had been detained longer on that Island. If poor Mr. *Randal* had remained among us, this Misfortune had not happened. He by his wise and prudent Care and Conduct, would have prevented this unlucky Accident. What must my poor Companions think that are left in a more miserable Condition than myself, if it be possible. I have no Compass, neither am I of myself capable of ruling the Vessel in a Calm, much less if there should a Storm happen, which are too frequent in this Climate.

After I had vented my Grief in a Torrent of Words and Tears, I began to think how the Vessel should have gone to Sea without my Knowledge; and by Remembrance of the Matter the Night before, found by our Eagerness and fatal Carelessness, we had forgot to fasten our Cables to the Geers; and pulling up the Halser that we had fastened to one of the *Burton* Trees on Shore, perceived that the Force of the Vessel had pulled the Tree out of the Earth. Then I too late found that a Hurricane had rose when I was found asleep; and stupified by too much Liquor, and carried off the Vessel. This Reflection wounded me deeper than before, which I followed with Curses on that Liquor that steals away our Senses, and makes worse than Beasts of human Creatures.

Now I began to call upon him that hears us in the Time of Trouble; even when the Wind blows
loudest,

loudeft, whofe Nod can fhake the Frame of Earth from off its Bafis; and with a Heart fincere, and vicious Thoughts correcled, I fent my Soul in penitential Words and Tears before his Throne of Mercy, imploring a fpeedy Ending of my Life or Troubles; when I began to be fomething better contented in my Mind, and thought of fuftaining Nature, almoft fpent with the Fatigue and Grieving. One great Comfort I had of my Side, which my poor (former) wretched Companions wanted, that was Provifion in Plenty, and frefh Water; fo that when I began to confider coolly, I found I had not that Caufe to complain which they had, who were left on a barren Ifland, without any other Provifion than that very fame Diet which I was forced to take up with, when firft thrown afhore; that is, the *Boobies*, whofe Numbers were mightily diminifhed before we defigned to leave the Ifland.

What made me moft uneafy, was to think what my Companions could judge of me, whether they fhould take it for Defign or Chance; but then I ftilled that Thought, by knowing they muft needs fee that the Tree was forced away with Violence beyond the Strength of Man. Befide, I had another fmall Comfort, that was the Company of my Dog, which lay on Board with me, which I ufed to talk to as if he were a rational Creature; and the poor Beaft would ftand and ftare me in the Face, as if he were fenfible of what I faid to him. It was a very handfome Creature of the *Danifh* Kind, but very good natured, and would often go to the Ca-

bin

bin where I lay, which was that of his old Mafter, and whine mightily.

I remained toffed upon the Sea for a Fortnight without difcovering Land ; for the Weather continued very calm, but yet fo hazy that I could not perceive the Sun for feveral Days. One Day fearching for fome Linnen that I had dropped under the Sacking of my Bed, (for I did not lie in a Hammock) I found an old Glove with 75 Pieces of Eight in it, which I took and fewed in the Waiftband of my Breeches, for Fear I fhould want it fome Time. or other I made no Scruple of taking it, for I was well affured it did belong to poor Mr. *Randal*. Befide I had heard the other People fay, that they were fure he had Money fomewhere; and after his Death we fearched for it, but could not find any.

January the 20th I difcovered a Sail to Leeward of me, but fhe bore away fo faft, that there was not any Hope of Succour from her, and I had not any Thing to diftinguifh me; and I fuppofed though I could fee them, yet they could not fee me by Reafon of my Want of Sail, which would have made me the more confpicuous. The next Day I difcovered Land, about fix Leagues to the S. W. of me, which I obferved my Veffel did not come nigh, but coafted along Shore ; but I was well affured it was the Province of *Jucatan* belonging to the *Spaniards*, and was the Place we came from. Now all my Fear was that I fhould fall into their Hands, who would make me do the Work of a Slave ; but even that I

thought

thought was better than to live in continual Fear of Storms and Tempests, or Shipwreck.

I coasted along in this Manner for two or three Days, and at last discovered Land right a-head, which I was very glad of; but yet mixed with some Fear, in not knowing what Treatment I should have. I began now to think of some Evasion, and not to tell them the Truth, of belonging to the *Log-wood* Vessel, but resolved to tell them that we were taken by a *French* Privateer, and after being rummaged, were turned off as useless.

January the 30th, I made the Bay and Town of *Francisco di Campechy*, as, it proved afterwards, and was almost upon it before I was met by any thing of a Ship, or a Boat; but at last two Canoes came on Board with one *Spaniard* and six *Indians*, who were much surprized when they understood my Condition by speaking broken *French*, which the *Spaniard* understood. They immediately carried me on Shore, and from thence to the Governor, who was at Dinner; they would have had me staid till he had dined; but he hearing of me, commanded me to come in, where he was at Dinner with several Gentlemen, and two Ladies; and though 'tis very rare any one sees the Women, yet they did not offer to veil themselves. I was ordered to sit down by myself at a little Table placed for that Purpose, where I had sent me of what composed their Dinner, which was some Fish and Fowls, and excellent Wine of several Sorts.

The

The chief Town of the Province of *Jucatan*, lies twelve Leagues from the Sea on either Side, which is a Bishop's See, and the Residence of the Governor of this Province. *Valladolid* is the second City; and *Campechy* the third; yet though but the third reckoned, it far exceeds the rest for Riches and Magnificence. It is a well-situated neat-built Town, and by Computation, contains near two thousand Houses. It is well fortified both by Art and Nature: By the former in a strong, well built neat Castle, that contains a hundred Brass Cannon, and several Mortars; and the latter by a Ridge of Hills, that runs all along the Side of the City. There is in the Center a very neat Piazza, consisting of about thirty high Arches. This Town has the chief Trade; for from this Place, the other Cities and Towns are furnished with all Necessaries that come from the *Havana*, and other Places in *America*; and likewise from *Old Spain*. Yet for all their Power, Riches and Strength, Capt. *Parker*, an *Englishman*, with one Ship, and a small Bark, and whose whole Crew contained but a hundred and forty Men, landed in the Middle of the Day, and in Spite of all their Forces, which were two hundred Horse, and five hundred Foot, took the Place, with the Governor and several other Persons of Quality, together with a rich Ship laden with Ingots and several other valuable Ladings, before they knew of the City's being taken. This Province of *Jucatan*, contains in Compass nine hundred Miles, and is situated between eighteen and twenty

Degrees

Degrees Northern Latitude. The Air is very hot, and not altogether fo wholefome as fome other Parts of *America* are. The Diftempers that reign here, are moftly Fluxes and Fevers, which carry off Abundance of new Comers. This Province was firft difcovered by *Ferdinando Cortez,* among his Conquefts of *New Spain*; and though not altogether fo fruit-ful, yet by the Induftry of the Inhabitants, 'tis as rich as any of the other Provinces of *New Spain*; for they are moft either Merchants or Tradefmen: And it is the vulgar Opinion, that thefe People are more hard and barbarous, than any other Part of the *Spanifh Weft Indies*; yet, for my own Part. I re-ceived more Civility from them, than if I had been among my own Friends in *England.*

There is a Tradition here among the Inhabitants that they ufed a Ceremony much like our Baptifm, and which had, in their Language, the Term of Regeneration, or fecond Birth, which they thought to be the Seed or Groundwork of all good and juft Things; and after being initiated, they were cer-tain it was not in the Power of the evil Spirit to hurt them in Body or Goods: Neither were they permitted to marry, without firft taking that Order upon them, which they ufed to diftinguifh by an *Oftrich's* Feather, larger and longer than any other they ufed to wear for Ornaments upon their Heads.

They have another Tradition, that this Province of *Jucatan* was firft inhabited and cultivated by a white-bearded People, that came from the Eaft;

after

after being toffed many Moons upon the Sea, and fuffering many Hardfhips for Want of Food and frefh Water, and other Neceffaries; yet relieved from Want and their Enemies, through the Power of the Deity they worfhipped, who even commanded the Sun to fhine, or not to fhine; who made it rain, or dry Weather; who could heal Sicknefs, or fend Diftempers; in fhort, a God that kept all the other petty Deities in Awe.

This Story, if true, feems to confirm an old Tradition of our *Welch* Chronicles, that tells us of one *Madoc ap Owen*, Son to *Guineth*, a Prince of that Country, who was drove, by fome Difguft, from his own Country, with feveral Companions; who, after various Adventures at Sea, were driven on an unknown Land to the Weft many hundred Leagues, where they had Communication in a friendly Manner with the *Indians*, and made a Settlement. Whereupon *Madoc ap Owen* returned for *Britain* again, and got to the Number of two thoufand Men and Women, befides Children, which mixed with the Natives, and left among them feveral of their Opinions and Manners; which they retained till the laft, when *Cortez* fubdued them; but now, by the Cruelty of the *Spaniards*, the Natives are almoft extinguifhed.

After they had feafted me for two or three Days, they fent me about with feveral Officers appointed by the Governor, to make a Gathering, which we did with Succefs; for in three Days we had got feven hundred and odd Pieces of Eight: And two
Merchants

Merchants there were at the Charge of fitting up my Bark, in order to fend it for my poor Companions. When it was finifhed, they gave me feveral Neceffaries for myfelf and Companions, to hearten us up; as fome Bottles of fine Wines; two Bottles of Citron-water, for a Cordial; Chocolate, and feveral other ufeful Things: But the Difficulty was to get Seamen to go with me: At laft they remembered they had five *Englifhmen* that were Prifoners there, and taken in the Bay of *Campechy*, upon Sufpicion of Piracy, but nothing could be proved againft them; which they freed without any Ranfom: 'This did not look like Barbarity or Ill-nature; for I received as much Humanity among them, as could be expected from any of the moft civilized Nations: But they have a greater Kindnefs for the *Englifh*, than they have for their Neighbours the *French*, for the *Englifh* are more open and generous (they fay), and don't ufe Stratagems to deceive them, as the *French* do frequently; though they only pay them in their own Coin, for there is no Nation under the Sun more fruitful than the *Spaniards* in Plottings and Ambufcades, (as they call them) to deceive their Enemies; which yet they think lawful.

On *February* the 15th, 1700, we fet Sail from *Campechy* Bay, after paying my Acknowledgment to the generous Governor, *&c.* but having nothing to prefent him worth Acceptance, but my *Ovid*, I gave him that, which he took very kindly, and faid he would prize it mightily, not only in the Efteem

he

he had for that Author, but in Remembrance of
me and my Misfortunes.

We plyed it to Windward very briskly, and in
fifteen Days difcovered the Ifles of the *Alcranes*;
but we durft not go within the Shoals, becaufe we
were all ignorant of the Channel. So we caft Anchor, and hoifted out our Boat, with two Men and
myfelf, and made to Shore, where we found my
three Companions, but in a miferable Condition,
and Mr. *Mufgrave* fo faint and weak, that they expected he could not live long.

When they awaked the next Day, after I was
drove off in the Dark, they were all in Defpair, to
find the Veffel gone, which they perceived was occafioned by a Hurricane, that they were affured was
violent, becaufe it had blown down their Tent,
though without awaking them. But when they began to confider they had no Food, nor but very little frefh Water, which was left in a Barrel without
a Head in the Tent, their Defpair increafed; but,
as no Paffion can laft long that is violent, it wore off
with their Care for Suftenance, which they dili-
gently fearched for; but not finding any Quantity
of Eggs, or *Boobies*, the dreadful Fear of ftarving
came into their Minds, with all its horrid Attend-
ants. Now they imagined that all that had happened
to them was, as I had thought, a Judgment of Divine Providence for the vile Sin of Drunkennefs,
when they fhould have rather implored Heaven's
Affiftance, in furthering them in their Delivery from
the Place where they were.

They

They had now been five Days without eating o
drinking, not for Want of Stomachs, but Food,
which they endeavoured to get, but all to no Purpofe; for the *Boobies* were retired, either out of
Fear, or Cuſtom, to ſome other Place. Neither
could they find one Egg more, and Weakneſs came
ſo faſt upon them, with Hunger and Drought, that
they were hardly able to crawl, ſo they thought of
nothing but dying; when at laſt they remembered
the Body of good Mr. *Randal*, that had been buried
a Week, which they dug up, without being pu-
trified; and that poor Wretch that helped to ſupport our Misfortunes when alive with his ſage Advice, now was a Means of preſerving their Lives,
though dead. They had by good Fortune left them
a Tinder-box in the Tent, (we having two) with
which they ſtruck a Light, and made a Fire, then
cnt off ſeveral Pieces of Fleſh of the Brawn of his
Arms and Thighs, broiled them on the Coals,
though with a great Deal of Reluctance; which was
the Means of keeping Life and Soul together, till
we came to relieve them from that deplorable Condition. Mr. *Muſgrave* we brought to a little Life
and Strength, by giving him ſome Citron-water in
ſmall Quantities. When I ſaw the Carcaſe of my
poor good Monitor lie for Food for human Creatures, my Horror at the Sight overcame my Reaſon,
and I believe I ſaid Things ſhocking enough; however, when I had calmly conſidered their Condition,
I was very ſorry for what I had ſaid, and begged
their Pardon. After we had refreſhed ourſelves,

we

we once more laid him in the Earth, having sewed his poor Bones in one of the Hammocks.

I must confess, I never think of that good Man, but Tears come into my Eyes, and Melancholy clouds all my Thoughts: For he was one whose Character came up to all we could desire in frail Man. Honest, without Interest; friendly, without Design; religious, attended with Reason; and not swaddled up so tight as to make it deformed: Pleasant in Conversation, courteous to all, hating nothing but Vice; gentle in reproving; bold in all Dangers, in being armed with an Innocence that inspired him with Success: In short, he was a Miracle of a Man, when we consider his Life had been always at Sea, among a Crew prone to all Manner of Vices, and where it was not possible to find a Pattern to follow of any Goodness.

He was a single Man, or rather indeed a Bachelor; for he had often told me, he could not bear to marry a Woman, to put her into Frights and Fears when the Wind blew hard, as every good Wife must certainly be concerned for the Danger of her Husband. Besides, as it was his Fortune to lead a Seafaring Life, he could not think of marrying, to be absent from his other Self so long (as he termed it); not but if he had had a sufficient Competency, he said, he believed he should have entered into the Marriage State in the latter Part of Life, that he might have settled his Mind, and, free from the Hazard and Turmoils of the Sea, slipped into his

F

Shrowd

Shrowd with Content, among his Friends and Acquaintance at Home.

He was an excellent Sailor, and knew moſt Parts of the World perfectly well; underſtood *French* and *Spaniſh*, and ſeemed to have a pretty good Knowledge in the *Latin* Tongue. His Journals were moſtly taken in Short-Hand: But he had one ſmall Manuſcript, containing about twenty-Leaves, *Spaniſh* on the one Side, and *Engliſh* on the other, all in his own Hand; which I ſuppoſe he had tranſlated for his Diverſion, and to paſs away his leiſure Hours. It was a Treatiſe of Herbs and Flowers, with other Rarities, to be found in the *Weſt-Indies*: On the Flat of his Book, he had writ in a large Hand theſe Words: *This Manuſcript in* Spaniſh, *I have tranſcribed from the Original of the Reverend Father* Pedro di Riberia, *of the Order of* Jeſus, *when I was Pilot in* Mexico. *The Tranſlation I have made at my leiſure Hours; and the Cures by the Simples, &c. mentioned in the ſaid Book, I have been an Eye-Witneſs to many of, and ſome were practiſed on myſelf.*

We now were got on Board once again, in order to ſail as ſoon as the Wind would riſe, it being ſtark calm, and continued ſo two Days; but at laſt it blew a little, and we weighed Anchor, and ſtood out to Sea; but made but little Way. I now was Maſter, or Captain of a Ship, and began to take upon me; we were in all nine Men, all *Engliſh*, that is, myſelf firſt, *Richard White, W. Muſgrave*, and *Ralph Middleton*, my old Companions; *John Stone*,

Stone, *W. Keater*, *Francis Head*, *W. Warren*, and *Joseph Meadows*, (all of *England*) the five Men given
me by Don *Antonio*, who, as I said before, were
taken on Suspicion of Piracy; whereupon a Thought
came into my Head, that had escaped me before: I
considered if these were really Pirates, being five to
four, they might be too powerful for us, and perhaps murder us. *Frank Head* we had made our
Cook, to dress our Provision, which he understood
a little One Day we all dined together upon Deck,
under our Awning, it being very calm Weather;
an *Awning* is only a Sail fixed at the Quarter-Deck,
and carried over the *Booms* (that is, spare Masts that
lie along from Quarter to Fore castle) to the Fore-
castle, to keep the Sun from our Heads: In Men of
War, and great Ships, they have one made of
several Kinds of handsome Stuff, for the Officers on
the Quarter-Deck; besides another on the Main
Deck, for the common Sailors. One Day, as I
said before, being at Dinner, for we all eat together, I asked the five Men, what was the Reason
they were taken by the *Spaniards* for Pirates? Upon
this they seemed nonplused, but *Warren* soon recovered himself, as well as the rest, and spake for the
others, in this Manner: We embarked on Board
the Ship *Bonaventure*, in the *Thames*, bound for
Jamaica, where we made a prosperous Voyage; but
after taking in our Lading, in our Way Home, we
were overtaken by a Storm, in which our Ship was
lost, and all the Men perished, but myself and four

F 2

Companions,

Companions, who were faved in the Long-Boat:
But the Reafon we were taken for Pirates was, that
making to Shore to fave ourfelves, we faw a Bark
riding at Anchor, without the Port of *Campecly*,
which we made to, in order to enquire whereabouts
we were, and to beg fome Provifions, our own being
gone; and entering the Veffel, found but two
People in it; the third, jumping into the Water,
fwam on Shore, and brought three Boats filled
with *Spanifh* Soldiers, which entered the Veffel
before we could make off. Make off! faid I.
What did you defign to run away with the Veffel?
No; anfwered *Warren*, with fome Confufion, but
we did defign to weigh Anchor, and go farther on
Shore, that we might land in the Morning (it being
late at Night): But we were prevented by their
coming on Board us, where we were found, being
armed, which we had taken Care of, when we
were in our Boat, to defend ourfelves, if we were
obliged to land among the *Savages*: And indeed
they had their Arms reftored them, when they
were freed and fent on Board with me.

I muft confefs, I did not like the Fellow being
nonplufed now and then, in not knowing what to
fay; but upon Confideration, thought it might be
for Want of Words to exprefs himfelf better, which
is the Occafion very often of People of common
Underftanding, Stammering, and Humming, and
Hawing, to put their Words in better Order; fo
for that Time I took no more Notice, not weighing

it

it in my Mind : But in the Evening Mr. *Middleton*
came to me, with a Face of Concern, and told me
he did not like thefe Fellows Tale. Why fo ? faid
I ; becaufe I obferve they herd together, anfwered
he, and are always whifpering and fpeaking low to
one another. Oh ! faid I, there cannot be any
Danger in them ; for if they had any Inclination to
run away with our Veffel, they might have done it
when they were five to one, before we took you in.
I know not, replied *Middleton*, I have a Heart fore-
bodes fomething. Pfhaw ! old Women's Fears ;
(faid I) for, as I faid before, they would have done
it when they had more Power, before I landed on
Defpair Ifland, (as I called it) if they had any fuch
Intentions. There is a Providence that rules over
all our Actions, anfwered *Middleton*, that we can no
more fee into, than the Book of Fate, but if a
foreboding Heart may fpeak, I am fure fomething
we fhall fuffer from thefe Fellows, that will be of
Danger to us. If fo, replied I, there's no refifting
the Will of Providence ; for what will come, will
come, and there's no fending againft it : But,
added he, this feems fomething like Foreknow-
ledge ; and to refift againft that, feems like ftrug-
gling againft the Will of Heaven, that warns us by
thefe Forebodings to prevent thefe Accidents of
Life. I believe God, purfued he, has fixed a
Period to our Breath ; but Accidents that happen in
this Pilgrimage of Life, may be avoided by a

F 3 timely

timely Notice : As we are all Partakers of free Will, and from that, forming our own Happiness, or Misery, it cannot be said but that the Actions of Life may be regulated by that Free Will. Our Maker never formed a Villain : Neither do their external Parts differ from a virtuous Man's ; if they did, they were to be easily avoided : But as an old Poet says, *There's no Art to find the Mind's Construction in the Face.*

Upon this Discourse, I began to stagger in my Opinion of their Honesty, and therefore we resolved to stand upon our Guard. We took no Notice of our Conference than to our two other Companions, but resolved to stay till Night, we having a better Opportunity, as we lay together in the Cabbin Aft; (which is as much to say in the Stern, or behind) when we were to go to Supper, we called one another to come, but five of the Sailors excused themselves, by saying they had dined so lately, that they had no Stomach as yet ; whereupon we had an Opportunity sooner to converse together than we designed. For being at Supper, we opened the Matter to our other two Companions, and they agreed immediately that we were in some Danger ; so we resolved in the middle Watch of the Night, to seize them in their Sleep. We were to have the first Watch, which we set at eight of the Clock ; then they were to watch till Twelve ; and then in their Watch, between One and Two, we had concluded to seize upon them as they slept ; that is,

four

four of them, for one of them watched with us, which was *Frank Hood*, the Cook; whom we agreed to seize and bind fast, towards the latter End of the Watch, and to threaten him with Death, if he offered to make the least Noise.

As soon as ever our first Watch was set, we sent Mr. *Musgrave* to prepare our Arms; in about half an Hour, or thereabouts, *Warren* called to *Hood* upon Deck, (they lying below) to get him a little Water, for he was bloody dry, he said; whereupon the other went down immediately with some Water in a Can to him. As soon as he was gone down, I had the Curiosity to draw as near the Scuttle as I could to hear the Discourse. Now you must know *Hood*, our Cook, had been employed that Day about searching our Provisions, our Beef Casks, and Pork, to see what Quantity we had, that we might know how long it would last; so that the others had not an Opportunity to disclose the Design to him. As soon as he was got down, I could hear *Will. Warren* say to him, G—d d—n ye, *Frank*, we had like to have been smoaked to-Day; and though we had contrived the Story that I told them, yet I was a little surprized at their asking me, because then I did not expect it; but we design to be even with them in a very little Time; For, hark ye, said he, and spoke so low that I could not hear him; upon which, the other said, there's no Difficulty in the Matter; but we need not be in such Haste, for you know, as we ply it to Windward, a Day or two

F 4

can

can break no Squares, and we can foon (after the effecting our Defign) bear down to Leeward to our Comrades that we left on Shore ; for I fancy, added he, that they have fome fmall Sufpicion of you now, (which in Time will fleep) and may be on their Guard ; therefore 'tis better to wait a Day or two: No, G—d Z——ds, we'll do it To-night, when they are afleep, replied *Warren*; whereupon there were many Arguments, *Pro* and *Con*; (as I fancied) but they fpoke fo low, that I could only hear a G—d D—n ye, now and then, and fomething of that Kind.

A little while after, *Hood* came up again, and after walking up and down, and fixing his Eyes often upon me, who in the mean Time was provided with a Couple of Piftols under my Watch-Coat, and indeed were their own, that we hung up ready charged in our Cabin ; which was one Reafon of their Defign to attack us in our Sleep, being they had no Arms till they could feize on them where they hung ; or elfe they were fuch defperate Fellows, they would have done it in the open Day. *Hood*, as I faid before, feemed to fix his Eyes frequently upon me, for till now I never watched in the Night ; at laft, faid he very foftly, if you pleafe Mr. *Falconer*, I have a Word or two to fay to you, that much concerns you all. What is it ? faid I. Why, anfwered he, I would have the reft of your Companions Ear Witneffes too ; with that I called them together ; but, faid he, let's

retire

retire as far from the Scuttle as we can, that we may not be heard by any below Deck; fo we went into the Cabin, and opened the Scuttle above, that Mr. *Mufgrave*, who fteered, might hear what was faid. When we were fat down upon the Floor, Mr. *Hood* began as follows. My four Companions below have a wicked Defign upon you; that is, to feize you, and put you into the Boat, and run away with your Veffel: But I thinking it an inhuman Action, not only to any one, but to you in particular, that have been the Means of their Freedom, therefore, I hope appointed by Providence, I come to let you know it, that we may think of fome Means to prevent it. Upon this, (finding his Sincerity,) I told him that we were provided againft it already; and with the Confent of my Companions, told him our Defign of feizing them in the third Watch; but, faid he, they intend to put their Project in Practice, their next Watch, therefore I think it will be more proper for us to Counter-plot them, and feize them this; but as they have no Arms, faid I, and we have, we need not fear them.

We had feveral Debates about this, which took up too much Time to our Sorrow; for *Warren* miftrufting *Hood*, it feems, got up and liftened, and when he found that we retired all of us to the Cabbin, he got upon Deck, and ftealing foftly, came fo clofe, that he overheard every thing we faid, which as foon as he underftood, he went immediate-

F 5

ly

ly to his Companions, who waited impatiently, (as they told us afterwards) and let them know all our Difcourfe; whereupon, without paufing, they refolved to attack us immediately, in the Midſt of our Confultation; which was no fooner refolved upon, but done: For we were immediately furprized with their feizing us, which they did with that Quicknefs, and fo unperceivably, that we were all confounded and amazed; they had whiped off two Piſtols in our Confternation, which they clapped to our Breaſts. In this Confufion, I had forgot mine that were at my Girdle, (or elfe we might have been hard enough for them;) neither did I remember them till they found them about me. They had' ſhut the Cabbin Door on the Infide, till they had' bound us, and never minded Mr. *Mufgrave* knocking and making a Noife, till they had fecured us. Which done, they opened the Door, and feized him, who came to know what the Matter was, for we had no Candle in the Cabbin, and he hearing a Noife, amongſt us, thought we were feizing *Head*, and called to us to forbear, (as he faid afterwards) and make hafte, for he was going to tack about, thorgh we did not hear him; on which he clapped the Helm a Lee, and came down to fetch us out, to haul off the Sheets, &c. and was feized, and bound with us; for they left us immediately, for the Sails fluttered in the Wind, by Reafon fhe was veering round, when the Helm was a Lee.

After they had fixed the Veffel, and it was broad Day, they came and unbound our Legs, and gave us Leave to walk upon Deck; whereupon I began to expostulate with them, particularly Mr. *Warren;* being he seemed to have a Sort of Command over the others. Pray, said I to him, for what Reason have you seized upon us, and bound us in this Manner? Have we done you any Injury? Why, said he, Self-Preservation; I found you were going to do the like by us, therefore you are but served in your Kind. And what do you design to do with us now you have your Desire? Do with you! Why, by and by we design to put you in the Boat, and turn you a Drift; but for that Son of a B—h, *Heed,* we'll murder him without Mercy; a Dog, to betray us; How, betray you! replied I? Yes! For I overheard all; then related the Manner of it as mentioned above. But as you have not so much injured us, we'll put you immediately in the Boat with a Week's Provision, and a small Sail, and you shall seek your Fortune, as I suppose you would have done by us. No, answered I, we only designed to confine you till we came to *Jamaica,* and there to have given you your Liberty to go where you had thought fit. Ay, ay, said *Warren,* shaking his Head, that is easily said, nor are we bound to believe you. Why, 'tis plain, said I, that our consulting to seize you, was but to prevent what has happened. We are not to enquire into the Matter, answered *Warren,* and now we have you in our Power, we'll do as we think fit. Why then, said I put us ashore at any Land that belongs to the *English,* and we shall think you have not done us any Injury. No, said he, we must go to meet our Captain and fifty Men upon the Main Land of *Jucatan,* where

our

our Veffel was ftranded not to be gotten off. Our firft Defign when we were taken in our Boat was to get us a Veffel to go a *Buccaneering*, which we had done at *Campechy*, if it had not been for the *Indian* that fwam on Shore unknown to us, and brought Succours too foon; which we could not avoid, the Sea Breeze blowing very ftrong all Night; fo we feeing our Danger, were forced to form the Lie we told the Governor, which had fome Appearance of Truth, for we did not ufe any Violence to the two old *Spaniards*, becaufe by good Words we thought to make them affifting to work our Bark back again to our Men. Now, purfued he, if you will ali refolve to go a *Buccaneering* with us, we'll venture to carry you to our Captain and Men; if not, we'll do as we have propofed. We looking one upon another, as if we were to know each other's Refolutions; he cryed, nay, if you paufe, you fha'n't have that Grace, if you defire it: Therefore prepare every Thing, perfued he, to one of his Companions, that they may be going, they won't be long before they come to their Journey's End.

When they had got every Thing ready, that is to fay, a Barrel of Bifket, another of Water, about half a Dozen Pieces of Beef, and as much Pork, a fmall Kettle, and a Tinder-Box; we were better provided than we expected, by much. Befides, they granted us four Cutlaffes, and a Fowling-piece, with about four Pounds of Powder, and a fufficient Quantity of Shot; together with all poor Mr. *Randal's* Journals, after their perufing them, and finding

ing

ing them of no Ufe to them · When this was done, he ordered them to tie *Hood* to the Maft of the Veffel, and was charging a Piftol to fhoot him through the Head, not confidering it was charged before, for it was one of them I had at my Girdle, and which they took from me; but in his Eagernefs and Heat of Paffion did not mind it. We all intreated for the poor Fellow, and he himfelf fell upon his Knees, and begged with all the Eloquence he had, to fpare him, and let him go with us; but *Warren* fwore bitterly, nothing fhould fave him. Said I, Mr. *Warren*, if you believe there is a Power, that formed this Globe, and fees every Action of Mankind, think what a Crime you commit by wounding of him, by murdering his Image: But if you are an *Atheift*, and believe in no Power fupernatural, yet confider what a Conqueft you will have gained over yourfelf by overcoming this headftrong Paffion. It may be your own Cafe another Time; and Murder you know is punifhed with Death. What the Devil have we got here, a preaching Puppy? Why, doft think that I mind thy ridiculous Cant? prythee mind thy own Bufinefs, and get thee gone, or perhaps I may begin with you, and fend you to the Devil before your Time. With that, he cocked his Piftol, and levelled it at *Hood*; but firing, it fplit into feveral Pieces, and one ftruck *Warren* into the Skull fo deep, that he was breathing his laft upon Deck; one of the Bullets grazed upon the Side of my Temple, and did but juft break the Skin; as for *Hood* he was not hurt; but with the Fright and Noife of the Piftol, (as we fuppofed)

laboured

laboured with such an Agony of Spirit, that he broke the Cords that tied him by the Arms, though as thick as a middle Finger, and fell down; but rose immediately, and not finding himself hurt, ran to us, and unbound our Arms, not perceived by the other two, who were busy about unfortunate *Warren*; and though they were called to him by them that steered, (who ran immediately to prevent it) yet they did not mind it, they were so concerned about *Warren*. And before he that steered came, *Hood* had unbound me, and stopped the Fellow (*Meadows*) by giving him a Blow with his Fist that knocked him down. In the mean Time, I had unbound *White*, *Musgrave*, and *Middleton*; and we went and seized upon the other two *Pyrates*, for now we called them nothing else. After we had bound in our Turn, we went to see what Assistance could be given to *Warren*, where we found that a Piece of the Barrel of the Pistol had sunk into his Skull, and that he was just expiring; but yet he sat upon his Breech with great Resolution; said he, you see you overpowered us, and I likewise see the Hand of Heaven is in it. I now with Horror find (added he) that what you intimated to me about Heaven, to be true; I see it more in this one Accident, than in all the Preachings of the Fathers. I was bred a *Roman*, had good honest Parents, *Romans*, whose Steps, if I had followed, would have made my Conscience easy to me at this Time; but I forsook all Religion in general, and now too late, I find that to dally with Heaven is fooling ones self; but yet in this one Moment of my Life, that's left, I heartily repent of all my past

Crimes.

Crimes, and rely upon the Saviour of the World, that died for our Sins to pardon mine. With that, he croffed himfelf, and expired.

I muft confefs, I was very forry for the unhappy Accident of his Death; but yet, glad that we were at Liberty; and were fomething eafy that the poor Soul repented before his Expiration; not doubting but the piercing Eye of Providence, faw that if he had furvived, he would have lived a good Chriftian. And fure the Almighty's infinite Stock of Bounty, has enough Mercy to fave the repenting Soul, though late before his Repentance comes.

After we had fecured our *Tartars*, we threw Mr. *Warren* over-board, and bore to the Wind; for after our firft tacking about in the Morning, when the Buftle happened, they bore away with Tack at Cat-head, as being for their Purpofe. The three Men that were left, defired us to let them have the Boat, and go feek their Companions; which we refufed, as not having Hands enough to carry our Veffel to *Jamaica*. But we promifed them, if they would freely work in the Voyage, they fhould have their intire Liberty to go where they thought fit without any Complaint againft them. Upon this, we began to be a little fociable as before, and they all declared, that that what they did was by the Inftigation of *Warren*.

The next Day we difcovered a Ship to Windward of us, that bore down upon us with crowded Sails. We filled all the Sails we had, and endeavoured to get away from her as faft as we could, but all to no Purpofe; we faw they gained upon us

every

every Moment, and therefore feeing it was not poffible to efcape, we backed our Sails and laid by
for them, that they might be more civil if they
were Enemies. As foon as ever they came up
with us, they hailed us, and ordered us to come
on Board, which we durft not deny; when Mr.
Mufgrave and I, with *Hood* and *White* for Rowers,
went on board them. We found by *Hood*'s knowing them, that they were his Captain and Comrades. Now, as *Hood* faid, we did not know how
we fhould behave ourfelves, or what we fhould fay
about *Warren*; but we only told the Captain how
we met with his Men, and that they were redeemed
upon my Account. He never afked particularly for
Warren, but how they all did; but when they fent
on board to fearch our Veffel, they foon came to
the 'Truth on't; for the other three told them the
Story, though not with aggravating Circumftances:
Upon which poor *Hood* was tied to the Main-maft,
lafhed with a Cat of Nine-tails moft abominably,
and after that pickled in Brine, which was more
Pain than the Whipping; but it kept his Back
from feftering, which it might otherwife have done;
becaufe they flay the Skin off at every Stroke, and,
to prevent it, they wafh it with Brine; which is
called *Whipping* and *Pickling*. After this they would
not keep him among them; but fent for the other
three Men from our Veffel, and ordered us all on
board, with another of their Men that was ill of a
dangerous Fever, which they feared might prove
infectious. They did not take any Thing from us,

as

as we expected at firſt, only gave us this ſick Man to look after, which we were very well contented with. So we parted with them very well ſatisfied, but much better when we were out of Sight, fearing they had forgot themſelves, and would ſend for us back, and take our Proviſion from us, or one Miſchief or another; for Pyrates do not often uſe to be ſo courteous.

Our ſick Man mended apace, for we took great Care of him, and by keeping him low, only with Water-gruel, his Fever left him; when I began to keep up his Spirits with my Cordials that I had by me, and in a Week's Time he was pretty hoddy, (as we call it at Sea). Now we began to converſe with him, and he ſeemed to be a ſenſible good-natured Fellow.

Among other Diſcourſe, we aſked him how Captain M———ll and his Crew got a Ship? Said he, I can only tell the Story as I have heard it (for I was ſick on Shore); which is as follows:

Sixteen of our Men got a *Paragua* from the *Indians*, who hate the *Spaniards*, being under their Subjection, and love the *French* and *Engliſh* very well; theſe ſet out to ſeize upon the firſt Ship that they thought they could compaſs; when after being five Days cruiſing along Shore, they ſpied a large Ship weathering *Cape Catoch*; but believing it to be too ſtrong for them, they reſolved to work by Stratagem, thus: Twelve Men laid down in the Boat, as if very faint and weak, and made a Signal to the Ship, as if in Diſtreſs, who very charitably

brought

brought to ; now they had no Arms with them, for when they refolved to ufe this Stratagem, they left them afhore, as making the Pretence more feafible ; fo that when they arrived at the Ship, they all went feebly up, as if not able to ftand ; nay, fome were obliged to be led, forfooth, to colour the Matter the better. They then told them that their Ship was caft away upon *Leggerhead's Key*, about three Leagues from *Cape Catach*, and faving themfelves in their Boats, they got fafe into the Cape ; but that wandering up in the Country, they were met by the *Indians*, who ufed them barbaroufly, killing eleven of their Number ; and would have ferved the reft fo, if they had not made their Efcape in that *Paragua* ; that they were fo harraffed for Want of Food, having been without eating two Days, that they feared fome of their Companions would never recover.

The poor *Spaniards* fwallowed the Bait, and their Captain, being a very good Man, refolved to relieve them, and afked him what they would have him to do for them ? They begged him to land them on the firft *Englifh* Colony or Ifland in their Way. He anfwered, he was bound for St. *Domingo* in *Hifpaniola* ; but that he would put in at *Jamaica*, though fomething out of his Way ; yet, faid he, I don't care for going to any of the noted Ports, becaufe there is a War talked of between *England* and *Spain*, and though it was not proclaimed, they might meet with fome Trouble. They were mightily obliged to him, they faid, but they did not

know

know how to return the Obligation, but by praying for him and his.

They sailed very lovingly with them for three or four Days, till at last Fortune gave them an Opportunity to put their Enterprize in Execution. They had Notice that the Ship leaked mightily, and that the Water came into the Bread-room; upon which, the *Spaniards* went down to remove the Bread to get at the Leak, and did not leave more than five Men and the Captain above, whom they instantly seized, and clapped down the Hatches upon the rest. When they had secured them, they armed themselves with Pistols and Lances, which were placed in the Steerage of the Ship, and so capitulated with them; but first, they steered their Course back again; that they might not lose any Time. As they came up, one by one, they bound them, till they were all so, but the Captain and the Pilot: The Captain they confined to his Cabin, with a Centry to guard him; but they let the Pilot go loose, that he might steer the Ship. O inhuman! cried I; thus the Snake in the friendly Bosom warmed turns and stings his kind Protector: Thus was their generous *Host* (if I may call him so) betrayed by his too much good Nature.

After they had brought the Ship safe to us, we embarked, and put the *Spaniards* ashore without a Morsel to help themselves; nay, if the *Indians* could conveniently meet with them, they would not leave one alive. I must confess, pursued the Man, that the barbarous Story shocked my very Nature,

and

and made me hate their Society; and I really believe the Abhorrence of this curfed Action brought my Diftemper upon me.

How much are fome Beafts Acknowledgments of Kindnefs more than Man? A poor Cur, fed but a Cruft a Day, will follow the bounteous Hand that gives it. Ingratitude is the Fountain of all other Crimes, for from thence flow all the reft. But all the Knowledge fome Men are endowed with, is but to find the beft Way to deceive. How happy it would be if fuch Creatures could fhake off their Humanity, and become Beafts in Form as well as Mind; then we fhould have a Mark to fhun them by. Our Creator has formed all Kind of Beafts in Shapes that tell us what they are: But Men differ in their Natures more than Beafts, or are indeed, under their human Form, the very Natures of the Brute Creation. How many Villains, under a fmooth Face and Tongue, betray their Brothers? The Father cheats the Son, the Son the Father; Mothers fquander the Dowry of their Daughters, and then proftitute them to gain them Bread, which is not Gain but Punifhment: But Ingratitude, like Murder, meets with its Punifhment on Earth, as well as in the other World; and an ungrateful Man fhould have a Mark, that all human Society may fhun him. I think the *Lacedemonians* ufed to punifh Ingratitude with Death, as a Crime equal to Sacrilege or Parricide.

After having taken all their Men on Board, (and leaving Directions on the Bark of a Tree, for the five

Men

Men that were gone upon the same Design another Way) we set Sail, and had not been out two Days before we met with you. Pray, said I, how came you among them, if you liked not their Design? Why, Sir, answered he, by Accident; embarking from *Bermudas*, bound for St. *Catharines*, or the Isle of *Providence*, we were met with by this Pirate, in a Ship of twenty Guns, and a hundred and twenty Men, who took us, and rummaging us, threatened to turn us adrift without Provision, if we would not embrace his Designs, which was Piracy. We, rather than undergo what he threatened us withal, consented with our Tongues; but our Inclinations were far from it. And from our first being with him, we were plotting to make our Escape the next Opportunity. But the other four (being but five in all our Vessel) were unfortunately killed in that Engagement, where they lost their Ship. What Ship was it they fought with? Why, Sir, a Man of War of twenty-six Guns, sent out on Purpose to take her; for the Captain had committed such Disorders wherever he came, that he obliged the Governor of *Jamaica* to send out the Ship called the *Experiment*, to cruise till she met with him: which she did about five Weeks ago. Our Captain, as soon as he saw her, guessed at her Design, and resolved to fight her to the last; well knowing if he could take or sink her, he might be pretty secure to range where he pleased, there being never another Ship of War nearer than *Barbadoes*; who never came so far West. After he had made a Speech to his

Men

Men to encourage them to fight it out, and told
them their Advantage, they confented to hoift the
bloody Flag, and neither to give or take Quarter.
As foon as ever the Man of War faw our bloody
Flag out, they hoifted theirs, and there enfued a
dreadful Fight. We began about Two o'Clock,
and fought till dark Night, without perceiving any
Advantage on either Side; and then by Confent lay
by till Morning without fighting: which we did fo
nigh, it being calm, that we could talk to one
another; but we did it only in threatning Language. As foon as the Morning dawned, we went
to it again, with more Fury than before, for our
People fought like defperate Madmen, well knowing if they fhould be taken, they muft all die. The
other Ship fought with a Bravery uncommon; but
I believe the Advantage was on our Side, though
we had killed on Board us thirty-fix Men.

We fought on till Noon, when we difcovered a
Ship about three Leagues to Windward of us,
which bore down upon us with all the Sail they
could. We foon conjectured, they could be no
Friends to us, fo without much Confultation, we
refolved to run it before the Wind, with all the
Sail we could make; as for the *Experiment* we
fought with, we had put it out of their Power to
follow us, for we had fhot their Main-Mast by the
Board, fo that if the other overtook us, we fhould
have but one to deal with. We by good Fortune
had all our Mafts firm, and we out-failed the other

Veffel;

Veſſel; but as ſoon as ſhe came up with the *Experiment*, (who never offered to follow us) ſhe laid by, as we ſuppoſe to aſſiſt her, and we obſerved through our Teleſcopes that ſhe had *Spaniſh* Colours out.

We ſoon loſt Sight of them, and then we deſigned to change our Courſe, but were prevented by the Men diſcovering two Feet Water in the Hold; who could not find out the Leak, though they ſearched with all the Diligence they could: So we were obliged to pump, but all that we could do, the Water ſtill gained upon us; we reſolved to bear away to *Jucatan*, a Province belonging to the *Spaniards*, and ſeek out ſome convenient Place, unfrequented by them, where we might find out our Leak, and ſtop it.

Notwithſtanding our Labour in pumping, the Water gained upon us; ſo we put out our Long-Boat, and our Pinnace, in order to put in our Proviſion; which by Morning we effected, and very happily for us; for it was agreed upon all Hands, that the Ship could not ſwim about eight Hours; and though we diſcovered Land, and were not above ſix Leagues off Shore, yet we were afraid we could not reach it, as the Ship was ſo heavy with Water. So all that could not ſwim, were ordered into the two Boats, with their Arms; which held in them thirty-ſeven Men with Officers. They that were left on Board, had Orders to pump as long as they could, and run directly in Shore to the Leeward of *Cape Catoch*; but within half a League of the Place,

the

the Ship funk, and the Men betook themfelves to fwimming, whom we met with our Pinnace, and took up.

I cannot omit one barbarous Action of the Captain's. There were five Men wounded, who begged to be taken into the Boat, but the Captain refufed them ; and this was his Reafon, as he gave to us in the Boat : Said he, thofe five that are wounded, will take up too much Room, for they cannot fit as we do, but muft lie along ; and another Thing is, they will take more Time in looking after, than we can well fpare. Befides, as I believe they will not recover, they will be fooner out of their Pain ; and if they fhould recover, added he, they would help us to devour our Provifion, which we muft take particular Care of, for we know not when we fhall get more. I muft confefs, this Ufage ftruck me to the Heart almoft, efpecially as to one of them, who feemed to have a Senfe of his Condition, and repented of all his paft Crimes.

After we came on Shore, we found that we had killed on Board us forty-three Men, befides the five that our Captain barbaroufly murdered, by leaving them in the Ship when fhe funk. Two of their Bodies were drove on Shore the next Day, but were ordered by the Captain to have Stones tied to their Feet, and carried off Shore and funk. As foon as we had made us two Tents with Sails that were put in the Boat for that Purpofe, they began to confult in what Manner they fhould get a Ship ; when one

Warren

Warren propofed to take the Boat, and four Men befide himfelf, with Arms, and a Week's Provifions, for he would not have any more, and go to the Bay of *Campechy* or *Campechy* Town, where he did not fear getting a Veffel for their Purpofe; for he faid, he had done fo upon the like Occafion before. Whereupon the Boat and four Men were ordered for him: but he ftaying longer than the appointed Time, they thought fome Mifchance had happened to him, fo took off their Thoughts of having any Veffel from him. One Day they 'fpied a large *Paragua* coming towards Shore with nine *Indians* and two *Spaniards* in it, and finding it come fo near, that they muft of Courfe fee them, they immediately refolved either to take or kill them all, for Fear they would difcover them to the *Spaniards*, before they had got a Veffel to go off again.

Though I muft confefs there was fome Reafon, yet I thought it barbarous to fee how they murdered the two *Spaniards* and nine *Indians*. They put out their Pinnace and ten Men well armed, to go and take this *Paragua*; as foon as ever they were difcovered by the *Indians*, they jumped over-board, and made towards Shore; but were fhot by our Men, or knocked on the Head with the Butt-End of their Mufquets. The two *Spaniards* had a new Kind of Death; they tied them Breaft to Breaft, and their Hands behind them, and threw them over board; where they ftruggled for fome Time, and at laft were drowned. I thought

G

this

this was a Cruelty exceeding all the Tyrants in the
World, and if I had had a Boat, and our People
never a one, I would have run any Hazard to have
faved them. Their *Paragua* was laden with Flower,
and dried Fiſh, with feveral Sides of dried Pork, or
Bacon; which was too good for the People that
had it. As for my own Part, but little of it came to
my Share, for I was taken ill the fecond Day after
we came there, and fo weak and feeble, that I did
not expect to overcome it; and if it had not been
for a Black, that was Trumpeter to the Captain, I
ſhould have periſhed for Want of Suſtenance; but
the poor Fellow frequently would bring me fomething or other to nouriſh me; and it is to him, under
God, that I owe my Life. He would often tell me that
he did not love that Sort of Life, and wiſhed he could
get rid of his Maſter; but faid he, if he did but
know I had fo much as a Thought that Way, he
would be the Death of me. I believe this was the
only poor Fellow that prayed in the whole Crew.
He was chriſtened at *Plymouth* in *England*, (and had
very good Notions of Religion) where he was given
to his prefent Maſter, who had made feveral Voyages into the *Weſt Indies*, for a *Plymouth* Merchant;
but at laſt finding Matters on Shore go but indifferently, and having killed a *French* Officer there,
feized upon the Ship he ufed to command, and with
a Crew of defperate Fellows made off to Sea, and
ſteered his old Courfe for the *Weſt Indies*, and there
                                    commenced

commenc.d Pirate; but had met with no other Succefs, than what has been related to you.

Said I, this Fellow's too wicked to have Succefs
in any Thing, efpecially when Succefs mufl be an
Addition to his Crimes: If it were poffible to know
his Fate, we fhould find that he would have fome
defperate End: For Men when abandoned by Providence Divine, though perhaps they may meet with
fome Succefs at firft, at laft find an End that's fitted
for fuch Wretches who deny a fuperior Being; and
even Atheifts, notwithftanding their human Form,
are no better than Brutes; nay, I take an *Atheift* to
have far lefs Right to Salvation, than thofe *Indians*
that pray to the Devil; for they do it through Ignorance, and worfhip him with a more fincere Devotion, becaufe they know 'tis in his Power to do
them Harm.   With what a fervent Zeal would they
ferve the true God, if they knew (as all who profefs
Chriftianity do) that it is in his Power to beftow
Bleffings, even after this Life? With what Devotion
they worfhip the Sun, who they take to be the fuperior Deity, becaufe it makes the Earth green, and
is the fecond Caufe of all the Good they enjoy?
Then, with how much more Reverence ought we to
give Praife to that Power that lends Light and genial
Heat to that Planet? If an *Atheift* would confider the
Works of Nature juftly, he would find it an Impof-
fibility to be fo any longer; and to fancy this World
was formed by Chance, or Accident, is to allow

G 2

Beafts

Beafts the Privilege of Nature and Reafon, to as great a Degree as we that pretend to Humanity.

John Roufe was the Name of this Sailor we took on Board, born at *Bermudas*. He offered us fome Propofals, if we would go along with him thither, but I declined it, as wanting to be with my old Ship's Crew, and thought of feeing my own Country again, as I believe all Travellers do, who bring nothing Home but Misfortunes, or the Vices of the Places they have travelled through. From this Man the faid *Roufe*, I had the following fhort Defcription of *Bermudas*, or the *Summer Iflands*.

Bermudas (the Place of my Birth) or the *Summer Iflands*, is fuppofed by fome, to take its Name of *Bermudas* from certain black Hogs that came out of a *Spanifh* Ship that was caft away on thofe Shores. And by others from one *John Bermudas*, a *Spaniard*, the firft Difcoverer of the Iflands. The Name *Summer Iflands*, is derived from *George Summers*, an *Englifhman*, who fuffered Shipwreck there. They are fituated in thirty two Degrees, and twenty five Minutes of Northern Latitude ; fixteen hundred Leagues from *England* ; twelve hundred from *Madeira*; four hundred from *Hifpaniola*; and about three hundred from *Bofton* in *New-England*. The *Spaniards* had it firft, and after them the *French* ; but the Supplies that were fent them from *France* mifcarrying by Shipwreck, they were obliged to abandon the Iflands. After this, one *Wingfield*, a Merchant in *London*, fent in two Ships, Captains *Gofnel* and *Smith*, with People to fettle there; but there was not much done

till

till 1612, when a Company was eftablifhed at *London* by Letters Patent, given by King *James* the firft, who immediately fent Captain *Moor* with fixty-five Men, where he was two Years in fortifying the Iflands againft the Attempts of any Invafion from either *French*, *Spaniards*, or *Indians*. In the mean Time a Sort of Rats fo increafed, that they devoured every Thing that was green in the whole Ifland, and had like to have ftarved the Inhabitants, if Providence had not timely fent a Difeafe among them that confumed them all. In about three Years after the firft Plantation by Captain *Moor*, there was fent them another Supply of Men and Provifion, by Captain *Bartlet*, who returned with a hundred Weight of Ambergreafe. The next Year, there arrived five hundred Men and Women, with Tradefmen of all Sorts. In 1616, one *Tuckard* fucceeded in the Government, and was very ferviceable to the Plantation, in bringing and planting feveral Trees, and Tobacco. He alfo divided the Country into Acres, and parcelled it out to the Tenants. It encreafed daily in Culture and Inhabitants. The Form of the Iflands, as they lie, refembles fomething of a Lobfter with its Claws off. The chief of the Iflands is called *George Ifland*, and is divided into eight Parts, befides the general Land. 1. *Hamilton Tribe*; 2. *Smith's Tribe*; 3. *Devonfhire Tribe*; 4. *Pembroke Tribe*; 5. *Paget's Tribe*; 6. *Warwick Tribe*; 7. *Southampton Tribe*; 8. *Sandy's Tribe*. The Iflands are all furrounded by Rocks, that at high Water are dangerous to Strangers. The chief Harbours are

G 3

Southampton

Southampton, *Harrington*, and the *Great Sound*. Upon
St. *George*'s *Island*, they have built feveral large and
ftrong Forts, whofe Chief are *Warwick* and *Dover*
Forts. The Soil in fome Places is fandy or clayed;
and in other Places Afh-coloured, White and Black;
about two Feet deep under the Afh, is found great
Slates, which the Inhabitants make Ufe of feveral
Ways; and under the Black is found a ftony Subftance, fomething like a Spunge, or Pumice-ftone.
The Wells and Pits, ebb and flow with the Sea,
yet produce excellent frefh Water. The Sky is generally ferene; but when 'tis over-caft they have
dreadful Thunder and Lightning. The Air is much
the fame as with you in *England*. They have two
Harvefts in the Year: They fow in *March*, and reap
in *June*; then they fow in *Auguft*, and gather in *Ja-*
nuary: And from that Month till *May*, the Whales
frequently fwim by them. They often find great
Quantities of Ambergreafe, and fometimes Pearl
Oyfters. No venomous Creature will live in any
of the faid Iflands. The yellow large Spiders have
not the leaft Venom in them. There's Plenty of all
Sorts of Cattle, both wild and tame, efpecially
Hogs, who have mightily encreafed fince their firft
landing; but they are not altogether fo fat as we
could wifh, feeding only on Berries that fall from
the Palmetto-Trees, which are very fweet. There's
Plenty of Mulberries, both white and red, which
produce prodigious Numbers of Silk Worms; who
fpin Silk of the Colour of the Berry. The Trees
are here of different Kinds; the Cedar is reckoned

the

the largeſt in the Univerſe. The Leaves are downy, and prickly at the End: The Berries that it produceth are of a pale Red which incloſe four white Kernels; the outermoſt Skin is ſweet; the innermoſt that contains the Kernel, is ſharp; and the Pulp is tartiſh. The Tree is always flouriſhing, being at the ſame Time full of Bloſſoms, green and ripe Fruit. The Berries when ripe begin to gape, and fall off in rainy Weather; leaving a round Stalk on the Boughs, which loſes not its Rind till that Time Two Years after. The Berry requires one Year before it comes to its full Ripeneſs, which happens about *December*. The Boughs ſhoot upwards, and in a little Time are ſo heavy, that they weigh down the Body of the Tree. There are many Plants, as the *Pickle Pear, Poiſon Weed, Red Weed; Purging Bean, Red Pepper, and the Coſtive Tree, and the Sea Feather,* which grows on the Brink of the Sea. . There is another Plant called *Nuchily,* which grows in the Niches of the Rocks, waſhed by the Waves of the Sea, and produces a Fruit like a Pear, which they call the *Speckled Pear,* from its Spots. For Fowls, we have all Sorts that *England* produces beſides a great Number of Cranes, larger than any I have ſeen elſewhere; with a Sort of Fowl that lives in Holes in the Rocks like Rabbits. As for Tortoiſes, they are as good there as any where. They catch them in this Manner; they watch for them at Night, when they come on Shore to dig Holes to bury their Eggs in; while they are doing of it, they turn them on their Backs, and not being able to get upon their

G 4

Legs

Legs again, they are eafily taken.   Some will have
a hundred Eggs in them about as big as a common
Tennis Ball, and very round; but a thin Skin, and
the Yolk lies on the Side of the Skin, or Shell, and
may be feen on the Outfide: Thefe hidden in the
Sand, are nourifhed by the Sun, and never minded
by the Tortoife that lays them; and as foon as ever
they have broke the Shell, they all run into the Sea.
Some fay they are full fix Years a hatching.   They
are excellent Meat, (for I can't call them Fifh) and
very nourifhing, and we ufe the Oil inftead of Butter, which will keep longer, and is reckoned much
wholefomer for many Ufes.   Befides, it is good to
bathe the Place that is ftung by a little Infect, called
Mufketo.   The largeft of thefe Iflands is *Long Ifland*;
the next, St. *George's Ifland*; after that, *Somerfet*, and
St. *David's*;   next, *Hibernia*,   or *Ireland Ifland*;
then *Longbeard, Cooper's,* and *Smith's Ifland*; *Non-
fuch Gates*; and the *Brothers Ifland*; with many others
as well inhabited, and provided with every Thing
for the Life of Man; which is elegantly defcribed by
your *Englifh* Poet, Mr. *Edmund Waller.*

 Bermudas, *wall'd with Rocks, who does not know*
That happy Ifland where huge Lemons grow,
And Orange Trees, which golden Fruit do bear?
Th' Hefperian Garden boafts of nnoc fo fair.
Where fhining Pearl, Coral, and many a Pound,
On the rich Shore, of Ambergreafe is found.
The lofty Cedar, which to Heav'n afpires,
The Prince of Trees, is Fewel for their Fires:

The

The Smoak, by which their loaded Spits do turn,
For Incenfe might on facred Altars burn:
Their private Roofs on od'rous Timber born,
Such as might Palaces for Kings adorn.
The fweet Palmettos, a new Bacchus yield,
With Leaves as ample as the broadeft Shield:
Under the Shadow of whofe friendly Boughs,
They fit caroufing where the Liquor grows.
Figs there unplanted through the Fields do grow,
Such as fierce Cato did the Romans fhow;
With the rare Fruit inviting them to fpoil
Carthage, the Miftrefs, of fo rare a Soil,
The naked Rocks are not unfruitful there,
But at fome conftant Seafons ev'ry Year,
Their barren Tops with lufcious Food abound,
And with the Eggs of various Fowls are crown'd.
Tobacco is the worft of Things, which they
To Englifh Landlords as their Tribute pay:
Such is the Mould, that the bleft Tenant feeds
On precious Fruits, and pays his Rent in Weeds:
With candied Plantanes, and the juicy Pine,
On choiceft Melons, and fweet Grapes they dine,
And with Potatoes fat their wanton Swine.
Nature thefe Cates with fuch a lavifh Hand
Pours out among 'em, that our coarfer Land
Taftes of their Bounty, and does Cloth return,
Which not for Warmth, but Ornament is worn:
For the kind Spring, which but falutes us here,
Inhabits there, and courts them all the Year;
Ripe Fruits and Bloffoms on the fame Trees live,
At once they promife, what at once they give.

G 5

So

So sweet the Air, so moderate the Clime,
None sickly lives, or dies before his Time.
Heav'n sure has kept this Spot of Earth uncurst,
To shew how all Things were created first.
The tardy Plants in our cold Orchard plac'd,
Reserve their Fruit for the next Age's Taste :
There a small Grain in some few Months will be
A firm, a lofty, and a spacious Tree :
The Palma Christi, *and the fair* Papah,
Now but a Seed, (preventing Nature's Law)
In half the Circle of the hasty Year
Project a Shade, and lovely Fruits do wear.
And as the Trees in our dull Region set,
But faintly grow, and no Perfection get ;
So in this Northern Tract, our hoarser Throats
Utter unripe, and ill constrained Notes :
While the Supporter of the Poet's Stile,
Phœbus *on them eternally does smile.*
O ! how I long my careless Limbs to lay
Under the Plantane's Shade———

'There is now in the Islands of *Bermudas*, near forty thousand Inhabitants, mostly *English*. The Laws are the same as in *England*. The Religion and divine Worship the same. There are three and twenty Parish Churches, besides Chapels. In the Year 1616, five Seamen set Sail from thence in an open Vessel of about three Tons, and after having suffered several Storms and Tempests, were safely landed at *Kinsale* in *Ireland*. The *French* and *Spaniards* have made several Attempts upon those Islands; but always were drove away with considerable Loss.

About

About a Month before I embarked for this unfortunate Voyage, we took a *French* Pirate, who was so insolent as to come into *Harrington's Sound*, even at Noon-day, and cut the Cables of a Merchant-man, richly laden, bound for *England*; but by good Fortune ran upon the Flats in the Mouth of the *Sound*, in going out again: So we had Time to man some Boats with some of the Soldiers of the Garrison, and send to their Relief, where there happened a desperate Fight for some Time; but more Forces going to the Affistance of the others, they took them after an obftinate Refiftance, killing twenty-feven of their Men, and lofing eleven of our own. The Captain made his Efcape in his Boat, in the latter End of the Engagement, when he perceived his Danger; but was obliged to go on Shore on *Ireland Ifland* for some Provifion, where he and four Men that were with him, were fecured, and fent to *Tucker's Town*; where they were to be tried the Day I came away.

'Two Nights after we had parted with the Pirate, we were encountered with a dreadful Storm, that lafted two Days without abating; and our poor Bark, which was none of the beft, was tumbled and toffed like a Tennis-ball, yet we received no Damage, but that fhe would not anfwer the Helm; so that we were obliged to let her go before the Tempeft, and truft to the Mercy of Heaven for Relief. This Storm, and the Danger we had efcaped from the Pirate, put me in mind of thefe four Lines of the forementioned Poet, the celebrated *Haller*:

Bold were the Men, which on the Ocean first
Spread their new Sails, when Shipwreck was the worst.
More Danger now from Man alone we find,
Than from the Rocks, the Billows, or the Wind.

We, in the middle of the Storm difcovered Land right a-Head, which put us all into our Panicks; we endeavoured to bring our Veffel to bear up to the Wind; but all to no Purpofe; for fhe ftill drove nearer to Shore, where we difcovered feveral Tokens of a Shipwreck, as Pieces of broken Mafts, and Barrels fwimming on the Water, and a little farther Men's Hats; then we began to think we fhould certainly run the fame Fate, when, as foon as thought, our Bark was drove on Shore in a fmooth fandy Bay, but where we had Opportunity to quit her, which was happy for us; for the Sea wafhed over her with fuch Violence, we had not any Hopes of her efcaping the Storm, but thought of courfe would be torn to Pieces.

When we were afhore, we all concluded it could be no other Part but the South of *Cuba ifland,* belonging to the *Spaniards.* We were then in a terrible Fright, left we were near any Part that belonged to the *Indians;* for Mr. *Mufgrave* affured me, that there were fome Parts of the South Side of *Cuba,* that *Indians* dwelt in, in Spite of the *Spaniards,* and maffacred them wherever they met them, or any other Whites. We lay all Night in terrible Fear, and though we found the Storm abated, or rather a

C.lm

Calm fucceeded, yet we durft not ftir till the Moon rofe, and then we all walked towards our Veffel, which we found all on one Side ; but by good Fortune moft of our Provifions were dry, which mightily rejoiced us ; but all the Veffel's Rigging and Mafts were fhattered and torn in Pieces, and fome Part of her Quarter wrung off, that fhe could not be of any Ufe to us if we could have got her upright. But we took out all our Provifion, and our Arms, with two Barrels of Gun-powder that was dry, the reft being damaged with Water and Sand that had got in. We had Arms enough, as having them that belonged to the three Sailors that were taken in the Pirate, which we fuppofed they had forgot; fo we were fix Men well armed, with each a Mufket, a Cafe of Piftols, and a Bayonet ; befides two Cutlaffes, if Need were.

By that Time we had taken every Thing out, Day approached, and then we defigned altogether, well armed, to go and view the Country. *John Roufe* was very well recovered of his Fever, but a little weak, yet his Heart was as good as the beft of us. So we refolved, if we were fet upon by *Indians*, to defend ourfelves to the laft Drop of Blood, choofing rather to die by their Hands in Fight, than to be tortured after the Manner as they inflict upon all the Whites they get into their Hands. But ftill we had fome Hopes that we were too far towards the Northward for them.

When we had placed our Provifion and other Neceffaries fafe behind a Tuft of Trees that grew

clofe

clofe by the Water-fide, we fixed our Arms, and ventured to walk up in the Country, which we did almoft every Way that Day, four or five Miles; but could not difcover any living Creature, nor any Sign of Inhabitants, only in one Place the Grafs feemed to be lately trodden, but whether by Man or Beaft we could not difcover, fo being pretty well tired, we went back again to our Station, where we ate heartily, and at Night we laid ourfelves upon the Grafs, and fell afleep; for we durft not lie upon the Sails we had got for that Purpofe, becaufe they were not dry, though fpread all Day long.

I was awakened the next Morning by a Company of *Lizards* creeping over me, which is an Animal frightful enough to look at, but very harmlefs, and great Lovers of Mankind; they fay, that thefe Creatures, if any Perfon lies afleep, and any voracious Beaft, or the *Alligator*, which comes on Shore often, is approaching the Place where you lie, will crawl to you as faft as they can, and with their forked Tongues tickle you till you awake, that you may avoid by their timely Notice the coming Danger. I got up, being roufed by thefe Animals, and looked about me, but faw nothing but an odd Kind of a Snake about two Feet long, having a Head fomething like a Weafel, and Eyes fiery like a Cat's; as foon as it fpied me it ran away, and my Dog after it; but I believe put it in a terrible Fright, for it made a Noife fomething like a

Weafel,

Weasel, but louder, which awakened my Companions. When I told Mr. *Musgrave* what I had seen, he said it was a small Serpent, but not very hurtful called the *Guabiniquinaze Serpent*, from eating a little Creature of that Name, something resembling a small Mole; and the *Indians* and *Spaniards* eat of them, and reckon them dainty Food.

We now resolved for another Walk, to discover what Inhabitants were our Neighbours, whether *Indians* or *Spaniards*; if *Indians* we designed to patch up our Boat, which had several Holes in it, and make off as fast as we could, and row Northward, till we came to some Place inhabited by *Spaniards*. But if we found the latter, to beg Protection, and some Means to get to *Jamaica*; whereupon we ventured out with these Resolutions. We met with several fine large Cedar Trees, and one particularly so large, that Mr. *Musgrave* and I could but just fathom it with our Hands joined.

We had not gone far before my Dog began to bark, when turning my Head on one Side, I beheld a Black approaching towards us, and being startled at the Sight, I cocked my Piece, and resolved to fire at him; but he called to me in *English*, and told me he did not come to do me any Harm, but was a poor distressed *Englishman* that wanted Food, and was almost starved, having eat nothing but wild Fruit for four Days. Upon that I let him come near, where he was soon known by Mr. *Rouse* to be *William Plymouth*, the Black that was Trumpeter to the Captain that commanded the

Pirate

Pirate Ship. Upon his knowing him, we fat down and gave him fome Provifion, which we had brought with us, becaufe we defigned to be out all Day.

After he had refrefhed himfelf a little, we afked him how he came into this Ifland? Why, anfwered he, we were cruifing about *Cuba*, in Hopes of fome *Spanifh* Prize, when a Storm arofe and drove us upon a Rock, where our Ship was beat to Pieces, and not above eighteen Men faved befides the Captain. And did that wicked Wretch efcape the Shipwreck, faid I? Yes, anfwered *Plymouth*, but to undergo a more violent Death. For, faid he, as foon as ever we landed we wandered up in the Country to fee for fome Food, without any Weapons but a few Cutlaffes, having loft our firft Arms; but however we ail got fomething or other to defend ourfelves on Shore, as long Clubs, which we got from the Trees we found in our Walks; our Captain refolved if he met with any *Indians* or *Spaniards* Huts, that he would murder all that he found in them, for Fear they fhould make their Efcape, and bring more upon us. Thus he encouraged his Men to follow him with their Clubs; faid he, we will walk till we find fome beaten Path, and there lie hid till Night, when we may go on to fome Houfes, and come upon them undifcovered; by which Means we may get Provifion and other Arms: For the *Indians* of *Cuba* ufe Fire Arms as well as the *Spaniards*, and are full as dextrous in ufing them as any *Europeans*, &c. After travelling
about

about ten Miles to the N. W. we difcovered a Path, upon which a Halt was commanded, and to retire into the Woods again till Night; which we did, and dined upon what Fruits we could get upon the Trees.

About two Hours before Night a Dog fmelled us out, and running away from us, barked moft furioufly; upon that we were afraid of being difcovered, which Fear proved true; for in half an Hour, or thereabouts, after the Dog left us, we were faluted with feveral Arrows and Mufquet-Shot, that killed us three Men, and wounded me in the Foot, but it proved the Means of faving my Life: For as foon as our Men perceived what had happened, they ran as hard as they could to meet the Danger, as knowing they could do no good till they came to Handy-Blows; I, in endeavouring to follow them, found my Hurt, which prevented my keeping up with the reft; but I could hear and fee them at it: There were about two hundred *Indians* fet upon our Men, and in about half an Hour killed them every one. I faw the Captain lay about him defperately, but at laft fell, being run through the Throat with a wooden Stake. As foon as ever they had conquered them, or rather murdered them, they fell to ftripping of them as faft as they could, and carried them off, together with their own Dead, which were many, for the *Englifh* fold their Lives very dearly.

After they were gone, which I found by their Screaming and Noife at a Diftance, I ventured to

fteal

steal out from behind a Row of Bushes, where I had placed myself to see what had happened; I went to the Place of Battle, where I found two of our Men that they had left, with all their Arms, and some of their own; so I took up one of their best Musquets, and a Cutlass, and made farther into Wood, for Fear of being caught; which I had certainly been, if I had staid a Quarter of an Hour longer, for I soon heard them come whooping, screaming, and hallooing back, to fetch the other two Bodies, and their Arms, as I conjectured.

I walked as far as my hurt Foot would let me that Night, and out of the Danger of the *Indians*, as I thought, and then laid me down to sleep as well as I could, being very hungry, and sadly tired, and slept pretty well till Morning, when I proceeded forward in my painful Journey, and directed my Course N. E. thinking that was the best Way to avoid the *Indians*, and probably to meet with some *Spaniards*, whom I knew inhabited towards the North, the *Havanna*, the capital City of the whole Island, being seated there. I wandered for four Days, eating nothing but Fruit in the Woods; but laying myself down about an Hour ago, to rest myself a little, I thought I heard the Tongues of *Englishmen*, which to my great Joy proved true. I left my Musquet behind the Bushes, for Fear of alarming you; but now, after returning God and you Thanks for this timely Nourishment, I'll go and fetch it, which he did; and we might easily know it to be an *Indian* Piece, for they had rudely

carved

carved it all over with feveral Figures of Birds and Beafts.

Now, faid I to my Companions, you fee the Reward of Wickednefs. He was not fuffered by Providence to go on long in his Crimes; though fome that are inured to Ills, yet they are overtaken at laft, when their Crimes are full blown; for though Juftice has leaden Feet, yet they always find fhe has iron Hands; and we too often fee that he who kills his Adverfary in a Duel, though he efcapes the Law, one Time or other meets the fame Fate himfelf.

After poor *Plymouth* had refrefhed himfelf, we fet forward, and walked along till we came to a Road that feemed to be the main Road of the Ifland, by the Largenefs. Here we confulted what we fhould do, whether we fhould go on, or return for more Provifion; but we refolved to go a little Diftance from the Road, for Fear we fhould meet with more of the *Indians*, and run the fame Fate with the other *Englifhmen*. But *Plymouth* told us, we were a great Way from that Place where his Countrymen were killed; (for *Plymouth*, though born in *Guinea*, would always call himfelf an *Englifhman*, as being brought over very young,) fo we refolved one and all to venture.

We fent up our Prayers to the Almighty for our Safety, and went on with a Faith that we fhould come off with Succefs; but we had not gone far when we heard the Reports of feveral Mufquets, and fhouting in a barbarous manner, behind us.

Looking

Looking that Way, we saw a *Mulatto* riding as fast
as ever his Mule could carry him; when he came
up to us, he stopped, and cried in *Spanish*, Make
haste, run, for the *Indians* are coming upon you,
they have killed several *Spaniards* already, and they
are fighting with them. Mr. *Musgrave*, who understood *Spanish* very well, interpreted what he said
to us; he asked him how far they were off? He
answered, just by; and hearing another Shout,
put Spurs to his Mule, and left us in an Instant.
We found by the Shouting and the Firing, that they
would be immediately upon us, so we retired out
of the Road to let them pass, and laid down upon
our Bellies that they might not discover us. Immediately came by about twenty *Spaniards* on Horse-
back, pursued by near a hundred *Indians:* Just as
they came by us one *Spaniard* dropped, and crept into a
Bush on the other Side of the Road; and presently
the *Indians* followed, shouting in a horrid Manner,
and overtook the *Spaniards* again, who being very
swift of Foot, out-run an ordinary Horse; and
they had thrown away their Fire-Arms, to make
them the lighter to run, as we supposed. The
Spaniards knew they would soon overtake them,
so only ran to charge their Pistols, and stand till
they came up; then discharged them, to put them
in Confusion, and run again, to prolong the Time,
in Hopes of some Aid. All this we understood by
the *Spaniard*, that crept into the Bush undiscovered
by the *Indians*, by Reason of the Horses Feet, and
the Dust together, he being the foremost in Flight.

He

He told us moreover that about three Leagues farther, there was a Fort belonging to the *Spaniards* to stop the *Indians*, they using to make Inroads before that Fort was built, even to the Gates of the City *Havanna*. Upon this we confulted and refolved to follow upon the Edge of the Road, to fee how we could be affifting; we foon came even with them, for they were in a narrow Place, and the *Spaniards* kept them at Bay pretty well; by good Fortune there was a high Hedge made by Trees all along as we went, which hindered us from being difcovered. Here we refolved to fire upon them all together, and then run further up, and if poffible get out into the Road and face them. Accordingly we agreed to fire four and three, and the firft four to charge again immediately. Mr. *Muf-grave*, Mr. *Middleton*, Mr. *White*, and myfelf, agreed to fire firft; then *Hood*, *Roufe*, and *Plymouth*; which as foon as we had taken good Aim, we did, and, firing at their Backs, killed four downright, and wounded feveral, for I had ordered them to put two Bullets into each Piece. As foon as ever we had fired our Mufquets, we let fly one Piftol each, and then the other three fired their Guns. As foon as *Plymouth* had fired, he ran and charged our four Guns, (he having never a Piftol) and then we let fly our other Piftols. With thefe Difcharges we had killed at leaft fifteen *Indians*, and put the reft into fuch Frights that they began to run; (for with the Duft and Buftle they made, they could hardly diftinguifh from whence the Fire came)

neither

neither did they ſtop till they met with the poor wounded *Spaniard*, who had crept out, hearing the Diſcharge of our Pieces, (as we ſuppoſed) ; they fell upon the poor Fellow with Shouts and Outcries, and tore him to Pieces, never minding the *Spaniards* purſuing them ; who cried *Miraculo ! Miraculo !* a Miracle ! a Miracle ! By this Time we got within twenty Yards of the End of the Hedge, where we ſeven fired our Muſquets, and left them to *Plymouth* to charge ; then we ran in upon them with our Piſtols, and diſcharged them cloſe upon them. With this laſt Fire we dropped them twelve Men, and they ſcreamed out, and ran away as faſt as they could. We did not think fit to follow them, for it was not to any Purpoſe, for they were ſoon out of Sight. We charged our Guns and Piſtols again, and the twelve *Spaniards* did the like, they having Nine in the laſt Conflict killed, and two deſperately wounded. They gave us Thanks for our Reſcue, and ſaid we were ſurely ſent from Heaven to their Relief ; they let us know they were Tax-gatherers for the King of *Spain*, and were obliged to go in Numbers, and well armed, for Fear of theſe deſperate *Indians* ; who, about nine Years ago, ſet upon them, and killed eighteen of them, and but two eſcaped, but never met with any Moleſtation from that Time till now ; ſo that this Time (thinking the Danger over) we leſſened our Number from fifty to thirty, which I ſuppoſe the *Indians* having Notice of, was the Occaſion of

their

their fetting upon us.   They faid it was to no Purpofe for to go back, for the reft of their Companions that were killed, which being a Mile off,
they had taken with them.

We had not gone above half a League onward,
but we heard dreadful Shoutings as before, and
looking behind us, it being a ftrait Road, we could
perceive a Cloud of Duft, and the *Indians* running
full Speed toward us.   Upon which we put down
our two wounded men that were on Horfeback,
and mounted upon the *Spaniards* fpare Horfes.
Now we being nineteen Horfemen, refolved to
ftand it : We divided into Ranks, four in a Rank,
which made five Ranks ; only there were but three
in the laft Rank.   So we refolved to keep directly
one behind the other, and when the firft File had
fired, to fall in the Rear, and charge again   The
Spaniards would make up the three firft Ranks, as
they faid they could not in Honour expofe us to the
firft Onfet, becaufe we ventured our Lives in coming
to their Affiftance. We had no Time to difpute, for
now they were juft upon us, and to our Surprize had
feveral Fire-Aims among them. As foon as they got
within a hundred Paces of us they fired, but not
above two of their Pieces went off, the reft were
clogged with Duft in running, that very happily for
us hindered their Difcharging. The Shot miffed
us providentially, and we would not give them
Time to charge again, but we moved forward and
fired in upon them, and did great Execution ; when
it came to our Turn to fire, we in the Heat forgot

our

our Orders, but after we had difcharged our Guns
and Piftols, we fell in with them with our Cutlaffes,
and being raifed above them by being on Horfeback, did great Execution ; and that with the *Spaniards* charging and firing again, put them to the
Rout ; but now we followed them being on Horfeback, and difperfed them, fo that it was impoffible
for them to rally any more that Night.   However
we took four of them Prifoners, and tying their
Hands behind them, faftened them to two of our
foremoft Horfes, the reft following after, that they
might not get loofe.

We were met in the Road by twenty *Spanifh*
Horfe, with each a Foot-Soldier behind them, . who
were upon the full Gallop to our Affiftance, being
alarmed by the *Mulatto* that rode by ; but I believe
fome were glad they came too late.   The Officer
and the reft faluted us very courteoufly, when they
heard how luckily we came to their Affiftance ; but
fell a whipping the poor naked *Indians* fo barbaroufly, that though they deferved it, I could not
bear to fee it done in cool Blood, and though the
Blood followed every Lafh, yet they never cried out.
This is the chief Caufe of the Hatred of the *Indians*,
when ever the *Spaniards* get any of them in their
Power, they put them to all Manner of Torture ;
but if, on the contrary, they would ufe them civilly, and difcharge them now and then, I am fure
they might live in perfect Friendfhip with them :
For the *Indians* are good natured, loving, and affa-
ble, till they are incenfed, and then they are implacable.

We

We arrived at the Fort about Evening, and were very well entertained. The Officer did not doubt but to procure us a Ship to tranfport us to *Jamaica*, though he had Orders from *Havannah* to fecure al^l *Englifh* Veffels, there being a War talked of between the *Spanifh* and *French*, and *Englifh* and *Dutch*. The next Day the Officer mightily bragged of being an old *Spaniard*, that is, born in *Spain*, and of an ancient Family; and Mr. *Mufgrave* made us very merry upon the Road, in interpreting the Don's Speeches. We found, all along from the Fort, a great many Gentlemens Houfes pleafantly fituated, and the Country all along yielded delightful Profpects.

We were well entertained at a Gentleman's Houfe at Dinner, with Provifions dreffed after the *Englifh* Way, and all Manner of Sweetmeats and cool Wines. The Gentleman had a Vault or Cellar thirty Feet deep under Ground. He fpoke pretty good *Englifh*, and had been a Factor feveral Years in *London*, and knew our Cuftoms and Manners very well, and preferred our Way of dreffing Victuals before their own. He had an *Englifh* Cook from a Tavern behind the *Royal-Exchange*, that he brought with him into *Spain*, and from thence to *Cuba*, where he had a vaft Eftate left him. His Cook's Name was *Hodges*, a good underftanding Fellow, and made very much of us, and would fain have had us to ftay with his Mafter longer. But as foon as we had dined, we were obliged to get on Horfeback, and away for the *Havanna*, which we reached about fix o'Clock in the Evening. We had

H

Rooms

Rooms allotted us, and several *English* and *Irish* Men came to see us that lived there.

Havanna is the capital City of the whole Island of *Cuba*, and has as great a Trade as any Place belonging to the *Spaniards* in the *West-Indies*. It has one of the finest Harbours in the Universe, not for its Greatness, but its Security, yet able to contain five Hundred Ships of the greatest Burthen. The Mouth of the Harbour is commanded by a Platform; and a square Fort, fastened together by a strong Boom, or Iron Chain, that no Ship can enter. The most shallow Part of the whole Harbour, is eight Fathom Water, and all its Banks paved round with fat Stone, so that a Vessel of a Thousand Tun may lay her Side to it and unlade. Just between the two Forts there stands a round Watch Tower, where they discover to the Town how many Vessels are coming towards the Harbour, by putting out a Flag for every Ship. This Place is the best fortified and garrisoned in all the *Indies*, to secure the Plate Fleet, and all other Ships that meet here, to set sail together for *Spain*. This City is very large, near as big as *Bristol* in *England*, and the Houses are handsomely built; but after the *Spanish* Fashion. There are two handsome Churches, fine, and well built, with Spires, and an Organ in each, besides several Chapels; and a Foundation laid for a third Church while we were there. This City, almost as soon as it was built, was sacked by a *French* Pirate in the Year 1536, who was driven thither by a Tempest, and landing his Men well armed, took the City in Spite of all their Resistance, and burnt

many

many of the Houses, they being most part Wood;
and had confumed them all, had not the *Spaniards*
redeemed the reft, by paying them a thoufand Ducats. Upon the receiving the Money, they made
out to Sea, and the fame Evening came into the *Havanna* three Ships from *Spain*, who hearing of what
had chanced, prepared to follow them, taking feveral Soldiers on board them; the Admiral, who failed beft, got the firft Sight of the *Frenchman*; but being fearful to attack him before the other Ships came
up, lay by. The *Frenchman* feeing that, boldly
fet upon the firft Ship, and took her without
fighting; the fecond feeing that, tacked about,
and ran afhore, which was taken by the Ship's
Boat; the third alfo run the fame Fate. Flufhed with
this Succefs, they returned to the *Havannah* the fecond Time, and exacted a thoufand *Ducats* more, or
elfe they threatened to level the City with the
Ground, which was paid them immediately. Then
they took their laft Leave with this rich Booty, and
failed for *Rochel* in *France*, where they fhared
their Prizes. After this they built their Houfes
with Stone, as they are now, which neverthelefs
the *Englifh* took about twelve Years after.

There are many fair Harbours befides the *Havannah*, in *Cuba*, as that of St. *Jago* City and Harbour,
which is a handfome Place, feated on the South of
the Ifland, and is alfo a Bifhop's See under the Arch-
bifhoprick of St. *Domingo*. Three Leagues from St.
Jago lie thofe famous Copper Mountains, called by
the *Spaniards*, *Sierra de Cobre*. There's another Town
and Harbour fituated on the Eaftern Part of *Cuba*,

H 2

called

called *Baracoa*, where they gather the beſt Ebony of all the *Indies*. There are many other good ones, as St. *Salvador*, *Trinedad*, *Puerto del Principe*, which has a Fountain near it, that ſome Times of the Year produces liquid Pitch.

Cuba was formerly divided into eight Provinces and Governments, and better peopled than any other Iſland in *America*, before the *Spaniards* invaded them; but now there are but few *Indians*, which inhabit ſeveral Parts of the Iſland unmoleſted by the *Spaniards*; but the Natives can never forget their Barbarity, which they have by Tradition from Father to Son. Nay, I have been informed that they keep a ſolemn Feſtival once a Year, which was the Time that the Maſſacre of the *Inaians* happened; and if they can get any *Spaniards*, they ſacrifice them to ſatisfy the *Manes* of their dead Anceſtors.

Hugh Linſcoten, the *French* Voyager, relates that a *Caſſick*, or one of the Lords of a Province, caught a *Spaniard* at their firſt Landing, and threw him into a River, to ſee if he would drown, which he did, and that ſatisfied him they were not immortal. Whereupon he encouraged his Men, and repulſed the *Spaniards* ſeveral Times with great Loſs; but at laſt run the ſame Fate with the reſt of the Natives. 'Tis reported that the *Spaniards*, firſt and laſt, had maſſacred ſixty thouſand *Indians* in the Iſland of *Cuba*.

La Caſes, a Biſhop in *New Spain*, that wrote the Hiſtory of the *Indies*, tells us this Story of another *Caſſick*, that was taken by the *Spaniards* in *Cuba*, and condemned to be burnt alive with green Wood, that his Torture might be the longer and more exquiſite.

exquifite. While he was tied to the Stake, before the Fire was lighted, the Fryar that was prefent preached to him the Truth of the Chriftian Religion, and that all who died in that Faith, and trufted in God that formed the Earth, and all the Creatures therein, fhould immediately after their Purgation afcend into Heaven, the Refidence of our Creator, there to converfe with Angels, and fuch as died in that Faith; but on the contrary, if they perfifted in Ignorance, and died in a contrary Opinion, they fhould defcend into Hell, and live in an Eternity of Torments. Upon this the *Caffick* afked him if there were any *Spaniards* in Heaven? And being anfwered there were many; then, faid the *Caffick*, let me go to Hell, for I would rather converfe with thofe you call *Devils*, than you *Spaniards* in Heaven; for I am fure you are the worft of Devils, and take Delight in nothing but tormenting us. Though the Fryar's preaching was certainly true, yet Men of any Reafon muft conclude, that no Religion can be propagated by Cruelty and the Sword, which was always the *Spaniards* Method with the *Indians*, wherever they came; and all their Excufe was, that if they had not ufed them in that Manner, they could never have made their Conquefts, for they were forced to leffen them, for fear their Numbers might overpower them; fo that in fhort, as *Dryden* fays, in his Conqueft of *Mexico* by the *Spaniards*, *You threaten Peace, but you invite a War*.

I met there with a Prieft, that I am fure harboured nothing of Cruelty in his Breaft, for he came to fee

H 3

us every Day, and in such a friendly Manner, that charmed us all. He was always sending us one good Thing or other, and would take us to divert us abroad. He understood *Latin* very well, and some *English*. On the *Sunday* he preached an excellent Sermon in *Spanish*, as Mr. *Musgrave* informed us, whose chief Heads ran upon us, and to excite Charity in the Auditors, to let us have what was necessary in carrying us to *Jamaica*. The next Day he brought us to the Value of fifty Pounds in *Spanish* Dollars, which were collected at the Church Doors for us. There was a small Vessel of about forty Ton upon the Stocks, that was bought of the Owners for us, and a Collection made in the Town for Money to pay for it. We told them of the Provision we had left on Shore, which by our Computation could not be above twenty Leagues off; but they told us it would be difficult to find it. One Day a *Spaniard* met us walking with Father *Antonio*, in one of the Cloisters of the Convent, and reprimanded him for favouring *Hereticks* (as he called us) so much. He thought none of us understood *Spanish*, so was more free in his Conversation. Said Father *Antonio*, We ought to use Charity even to Brute Beasts, and much more to our Fellow Creatures, who wear with us our Creator's Image; I would not be thought to make a Schism in our Religion, which I am sure is the holiest and most pure; but yet I cannot consent in my Thoughts, that all who are out of the Pale of our Church must suffer Damnation; it would be horrid to think it,

and

and would take away from the Lustre of our Opinion, which shines so brightly.   If they are in any Errors, concerning their Belief, God, in whose Breast it lies, can open their Eyes when he thinks fit, that they may see those Errors.   Then added the *Spaniard*, with the same Reason you may say the *Indians* and Natives may still remain in Ignorance, till Heaven shall think fit to open their Eyes, as you say; and if so, the *Missionary* Fathers may spare their Trouble.   No, replied the Father, We are there appointed by Providence to bring them out of the Cloud that dims their Sight.   But of People that own Christ, and serve the same God with us, who differ but in a few outward Forms of Worship, it is very hard to believe that those instructed in that Worship, must inevitably sink into Damnation.   I can't tell what the *Spaniard*'s Thoughts were upon this Discourse, but I am sure he was more charitable than before, for he pulled out of his Purse a *Moidore*, and gave Father *Antonio* for our Use, which it seems he had refused to do, when he went about collecting for us.   After he was gone, he told us his Discourse *pro* and *con*, and what he could not make out in *English*, Mr. *Musgrave* cleared to us from the other's telling him in *Spanish* what he meant.

We were told our Vessel was ready, and therefore might be going when we pleased.   It was a very neat one as ever was built by the *Spaniards*, and carried between thirteen and fourteen Ton.

H 4

We

We had all Sorts of Provision sent on Board for
half a Year, or more, so that we only staid for the
Wind to rise, it being quite calm.

While we staid there, the four unfortunate *Indians* were to be executed in the Midst of the *Parade*.
They were first to be dragged by four Horses, naked, along the great Street to the *Parade*, and then
to be chained to a Post, fixed for that Purpose, and
burnt to Death: I must confess, when I saw with
what barbarous Cruelty they designed to use them,
I repented my being an Instrument in the taking of
them.   This Execution was ordered to be between
seven and eight in the Evening, being then it was
cooleft: All the *Indian* Slaves that served *Spanish*
Masters in the Town, were ordered to go and be
Spectators of the Tragedy, that they might see
what they must expect, if they ever offered to rebel
in the like Manner. When the Time came, the
whole Street was crowded with a vast Number of
People of all Conditions. But such a Sight I never
desire to see again; each *Indian* was tied by the Feet
to the Harness of the Horse, and so dragged from
the Prison to the Place of Execution upon the bare
Stones naked, their Arms tied upon their Breasts,
and fastened upon their Backs, that they might not
lift them up to save themselves as they were dragged
along the Stones; but by that Time the poor Creatures came to the *Parade*, the Skin of their Legs,
Thighs, and Back, was almost stripped off, yet
without the least Complaint; as soon as they were
tied fast to the Stake, they took from a Pot of liquid

quid Pitch, boiling hot, a Stick with fomething faftened to the End on't, and rubbed over their naked Bodies. One of them then, I obferved, began to faint, but was rated by another of his Fellow-Sufferers in their own Language, which none underftood but *Indians*, and the Fellow feemed to bear it much better. Before the Fire was put to the Pile, a Fryar ftepped up to them, and in *Spanifh* fpoke to the *Indian* that was ready to faint before, who had been Servant in the Town, but run away from his Mafter, and underftood *Spanifh*. The Fryar defired them, if they would be happy in the other World, to acknowledge themfelves Chriftians, and go out of the World in that Faith. Upon this the *Indian* anfwered, ' When I lived among you ·(faid ' he) and was taught to worfhip your God, you ' told me he was an upright God, and a juft God ' to them that ferved him faithfully, but an aveng- ' ing Power to thofe that once offended him; if ' fo, how comes it to pafs that he has not punifhed ' you for all your Crimes ? You have taught me, ' that Whoring and Adultery were Sins not to be ' pardoned, and yet you commit thofe Sins, as if ' you were in no Fear of any Punifhment. Murder is ' one of your Commandments not to be forgiven, ' when at the fame Time you'll hire a Bravo to kill ' a Stranger that looks but wantonly on your ' Wives. In fhort, I know not any one Thing ' that I have heard preached to us poor *Indians*, that ' you practife yourfelves. Therefore if your *Spanifh*

H 5   ' God

‘ God be as you defcribed him to us, the Curfe muſt
‘ fall upon you if we cannot believe in him, being
‘ we are deterred by the Cruelties you inflict upon
‘ us, in ferving him as you would have us, when
‘ we find your Actions and Words differ more than
‘ our Complexions. You preach up Holinefs and
‘ Righteoufnefs, but you practife Debauchery and
‘ Lewdnefs.’

He faid more, which was to excite the *Indians*
to rebel, but they put a Stop to it, by putting Fire
to the Wood, which being compofed of feveral
combuſtible Matters, foon confumed the poor
Wretches.

When all was over, Father *Antonio* took us home
to his Lodgings, to give us a fmall Collation for the
laſt Time, being the next Day we did all defign to
lie on Board, in Expectation of the Wind’s rifing.
We told him by Mr. *Mufgrave*, that we thought it
a great Weaknefs in them to preach in that Manner
to *Indians* in their Condition, and it would be apt
to make others defpife their Religion ; faid Mr. *Mufgrave*, it is like courting a Woman to Love by
Stripes (pardon the Comparifon) : Why, faid Father *Antonio*, I muſt confefs it is not what any of our
Fathers like, but it is what we are ordered to do,
and therefore muſt not be denied. Befides, at firſt, it
was a Piece of barbarous Policy in the firſt Conquerors of the *Indies*, they would order the Miffionaries
to preach to all *Indian* Criminals, but out of hearing of any Spectators ; fo as foon as they were executed, they would declare to all the *Indians* that
they

they died Christians, and were happy. Mr. *Musgrave* asked him, What made them use them so inhumanly, was it not enough that they suffered Death, but must be tortured in that barbarous Manner? He replied, it was done to terrify the other *Indians* from any Violence. Mr. *Musgrave* answered, That was certainly wrong, for as they are an implacable Sort of People, and have handed down to them from Father to Son, the first Massacre, though almost two hundred Years ago, they must needs remember these Cruelties of so fresh a Date, which revive in their Memories the former, if they had any Mind to forget them: He could not say much to it, he said, but evaded the Discourse, by bidding us be merry, that is, innocently and inoffensively so, for he did not allow of Disorders in any one; so we refreshed ourselves, and took our Leaves of the good Father, who blessed and embraced us, and said he would pray to Heaven for our prosperous Voyage. So on the next Day we paid our hearty Acknowledgments to all our Benefactors, and went on Board; where we had not been a Quarter of an Hour, before an extraordinary Message came from the Governor for *Plymouth*, our Black, who went with them without any Hesitation, and returned with a Present from the Governor, of several Bottles of Arrack, *Spanish* Wines, Fowls, Rice, and Brandy, with twenty Pieces of *Spanish* Gold, as the Messenger told us, in Recompense for the Loss of one of our Companions; for the Governor had sent for *Plymouth*, to know if he would serve him in

H 6

Quality

Quality of his Trumpeter, and he would settle a Penfion upon him for Life. *Plymouth* thought fit to accept of it, as having no Mafter, nor knowing when he fhould have one : But he got Leave to come on Board to bid us farewel, which he did in a very affectionate Manner. I bid him have a Care to pleafe the Governor, and then he need not fear doing well; fo we parted with *Plymouth*, with our hearty Thanks recommended to Father *Antonio* for all his Favours. *Plymouth* had a Trumpet given him by the Governor, as foon as he came on Shore, which he brought with him, and founded all the Way in the Boat, as he went back again to oblige us ; for really he founded extraordinary well, and had learned to play on feveral other Inftruments, having a tolerable Underftanding in Mufick. We were forry to part with *Plymouth*, as being a faithful honeft Fellow, yet glad he had got fo good a Mafter. The Wind rifing, we weighed Anchor, and left the Port with three Huzza's, and a Volley of fmall Arms, (we having no Cannon) and in two Days loft Sight of the Ifland of *Cuba*.

This famous Ifland, *Cuba*, which was firft called *Joanna*, by *Columbus* the firft Difcoverer, afterwards *Fernandina*, then *Alpha* and *Omega*, as being the firft and laft Ifland the *Spaniards* touched at : But afterwards was called *Cuba*, and ftill retains that Name. This is reckoned one of the four Iflands of the *Barlovento*. The others are *Hifpaniola*, *Jamaica*, and *Porto-Rico*. The North Side of *Cuba* is

fortified

fortified with a vast Number of small Islands, called the *Lucaies*, which some Geographers have taken for a Part of the main Land. The chief is *Bahama*, which forms the Gulph of *Florida*, the Passage that all Ships go through when they come out of the *West-Indies* into *Europe*.

Cuba has on the North, *Jucatan*, a Province on the main Land, distant about 50 Leagues; and on the South *Jamaica*, about 40 Leagues: In Length 220, and in the broadest Part about 56. The Soil in most Parts, that are inhabited by *Spaniards*, is fruitful, and much more healthy than *Hispaniola*. The Tobacco is reckoned the best in the *Spanish West-Indies*. I have seen very large Vines there, which bear excellent Grapes, but not fit to make Wine; many have tried, but it turns sour in a few Days. And for Birds, Beasts, and Fishes, it comes up to, if not exceeds any of the other Islands. The Bird *Flamingo* is a Fowl something bigger than our ordinary Geese, but Legs and Neck twice as long, and all over red, and generally go in a Body. At a Distance they look like a Company of Soldiers marching. The *Spaniards* have a Proverb here, That the Time will come that *Englishmen* will walk as freely in their Streets, as the *Spaniards* do now; if it were so, it would be of a prodigious Advantage to the *English*, being the *Havannah* is a Strait that commands all the Ships that come out of the *Indies* for *Europe*, and I really think from what I have seen, that it would be in the Power of ten thousand Men, with a Fleet pro-
portionable,

portionable, to overcome the whole Island in a little Time. Besides it is observed, that there are more Prizes brought into the *Havannah*, than any four Havens in the *Indies*.

While we were at the *Havannah*, a *Spaniard* carried two strange Beasts about the Streets for a Show, that he brought from *Brazil*, the one was called *At*, with a Head something resembling that of a Man's, and covered with rough short grey Hair: Each Foot has three Claws close together, about a Finger long, very sharp Teeth, with a smooth high black Nose, very small sleepy Eyes, and no Ears, with a Tail small above and broad at the Bottom, with Hair all over the Body of an Ash Colour. This Beast is about the Size of a large Fox, but so lazy a Creature, that when it gets up a Tree, it never comes down till it has devoured every Leaf, and when it has done, it will sit there twenty Days together without eating, and almost starved before it will take the Pains to go down to feed. It cannot travel or creep in a whole Day not above a Quarter of a Mile. This that was shown to us, never would stir till roused with a Stick, and it would be asleep again in an Instant.

The other Creature was something like a *Baboon*, but considerably larger, with a Face and long Beard, like an old Man's, and hairy like a Goat, all over the Body; his Ears bald, his Eyes black, large, and sparkling. He that showed it to us, called it a *Cayon*: its Tail is about four or five Feet long,

which

which they twift round a Tree, and so fling themfelves to the next They are very fierce and fubtile,
and when wounded, will fet upon their Adverfary
without any Fear; and if forced to climb the
Trees, they carry their Mouth and Hands full of
Stones to throw at Travellers as they pafs by; and
when wounded, they fet up a Shriek, that immediately brings all of their Kind, within Hearing,
to their Succour, who ftop the Wound with Leaves
and Mofs, which will foon be healed. This that
we faw was brought up very young by the Perfon
that had him, and would play many comical
Tricks; as he was fhown to us, he urined in his
Paw, and threw it in our Faces, before we were
aware, and while I was wiping mine, he gave me
fuch a Salute with his Tail, that made me ftand
farther off, which feemed to pleafe him mightily,
for he looked at me and chattered, as much as to
fay, I have given it you. The *Spaniard* told us,
they ufed to play at a certain Game with the Natives for Money, and would often win, and then
go fpend what they had got, upon a Liquor that
made them drunk, and as foon as they found themfelves fo, they would retire very decently, and take
a Nap, by which they were very often caught.

Jofeph de Acofta, that wrote the Hiftory of the
Weft-Indies in *Spanifh*, tells us a Story of one of
thefe Sort of Creatures going to a Tavern, with a
Pot, and Money to pay for his Wine, yet would
not part with his Money, till they had filled his
Pot with the Wine; but in the mean Time beat

four or five Boys, that did their Endeavour to take
it from him, and carried it fafe to them that fent
him.

Peter Martyr relates another Story of one of
them, that feeing a *Spaniard* going to fire a Gun
at him, fnatched up a little Child that was there,
and held it before him as a Buckler, and would not
let it go before the *Spaniard* was retired ; then he
laid the Child gently down, and ran away, after
having firft urined upon it.

The Fellow that fhowed them, fold them to the
Governor of *Havannah* for two hundred Dollars,
and would have gone with us to *Jamaica* or any
where; but we durft not take him without an Order
from the Governor, who does not fuffer any one to
go out of the Ifland without a Pafs from him,
which cofts a Dollar, and brings into his Purfe a
great deal of Money in the Year, having no other
Revenue from the King of *Spain*, only fo much a
Year for a Table, and a Palace ready furnifhed
with every Thing that is neceffary, befides Servants.
Every Ship that comes in pays two Dollars, and at
going out four more, fo that the Government of
this Ifland exceeds in its Profit any other Government (except the Vice-Roy of *Mexico*) in the *Spanifh
Weft-Indies*.

The Weather continued favourable, fo that we
arrived at *Jamaica* without meeting any thing remarkable in our Paffage. As foon as we had caft
Anchor, I ordered the Boat to be made ready to

carry

carry me on Board my own Ship, which I faw ride there. But when I got up the Ship's Side, I found my Cloaths felling at the Maft, at, *Who bids more?* Which is the Method, as foon as a Perfon is dead, or killed; the firft Harbour they anchor in, the Cloaths of the Deceafed are brought upcn Deck, and fold by Auction, the Money to be paid when they come to *England*, for it generally happens that Sailors have not any till they come Home again.

They were at the laft Article, when I came up the Ship Side; which was a Pair of black Worfted Stockings that coft I believe about four Shillings, which went at twelve and Six-pence, though they had been worn. As foon as I was feen by them, fome cried out, a Ghoft! a Ghoft! and others ran away to fecure the Cloaths they had bought, fufpecting that now I would have them again. When they were fatisfied of my being alive, and were told my Story, they were all rejoiced at my good Fortune, but none would be prevailed upon to let me have my Cloaths again. So I took up the Slop-Book, and caft up what they were fold for, and found, that what coft me about twenty Pounds, were fold for four times the Money: When I was fatisfied in that, I called every Perfon, one by one, that had bought any of my Cloaths, and ftruck a Bargain with them for ready Money, and bought them for about ten Pound; but the ready Money pleafed them mightily.

Captain

Captain *Wase* being sick ashore, I went to pay him a Visit, where he was mighty glad to see me, as believing I had perished; he told me that the Vessel hung Lights out for several Hours, that I might know where to swim, and laid by as long as the Wind would permit, as the Crew acquainted him when they came into Harbour. The Captain told me, That he did not think he should live long, therefore was mighty glad I was come to take Charge of the Ship, which had sailed before, if he had been in a Condition to bear the Sea. From thence I went on Board my new Bark, and settled my Affairs there with my Companions, who were mighty sorry to think of parting with me. *Hood* and *Rouse* desired they might be received on Board as Sailors, and go for *England* with us; for *Hood* was an *Englishman*, I mean born in *England*, and *Rouse* had Friends there. Besides it was as easy to go from *England* to *Bermudas*, as from *Jamaica*. So I spoke to the Captain, who was very well pleased to receive them, for he had lost five Men by the Distemper of the Country. The poor Captain died in a Week after my coming, and left me Executor for his Wife, who lived at *Bristol*.

As soon as we had buried him, I went on Board with my two Men, and did design to sail in three Days at farthest, which I would have done before, but that I was hindered by wanting a Chapman for our Bark, being we had Shares to dispose of; when I came on Board, the Master told me he had no Occasion for the two Men to add to their Charge;

said

said I, that is as I shall think fit, for the Power is in my Hands now; and who put that Power into your Hands? (said the Master). He that had Power so to do (said I) the Captain, whereupon I shewed him in Writing. He told me it did not signify any thing, and that he would find no one of the Sailors would obey a Boy, uncapable to steer a Vessel. Said I, I don't desire to have any Command over you, but only to represent the Captain that is deceased: We have no Want of any Representatives (replied the Master), and you shall go in your own Station, or not at all. It would be a pretty Thing, added he, for my Mate to become my Captain, and as I was design'd by the Captain to have the Command of the Vessel before you came, so I intend to keep it. But, said I, this Paper, signed by his own Hand, is but of two Days Date, and you cannot shew any thing for the Command, as you pretend to: Therefore (said I) I'll make my Complaint to the Governor, and he shall right me. Ay, ay, do so! (said he) I'll stand to any thing he shall command. Whereupon *Rouse*, *Hood*, and myself went into the Boat again, and rowed immediately on Shore; but the Governor was six Miles up in the Country, and it being pretty late, we designed to wait for his coming Home, which we were told would be in the Morning early. So I went on Board the Bark, and lay all Night, the Ship lying beyond the Keys two Leagues from the Harbour, in order to sail. The next Morning getting up with an Intent to wait

upon

upon the Governor, and looking towards the Place where the Ship lay over Night, found she was gone, and casting my Eyes towards Sea, saw a Ship four or five Leagues distant from us, which we supposed to be ours. I immediately went on Shore, and found the Governor just come to Town, and made my Complaint. He told me there was no Remedy, but to send immediately to *Blewfields Bay*, where he supposed they would stop to get Wood, which was usual with our Ships that were bound for *England:* Whereupon there was a Messenger ordered for *Blewfields*, which I accompanied, to give Instructions to the Officer that commanded at the Fort, to seize the Master of the Ship, and order him before the Governor at *Port Royal:* So we got on Horse-back, and reached it in three Days, it being almost a hundred Miles. When we came there, we found several Ships in the Harbour, but none that we wanted: So we waited a Week, but all to no Purpose, for she passed the Bay, as mistrusting our Design; upon this we were obliged to return with a heavy Heart, and tell the Governor of our ill Success, who pitied me, and told me he would see me shipped in the first Vessel bound for *England:* So I went on Board my own Bark, where they were all glad to see me, though sorry I was so disappointed. Now I was very glad that I had not disposed of my Bark, for I thought now it might be of Use to me. We consulted together, to know what was best to do; at last I made a Bargain with them, if they would

venture

venture with me in our Bark to *England*, I would
give them not only my Share of her, but as much
Money as came to the other two Shares, if they
would be wiiling to part with them : Upon this
we agreed, and with what Money I had, I began
to lade my Veſſel with Things to traffick with.   I
bought a good Quantity of Indigo, ſome Cotton,
Sugar, and Rum.   In ſhort, I laid out the beſt
Part of my Money ; and on *June* the 1ſt, 1700, ſet
ſail, and ſteered our Courſe for *England*.

Before I leave *Jamaica*, I think it will not be a-
miſs to give ſome Account cf the dreadful Earthquake
that happened there in 1692.   I am ſure it is a true
Account of it, for it was wrote by the Rector of
Port Royal's own Hand, who was upon the Place
when the Accident happened.   You ſhall have it in
his own Words.

' From on board the *Granado* Merchant in
Port Royal Harbour, *June* 22, 1692.

' *Dear Friend,*

' I DOUBT not but you will hear both from
'   *Garret*'s and *Bris*'s Coffee-Houſe, of the
' great Calamity that hath befallen this Iſland by a
' terrible Earthquake on the 7th Inſtant. Which
' have thrown down almoſt all the Houſes, Church-
' es, Sugar Works, Mills, and Bridges, through
' the whole Country ; it tore the Rocks and Moun-
' tains, and deſtroyed ſome whole Plantations, and
' threw them into the Sea ; but *Port-Royal* had much
' the greater .Share in this terrible Judgment of
' God.

‘ God. I will therefore be more particular in giving
‘ you an Account of its Proceeding, that you may
‘ know what my Danger was, and how unexpected
‘ my Prefervation. On *Tuefday* the 7th of *June* I had
‘ been at Church reading of Prayers, (which I did
‘ every Day) fince I was Rector of *Port-Royal,* to
‘ keep up fome Show of Religion amongft a moft
‘ ungodly, and debauched People.   When Prayers
‘ being ended, I went to a Place hard by the Church,
‘ (where Merchants ufe to meet) where the Prefident
‘ of the new Council, who acts in Chief till we have
‘ a new Governor, came into my Company, and
‘ engaged me to take a Glafs of Wormwood-Wine
‘ with him, as a Whet before Dinner.   He being
‘ my very good Friend, I ftaid with him; upon
‘ which he lighted a Pipe of Tobacco, which he
‘ was pretty long taking, and not being willing to
‘ leave him before it was out, I was detained from
‘ going to one Captain *Rudders*’s where I was to dine;
‘ whofe Houfe upon the firft Concuffion funk into
‘ the Earth, then into the Sea, with his Wife and
‘ Family, and fome others that came to Dinner with
‘ him.   But to return to the Prefident and his Pipe
‘ of Tobacco; before it was out, I found the Ground
‘ rolling and moving underneath my Feet; upon
‘ which I faid to him, Lord, Sir! What’s this? He
‘ replyed very compofedly, being a very grave Man,
‘ it is an Earthquake, be not afraid, it will be foon
‘ over; but it did encreafe every Minute, and we
‘ heard the Church and Tower fall, upon which we
‘ ran to fave ourfelves: I quickly loft him, and
                              ‘ made

' made towards *Morgan*'s *Fort*, which being a wide
' open Place, I thought to be there more fecure from
' the falling Houfes; but as I made towards it, I faw
' the Earth open and fwallow up a Multitude of Peo-
' ple, and the Sea mounting in upon us over the For-
' tifications. I then laid afide all Hopes of efcaping,
' and refolved to make towards my own Lodging,
' and there to meet Death in as good a Pofture as I
' could, but I was forced to crofs and run through
' two or three narrow Streets, the Houfes and Walls
' fell on each Side of me, fome Bricks came rolling
' over my Shoes, but none hurt me: When I came
' to my Lodging I found all Things in the fame Or-
' der I left them in, not a Picture (of which there
' were feveral fair ones in my Chamber) being out
' of its Place. I went to the Balcony to view the
' Street in which our Houfe ftood, I faw never a
' Houfe down, nor the Ground fo much as cracked.
' The People feeing me there cried out to me to
' come and pray with them. When I was come in-
' to the Street every one laid hold on my *Cloaths*,
' and embraced me, that with their Fear and Kind-
' nefs I was almoft ftifled. I perfuaded them at laft
' to kneel down, and make a large Ring, which
' they did: I prayed with them near an Hour; when
' I was almoft fpent with the Exercife, they brought
' me a Chair; the Earth working all the while with
' new Motions, and trembling like the rolling of the
' Sea; infomuch that fometimes whilft I was at
' Prayer, I could hardly keep myfelf upon my Knees.
' By that Time I had been half an Hour longer,

fetting

‘ fetting before them their many and heinous Sins,
‘ fome Merchants came to me, who defired me to
‘ go aboard fome Ship in the Harbour and refrefh
‘ myfelf; they told me they had gotten me a Boat to
‘ carry me off. Coming to the Sea, which had en-
‘ tirely fwallowed up the Wharf, with all thofe
goodly Houfes on it, moft of them as fine as thofe
‘ in *Cheapfide*, and two entire Houfes beyond it, I
‘ upon the Tops of fome Houfes that lay level with
‘ the Water, got firft into a *Canoe* and then in a long
‘ Boat which put me aboard a Ship, called the *Siam*
‘ Merchant, where I found the Prefident fafe, who
‘ was overjoyed to fee me: I continued there that
‘ Night, but could not fleep for the Returns of the
‘ Earthquake almoft every Hour, which made all
‘ the Guns in the Ship to jar and rattle. The next
‘ Day I went from Ship to Ship to vifit thofe that
‘ were taken up in Boats bruifed and dying, and to
‘ pray with them ; alfo to do the laft Office to them,
‘ in faying the Form of Prayer that is ufed at the
‘ Burial of the Dead, which hath been my forrow-
‘ ful Employment ever fince I came aboard this Ship,
‘ with Defign to come for *England:* we having no-
‘ thing but Shaking of the Earth, Thunder, Light-
‘ ning, and foul Weather ever fince. And the Peo-
‘ ple being fo defperately wicked, it makes me afraid
‘ to ftay in the Place ; for that very Time this ter-
‘ rible Earthquake was, as foon as it was Night, a
‘ Crew of lewd Rogues, which they call Privateers,
‘ fell to breaking open Warehoufes, with Intent to
‘ rob and rifle their Neighbours, whilft the Earth
‘ trembled under them, and fome of the Houfes fell
                                        ‘ on

‘ on them in the Act, and thofe that remain ſtill in
‘ the Place, are as impudent and drunken as ever. I
‘ have been twice aſhore to pray with the bruiſed and
‘ dying Perſons, and to chriſten their Children, where
‘ I met too many drunk and ſwearing. I did not
‘ ſpare them, nor the Magiſtrates who have ſuffered
‘ Wickedneſs to grow to ſo great a Height. I have,
‘ I bleſs God, to the beſt of my Skill and Power,
‘ diſcharged my Duty in that Place, which you
‘ will hear from moſt Perſons that come from hence;
‘ I have preached ſo ſeaſonable to them, and ſo
‘ plain, in the laſt Sermon I preached in the
‘ Church, by ſetting before them what would be
‘ the Iſſue of their Impenitence, that they have
‘ ſince confeſſed it looked more like a Propheſy
‘ than a Sermon. I had, I confeſs, an Impulſe to
‘ do it, and many Times I have preached in the
‘ Pulpit, Things that I never meditated at Home,
‘ and could not methought do otherwiſe. The
‘ Day (when all this befell us) was clear, afford-
‘ ing not any Suſpicion of the leaſt Evil; but in
‘ the Space of three Minutes, about half an Hour
‘ after Eleven in the Morning, *Port-Royal*, the
‘ faireſt Town of all the *Engliſh* Plantations, the
‘ beſt Empire and Mart of this Part of the World,
‘ exceeding in its Riches, plentiful of all good
‘ Things, was taken and ſhattered to Pieces, ſunk
‘ in, and covered for the greateſt Part by the Sea,
‘ and will in a ſhort Time be wholly eaten up by it;
‘ for ſome of thoſe Buildings that yet ſtand, and are
‘ left, we every Day hear fall, and the Sea daily

I   ‘ encroaches

‘ encroaches upon the Town. We guefs, by the Fal-
‘ ling of the Houfes, and Opening of the Earth,
‘ and Inundation of the Waters, that there are kil-
‘ led fifteen hundred Perfons, and many of good
‘ Note, of whom are my good Friend Attorney-
‘ General *Mufgrave*, Martial *Reeves*, *William Tur-*
‘ *ner*, *Thomas Turner*’s Brother is loft; I have loft
‘ the beft Living that ever I had or fhall have. I
‘ came, as I told you, aboard this Ship, in order
‘ to come Home; but the People are fo importunate
‘ with me to ftay, I know not what to fay to them;
‘ I muft undergo great Hardfhips if I ftay here, the
‘ Country being broken all to Pieces; I muft now
‘ live in a Hut, and eat Yams and Potatoes for
‘ Bread, which I could never endure; drink Rum
‘ Punch and Water, which were never pleafing to
‘ me. I have wrote as effectually as I could to my
‘ Lord Bifhop of *London* to fend a younger Perfon,
‘ who may better endure the Fatigue of it, than I
‘ can: Now it would look very unnatural in me to
‘ leave the People in their Diftrefs, and therefore
‘ whatever I fuffer, I would not have fuch a Blame
‘ lie at my Door. I have acquainted my Lord of
‘ *London*, That, by Reafon of the prefent Diftrefs,
‘ I am willing to continue a Year longer. They are
‘ going to build a new Town near the Rock in *Li-*
‘ *guinea*, the Garden of the Ifland. The *French*
‘ from *Petiganies* did attack the Ifland on the North
‘ Side, but were all defeated and deftroyed, it be-
‘ ing near the Time of the Earthquake.

June

June 28, 1692.

‘ EVER since that fatal Day (the most terrible
‘ that ever I saw) I have lived on Board a
‘ Ship, for the Shaking of the Earth returns every
‘ now and then : Yesterday we had a very great one,
‘ but it seems less terrible Aboard than on Shore.
‘ Yet I have ventured to *Port Royal* three Times
‘ (since its Desolation) among the shattered Houses
‘ to bury the Dead, and christen their Children.
‘ *Sunday* last I preached amongst them in a Tent;
‘ the Houses that remain being so shattered, that I
‘ durst not preach in them. The People are over-
‘ joyed when they see me amongst them ; and wept
‘ very bitterly when I preached to them. I hope by
‘ this terrible Judgment, God will make them re-
‘ form themselves, for there was not a more un-
‘ godly People upon the Face of the Earth. It is a
‘ sad Sight to see such a fair Harbour covered with
‘ the dead Bodies of the People of all Conditions ;
‘ for our great and famous Burial-place, the Pal-
‘ lisadoes, was destroyed by the Earthquake, and
‘ the Sea washed the Carcases of those that were
‘ there buried, out of their Graves. Their Tombs
‘ being dashed to Pieces by the Earthquake, of
‘ which there were hundreds in that Place. Many
‘ rich Men are utterly ruined, whilst many, by
‘ watching Opportunities, searching the sunk
‘ Houses, even almost whilst the Earthquake lasted
‘ (while Terror and Amazement had seized on all

I 2   ‘ the

‘ the confiderable Perfons) have gotten grea: Riches.
‘ We have had an Account from feveral Places of
‘ the Ifland, of Mifchiefs done there by the Earth-
‘ quake : From St. *Anne*’s we hear, that above a
‘ thoufand Acres of Woodland are wafhed into the
‘ Sea, carrying away whole Plantations in divers
‘ Places, but none fuffered like *Port Royal*, where
‘ Streets were fwallowed up by the Opening of the
‘ Earth.   The Houfes and Inhabitants went down
‘ together. Some of them were driven up again by the
‘ Sea, which arofe in the Breaches of the Houfes, and
‘ wonderfully efcaped. Others were fwallowed up to
‘ the Neck, the Earth fhut upon them, and fqueezed
‘ them to Death.   And in that Manner feveral are
‘ left buried with their Heads above Ground, only
‘ fome Heads the Dogs have eaten. They are co-
‘ vered with Duft and Earth by the People, which
‘ yet remain on the Place, to avoid the Stench.
‘ Thus I have told you a long ard fad Story, and
‘ God knows what worfe may happen yet. The
‘ People tell me they hear great Bellowing and
‘ Noifes in the Mountains, which makes fome very
‘ apprehenfive of an Eruption of Fire ; if fo, I fear
‘ it will be more deftructive than the Earthquake. I
‘ know not how to ftay, and yet I cannot tell how,
‘ at fuch a Juncture, to quit my Station.’

Yours, &c.

I believe

I believe this was the most terrible Earthquake that has ever happened since the Creation of the World, and did more Damage. They tell a Story of a wicked Fellow, that in the Time of the Earthquake ravished a Merchant's Daughter, and after murdered her, that he might not be discovered; but a Black, that happened to be in another Room, and hearing what had happened, ran away to the Ship where her Father was, to give him Notice, that he might come and apprehend him. But when he came and found his Daughter murdered, and the Villain gone, he was almost distracted, and the House tumbling with the Earthquake, he perished in the Ruins bemoaning his Daughter. The execrable Wretch was soon overtaken with divine Vengeance; for going to make his Escape, a large Stone from one of the falling Houses dropped on his Back and broke it, where he was taken up in such Misery, that he prayed for some one to knock him on the Head to put him out of his Torture. The Pain was so violent, that it took away his Senses, and in the Height of his Raving, discovered himself to be the Author of the horrid Fact mentioned; but he died without Repentance, cursing every body.

Another Story that was told me, was, That a Gentlewoman had come out of the Country to lie in there, being she would be better accommodated, and was brought to Bed but two Days before. The Husband was gone out; and at the first Shock of the House all her Servants left her, with the Infant with her, which with the Violence of the Shock, was

I 3

overturned

overturned in the Cradle : With this Accident, the Gentlewoman in a Fright rofe out of her Bed, though in a weak Condition, and took up her Child, and feeling the Houfe totter, ran down Stairs in her Shift, with her Infant in her Arms, where fhe was met by her Hufband, who took her in his Arms to carry her away, juft as the Houfe fell upon them all, where they were drawn out, but the Child was dead, and the Mother died in Half an Hour, the Hufband mightily bruifed, with much Pain lingered out to the next Day, and then expired, and were all three buried together in one Grave.

One *Abraham Matthews*, an Inhabitant of *Port-Royal*, that was alive when I was there, told me of a remarkable Providence that happened to him, as he was packing up feveral Things to carry on Board fome Veffel that was in the Harbour, for the more Security.   He had no fooner come out of the Houfe where he lodged, but it fell down and fmothered feveral People within.   Juft as he got to the Water-fide, the Boat was going off, and as he put one Foot into the Boat, the Boat-man pufhed him out again, and told him he muft ftay till he came back, being the Boat was full.   The Boat, in turning the Point by the Fort, was over-whelmed by a Point of the Shore, which fell upon it, and all that were in it perifhed.   This was the fecond Deliverance.   When he faw what had happened, he retired to the Church, which was open, to return God Thanks, and beg his farther Protection ; or if Death happened, he could not choofe a better Place

to

to die in. While he was at Prayers, he saw one of
the *Buccaneers*, or Thieves, stealing away his Bundle,
which he immediately followed, seized, and took
it from him : As soon as he was out of the Church,
that fell to the Ground. When he had got the Bundle, he kneeled upon the Earth to tie it faster, the
adjacent House sunk down also, and smothered the
Fellow, with several others that were in it. Going
a little farther, he met some of his Acquaintance,
who were getting a Canoe ready to convey themselves on Board a Ship in the Harbour, where he
safely arrived, and gave God Thanks for his many
and happy Deliverances.

We put in at *Blewfields Bay*, for the Conveniency
of Wood and Water, and when we were provided,
steered our Course onward for *England*. But as we
came within ten Leagues of the *Havanna*, a *Spanish*
Man of War of forty Guns came up with us, who
commanded us to strike our Sails, which we did
immediately, and coming on Board us, were surprized to find us all *Englishmen*, not expecting other
than *Spaniards* from the building of our Vessel.
Whereupon they made us all Prisoners, and sent
fifteen Men on Board us to carry the Vessel into the
Havanna. Telling them how we came by the Vessel did not signify any Thing, for they said we were
Pirates, and had seized it. And our Pass which we
had from the Governor of *Havanna*, not being to
be found, made Things appear but with an indifferent Face ; we were afraid we should find many
Difficulties in getting our Liberty, especially if they

I 4   went

went to their Station, which was St. *Jago*. But it happened better than we expected, for she made directly to the Port of the *Havanna*, where we knew every Thing would be placed in a true Light again. When we were anchored, and the People could come on Board us, we were soon known, and the Captain going to the Governor, was soon informed of the Matter; so we were released immediately, and had a Visit made us from Father *Antonio*, and honest *Plymouth*, who were mightily rejoiced to see us.

We were detained two Days, before we could get away. And then we set Sail with a brisk Gale, first saluting the Town with our four Guns, and four Patteraroes, which I had forgot to mention our buying at *Port Royal*.

In two Days after our first Sailing we made Cape *Florida*, and entered the Gulph that bears the same Name, and passed it without Danger. But here a sudden Calm overtook us, as frequently happens when you are past the Gulph; and the Current set strong to Westward, occasioned, as we supposed, by the Opening of the Land upon that Coast. The Calm lasting for four Days, we were insensibly carried within half a League of the Shore, but a little Breeze rising from Land, helped us farther out again; But still our Danger more encreased, for we soon perceived three large *Canoes* making towards us, full of *Indians* armed. We had not much Time to consult what to do, for they gained upon us every Moment. Now Death, or something

worse

worſe than Death, glared us in the Face, and moſt
of us thought this the laſt Day we had to live.
Come, Friends, (ſaid I) if we muſt die, let us die
brave like *Engliſhmen*. To die is juſt as common as
to live, only Life is Choice ; but Death we ſtill
purſue, and every Step we take ſhortens our
Journey. If then we follow Death, why ſhould we
fear it ? Or if we ſhould fear, what would that
avail ? ſince Fearing cannot put back the fated
Hour. Then let us, like thoſe that would diſpoſe
of ſomewhat, do it to the beſt Advantage. We
charged our four Guns with double and round, and
our Patteraroes with Muſket-balls : The reſt of our
Arms we got in Readineſs, and reſolved to die fighting, and not ſuffer ourſelves to be taken, to be
miſerably butchered, as all the *Indians* of *Florida* do,
when they get any Whites in their Power. We
reſolved to fire our ſix Muſkets upon them as ſoon
as they came within Reach ; ſo we took our Aim,
two at each *Canoe*, and fired upon them, which did
them ſome Damage, for they ſtopped upon it,
which made us make the beſt of our Way ; but they
ſoon purſued us with loud and rude Shouts. By this
Time we had charged our Muſkets again, and fired
as before at the ſame Diſtance ; but whatever Damage
we did them, they came on as faſt as they could,
but not before we had charged our Pieces the third
Time, which we fired as before, but did more
Execution, as being nearer to us ; and now we
charged them the fourth Time, and laid them
along upon the Deck for a farther Occaſion ; for

I 5

they

they being fo nigh, that our great Guns would
reach them with our double and round, which we
fired, one at a time; the firft we fired at was the
largeft *Canoe*, which put them in fuch Confufion,
that they fell foul of one another, and being in a
Huddle together, we fired the other three, that
made a mighty Havock among them. We now
thought of a Victory, inftead of being made Slaves,
and bore up to them, that we might make our Patteraroes of Ufe to us, which we fired upon them
with Partridge (or Mufket) Shot, that anfwered our
End; for now they began to turn Tail, which we
feeing, fired our Mufkets the fourth Time, which
killed them two *Indians*; and charging our great
Guns with fingle Balls, of 3 Pound Weight, (or
3 Pounders, as they call them at Sea) and firing at
their Boats (or Canoes) we funk one of them; but
the Men fwam to the other Canoes, and taking
hold of the Sides, with their Weight turned it over.
Mr. *Mufgrave*, and the reft of our Men, advifed to
make up to them, and in this Confufion kill them
all. But I was fatisfied with the Difappointment
they had met with, and as it was not in their
Power to hurt us farther, refolved to make the beft
of our Way; but looking towards the Shore, faw
eight more of their Canoes making up to us. This
put us upon making all the Sail we could, and the
Sea-breeze being now pretty ftrong, we made good
Way. We thought the Canoes would ftay when they
came up with the other three, but they made after
us along with thofe *Indians* that they had taken up.
                                                    We

We had charged our great Guns with great Shot,
and fired at them, but miffed them; we charged
them the fecond Time, and one Shot, by good
Fortune, took the firft Canoe, and overfet her,
which put them into more Confufion than before;
but ftill five of them purfued us, which were met
with by fome of our Mufket Balls, that gave two
of them their *Quietus eft*; and firing our great Guns
once more, funk one of their Canoes; but the
Men foon got into the other, and followed us ftill.
Seeing this, we refolved to make one ftrong Effort,
and make the beft of our Way: fo we backed our
main Sail, and laid by for them, and brought our
four Guns to one Side, and our four Pateraroes to
bear accordingly, we charged our Mufkets once
more, and laid them in Readinefs, with two Half-
pikes, and our Cutlaffes; and now we refolved not
to fire till every Gun might do Execution. We
ftaid till they came within two Ships Length of us,
and then we fired upon them as faft as ever we
could, which proved effectual, for we killed them
at leaft twenty. Upon which, they fet up dreadful
uncommon Noifes, and rowed back as faft as ever
they could; we gave them our farewell Mufket-
fhots, and made the beft of our Way. By a moderate Computation, we killed them at leaft 50 *Indians*, without their once firing at us; neither could
we conceive how they intended to affault us, or
whether they had any Fire-Arms, for we faw none.
After we had brought our Veffel to rights again,
we affembled ourfelves to Prayers, and returned

our

our fincere Thanks to the Defender of the weak, and Giver of all good Things, for our happy Deliverance. We faw the Canoes paddling towards Shore, and were met by feveral others, with a Defign, as we fuppofed, to affift them ; but we were now too far for them, and there was nothing more to be feared ; fo we failed on with a profperous Gale, and met with nothing worth Note, till *Thurfday, July* the 15th, we difcovered Land, which amazed us all, for we did not think of falling in with any Shore till we faw *England.* We went to confult our Charts, and faw we were near *Newfoundland,* and finding that we fteered directly into St. *John*'s Harbour, which is the Capital of the Ifland, I mean of that Part which belongs to the *English.* The Harbour is large, fair, ftrong, and commodious, commanded by feveral good Forts, and a ftrong Bomb that fhuts it up. The Town confifts of about 800 Houfes, but after the Manner of the Houfes in *England.*

Newfoundland, or *Terra Nova,* was difcovered by *Sebcftian Cabot,* for King *Henry* the VIIth of *England.* This Ifland is feated in fifty-two of Northern Latitude, and divided from the Continent by an Arm of the Sea, about 20 Leagues over. It is larger than *Ireland* ; the Climate is much the fame as in *England,* very wholefome, has feveral commodious Harbours. The *English* poffefs one Part, and the *French* the other : but the *English* are more populous. This Ifland is of great Benefit to the *English,* as well as other Nations, from the vaft Quantities of Fifh that

are

are caught upon the Banks of *Newfoundland*. This is a very large Bank of Sand, which extends a hundred and twenty Leagues to the West, near the Continent, and about twenty Leagues broad in the middle, and sharpens to each End. It is reckoned the most extraordinary Thing found in the Sea of that Kind; for Ships may anchor, though twenty or thirty Leagues from Land. The Fruits are the same as with us in *England*, and the Soil so very rich, that it will bear Pease, Beans, &c. without Tillage, which are as good as any in *England*. The Beasts the same, only the Bear, which is found there. In short, *Newfoundland* resembles *England* in every Thing so much, that if a Man could be carried from thence in his Sleep, he would only think he was strayed somewhere out of his Knowledge. There is only this to be said, that there is not so many Inhabitants, so there is more Plenty of every Thing for human Life. Their chief Trade is Fish, but they send great Quantities of Musk, Sables, and other Furs. There is not one *Indian* to be found upon the whole Island, but what are brought from other Countries, and used as Servants; though it is reported, about twenty Years ago, towards the North-west Parts, the *French* met with some *Indians*, that used to help them to cure their Fish, and make their Oil. They describe them a civil Sort of People, but no Knowledge of a superior Deity; and when attempted to be taught, they would answer, We are well contented with our own God, neither do we desire any other; Why should we

offer

offer to change? We think our Forefathers wiſer than we are, and they worſhipped the ſame with us: Therefore, as we think of going to the ſame Place where they are, we muſt worſhip the ſame Power. You have your God, and we have ours; every Nation muſt have a God according to their own Language. Should we pray to your God in our *Indian* Language, how ſhould we be underſtood? Or ſhould you pray to ours, what would it avail you, ſeeing he would not know what you ſaid to him. Now we have not one God only, but many; as one for Fiſhing, one for Fowling, and another for Huſbandry; and when we are about any of theſe particular Buſineſſes, we pray to that God; for it would be too much for one to mind them all. Would it not ſeem ridiculous for one of us, if we wanted Succeſs in Hunting, to pray to him that takes Care of Fiſhing? Or you that wear Cloaths, would you go to a Fiſherman to bid him cloathe you? You tell us, there are a vaſt Number of Wor-ſhippers of your God in all Countries; then what need you any more? We will ſerve you as well and as faithfully as if we had but one God, and pray to our Gods to give you Succeſs in whatever you un-dertake. If you fiſh, we'll pray to that God; if you go to fell Timber, we'll pray to that; and ſo on, to whatever you employ yourſelves in. When you are out of their Dominions, you muſt pray for yourſelves to your own God. In ſhort, there is neither fair Means nor foul, will ever bring theſe poor Creatures to the Knowledge of the true God.

If

If you are angry with them, they will comply with you, and fay, Well, well, we will do as you would have us; but never think of it afterwards: If you reafon calmly with them, then they anfwer you as above.

After being here two Days, we fet fail, and made our Courfe for *England*, *July* 25, 1700. We met with no extraordinary Accident in our Paffage, till we difcovered the Land's End, *Auguft* the 21ft. How rejoiced I was to fee my native Country, let them judge that have been in the fame Condition as I have been; and I may with Truth fay, that the Tranfports felt in firft feeing the white Cliffs of the Ifland that gave me Birth, exceeded the Joy I received when I was delivered from the moft imminent Danger. Here we confulted, whether it were better for us to go to *London*, or to *Briftol*; but every one allowed *London* to be the beft Mart for our Goods; fo we made for the *Thames*, and the Weather being fair, and a brifk Gale, we anchored over-againft *Shadwell* Dock. Now all that we had to do was to get a Chapman for our Goods, I applied myfelf to a Merchant upon '*Change*, who foon ftruck a Bargain, and, with the Confent of my Companions, fold the Lading, Bottom and all, for nine hundred and twenty Pounds, reckoning the Lading feven hundred Pounds, which was my own, and two hundred and twenty for the Veffel, and every Thing befides. They were all contented with their Dividend, but ftill refolved to go with me to *Briftol*, to fee after my Affairs there. So we fet out on Foot, intending

tending to walk it, and be a little merry upon the Road, for we expected more Diversion by walking it leisurely, than going in any other Manner. I had turned all my Money into Bank Bills, which amounted to 800*l.* with my Money that I had for my Goods, and sewed them in the Waistband of my Breeches, not that there could be any Danger, being so many in Company. We took the *Salisbury* Road, though something out of our Way, I being resolved to carry my Friends to *Bruton*, the Place of my Birth. Coming through *Basingstoke*, a Sailor met us, begging Charity for God's Sake. I gave him Sixpence, which he returned me many Thanks for; I asked him how it came to pass, that a lusty Sailor as he was did not go to Sea? (especially now War being talked of between the *English* and *French*) he answered, he was going to *London* for that Intent, but was obliged to be beholden to good Men to assist him in his Journey. Why, (pursued I) have you no Friends? your Cloaths are good, you don't seem to have begged long. No, answered he, this is my first Day; I have made an End of the little Money I had last Night. Have you been long from Sea, (said I)? But a Week, answered he. I had the Misfortune to be cast away in Sight of Harbour. From whence came you, (asked I)? Said he, We came from *Jamaica*, and were bound for *Bristol*; but a violent Storm overtook us within six Leagues of the Mouth of the River *Severn*, and drove our Ship upon some Rocks in the Mouth of the Bay, and all the Men perished but myself. From *Jamaica*, (said

I),

I), pray what Ship? The *Albion* Frigate, replyed he. Who was your Captain, added I? The Captain died at *Jamaica*, but the Master supplied his Place, one *Jacob Bingley*. Did you ever hear of one *Falconer?* Yes, he was the Mate, supposed to be left in a Voyage he made to the Bay of *Campechy*, but coming safe into Harbour afterwards, the Captain before his Death gave him the Command of our Ship; but the Master not approving of such a young Man to have the Power over him, set Sail without him. This I learned on Board afterwards; for I and another Sailor were hired for the Voyage that Afternoon, before the Morning we set Sail. We had but an indifferent Passage the whole Voyage, which was made up with nothing but Storms and Calms, that caused much Uneasiness, and our Provision received Damage by the Salt-water, which drove us to the last Extremity; and when we were raised in our Hopes of setting our Feet upon our native Country, we were devoured by the tempestuous Waves. I myself was taken up for dead upon the Shore by a Fisherman. Have you any Friends (said I) at *London?* None, (replied he) every Place to me is Home, a Sailor is never out of his Way. If so, (said I) return with us to *Bristol*, where we are bound, and I'll promise you, if I cannot get you a Ship, I will give you wherewithal to carry you to *London* without begging. We easily agreed upon the Matter, and honest Tarr went on with us. I asked him why he did not endeavour to get a Ship at *Bristol?* he answered, He would rather chuse to go in a Man of War than a Merchant-man,

since

since War was approaching, and he heard there was a Fleet fitting out for the *West Indies*; and if so, (said he) there may be some Hopes of getting something there, either of *Jack Spaniard* or *Jack Frenchman*. We came to *Bruton*, and took Lodgings in the *Mag-pye-Inn*, where I visited all my Acquaintance; and from thence we went in the same Manner to *Bristol*, where the first Thing was to enquire after my poor Father; but I was informed by Capt. *Puilney*, that he thought he was certainly dead; though he had seen him but once since I had been abroad, and that was in the *January* before, when he came privately to him, and told him he was settled in a small Village near *Hereford*, and went by the Name of *Hawkins*. What convinces me he is dead is, that about two Months ago, he sent me a Letter, which I'll show you. He went up Stairs and fetched it, which contained these Words:

SIR,

WHEN I had settled myself in my little Tenement, I began to think of turning Farmer, that I might have some Employment to pass away the tedious Hours of my voluntary Banishment; but going the other Day to view a hollow Place, where we had our Marl to marl our Ground, the Earth on a sudden fell upon me, and I was scarce taken out alive, my Back broke, and bruised all over in a piteous Manner. This is the first Day of Rest or Ease that I have had from my intolerable Pain. It is allowed, and I am very well satisfied, that I cannot survive it. Pray be kind to my dear **Dick**, if he ever lives to come home, if not,

what

what I have deposited in your Hands, let it remain with you for your own Use, since my Daughter is provided for. If I should, against the Expectation of every Body, recover, you shall hear from me very soon; if not, believe that I am returned to Earth, from whence I came. I hope I need not caution you once more to be kind to my poor Boy, if he should return, and be a Father to him; comfort him amidst his Affliction, and restore to him what I left with you, with a dying Parent's Blessing, that he may be as happy, as his wretched Father was miserable; which is the hearty Desire of your Friend and Servant,

FALCONER.

Grief so overcame me for a Time, that I was not able to speak; to be robbed of a Father, and a Father I loved so dearly, was a cutting Stroke; and I was constrained to make Use of all my young Philosophy to support it. My Father had left the Writing of his Estate with Captain *Pulney*, he having only mortgaged it before for five hundred Pounds to a Friend, to prevent its being seized on by the Crown which was redeemed by the Captain, by my Father's Appointment, when he came to see him last. I paid him his five hundred Pounds, and would have given him Interest for it, but he would not accept of it, but advised me to part with it, without I designed to settle in *England*, which I thought was the best Way, whether I staid in *England* or not. The Captain undertook the Matter, and sold it for four thousand Pounds. But whilst he was busy about it, I got Mr. *Musgrave*,

who

who was always my Bofom Friend, to go to *Hereford*, and if it were poffible, to find out where my dear Father was buried, and to fee how Matters ftood there. Accordingly we hired a Couple of Horfes, and fat out : when we arrived at *Hereford*, we found it not a little difficult, but at laft, through the Means of one Mr. *Hall*, Organift of the Cathedral Church, we had Sight of the Place, which was about half a Mile from the City. Mr. *Hall* came by the Knowledge of it by the Means of an honeft Clergyman, that my Father had contracted a Friendfhip with, before that unhappy Accident befel him, that deprived him of his Life. He brought us to his Houfe, where the Gentleman was laid up with a Fit of the Gout. As foon as we were private, I let him know who I was, upon which he tenderly embraced me, and was mightily joyed to fee the Son of his late Friend. Said he, I fhould have been at *Briftol* ere now, but that the Gout prevented me. Your Father was a Perfon I had but a fhort Acquaintance with, yet that little Time difcovered him to be a Man of Integrity, Honefty, and Honour. When he was upon his Death-bed, he told me his real Name and Circumftances, and what Misfortunes had brought him to this Part; he told me alfo, that he had a Son at Sea, and begged of me to difpofe of his little Fortune he had here, and fee it put into the hands of Captain *Pultney* at *Briftol,* which I had done, but was prevented, as I faid before, by this fudden Fit of the Gout. I have taken Care of all your Father's Effects, and the little Farm I have

bought

bought myself, it being for my Turn. Upon that he
sent his Maid for a little Box, which he unlocked, and
told me out two hundred Guineas. This is what your
Father left in ready Money behind him; his Farm, &c.
I rate at two hundred and fifty Pounds more; there
are the Writings, and there is the Money; by the
Writings I saw it cost my Father but two hundred
Pounds. As for his Apparel, and other little Necessaries, I gave them, by his Order, to a Maid
Servant, and a Man that he hired; and for his
Goods, there are but few, nor have we made any
Estimate of them; but if you'll have them ap-
praised, I will give something more than what
they are valued at, being I would willingly have
them along with the House; Said I, neither
shall they be parted; and if you please to accept
of them, be they what they will, you shall be
heartily welcome. He refused them obstinately,
but I prevailed with him to take them with much
ado. He also gave me a Ring, which I prized
mightily, because it had been my Father's from his
Infancy, given him by my Grandfather. When he
had settled every Thing, I went to see the Place
where my Father's Bones were laid, which filled me
with such awful Sorrow, that I could not refrain from
weeping, in Spite of my Resolution to the contrary. I would have erected a Tomb or Monument
for him, but it was his last Request, that he might
be buried as obscurely, as he designed to live there.

After parting with my Father's Grave with a
Load of Sorrow, we took Leave of my Friend the
Parson, and Mr. *Hall*, and rode for *Bristol* again,

but

but were overtaken about fix Miles from *Hereford*,
by three Gentlemen of the Pad, that had got fome
Notice of the Booty they fhould gain if they could
rob us ; for I was fo inadvertent as to put all my
Money into my Bags, which I wore before me at
my Saddle. They paffed us firft, but looking wifh-
fully upon us, gave us fome Sufpicion of what they
were. Mr. *Mufgrave* advifed me to ride back again,
and ftay till we had more Company; but I told
him they would foon overtake us, and, feeing us
fearful, would make them more refolute ; fo I rather chofe to face them, for we obferved they were
returning to meet us. We refolved to be before-
hand with them, and we drew out our Piftols ready,
and if they offered to come too near us, to begin
with them. As foon as they came within twenty
Yards of us, I called to them, and afked them
what they wanted ; if it was our Mcney, they
fhould firft take our Lives. They anfwered, they
had no fuch Intention. Then what is your Reafon
of paffing us firft, and then meeting us again ?
They anfwered, one of their Companions in alight-
ing to eafe himfelf below the Hill, had dropped
his Watch, and they were returning to find it if
they could. Why then pafs by in the Name of
God, (faid 1), and accordingly they did ; but we
were cautious of letting them come too near us. As
foon as they were paft us, we fet Spurs to our
Horfes, and got over the Heath before we looked
behind us; but riding leifurely through the Village, we faw them coming after a full Gallop.
Now we repented we had not ftayed in the Village,

but

but we refolved, as before, to encounter them if they affaulted us. They foon overtook us, and coming even with us, told us their Companion had found his Watch, which he pulled out and fhowed us. They faid they could not blame us in taking them for Highwaymen; but they affured us they were Travellers, as we were, and were going to *Worcefter*. We did not make any Words with them, but rode along with them, indeed, becaufe we could not help it. They rode with us for about a Mile, and then the Road going narrow, one of them pretending to go foremoft, feized hold of my Bridle; with the Surprize, my Horfe, being a very good one, rofe up an End; and he difcharging his Piftol, the Ball grazed upon my Cloak-bag, and did not do any farther Damage. Upon this I fired one of my Piftols, but miffed him; but I threw it at him with all my Force, which hit him on the Head fo full, that he ftaggered a little, and fell from his Horfe. The other difcharged a Pocket-Piftol at me, and wounded me flightly in the left Shoulder; but going to difcharge another, I fet Spurs to my Horfe, and had the good Fortune to fnatch it from him; but in the Buftle between us it went off, and fhot the other Highwayman's Horfe in the Head, which fo enraged him, that he ran away with him in Spite of all he could do to ftop him. Mr. *Mulgrave*, who engaged with him, followed him, but confidering he had left me with two, re-turned again, and in very good Time; for the other Fellow that I had knocked down with my

Piftol

Piftol, had got up again, and had juft caught his Horfe that was grazing under the Hedge. His other Companion that I had taken the Piftol from, had drawn a broad cutting Sword, and was laying at me. I, by good Fortune, had before me a great Coat for Fear of Rain, and the Ball of his Piftol had broke the Strap, fo that I wrapped it round my left Arm, and received his Blow, which did me no Damage, and in the mean Time thruft my Sword into his Side up to the Hilt, which neverthelefs did not kill him. But he called to his Companion, Come, *Harry*, let's make off, for by God I believe I am killed. Accordingly they fled as faft as ever they could back again, the Way we came, with my Sword in his Breaft ; for when he received the Wound, he turned fo fhort with his Horfe, that wrung the Hilt out of my Hand. Mr. *Mulgrave* was for following them, but I found fome Pain in my Shoulder, and it began to grow ftiff, being cold, and chofe to go on; but in our riding and talking of the late Accident, we loft our Road, and had taken that which led to *Gloucefter* ; and riding on, we met the third Highwayman, whofe Horfe had run away with him, who was coming back, as we fuppofed, to fee how Things went. As foon as he faw us, he turned his Horfe, and rode away as hard as he could, and we rode as faft after him, it being, as we thought, our Road. We followed him through feveral Villages, and called to the People to ftop him, but to no Purpofe ; at laft his Horfe ftumbled, which gave us Time to come

pretty

pretty near him; when he found he could not escape us, he turned about, and discharged a Pistol at us. I had one Pistol that I had not fired yet, which I drew from the Housing, and let fly at him, and wounded him in the Neck. He fled as fast as he could, and our Horses beginning to tire, he got out of our Sight. We asked several People we met, whether they had seen any such Person, and they told us he was gone into *Gloucester* Town before them. We followed, and got into *Gloucester* immediately, and were told such a Man was seen to ride through the Town; so we pursued him no farther, our Horses being very much tired; but they sent a Hue-and-cry after him, but to no Purpose, for they returned no wiser than they went out. We stayed at *Gloucester* two Days to have my Wound dressed, and then rode to *Bristol*, where all our Friends waited impatiently for us, because we had exceeded our Time three Days. After having settled my Money in the Hands of People that the Captain appointed to improve it for me, I resolved to make a Trip to *Ireland*, to see my Sister, who was married very well to a Merchant there. But hearing of the grand Fleet making Preparation for some Expedition, put us all agog, and my natural Genius for Travel, made me once more resolve to be gadding. I opened my Mind to Captain *Pultney*, who advised me to the contrary; but I told him I was so much concerned for my Father's Death, (as indeed I was) that I should sooner wear it off at Sea, than on Shore, because here every Object that I saw put me in Mind of

K

him.

him. He was very well fatisfied with my Reafons
at laft; but, faid he, I would not have you go in
any Poft, but as a Volunteer, that you may not be
confined to ftay longer than you fhould defire. I
thought this the beft Way, therefore refolved for
London with all my Companions, and got us a Ship.
I had Letters of Recommendation to Secretary *Bur-
chet,* and feveral Gentlemen that had the Manage-
ment of the Navy. We arrived at *London, February*
the 8th, 1701. Mr. *Mufgrave* and I entered on
Board the *Breda,* Captain *Fog* Commander, becaufe
we were informed Admiral *Benbow* would hoift his
Flag in that Ship. Mr. *Mufgrave,* having formerly
had fome Acquaintance with the Admiral, waited
on him, and had a Warrant for a Quaiter-mafter
given him. The reft of our Companions entered before the Maft, that is, common Sailors, in the fame
Ship. *Hood* was foon made Cook's Mate, and the
reft of them got fome little Office, that raifed them
fomething above the common Sailors, though they
entered as fuch, and all by the Means of Mr. *Mufgrave,* who acquainted the Admiral with their Fortunes. When we had fent all our Things on Board,
and not knowing when they would fail, Mr. *Mufgrave* and I got Leave to go to *Portfmouth* by Land
where we arrived on *Saturday, March* the 3d, and
ftayed there till the *Englifh* and *Dutch* Fleet arrived.
A Squadron was ordered out to cruife, of which our
Ship was one, but an unlucky Accident hindered,
my going with her, (but Mr. *Mufgrave* was forced
to go againft his Inclinations, and leave me behind
him;)

him;) which was as follows: One Evening, coming from feeing a Play at the Bull-Head, a Gentleman coming out with a Lady, the Crowd by Chance
joftled me againft the Lady, which this Gentleman,
Mr. *Martin* (Nephew to *Johnny Gibfon*, Governor
of the Place) took as an Affront put upon him, being he had the Care of the Lady; but I begged her
Pardon, and told her it was an Accident I could
not help; but he being in a ftrange Paffion, called
me feveral ungenteel Names, as Rogue, Rafcal, and
fuch like, and ftruck me over the Head with his
Cane. Though I did not much mind his Words, I
did not care to take his Blows without a Return,
which I did with Intereft, and we were foon parted.
But an Hour after, being at the aforefaid Bull-
Head at Supper, the Drawer came up and told us,
there was a Gentlemen below defired to fpeak one
Word with Mr. *Falconer*. There was one Mr. *Lang-
ley*, Lieutenant to the *Windfor* Man of War, that I
had made an Acquaintance with at the Play, who
promifed to come and fup with us, and I took the
Meffage to come from him, but was furprized to
find it the Gentleman that I had the Buftle with.
He wanted to drink a Glafs of Wine with me, he
faid, and led me into a Room. When we were
there, he told me he came for Satisfaction for the
Affront I put upon him about an Hour ago; therefore draw, added he, or I'll run you through. I
endeavoured to pacify him with good Words, yet
all to no Purpofe; he made fo many Thrufts at me,
that I was in Danger of my Life; but at laft I dif-

K 2

armed.

armed him, but not without a little Wound in my
Arm.   As soon as I gave him his Sword again, he
pushed at me with all the Malice imaginable; and
hearing the People from all Parts of the House,
coming to see what was the Matter, he clapped his
Back against the Door, to keep them out, which
they on the other Side broke open, and giving him
a Push, his Breast ran against the Point of my
Sword, which appeared at his Back, and he fell
down without any Sign of Life.   The People coming in, I was immediately secured, and carried to
Prison, till they knew whether he would live or die.
I was mightily concerned, not that any Danger was
to be feared, but that it would be a Hindrance to
my Voyage.   The Gentleman continued in a violent Fever a great while, and his Life was despaired
of; but at last, after a tedious Illness, recovered,
but continued weak.   One Day he came to visit me
in a Chair, where I was confined, and told me he
was very sorry for what had happened, and that
to-day I should be at Liberty; and accordingly an
Order came in the Afternoon for my Freedom,
without paying any Fees.   But to my great Grief
the Fleet was sailed, and *Benbow*'s Squadron designed for the *Indies*.   But Mr. *Martin* begged me
to be patient, and he would procure me a Passage
in a Storeship, that would sail in a Week at farthest
for *Jamaica*; and he was as good as his Word; for
the next Day he carried me to Captain *Young*, Commander of the *Tyger* Store-ship, and entered me immediately.   Then my Heart began to be at Rest,

and

and I gave him Thanks; and for the Time we
ftayed there, Mr. *Martin* and I were very intimate,
and he expreffed himfelf fo genteelly about our former Encounter, that he gained my Efteem.

Paffion, indeed, is certainly a Madnefs; and
therefore what was done in that Heat ought to be
forgot, if the Perfons themfelves repent of it. But
how humane would it be, if in the Midft of that
Fire of Paffion which blazes out, they could fprinkle
the cool Water of Reafon, and quench it? For nothing more deforms the Mind or Body than Paffion,
and 'tis then we lofe our human Form, and are
metamorphofed into Beafts. How many great and
good Men have done fuch Things in a Paffion, that
they have repented of all their Lives after; therefore Paffion may well be termed a pilfering Devil,
that fteals away our Senfes, and prompts us to do
Actions unbecoming the Form we bear.

We fet Sail from *Spithead*, *May* the 18th, 1701,
and our Captain gave us Hopes of overtaking the
Fleet, by Reafon, he faid, one Ship could better
make Way than a whole Fleet, becaufe they were
obliged to wait for one another. We met with nothing extraordinary but a Storm, that drove us almoft upon the Ifland of *Madeira*, which being fo
nigh, our Captain refolved to anchor at, and accordingly we did, in the Bay of the City of *Funial*,
the Capital of the Place. Captain *Young* and I
went on Shore to view the Town.

Funzal, the Capital of this Ifland, is a large handfome City, with one Cathedral and four other

K 3 Churches,

Churches, all neatly built; two Cloisters, one for the Men, and the other for the Women. The City contains 1600 Houses. There is also computed to be upon this Island 100,000 Inhabitants. I bought a *Portuguese* Book here, that gives a better Account of the first Discovery of this Island, than any I have seen extant, which Mr. *Musgrave* translated for me into *English*. I have seen it in *French* since, but not truly translated, because there was something left out concerning King *Edward* the Third, that conquered *France*. And as the Honour belongs to the *English*, as the first Inhabitants, I shall here give it you faithfully translated. It being but short, I hope it will not be found tedious; for in all my Voyages I avoid Prolixity, as being offensive to all Readers, and the Places I describe are generally such as are not frequented by the *English*, it being my Fortune to be carried there.

T H I

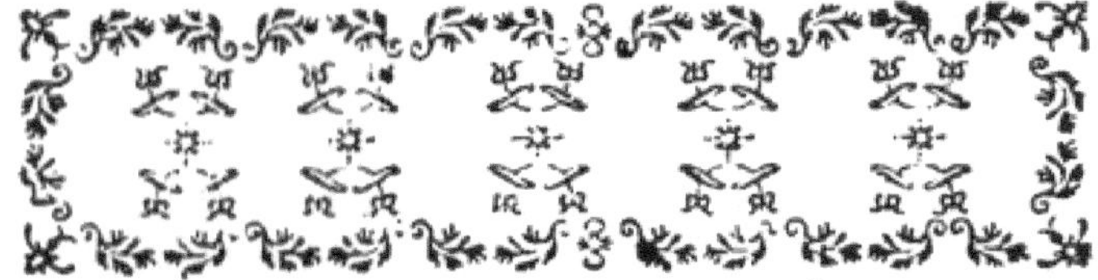

THE

HISTORY

OF THE

DISCOVERY of the Island of

MADEIRA.

Written originally in Portuguese *by* Don Francisco de Alcafarado, *and translated into* English *by* W. Musgrave, *Native of* Jamaica.

WHEN *England* was settled in a lasting Peace, after the Turmoils and Hazard of a dangerous War, King *Edward* the Third, who conquered *France*, and fixed his Royal Standard in the City of *Paris*; he who had felt the Inconveniences of War, knew how to encourage the Pleasures of Peace; and *London*, the Metropolitan City of the Kingdom, became the Seat of Mirth and Jollity. All Thoughts of War were banished;

K 2   the

the Enfigns now were furled, and Swords were wore for Ornament, not Ufe. Among the reft that embellifhed the Court, was one *Lionel Machin*, the youngeft Brother of a noble Family, and confequently not over-rich; yet a Gentleman (which often happens in younger Brothers) that was reckoned the only Ornament of the Root from whence he fprung. This Gentleman fell defperately in Love with a Lady, beautiful to Perfection, and the only Toaft of her Time. But there was a vaft Difparity in their Fortunes; for fhe was the only Daughter to a Nobleman, whofe Riches exceeded moft of his Rank, and confequently courted by thofe that could make her a Jointure, equal to the Fortune her Father would give her. But neverthelefs the Force of Love is fuch, that it never minds Intereft nor Duty; and the young Lady, whofe Name was *Arabella*, was fo much taken with the winning Behaviour of *Lionel*, that fhe placed her entire Affection upon him, who was indeed, bating his flender Means, the moft deferving of her. But the Parents of *Arabella* hearing of the Amity that was between them, complained to King *Edward*, and begged that he would interpofe his Royal Authority. The King ufed many Perfuafions to *Lionel* to withdraw his Affections, but it was like bidding the Sun ftand ftill, or the Wind, or Rain to ceafe; for their Affections were fo ftrongly united, that nothing could ever part them. The Father having provided a fit Match for his Daughter, intreated the King to fecure *Lionel* till the Marriage was·

folemnized,

folemnized, who granted his Requeſt, and clapt *Lionel* in Priſon under Pretence of ſome treaſonable Practices. When immediately the Marriage Rites were performed, and *Arabella* was conſtrained to give her Hand where it was not in her Power to give her Heart; and Parents are to blame to force their Children to marry againſt their Inclinations, for from thence ſpring ſuch Diſorders in Families that are not in their Power to compoſe. As ſoon as the Ceremony was over, the Huſband carried his Lady to a Palace, ſeated upon the River *Severn*, near *Briſtol*: When done, *Lionel* was releaſed out of Priſon, but with a heavy Heart, for the Loſs of his dear *Arabella*. But ſtill his Love encreaſed from the Difficulties he found to obtain his Deſire, and knowing it impoſſible to live without her, thought of a Stratagem that gave him Hopes of conquering all Difficulties. He ſummoned about thirty young Gentlemen, all reſolute, bold, and fit for any Undertaking. When he had got them all together, he made this ſhort Oration to them:

Moſt here are my Relations, or what is a nearer Tye, my boſom Friends: You all know the Indignity I have ſuffered, by Arabella's *forced Marriage; therefore I require you all to aſſiſt me in whatever I ſhall undertake (without tainting your Honour) to be revenged for the Affront put upon me.*

To this Requeſt they all agreed to ſerve him with their Lives and Fortunes. Whereupon it was reſolved to part and take ſeveral Ways to *Briſtol*:

K 5

Whea

When they all arrived at their Place of Rendezvous, they confulted together, and refolved to feize any Ship in the River, that they found was fit for their Turn. *Lionel* thought nothing difficult when Love was to be the Reward; but now he wanted fome Means to let *Arabella* know their Defign: But at laft it was agreed, that one of their Company fhould enter into the Service of the Hufband, which fell out as they could wifh, and a proper Perfon was hired to be Groom, where he had the Care of a fine fpotted Horfe, that ufed to carry the Lady abroad, to vifit her Neighbours: The Wind proving fair, Notice was given that the Project was to be put in Execution; the pretended Groom, to favour the Bufinefs, had omitted giving *Arabella*'s Horfe any Water, when *Arabella* had Notice of the Hour, fhe ordered her fpotted Horfe to be faddled under Pretence of taking the Air, attended with her Groom and two more of her Domefticks. When they came near the Cape of Land, where *Lionel* and his Companions waited for her, the Horfe, by the beating of the Waves againft the Shore, heard and fmelt the Water, and made down to it to drink, where *Lionel* immediately laid hold of the Lady, (who feemed to be mightily frightened) and put her in their Boat and made off. Now the Day that they had feized the Lady, was alfo pitched on to feize the Ship they had a Defign upon; which was eafily done, as their Crew were moft of them afhore. They cut her Cables, and made off to Sea with all the Sail they could bear, and foon got out of Sight, and directed their Courfe

for

for *France*, but a Storm met them and drove them quite contrary. *Lionel*'s Friends now began to repent of their Undertaking, and *Lionel* was mightily concerned for the Danger of her he loved more dear than Life; who though mightily difordered with the Sea, yet feemed contented in having the Object of her Defire with her. Thirty Days they were the Sport of the Waves, every Day expecting Death; but one Morning they difcovered Land, high, craggy, and very woody, which filled them with Joy, more efpecially *Lionel*, for now he hoped a refting Place for his dear *Arabella*. None in the Ship could guefs what Land it could be, for they knew it was not inhabited, becaufe Birds of all Sorts were fo tame, that they would fuffer themfelves to be taken with the Hand. The Place they chofe for their Habitations was a fine Grove of Laurel-Trees that were very delightful, as was alfo every Part of the Country they had rambled over. Finding they were to ftay there a great while, they got out of their Ship feveral Neceffaries, and lived very pleafant for about thirteen Days, defigning to commit themfelves in a Day or two to the Mercy of the Waves, for though the Ifland was delightful to live in, yet it feemed tirefome to thofe that wanted many Things they enjoyed in their own Country.

The Night before they defigned to embark, a violent Storm arofe, and drove the Ship from the Ifland with about fixteen Men that were preparing all Things for failing the next Day. Thefe were

toſt by the Winds and Sea for many Days, but at
laſt, to their great Joy, diſcovered Land, where
they ran their Ship on Shore, for ſhe was ſo leaky
ſhe could hardly ſwim. But their Joy for being
ſaved from the watry Element, ſoon changed to
Sorrow, when they found themſelves taken by the
Moors, they being landed on the Coaſt of *Africk*.
Their new Maſters (after hard Uſage) arrived at the
City of *Morocco*, with their Purchaſe, where they
ſold them in the Market like Cows, or Oxen; but
all declaring they were Men of Rank, they were
impriſoned, in Hopes of large Ranſoms.

When *Lionel* and *Arabella*, and the reſt that were
left on Shore, diſcovered the next Morning their
fatal Diſaſter, Grief ſeized them with ſuch a Force,
that ſome of them loſt their Senſes, running fran-
tick up and down the Woods, and raving, killed
themſelves. Poor *Arabella*'s Grief ſunk inward,
and preyed upon her Life with ſuch Violence, that
Death appeared to her Reſcue: She never upbraided
Lionel with her Misfortunes, but cloſed her Eyes
with a true Repentance of her Failings.

Lionel was like a diſtracted Man, laid himſelf
down at her Feet, and could not be removed till
Death gave him his Releaſe. His Companions buried them together in one Grave, and at the Foot
erected a Croſs, to ſhew theſe that were interred
there, died under the Banner of Chriſt: Upon the
Bark of the Tree, they cut in Letters the whole
Story of their Misfortunes. The reſt that remained
upon the Iſland, propoſed to themſelves of ven-
turing

turing into their Boat (which by good Fortune was left on Shore) and steer their Course to the nighest main Land, where they happily arrived without Danger, but ran the same Fate with their other Companions that were thrown on the same Coast in the Ship, that they all thought was cast away. All the Comfort they received in their Misfortunes, was, that they were committed to the same Prison, that their Companions were in. They were over-joyed to find those alive that were thought dead, but mourned to think of meeting in such a melancholy Place. In the same Prison was one *Juan de Morales*, a noted Pilot, and an excellent Navigator; this Man was mightily pleased with the Tales of these *English* Gentlemen, and so often begged them to repeat their Adventures, that he had every Mark of the Island exact, and perfectly saw it in Imagination. In the Year 1416, *Don Sancho*, Son to *Ferdinand* King of *Arragon*, died in *Castile*, and left considerable Sums of Money to redeem *Spanish* Prisoners that were Captive in Barbary; among the rest was *Juan de Morales*; and at the same Time the *English* Gentlemen got their Ransom, and safely arrived in their own Country, with a Pardon for their Offence from the King of *England*, and the Husband of *Arabella*. *Morales*, and all the Ship's Crew, were taken by the *Portuguese*, who met with them cruising in those Seas, but all, excepting *Morales*, had their Liberty given them, who was detained for his Knowledge in the

Mathematicks,

Mathematicks, and Promises were made him of great Recompence, if he would serve King *John* of *Portugal* in his Discoveries.

As soon as they were arrived at *Lisbon*, *Morales* was presented to the King, by *Don Henry* the *Infant*, who was a great Encourager of new Discoveries, where he opened the whole Story of *Lionel* and *Arabella*: Which was so generally received, that a Fleet was ordered immediately for this new Voyage, and June the 2d, 1420, set out to Sea well armed. They designed first for *Porto Sancto*, as being nigh the Island, as *Morales* conjectured, the *English* abandoned.

When they arrived there, the Inhabitants advised them not to go any farther in their Discoveries towards the N. E. being there was a black Cloud which would terminate their Navigation, because there was not any one that ever attempted it, but lost their Lives for their Presumption, and were never heard of more. Notwithstanding *Gonsales* the Admiral, and *Morales* the Pilot, were well assured that very Cloud was the Island they wanted to find, they were the more convinced in it, by Reason the Cloud continued of the same Colour through every Change of the Moon. But the rest of the Ship's Crew were of the contrary Opinion, and mutinied against *Morales*, telling him that he being a *Castilian*, (and consequently their Enemy) did it to disgrace them; and that it was a presumptuous Thing to pretend to search into the Secrets of Providence.

Notwithstanding

Notwithstanding their Grumblings, they set sail from *Porto Sancto*, and made forward for their Discovery; but the nearer they approached this Cloud, the more frightful it grew, which caused a terrible Fear in all the Sailors, intreating *Gonsales* to return, and not to be the Death of so many innocent People. But still they held their Course for all their Clamours; yet *Gonsales*, to encourage the Sailors, assured them it must be firm Land, and to dissipate their Fears made them this following Oration:

Why should I be more hardy than you, but that I am confirmed it is as I tell you? If there should be any Danger, have I any Means to extricate myself more than yourselves? Is not my Life as precious to me, as any of yours, my Companions? A Fool Hardiness does not become us, it is true; but a firm Courage is what all Men should be endued with. Every Person here has ventured his Life for his King in Battle before now, without half the Recompense or Honour that will be gained by this Expedition, if we succeed, as we certainly shall, if we arm ourselves with Resolution to overcome all Difficulties: Banish your Fears, and call your Reason to your Aid, and let us proceed in the Name, and for the Honour of God, and our King.

They proceeded cheerfully, animated by this Oration, and in a little Time entered the Cloud, or settled Fog; but the Tide driving the Vessel too far North, they put out their Boats to tow their Ship in the midst of the Cloud; but the farther they rowed, the Cloud seemed to decrease, and presently after they discovered Land to their great Joy, being it was what but few of them expected: The first

Cape

Cape they difcovered, was called by *Gonfales*, Cape
St. *Lawrence*, which they doubled, and faw a fine and
fertile Country full of fair and lofty Trees, that
made the Profpect delightful. Sailing on, they difcovered a large Bay, which *Morales* judged to be the
Place where the *Englifh* were thrown; but it being
late, *Gonfales* ordered to let fall the Anchors, not
caring to land till they had the whole Day before
them.   The next Morning they landed, and found
it to be the fame Place where *Lionel Machin* and *Ara-*
bella were buried.

When they had given Account to the Admiral of
the State of Things, he landed and took Poffeffion
of the Ifland for his Mafter, *John* the firft, King of
Portugal.   They erected an Altar upon the Tomb of
the two Lovers, faid Mafs, and returned God
Thanks for their happy Succefs.

Gonfales termed the Ifland *Madera* from the Quantity of its Wood (which in the *Portuguefe* Language
fignifies Woody) that was found all over the Ifland,
but no human Inhabitants.

After they had fearched well on Shore, Boats were
ordered to row round the Ifland, being it was dangerous for their Ship, by Reafon of many Rocks
and Shallows that lay in the Water. So fteering Weft,
they difcovered four fine fmall Rivers running into
the Sea, the Water being extremely clear. *Gonfales*
ordered fome to be bottled to prefent to the King of
Portugal his Mafter at his Return.

Going farther, feveral Soldiers were landed in a
Valley, which was watered by a fine River, and a
noble

noble Grove of Trees that made a perfect Harbour, where *Gonsales* erected a large Cross.

Sailing on, they came to a Point of Land that ran a great Way into the Sea, which was inhabited by such a Number of great different Birds, that the Men were afraid of being devoured by them. This Place was named *Punta des Gralhos*, from the large Number of Birds.

Going forward, they discovered a Valley covered with fine large Cedar-Trees; next to that they found another large one, where was a great Lake or Pond, from whence they could perceive the Bay they set out from. In searching the Country, they discovered a large Plain, which overlooked the rest of the Island, free from Trees, but covered over with a beautiful Fennel, called by the Portuguese *Funchall.* Upon this Plain they built a City, and called it *Funchall*, from the Quantity of Fennel that was found there, which was formerly a Bishop's See, but is still the chief Place for Temporal Affairs.

From this Plain run three Rivers into the Sea, which form an Island, and landlock the Haven, secure from Storms and Tempests.

Gonsales still sent out more Men for Discoveries in the Island, where they found a white Rock, called by the Portuguese *Praya Formosa*, or the fair Rock; below which was a fierce Torrent of Water, so clear, that obliged them all to observe it. Two resolute Soldiers pulled off their Cloaths, and attempted to swim across the Stream, but were hurried away with the Current in such an impetuous Manner, that they

had

had perifhed if they had not been timely fuccoured by their Companions by Ropes, which they threw in, and pulled them up againft the Violence of the Stream. This Torrent they named *Soccorides*.

The moft remarkable Thing they found in their Voyage, was a great Number of Sea-Wolves, which rufhed out of a Cave into the Water when they approached them. *Gonfales* gathered all Sorts of Plants, Roots, Flowers and Minerals, together with all Sorts of Birds, and a large Parcel of the Earth, and embarked for *Portugal*, where he fafely arrived *Auguft* the 2*d*, the fame Year 1420, where he was received with all the Favour imaginable.

In *May* 1421, *Gonfales* was made Governor of the whole Ifland, with an additional Title of *Count*, and in the fame Month fet Sail with his Wife and two Daughters, and many more, for the inhabiting the fame, where he happily arrived, and laid the Foundation for the prefent Capital of *Funchall*, or *Funzal*; but to honour *Lionel Machin*, who was there interred, he called the Place *Porto Machino*, and over the Grave he erected a noble Church. Some Writers relate that *Gonfales* fet the Woods on Fire, that continued burning for feven Years, which made Wood fcarce in that Ifland; but there is fuch Plenty of all Sorts, that I look upon that Story but as a Fable. The Ifland daily increafed in its Inhabitants, till it came to the now flourifhing State it remains in.

Madera is fituated in thirty Degrees and thirty one Minutes. In Circumference about forty Leagues, twelve in Length, about two broad. The Air fo
temperate,

temperate, that neither Heat nor Cold is trouble-some, and the Soil so fertile, that it yields more Corn for the Bigness of the Place than any other Is-land as large again. The Grass shoots up so high, that they are obliged to burn it, and in the Ashes they plant Sugar-Canes, which in six Months Time produce Sugar. The Inhabitants are more civilized than any of the *Canary* Islands.

After we had made an End of our Affairs, we set Sail from thence, and directed our Course for *Tene-riff*, one of the *Canary* Islands, or the *Insulæ Fortu-natæ* of *Ptolemy*, where we safely arrived. This Island lies in twenty-seven Degrees, and thirty Minutes; about fourteen Leagues in Length. *Santa Cruz*, the Place where we anchored, is the chief Harbour. It is an Island very well inhabited, con-taining three Cities, or large Towns, besides a great Number of Villages. But what it's famed most for is the Pike, or high Mountain, that rears its Head above the Clouds, and seems to scale even Heaven itself. I have seen many People that have told me they have been at the Top of this Moun-tain : But none give so good a Description of it (and even the whole Island) as the Right Reveren Dr. *Sprat* in his *History of the Royal Society* ; which : as follows :

' Having furnished ourselves with a Guide, Su
' vants and Horses, to carry our Wine and Prov
' sion, we set forth for *Oratava*, a Port-Town i.
' the Island of *Teneriff*, situated on the North-side
' two Miles distant from the main Sea, and travelled
' from

‘ from twelve at Night till eight in the Morning;
‘ by which Time we got to the Top of the firſt
‘ Mountain, towards the *Pico de Terraira:* There,
‘ under a very large and conſpicuous Pine-tree, we
‘ took our Breakfaſt, dined and refreſhed ourſelves
‘ till two in the Afternoon : Then we paſſed
‘ through many ſandy Ways, over many lofty
‘ Mountains, but naked and bare, and not covered
‘ with any Pine-Trees, as our firſt Night’s Paſſage
‘ was. This expoſed us to exceſſive Heat, till we
‘ arrived at the Foot of the *Pico,* where we found
‘ many huge Stones, which ſeemed to have fallen
‘ from ſome upper Part : About ſix in the Evening
‘ we began to aſcend the *Pico,* but we were ſcarce
‘ advanced a Mile, and the Way being no more
‘ paſſable for Horſes, we left them with our Ser-
‘ vants. In the Aſcent of one Mile, ſome of our
‘ Company grew very faint and ſick, diſordered by
‘ Fluxes, Vomitings, and agueiſh Diſtempers, our
‘ Horſe’s Hairs ſtanding upright like Briſtles ; and
‘ calling for ſome of our Wine, carried in ſmall
‘ Barrels on a Horſe, we found it ſo wonderfully
‘ cold, that we could not drink it till we had made
‘ a Fire to warm it, notwithſtanding the Air was
‘ very calm and moderate. But when the Sun was
‘ ſet, it began to blow with ſuch Violence, and
‘ grew ſo cold, that taking up our Lodging among
‘ the hollow Rocks, we were neceſſitated to keep
‘ great Fires in the Mouths of them all Night.
‘ About four in the Morning we began to mount
‘ again ; and being come another Mile up, one of
‘ our

‘ our Company failed, and was not able to pro-
‘ ceed any farther. Here began the black Rocks.
‘ The rest of us pursued our Journey till we came to
‘ the Sugar-Loaf, where we began to travel again
‘ in a white Sand, being fitted with Shoes, whose
‘ single Soles are made a Finger broader than the
‘ upper Leather to encounter this difficult Passage.
‘ Having ascended as far as the black Rocks, which
‘ lay all flat like a plain Floor, we climbed within
‘ a Mile of the very Top of the *Pico*, and at last we
‘ gained the Summit, where we found no such
‘ Smoke as appeared a little below, but a continual
‘ Perspiration of a hot and sulphurous Vapour, that
‘ made our Faces extremely sore. All this Way we
‘ found no considerable Alteration of the Air, and
‘ very little Wind, but on the Top it was so impe-
‘ tuous, that we had much ado to stand against it,
‘ whilst we drank the King’s Health, and fired each
‘ of us a Piece. Here also we took our Dinner,
‘ but found that our strong Waters had lost their
‘ Virtue, and were almost insipid, while our Wine
‘ was more spirituous and brisk than before. The
‘ Top on which we stood being not above a Yard
‘ broad, is the Brink of a Pit, called the *Caldera*,
‘ which we judged to be a Musket-shot over, and
‘ near fourscore Yards deep, in Form of a *Cone*,
‘ hollow within like a Kettle, and covered with
‘ small loose Stones, mixed with Sulphur and Sand,
‘ from among which issued divers Spiracles of Smoke
‘ and Heat; which being stirred with any Thing,
‘ puffs and makes a Noise, and so offensive, that we
‘ were

‘ were almoſt ſuffocated with the ſudden Emana-
‘ tion of Vapours, upon the removing one of theſe
‘ Stones, which were ſo hot as not eaſily to be
‘ handled. We deſcended not above four or five
‘ Yards into the *Caldera*, becauſe of the Slipperi-
‘ neſs under Foot, and the Difficulty; but ſome
‘ have adventured to the Bottom. Other Matters
‘ obſervable, we diſcovered none, beſides a clear
‘ Sort of Sulphur which lay like Salt upon the
‘ Stones. From this renowned *Pico* we could ſee
‘ the *Grand Canaries*, 14 Leagues diſtant; *Palma*
‘ 18; and *Gomera* 7; which Interval of Sea ſeemed
‘ not much wider than the *Thames* about *London*. We
‘ diſcerned alſo the *Herro*, being diſtant about 20
‘ Leagues, and ſo to the utmoſt Limits of the Sea
‘ much farther. As ſoon as the Sun appeared, the
‘ Shadow of the *Pico* ſeemed to cover not only the
‘ whole Iſland, and the *Grand Canaries*, but the Sea,
‘ to the very Horizon, where the Top of the *Sugar-*
‘ *Loaf* or *Pico* viſibly appeared to turn up, and caſt
‘ its Shade into the Air itſelf, at which we were
‘ much ſurprized; but the Sun was not far aſcend-
‘ ed, when the Clouds began to riſe ſo faſt, as that
‘ they intercepted our Proſpect both of the Sea, and
‘ the whole Iſland, except the Tops only of the
‘ ſubjacent Mountains, which ſeemed to pierce them
‘ through. Whether theſe Clouds do ever ſurmount
‘ the *Pico*, we can’t ſay, but to ſuch as are far be-
‘ low they ſeem ſometimes to hang above it, or
‘ rather wrap themſelves about it, as conſtantly

' as the Weſt Winds blow ; this they call the *Cap*,
' and is the infallible Prognoſtick of enſuing Storms.
' One of our Company who made this Journey
' again two Years after, arriving at the Top of the
' *Pico* before Day, and creeping under a great Stone
' to ſhroud himſelf from the cold Air, after a little
' Time found himſelf all wet, and perceived it to
' come from a perpetual Trickling of Water
' from the Rocks above him.   Many excellent and
' exuberant Springs we found iſſuing from the Tops
' of moſt of the other Mountains, guſhing out in
' great Spouts almoſt as far as the huge Pine-Tree
' which we mentioned before.   Having ſtaid a-while
' at the Top, we all deſcended the ſandy Way, till
' we came to the Foot of the *Sugar-Loaf*, which be-
' ing ſteep, even almoſt to a Perpendicular, we ſoon
' paſſed ; and here we met with a Cave about ten
' Yards deep, and fifteen broad, being in Shape like
' an Oven, or Cupola, having a Hole at the Top,
' near eight Yards over.   This we deſcended by a
' Rope that our Servants held faſt at the Top,
' while with the other End (being faſtened about
' our Middles) we ſwung ourſelves, till being over
' a Bank of Snow, we ſlid down, lighting upon it ;
' we were forced to ſwing thus in our Deſcent, be-
' cauſe in the Midſt of the Bottom of this Cave,
' oppoſite to the Aperture at the Top, is a round
' Pit of Water, like a Well, the Surface whereof is
' about a Yard lower, but as wide as the Mouth at
' Top, and about ſix Fathom deep.   We ſuppoſed
' this

' this Water not a Spring, but diffolved Snow
' blown in, or Water trickling through the Rocks.
' About the Sides of the Grot for fome Height there
' is Ice and Icicles hanging down to the Snow. But
' being quickly weary of this exceffive cold Place,
' and drawn up again, we continued our Defcent
' from the Mountains, by the fame Paffage we went
' up the Day before, and fo about five in the Even-
' ing arrived at *Oratava*, from whence we fet forth;
' our Faces were fo red and fore, that to cool them,
' we were forced to wafh and bath them in Whites
' of Eggs.   The whole Height of the *Pico* in Per-
' pendicular is vulgarly efteemed to be two Miles
' and a half; no Trees, Herbs, nor Shrubs did we
' find in all the Paffage, but Pines; and among the
' whiter Sands, a Kind of Broom, being a bufhy
' Plant; and on that Side where we lay all Night,
' a Kind of *Coalon*, which had Stems eight Feet
' high, and the Trunk near a Foot thick, every
' Stem growing in four Squares, and emerging
' from the Ground like Tufts of Rufhes; upon the
' Edges of thefe Stems grow very fmall red Buttons,
' or Berries, which being fqueezed, produce a poi-
' fonous Milk; which falling upon any Part of a
' Horfe, or other Beaft, fetches off all the Hair
' from the Skin immediately; of the withered
' Sticks of this Vegetable we made our Fire all
' Night. This Plant is alfo unive rfally fpread
' over the Ifland, and is perhaps a Kind of *Euphor-*
' *bium.*

' Of

‘ Of the Ifland *Teneriff* itfelf, this Account was
‘ given by a judicious and ingenious Man who
‘ lived twenty Years in it, as a Phyfician and
‘ Merchant: His Opinion is, that the whole Ifland
‘ being a Soil mightily impregnated with Brimftone,
‘ did in former Times take Fire, and blow up all,
‘ or near all, at the fame Time; and that many
‘ Mountains of huge Stone, calcined and burnt,
‘ which appear all over this Ifland, efpecially in
‘ the South-Weft Part of it, were caft up, and raifed
‘ out of the Bowels of the Earth, at the Time of
‘ that general Conflagration; and that the greateft
‘ Quantity of this Sulphur lying about the Center of
‘ the Ifland, raifed up the *Pico* to that Height at
‘ which it is now feen; and he fays, that any one
‘ upon the Place, that fhall carefully note the Situ-
‘ ation and Manner of thofe calcined Rocks, how
‘ they lie, will eafily be of that Mind; for they lie
‘ (fays he) three or four Miles almoft round the
‘ Bottom of the *Pico*, and in fuch Order one above
‘ another, almoft to the *Sugar-Leaf*, as it is called,
‘ as if the whole Ground fwelling and rifing up
‘ together, by the Afcenfion of the Brimftone, the
‘ Torrents and Rivers of it did, with a fudden
‘ Eruption, roll and tumble them down from the
‘ reft of the Rocks, efpecially (as is faid before) to
‘ the South-Weft, for on that Side from the very
‘ Top of the *Pico*, almoft to the Sea-Coaft, lie huge
‘ Heaps of thefe burnt Rocks one under another;
‘ and there ftill remain the very Tracts of the
‘ Brimftone Rivers, as they run over this Quarter of

L   ‘ the

‘ the Island, which has so wasted the Ground
‘ beyond Recovery, that nothing can be made to
‘ grow there but *Broom:* But on the North Side
‘ of the *Pico* few or none of these Stones ap-
‘ peared; and hence he concludes, that the
‘ *Volcano* discharged itself chiefly on the South-
‘ West Side.   He adds farther, That at the
‘ same Time Mines of several Metals were blown
‘ up, some of those calcined Rocks resembling
‘ Iron Ore, some Silver, and others Copper; par-
‘ ticularly on the South-West Parts, called *Azuleois,*
‘ being very high Mountains, where never any *En-*
‘ *glishman* but himself (that ever he heard of) was.
‘ There are vast Quantities of a loose bluish Earth,
‘ mixt with blue Stones, which have a yellow Rust
‘ upon them, like that of Copper, or Vitriol; as
‘ also many small Springs of Vitriol Water, where
‘ he supposes a Copper Mine; and he was told by
‘ a Bell-founder of *Oratava,* that he got out of two
‘ Horse Loads of this Earth, as much Gold as made
‘ two large Rings: And a *Portugueze* who had been
‘ in the *West-Indies* told him, that his Opinion was,
‘ there were as good Mines of Gold and Silver
‘ there, as the best in the *West-Indies.*   Thereabouts
‘ also are Nitrous Waters, and Stones covered over
‘ with a deep Saffron-coloured Rust, tasting of
‘ Iron; and farther, he mentions one of his
‘ Friends, which of two Lumps of Earth or Ore,
‘ brought from the Top of this Side of the Moun-
‘ tain, made two Silver Spoons.   All this he con-
‘ firmed by the last Instance of the *Palm*-Island, 18
‘ Leagues from the *Teneriff,* where, about 12 Years
‘ since,

' fince, a *Volcano* was fixed, the Violence thereof
' made an Earthquake in this Ifland, fo great, that
' he and others ran out of their Houfes, fearing they
' would have fallen upon their Heads ; they heard
' the Noife of the Torrent of flaming Brimftone,
' like Thunder, and faw the Fires as plain by
' Night, for fix Weeks together, as a burning
' Torch, and fo much Sand and Afhes, brought
' from thence by the Wind and Clouds, fell upon
' his Hat, as would fill the Sandbox of his Ink-
' horn.

 ' In fome Places of this Ifland grows a crooked
' Shrub called *Legnan*, which they bring to *England*
' as a fweet Wood. There are likewife *Apricots*.
' *Peach-trees*, and others, which bear twice a Year ;
' alfo *Pear-trees* as pregnant, *Almonds* with a ten-
' der Shell ; *Palms*, *Plantains*, *Oranges* and *Lemons*,
' efpecially the *Paegnadaes*, which have fmall ones
' within them, from whence they are fo denomi-
' nated. Alfo they have *Sugar-Canes*, and a little
' *Cotton*, *Colloquintida*, &c. The Rofes blow at
' *Chriftmas* ; there are good *Carnations*, and very
' large, but no *Tulips* will grow or thrive there ;
' *Samphire* cloaths the Rocks in Abundance, and a
' kind of Clover the Ground. Another Grafs
' grows near the Sea, which is of a broader Leaf, fo
' lufcious and rank, that it will kill a Horfe that
' eats of it, but no other Beaft. Eighty Ears of
' Wheat have been found to fpring from one Root,
' but grows not very high ; the Corn of this is
' tranfparent, like the pureft yellow Amber, and
L 2
one

' one Bushel has brought forth an hundred in a sea-
' sonable Year.

' The Canary Birds which they bring to us in
' *England*, breed in the *Baranco*'s or *Gills*, which the
' Water has fretted away in the Mountains, being
' Places very cold. There are also *Quails*, *Par-*
' *tridges* larger than ours, and exceeding beautiful
' large *Wood Pidgeons*, *Turtles* at Spring, *Crows*, and
' sometimes the *Falcons* come flying over from the
' Coast of *Barbary*.

' Bees are carried into the Mountains, where they
' prosper exceedingly, and there they have wild
' Goats which climb to the very Top of the *Pico*
' sometimes; also Hogs, and Multitudes of
' Coneys.

' Of Fish, they have the *Cherna*, a very large and
' excellent Fish, better tasted than any we have in
' *England*; the *Mera*, *Dolphins*, *Lobsters* without
' great Claws, *Muscles*, *Periwincles*, and the *Clacas*,
' which is absolutely the very best Shell-Fish in the
' World; they grow in the Rocks, five or six
' under one great Shell, through the Top-Holes
' whereof they peep out with their Nibs, from
' whence (the Shells being broken open a little
' more with a Stone) they draw them; there is
' also another Sort of Fish like an *Eel*, which hath
' six or seven Tails of a Span long, united to one
' Head and Body, which is also as short; besides,
' there they have *Turtles*, and *Cabrido*'s which are
' better than our *Trouts*. The Island is full of Springs
' of fresh Water, tasting like Milk; which in *Inla-*
' *	Inla-*

' *La-ma*,

' *gima*, where the Water is not fo clear and lympid,
' they cleanfe by percolating it through a Kind of
' fpungy Stone, cut in Form of a Bafon.   The
' Vines which afford thofe excellent Wines grow
' all about the Ifland within a Mile of the Sea;
' fuch as are planted farther up are not fo much
' efteemed, nor will they thrive in any of the other
' Iflands.   Concerning the *Guanchio*'s or ancient
' Inhabitants he gave this full Account: The 3d of
' *September*, about 12 Years fince, he took his
' Journey from *Guimar*, a Town for the moft Part
' inhabited by fuch as derive themfelves from
' the antient *Guanchio*'s, in the Company of
' fome of them, to view their Caves, and the
' Corps buried in them : (a Favour they fel-
' dom or never permit to any, having the Corps
' of their Anceftors in great Veneration, and like-
' wife being extremely againft any Moleftation of
' the Dead) but he had done feveral eleemofynary
' Cures among them, for they are very poor (yet
' the pooreft think themfelves too good to marry
' with the beft *Spaniard*) which endeared him to
' them exceedingly ; otherwife it is Death for any
' Stranger to vifit thefe Caves and Bodies.   The
' Corps are fewed up in Goats Skins, with
' Thongs of the fame, with very great Curiofity,
' particularly in the incomparable Exactnefs and
' Evennefs of the Seams ; and the Skins are made
' very clofe and fit to the Corps, which are for the
' moft Part entire, the Eyes clofed, Hair on their

L 3

' Heads,

' Heads, Ears, Nose, Teeth, Lips and Beard, all
' perfect, only discoloured and a little shrivelled,
' likewise the Pudenda of both Sexes.   He saw
' about three or four Hundred in several Caves,
' some of them standing, others lying upon Beds of
' Wood, so hardened by an Art they had (which
' the *Spaniards* call *Curay*, to cure a Piece of Wood)
' that no Iron can pierce or hurt it.   These Bodies
' are very light, as if made of Straw, and in some
' broken Bodies he observed the Nerves and Ten-
' dons, and also the Spring of the Veins and Ar-
' teries very distinctly.   By the Relation of the
' most ancient of this Island, they had a particular
' Tribe that had this Art only among themselves,
' and kept as a Thing sacred, and not to be com-
' municated to the Vulgar; these mixt not them-
' selves with the rest of the Inhabitants, nor mar-
' ried out of their own Tribe, and were also their
' Priests and Ministers of Religion.   But when the
' *Spaniards* conquered the Place, most of them were
' destroyed, and the Art perished with them, only
' they held some Traditions yet of a few Ingredi-
' ents that were used in this Business; they took
' Butter (some say they mixed Bear's-grease with it)
' which they kept for that Purpose in the Skins;
' wherein they boiled certain Herbs, first a Kind of
' wild Lavendar, which grows there in great
' Quantities upon the Rocks; secondly, an Herb
' called *Lara*, of a very gummy and glutinous Con-
' sistence, which now grows there under the Tops
' of

‘ of the Mountains ; thirdly, a kind of *Cyclamen*,
‘ or Sow-bread ; fourthly, wild Sage, which grows
‘ plentifully upon this Ifland ; thefe with others,
‘ bruifed and boiled up with Butter, rendered it a
‘ perfect Balfam ; this prepared, they firft unbowel
‘ the Corps (and in the poorer Sort, to fave
‘ Charges, took out the Brains behind) : after the
‘ Body was thus ordered, they had in Readinefs a
‘ *Lixivium* made of the Bark of Pine-trees, where-
‘ with they wafhed the Body, drying it in the Sun
‘ in Summer, and in the Winter in a Stove, this re-
‘ peating very often ; afterwards they began their
‘ Unction, both without and within, drying it as
‘ before ; this they continued till the Balfam had
‘ penetrated into the whole Habit, and the Mufcles
‘ in all Parts appeared through the contracted Skin,
‘ and the Body become exceeding light ; then they
‘ fewed them up in Goats Skins, as was before
‘ mentioned. The Ancients fay, that they have
‘ above twenty Caves of their Kings and great Per-
‘ fonages, with their whole Families, yet unknown
‘ to any but themfelves, and which they will never
‘ difcover. Laftly he fays, that Bodies are found in the
‘ Caves of the grand *Canaries* in Sacks, quite con-
‘ fumed, and not as thefe in *Teneriff*. Antiently
‘ when they had no Knowledge of Iron, they made
‘ their Lances of Wood, hardened as before men-
‘ tioned. They have earthen Pots fo hard that they
‘ cannot be broken. Of thefe fome are found in
‘ the Caves, and old *Bavances*, and ufed by the
‘ poorer People that find them to boil Meat in.

L 4

‘ Their

‘ Their Food is Barley parched, and then ground
‘ with little Stone Mills, and mingled ith Milk
‘ and Honey, which they always carry with them
‘ in Goats-ſkins at their Backs: To this Day they
‘ drink no Wine, nor care for Fleſh; they are very
‘ ingenious, lean, tall, active, and full of Courage,
‘ for they leap from Rock to Rock, from a pro-
‘ digious Height, till they come to the Bottom,
‘ ſometimes making ten Fathoms deep at one Leap,
‘ in this Manner: Firſt they tertiate their Lances,
‘ which are about the Bigneſs of a half Pike, and
‘ aim with the Point at any Piece of a Rock, upon
‘ which they intend to light, ſometimes not half a
‘ Foot broad; in leaping off they clap their Feet
‘ cloſe to the Lance, and ſo carry their Bodies in
‘ the Air; the Point of their Lance comes firſt to
‘ the Place, which breaks the Force of their Fall;
‘ then they ſlide gently down by the Staff, and
‘ pitch with their Feet on the very Place they firſt
‘ deſigned, and ſo from Rock to Rock, till they
‘ come to the Bottom; but their Novices ſometimes
‘ break their Necks in the learning. He told alſo
‘ (and the ſame was very ſeriouſly confirmed by a
‘ *Spaniard*, and another *Canary* Merchant there in
‘ the Company) that they whiſtle ſo loud, as to be
‘ heard five Miles off, and that to be in the ſame
‘ Room with them when they whiſtle were enough
‘ to endanger the breaking the Tympanum of the
‘ Ear; and added, that he being in Company of
‘ one that whiſtled his loudeſt, could not hear per-
‘ fectly in 15 Days after; he affirms alſo, that they
‘ throw

‘ throw Stones with a Force almoſt as great as that
‘ of a Bullet; and now uſe Stones in all their
‘ Fights as they did antiently.

This Account was given to that Ingenious and
Reverend Divine, Dr. *Sprat*, Biſhop of Rocheſter,
by ſome *Engliſh* Merchants, who had the Curioſity
to aſcend the *Pico*, one of the higheſt Mountains in
the World; neither could I find him out in any
Thing, but in the Height; he allows it to be but
two Miles and a half; but all the Inhabitants agree
to make it a full League high.

Capt. *Young* and I attempted to aſcend it; but
there was ſuch a thick Fog, that we were perſuaded
to the contrary; we went up about a Quarter of a
Mile, but were ſo wet with the Fog, that we had not
a dry Thread about us.

When we had ſatisfied our Curioſities as far as we
could, we ſet ſail from *Teneriff* and made our Courſe
for the *Weſt Indies*. We met a *Dutch* Ship from *Ba-
tavia* that was drove by ill Weather ſeveral Degrees
out of her due Courſe; we ſpared them what Necef-
ſaries we could, being they were in great Want, and
took our Leaves of them. The ſame Evening a
Storm overtook us, and drove us out of our Courſe,
but in the Night it turned ſtark calm. The next
Morning we diſcovered a Galley with *Turkiſh* Colours
out, rowing up to us with all their Strength; we
were all ſurpriſed and amazed, and couid hardly
give Credit to our Eyes, as no one on Board us ever
heard of a *Turkiſh* Galley ſo far from their own
Coaſt; but it ſeems we were nigher *Africk* than we
ſuppoſed, as it proved afterwards. Our Captain

L 5

told

told us we had nothing to do but fight it to the laſt ;· for if we were taken, we might be Slaves all our Lives long. I adviſed our Captain to put out our Boat, and tow our Ship from them : For, ſaid I, if a Wind does not riſe in the mean Time, that we may eſcape them, we ſhall gain more Time to put ourſelves in Readineſs to receive them, when they come up with us. This Advice was approved of, and the Boat was got out immediately with ſix Men to row, and I obliged myſelf to go along with her to ſteer her right, that they might row with all their Strength. We rowed ſo tightly for an Hour, that we made pretty good Way with our Ship ; but for all our Endeavours, we found that in about another Hour they would get up with us ; but we deſigned to row, till they were within a Quarter of a Mile of us, and then go into the Ship again. In the mean Time our Men on Board had prepared every Thing, and were in good Order to receive them. We had ſixteen Guns, and forty Men, and Ammunition enough. We were preparing to come on Board, when we found they were almoſt up with us, but our Captain adviſed me not, and ordered us to have Arms in the Boat, with ſome Hand-Granado's ; and as ſoon as we ſhould ſee them engaged, to go to the contrary Side of the Enemy, and fire upon them, and by that Means we ſhould amuſe them, that they would not venture to board us. Immediately it was agreed, and two more Men, together with our Arms, were put into us. The Galley came up with us in an Inſtant and hailed us in *Engliſh*, and bid

us

us ſtrike our Colours immediately, or it ſhould be
worſe for us, but were anſwered by us with our Cannon, inſtead of our Voices, and we went to it.
Now to obey my Orders, I looſed my Tow-Rope,
rowed to get on the other Side of the Galley, but
was mightily ſurprized to find their Boat out, and
about the Number of twenty *Turks* getting into her;
our Men in the Boat adviſed immediately, to return,
but I told them it was too late, for it would be
worſe for us if we did: Nay, our Captain called us
to come on Board, but I thought they would do us
more Injury in getting up the Ship's Side, than if
we ſtood them boldly, which we reſolved to do:
There were nine of us, and we had Arms enough;
ſo before they could fire at us, we diſcharged our
Muſkets at them, and laid ourſelves under the Gunnel of our Boat to charge again: When we were
prepared, I ordered them not to ſtir till the *Turks*
had fired; and as ſoon as they had done ſo, to ſet
Fire to the Fuzee of their *Hand-Granado*'s, and throw
them in upon them; as ſoon as we heard the *Turks*
fire, which did us no Damage, we ſet fire to our
Hand-Granado's as agreed upon, and threw them in
upon them: but they ſuſpecting ſomething, it ſeems,
ordered but half their Number to fire firſt, and the
other half fired upon us ſo unluckily, when we roſe
to diſcharge our *Granado*'s, that they killed three of
my Men out-right, wounded another dangerouſly,
and myſelf in the left Arm. It is true our *Granado*'s killed them four, and wounded ſeveral; but
ſtill their Number doubled ours, and now they pre-

L 6

pared

pared to board us. My four Companions and myfelf fired upon them with our Pieces, but could not
prevent them boarding us; yet we clubbed our
Muſkets on both Sides, and fell to work; but a
Turk coming behind me while I was engaging with
another, ſtruck the Cock of his Piſtol into my
Skull, and I dropped down for dead; but when I
came to myſelf, which was not in ſeveral Hours, as
I was told, I found myſelf on Board the Galley.

They had ordered a Surgeon to dreſs my Wounds,
which were three; one in my left Arm, that in my
Skull, and another upon the Side of my Throat,
which I did not feel in the receiving. I was ordered
to be taken particular Care of; for as I was not in
a Sailor's Habit, they thought I was ſomething
above the reſt, and therefore hoped to get a confiderable Sum for my Ranſom. The Surgeon that
dreſſed me was an *Engliſh* Renegado, whoſe Name
was *Matthews*. The Captain was an *Engliſhman* too,
born at *Deptford*, but the vileſt Wretch ſure that ever
breathed. There were ſeveral other *Engliſh* Renegadoes on Board, moſt of them profligate Wretches.
I underſtood from my Surgeon, that the two Veſſels parted after a deſperate Engagement, and the
Turks had about fifty Men killed and wounded:
Three of my Companions were Priſoners likewiſe;
the fourth being killed in the laſt Conflict, and the
other expired in the Boat with his Wounds. When
I began to mend, I walked upon Deck, and looked
about me a little; the other three (being well) had
renounced their Saviour Jeſus Chriſt; he who died

for

for their Sins, and took upon him the State of Man, that he might redeem us miserable Sinners from the Curse of the Serpent. What must be their Punishment, who for a little Ease in this World, forego their Portion of eternal Life? If the Tortures of Hell have their Degrees, the last and greatest must be their Lot. The Captain of the Galley ordered me one Day to be brought before him on the Deck, where he told me, If I did not in a Twelvemonth procure him to the Value of eight hundred Pounds for my Ransom, I should be chained to the Oar, and be a Slave all my Life; (it seems one of the three that was taken with me, had told him of my Abilities, and that I was possessed of a plentiful Fortune.) I answered, I would send to *England*, and do my Endeavour to get that Sum; but I told him it was more than I was worth, and there was no Hopes of so much Money for my Ransom, unless my Friends would out of Charity contribute towards it. I added, I believed I could raise a hundred and fifty, or two hundred Pounds: But he stuck to his Text, and told me, He would bate me nothing of that; and when the Time was expired that he had fixed, if the Money did not come, I should never have my Liberty. I told him, I would do my Endeavour to procure it for him when we came into Port, and had Liberty to write to my Friends in *England*.

The Captain did design to cruize a Month longer, that he might take some Prize to make him Amends for his last Disappointment. He never importuned

me

me to forſake my Religion ; being, if I had been as
vile as the others, he would not have had any Hopes
of my Money to redeem me. We coaſted off the
Shore of *Africk* a Fortnight or three Weeks, but met
with no Prize ; which enraged the Captain very
much. One Day the Surgeon dreſſing the Wound
in my Head, ſlipt into my Hand a Letter, which
he bid me read cautiouſly, and give him an Anſwer
the next Day. I had not an Opportunity for ſeveral Hours to read the Contents ; at laſt I counter-
feited a ſudden Weakneſs, and retired to my Cabbin, which was in the Place we call the *Forecaſtle*.
When I laid myſelf down, and found no one was
near me, I opened my Letter, and read the Contents to this Effect :

*We whoſe Names are ſubſcribed to this have reſolved
upon a Stratagem for our Liberty, there is ſeven of us,*
English, *beſides yourſelf ; and the Galley-Slaves are
twenty in Number, who have Notice of the Project.
One of the* English, *that has the Keys of the Galley-
Slaves Chains, is alſo one of our Number. Our Project
muſt be put ſpeedily in Execution, being they will go into
Harbour in ten Days, and then it will be impoſſible to
effect it. We will procure Arms, and give you further
Notice of the Hour. We muſt not ſeem to converſe together, neither muſt you take it ill if you find we give you
ill Language now and then, it being only to inſinuate
ourſelves into the good Eſteem of the* Turks. *When we
have redeemed the Slaves, we ſhall be twenty-eight in
Number, which will be a ſufficient Strength to cope with*
the

the Turks, *they being but forty-one in all. We will convey Arms into your Cabbin by the Means of Mr. Matthews, and we doubt not but we shall effect our Liberty under God.*

Signed,

Ralph Smallwood,	*George Jenkins,*
George Kirk,	*William Ashton,*
Richard Shan,	*Edward Wilkins.*
	Anthony Matthews.

After I had read it, I prayed to God to aid us in our Design. The next Day Mr. *Matthews* came to dress me as before; I gave him to understand that I had read, and considered the Letter, and told him my Opinion was to execute it as fast as ever we could, for Fear of any Accident that might happen : For, said I, it is not impossible but we may meet with one of their own Galleys, and then we shall find it to be a fruitless Undertaking. Said he, we must wait a convenient Time ; for if we should fail, we must expect the worst of Torments. He went from me upon this, being some of the *Turks* came to look upon my Wound. The Captain asked him how my Hurts fared? Ah! Damn him, said he, the Christian Dog will do well enough I warrant him : So much the better, answered the Captain, for I am informed he is worth a great deal of Money, and I shall set his Ransom at a higher Rate than what I first determined. All this Discourse I heard, being upon Deck, talking with my three Companions that

were

were taken with me, who treated me with ill Language, and called me Chriftian Fool, that would not turn *Mahometan*, when I might have all the Liberty I defired. One of them carried the Jeft fo far, that he gave me two or three good Strokes with his Hand; but the Captain feeing them (laughing) Let the Fool alone, 'tis not worth your while to foul your Fingers about him. I faid fo much to them, concerning *Mahomet* their falfe Prophet, that if the *Turks* had underftood me, I might have run the Danger of being murdered. But generally the *Renegadoes*, (that is, thofe that forfake the Chriftian Faith, and turn *Turks*) have fo little of any Religion in them, that they laugh at thofe that have any at all. At Night Mr. *Matthews* told me in *French* very low, that the next Morning early was defigned for their Enterprize, being it was fome Faft-day with them, that they ufually at four o'Clock in the Morning rife, and wafh themfelves all over, and pray to their Prophet for fome Time; and this being to be done below, they thought then would be the right Time. Accordingly all that Night they fpent fecretly in preparing every thing. He that commanded the Slaves (which was *Jenkins*) found Fault with them for fomething, and chaftifed them as ufual, but took the Opportunity to unlock them all, and ordered them to lie ftill as if their Chains were faft, till they had Command to do otherwife. Every Thing fucceeded to our Wifhes, for the *Turks* got up to their Devotion fooner than we expected, even before it was Light; and hud-

dling

dling down together, we clapt down the Hatches, and secured the best Part of them. The Captain, with two *Englishmen*, and one *Frenchman*, were seized in the Cabbin, and bound Hands and Feet; and this without any Noise. About eight others that had not got up as early as the rest, our Galley-Slaves seized; and before we could prevent them, had killed them all, and begged they might serve the Captain and the whole Crew in the same Kind.

The Bustle the Slaves made in killing the eight *Turks*, rouzed the others below from their Prayers; and when they found they were shut down, they made a Noise, and knocking to be let out, which we did; but first we loaded a great Gun with Musket-shot, and turned the Muzzle towards the Scuttle. Then as they came up, we bound them; but being but few *English*, we could not hinder the Slaves from killing several of these too. At last we bound them all, being twenty-five, there being killed by the Slaves sixteen, and, afterwards, by the Consent and Agreement of all, we chained twenty of them to the Oar in the Room of those we had released; but they began to be very stubborn at first, but we put the Slaves to them, and they soon made them work, by giving them the same Usage as they generally used to receive from them.

When we had secured them, we returned God Thanks for our happy Success, and then consulted which Way we should steer. We *English* agreed to go for *England*, but the Slaves we redeemed, being mostly *Spaniards* and *Portugueze*, were for going to

Spain;

Spain; in short there was no agreeing, for they being the greater Number, they pretended to have the Command over us, never considering it was to us they chiefly owed their Liberty. I must confess I was very much dissatisfied at their Ingratitude, but could not find any Means to help ourselves. Mr. *Matthews* spoke to them in *Spanish*, and laid before them the Benefit it would be for them to go for *England*; but it was like preaching to so many Beasts, for they regarded him not, but resolved to follow their first Design of directing their Course for *Spain*. When we found there was no Remedy, we desired them to touch at *Lisbon* in *Portugal*, and set us ashore there; which they consented to with much Intreaty. If we had been of an equal Number, we would have endeavoured to have forced them with us for *England*, that they might have repented their Ingratitude.

They would not let any of us have the Command of the Vessel, but one *Velasques* a *Spaniard* was chosen Captain, who immediately turned out Mr. *Matthews*, that we had given the Captain's Cabin to, and took Possession of it himself. This set us all a murmuring, and we consulted to contrive some Way to be even with 'em; but they were so watchful and always upon their Guard, that it was to no Purpose to plot any thing. They used to put Centinels upon us every Time we went to rest. One Night we were awakened out of our Sleep by Orders from our new Captain *Velasques*; when we were upon Deck, he told us there was a Ship discovered

to

to Windward of us.   Now my Reason of sending
for you, said the Captain, is, we design to attack
her, and make a Prize of her, let her be of what
Nation she will, excepting *Spanish*. When Mr. *Mat-*
thews had told us in *English* what he said, my Indignation rose that I could hardly forbear rushing
upon him, and tearing his Throat out; but at last my
Reason conquered my Passion, and I became calm.
I bid Mr. *Matthews* let him know he could not expect us to fight, if they were *English*, our Countrymen : But he swore we should fight, or be killed, if
they were our own Fathers.   I bid Mr. *Matthews*
tell him, as for my own Part, I would not fight a
Stroke, let it be what Nation it would ; and for his
threatening to kill us, I did not know but it would
be better to die, than to associate with such an ungrateful Crew as they were.   The Ship now instead
of keeping her Course, as she did at first, made all
the Sail she could, and bore down upon us, which
they did not mind in our disputing.   The Captain
then began to change his Tone, and thought it the
wisest Way to steer away before the Wind, and endeavour to get from 'em.   Whereupon he crowded
away, and belaboured the poor *Turks* with his Bas-
tinado to row with all their Strength, that I pitied
them.   Looking towards the Ship that pursued us,
we could perceive *English* Colours out, which rejoiced us *English* mightily.   We now consulted how
we should stop the Galley ; for with sailing and rowing we went faster than they.   At last I resolved to
take a Pistol and shoot him through the Head, let
the

the Confequence be what it would. So I laid hold of one of the Piftols unperceived, (they having prepared their Arms for the Engagement) went up to *Velafques*, and took him by the Throat with my left Hand, and holding the Piftol to his Breaft with my Right, I threatened to fhoot him dead if he or his Men offered to ftir. Several of his Companions were running to his Affiftance, but were ftopped by Mr. *Matthews*, telling them if they offered to ftir, their Captain was a dead Man. This Buftle caufed the *Turks* to lie upon their Oars, and in the mean Tim: Mr. *Sloan* brought the Galley to the Wind, and lay by, and the Ship got up with us in an Inftant, and without hailing us, poured in a Broadfide upon us, which killed us two of the *Turks*, and five of our *Spaniards*, among which was that ungrateful Monfter *Velafques*, and the Wind of one of the Shot threw me down upon Deck without any further Hurt; we had no Colours up at all but the Vane upon the Top-maft Head, which fhewed us to be a *Turkifh* Veffel; I fent up *George Kirk* to take down that, which prevented their firing again; upon this they hailed us : But after we told them we were *Englifh*, they fent immediately two Boats well armed on Board us, and when we had fatisfied them how it was with us, we feized upon our vile *Spaniards* and *Portuguefe*, and bound them ; we faw it was an *Englifh* Man of War, and upon an Enquiry found it was the *Ruby*, Captain *Walton* Commander, bound after the Fleet for the *Weft Indies*. They had met with Captain *Young* and his Crew fteering their

Courfe

Courfe for *England*, being they were fo difabled with the Engagement they had with the Galley of the *Turks* that we were in, they durft not hold on their Way for the *Weft Indies*. So the Stores were moft of them put on Board the *Ruby*, and the reft were to follow as foon as they could fhip them in another Veffel. Now there were two Men, that were Paffengers in Captain *Young*'s Ship, put on Board the *Ruby* to purfue their Voyage, and they feeing the Galley, knew her to be the fame that engaged with Captain *Young* in the *Tyger*, and that was the Reafon they fired upon us without hailing, as is ufual in thofe Cafes.

I was very glad of an Opportunity to purfue my Voyage; I made my Addrefs to Captain *Walton*, who very friendly received me; while we were confulting what we fhould do about our Prifoners, the Galley feemed to lie deeper in the Water, and going to examine her, found a Shot had pierced her between Wind and Water, but it was impoffible to come to it to ftop it; fo we took what we could out of her, and going to unlock the Galley-Slaves Chains, the Key was not to be found, and the Galley was finking every Minute, and before we could break the Chains fhe funk downright with the whole twenty poor unfortunate *Turks*, and all the *Spaniards*, who being tied, could not help themfelves, neither had we Time to give them any Affiftance. I muft confefs I was very much concerned to fee fo many poor unfortunate Creatures meet with

Death

Death, when it was in our Power ten Minutes before to have faved them.   Captain *Walton* was really
grieved at it, and ſhowed a Temper full of Humanity.   We had juſt brought on Board the Captain,
and two more *Engliſhmen*, with the *Frenchmen*, Renegadoes. The Captain was ſo ſullen that he would
not eat or drink, but intended (as we ſuppoſed) to
ſtarve himſelf to death.   Captain *Walton* uſed all
gentle Means poſſible to bring him into Temper,
but to no Purpoſe, for he would not ſo much as give
any Anſwer to what was aſked him ; and in about a
Week or eight Days after we took him on Board, he
was found dead in his Hammock : One of the *Engliſhmen* told us he had poiſoned himſelf, for he always ſaid if he was ever taken by the *Engliſh* he
would make away with himſelf, to prevent the Puniſhment he ſhould undergo.   The other four *Engliſhmen* that were inſtrumental in our Deliverance,
were all *Mahometans* in Appearance, as I ſaid before,
that is, they forſook their Chriſtianity in outward
Shew, but were really Chriſtians in their Hearts, as
were likewiſe my three Companions that were taken
in the Boat with me, but as they told me they only
did it to have ſome Opportunity of getting their
Liberty, and the Words that were uſed, though it
was in a Speech they did not underſtand perfectly,
ſhocked them in their Utterance, and they all hoped
their Peace was made with God for their Crimes,
with a ſincere Penitence from the Moment they had
committed it.

Mr.

Mr. *Matthews* the *Surgeon*, *George Jenkins*, *William Ashton*, and *Ralph Smallwood*, were taken in a Ship called the *Two Brothers* of *Bristol*, bound for *Scanderoon*, after an obstinate Fight, where all were killed, excepting the abovementioned four, who were taken and sold for Slaves, and continued so for some Years; but seizing on a Boat with the four *Frenchmen* that did design to venture for their Liberty with them, they put to Sea, and rather chose to trust in the Waves, and an open Boat, than stay there to be Slaves for ever. But *Hamet* the Renegado, whose Christian Name was *Lewis Gordon*, having Notice of their Flight, followed them with a swift Galley, and got Sight of them: Mr. *Matthews* (who relates the Story in this Manner) and his Companions seeing it impossible to make their Escape, thought of a Stratagem for four of them to get the Good-will of the Renegado *Hamet*; which was this: Seeing no Likelihood of getting clear off, the four *English* proposed to the *French* to cast Lots, and that should decide which four should be bound, and the other four should immediately row back, as if they had no Design of running away, and make out their Story as well as they could; accordingly we drew, and the Lots fell upon the four *Frenchmen*. Immediately we bound them, and rowed back, and were soon met by the Galley, where we made our Tale good, by telling the *Turks*, that going a Fishing with the four *Frenchmen*, they would have compelled us by Force to have rowed with them in their Boat for Spain;

but

but we being not willing, fell to grappling with them, and overcame them by main Force, tied them, and were bringing them back. The *French-men* kept true to their Promife, and never contra-dicted us in our Story. *Hamet* upon this became very civil to us, and put us in Truft: He made me immediately Surgeon to the Galley, Mr. *Jenkins* Mafter of the Slaves, and our two other Companions had fome little Office that pleafed them. We went feveral Voyages with him, and took many Veffels, but never met with any *Englifh* Ship before the *Tiger* that we had the defperate Engagement with. The four *Frenchmen* were made Slaves to row in another Galley, which was taken about two Months ago by a *Spanifh* Man of War, and by that Means got their Liberty.

The other two *Englifhmen,* and *Frenchman,* that were taken in the Cabin, confeffed that they had been guilty of many Crimes, but more efpecially in denying their Saviour, but they now felt in their Hearts and Minds a yearning to Repentance, and begged that Captain *Walton* would forgive them, and not take their Recantation for a Falfhood, be-caufe they were in fome Danger, but a true Light of the divine Brightnefs. Captain *Walton* freely forgave them, and having a Chaplain in the Ship, we rechriftened them; and the Fellows feemed ever afterwards to have a true Senfe of their happy Condition. Captain *Walton* and myfelf were God-fathers for them all. Therefore it behoved us to fee, that they were now inftructed in their Faith;

though

though these were of sufficient Years to know their Duty without Sureties for them. We have many People that undergo that Office, but never consider what their Duty is, and, in short, make it nothing but an outward Ceremony, when if they thought of it, as they ought to do, they would find it of the utmost Concern; for the true Office of Sureties, or Godfathers, &c. is to train up the young Plant, till it is capable of bearing Fruit itself of good Works. But many now a-days do as the Turtles do by their Eggs, lay them, cover them with Sand, and never more regard them.

We came into our old Course again, and pursued it with Success · when we were got into the Latitude of the Tropick, we ducked our Men as before; but there was a great Mutiny of the Sailors: The Captain had three Dogs on Board, and they would have them ducked as well as themselves, unless he would pay the usual Rate; which being promised them, they were composed again, and the Sailors and Dogs were reconciled without going together by the Ears.

We overtook an *English* Vessel that had suffered much by an Engagement with a *Spanish* Pyrate; she had lost all her Masts, but had raised a Jury-Main-Mast, yet could make but little way, by Reason of her Leaks. Our Captain sent a Boat on Board, and gave them all the Assistance he could; but finding it was but two Days since the Engagement, we had some Hopes of coming up with her, for we learnt from the other Ship she was mightily disabled as

M

well

well as themfelves. So we crowded all the Sail we could; and though it was in the Night, we made the beft of our way. The Veffel we left, faluted us with five Guns to take their Leave, which we anfwered with three; and in a quarter of an Hour afterwards heard feveral Guns fired now and then, as if fome Veffel was in Diftrefs, and in an Hour more difcovered a Light, which we made directly towards, and coming up with it, found it to be the *Spanifh* Veffel that had engaged with the other *Englifh* Ship two Days before; the Light that they made was only a large Lanthorn fixed on their Main Top-Maft-Head, that we might the fooner perceive them. We immediately hailed them, and commanded them to furrender: They readily obeyed and begged our Affiftance, which they had great Need of; for the Water gained upon them every Moment, and in an Hour's time the Ship funk, but we preferved all the Men, being in Number 23. having loft in the Engagement with the *Englifh* Ship 27, and received feveral Shot between Wind and Water, which they did not perceive till they difcovered two Feet Water in the Hold, and found no Hopes of being faved from the mercilefs Enemy the Sea, if we had not fortunately for them come timely to their Affiftance. But to allay their Joy for their Deliverance from Death, they were made Prifoners, and being Pyrates (as we fuppofed) for there was no War declared between the two Nations; and therefore they might very

probably

probably think they were to be punished with Death when they came on shore.

The Ship sunk so fast, that we could save nothing but the Men, which took us up about four Hours, and then we pursued our Course, and about four in the Evening made the Island *Barbadoes*; where we set our *Spanish* Prisoners on shore. Captain *Walton* gave the Governor an Account of what had happened, and left it to his Discretion to do with them as he thought fit.

On *June* the twenty-third we set sail for *Dominico*, where we arrived without any Accident. Here I went on shore along with several of our Men to get Wood and Water for our Ship. The Natives seemed very civil, and came on Board us in their *Canoes*.

These *Indians* are most of them tall, lusty Men, well featured and well limbed, but poor Brains, for an ordinary Glass of Rum will make them drunk: They mightily like this Liquor, and will call for it as soon as ever they come on Board you: They wear no Cloaths, but a little Skirt about their Waist; but most of them have Pieces of Brass in the Form of a Three-quarter Moon in their Nose and Ears. I gave one of these *Indians* a Pair of Breeches, and he made an Essay to put them on in this Manner. He first put his two Arms into the Thighs of the Breeches, and desired one of his Companions to button the Waistband about his Neck; but when we shewed him the right Way, and he had put them on, he walked as if he had formerly worn Irons,

and

and was so uneasy with them that he pulled them off, and made Signs to have some Linnen in Exchange: In Return I gave him a long Cravat, and tied it properly about his Neck: But to see how the Fellow strutted, one would have taken him for one of the Captains of the Trained Bands ready to march.

I rambled with these *Indians* several Miles up in the Country, and saw their Huts, that were digged about three Feet deep in the Earth, and then raised about six Feet high above the Surface, and covered with Barks of Trees, and sometimes divided into Apartments by a Couple of long Poles, and Fathers, Sons and Daughters, lie promiscuously together.

The Day before we sailed, (after we had provided ourselves with Wood and Water) I went up to the *Indian* Huts to exchange a Trifle or two for one of their Bows and Arrows; and returning towards the Ship, by myself, lost my way; and though I directed my Course (as I thought right) I came to that Part of the Shore where was no Ship to be found; but endeavouring to go more West along the *Strand*, my Way was intercepted by some high pointed Rocks, which I made several fruitless Essays to pass: I then endeavoured to make a Compass within Land to get by the Rocks; which I did, but could not find the Bay where the Ship rode. I was now in a deep Perplexity, and though very much tired, yet resolved to look for the Track that would carry me back to some of the Huts, where I might get an *Indian* to direct me; but there were so many various ones, that

I knew

I knew not which to chufe. At laft I pitched upon
one that brought me to feveral of them, but not
thofe from whence I came: I fearched them, but
could find no *Indians* in them.   I from thence walked a little farther, but was furprized with a Sight
that fhocked me with Horror.   Near the Skirt of a
thick Wood I found one of our Men killed, with an
Arrow in his Throat; and by the Pofture he lay in,
I found it was done when he was eafing Nature.
The Object fo overcame me, that I thought not on
my own unhappy Condition, till I was awakened
from my Stupidity by a Noife and Gabbling I heard
in the Wood on my Right.   This put me into a
terrible Fright, which made me run as far from the
Noife as I could; for I made no doubt, that if they
caught me, I fhould run the fame Fate with the
poor unfortunate Fellow, who perhaps might lofe
his Life by his feeking me. When I had got a confiderable Diftance, I entered the Wood, and ventured to look out, where I could perceive (though
it was almoft dark) what they were doing.

They cut off the poor Fellow's Head, and tore
out his Bowels in a moft inhuman Manner. Let any
one judge what my Condition muft be; I'm fure my
Thoughts were fo confufed, that I might juftly fay
I never thought at all. I obferved when they had
done, they carried him between Eight of them upon
four Staves, and went towards their Tents. When
they were gone, and I had Leifure for Reflection,
every Thought was a Dagger to me; but yet when
my Senfes were compofed, I put my Truft in God

M 3

that

that he would deliver me from this Danger, as well as several other immediate ones, which through his Mercy I had overcome.

I crept farther into the Wood to rest my Limbs, but my Thoughts kept me waking all Night. When Day approached I went still farther into the Wood, not only to avoid those barbarous *Indians*, but to see if, when on the other Side, I could find some Path that would lead me to the Bay where our Ship rode; but before I could get out of it I heard a Cannon discharged, that both rejoiced and grieved me; it joyed me to know that the Ship could not be far off, and grieved me to think that it was certainly the Signal for the Boat to come on Board, and perhaps they might be that Moment under sail. I ran with all the Haste I could; but with a Mind mixed with Hope and Fear. I got out of the Wood at last, and I directed my Course to that Part as I thought the Noise of the Gun came from, but could find no Path; yet at last I got to the Top of a Rock from whence I could behold the Sea, and with great Grief saw our Ship under Sail not half a League from the Shore. I immediately pulled off my Shirt, and hung it on a Stick I had broke to support me in my Walking; but my Signal did not do me any good, for they saw nothing of it. My Despair began to be predominant over my Reason, and I had often resolved to throw myself down from the Rock to end my Misery; but still my Conscience would give me a secret Check; and at last I resolved with myself to submit to whatever should befall me, with a thorough Resignation

fignation to the Will of Heaven. As foon as the
Ship was out of Sight, I went down from the Rock
(nct having Power to ftir before) and endeavoured
to find fome Food, but was prevented by a hideous
Noife I heard, which drove me to Shelter in the
Wood again; but the farther I went, the plainer I
heard the Noife, fo that I knew not what to do, for
at laft it encreafed on every Side: fo that coming to
a thick Parcel of Shrubs, I laid myfelf down, and
couched fo clofe, that it was impoffible for them to
fee me, unlefs they came into the very middle of it.
I had thrown my Bow and Arrows away, as being
of no Ufe to me; but I had my Sword, which, however, I did not defign to ufe. The Noife came fo
nigh me, that I could hear the Tread of their Feet,
and the Boughs ruftle about me; but at laft it went
iofenfibly away, fo that I heard no more of them for
fome Time.

When I found all was ftill, I began to get up and
look about me, where I faw them in the Plain engaged with feveral other *Indians*, whom I thought
I knew, though at a good Diftance. I faw feveral
of them fall upon the Ground. At laft thofe *Indians*
that went hallooing through the Wood feemed to
me to have the worft of it, and were drove by the
other Party quick back again; but did not purfue
them any farther, only let fly their Arrows at them;
and one of them came among the Shrubs where I
lay, which ftartled me, for I was afraid they would
come to look for their Arrows, and fo find me.
After the Hurlyburly was over, I refolved to go out

of

of the Wood, and follow thofe *Indians* that were Vanquifhers, with this Hope, That they might be of a milder Nature, and not fo barbarous as the others who run through the Wood; who to my thinking had more ftern Looks than thofe *Indians* I had feen upon that Part of the Ifland where we ufed to land to get Wood and Water. So as I faid, I got up, and directed my Courfe out of the Wood after the *Indians*, but foon difcovered two *Indian* Men, and four Women coming towards me, (which I fuppofe had hid themfelves during the late Conflict:) It was to no Purpofe for me to fly, for they had got Sight of me; or if I had, they would have foon fent one of their winged Meffengers after me; fo I chofe boldly to meet them. When we were come within forty Paces of each other, one of the *Indians* was going to fhoot at me, but was with-held by one of the Women: As foon as ever I came clofe to them, they looked upon me with ftrange Geftures, and diftorted Countenances: I put my Hand to my Head and Breaft, which is the Token of Submiffion with the *Indians*; and they let me know by Signs that I muft go with them, which I did not deny; for if I had, I knew I fhould be forced; fo I went willingly enough. When we had got through the Wood, one of the *Indian* Men would have my Coat and Waiftcoat off, which I durft not refufe: The Coat he put upon his Companion, and the Waiftcoat on himfelf, and ftrutted ftrangely. I gave my Handkerchief and Neckcloth to the Woman that hindered the *Indian* from fhooting at me, who received it with a

great

great deal of Joy, and seemed mightily pleased with me. When we arrived at their Huts, there came out at least a hundred frightful-looking *Indians*, who came about me, and had a great deal of Talk with those that brought me with them; but the two *Indians* were forced to part with their Cloaths they had taken from me, to two of the oldest *Indians*, who immediately put them on, and seemed mighty proud of themselves. They gave me some Rice, and another Sort of Victuals boiled; but what it was composed of, I could never learn, neither did I eat any of the same all the while I was among them. When Night came, I was sent into a Hut by myself, and the Door shut upon me, I had a Piece of Mat to lie on, but nothing to cover me. Now I had Leisure to reflect upon my Misfortunes, which I could not do before, by Reason of the Fears I was in. I thought my Condition was now worse than ever it was, for I really believed they designed to make a Sacrifice of me, for I thought to myself they were Cannibals, or Men-Eaters. I passed the Night with a thousand Anxieties and Inquietudes; but nevertheless my Senses were so tired, that I slept whether I would or no; and in the Morning was awakened by four of the eldest *Indians* that came to visit me, who made Signs to me to follow them, which I did without any Hesitation; when I was out in the midst of the plain Place before the Doors of their Huts, they brought before me several of their Women, and gave me to know by Signs that I should take one of them to be my Mate, or Bed-fellow, or suf-

M 5

for

fer Death. I muſt confeſs I was mightily ſhocked, but not giving myſelf much Time to weigh, or think of the Matter, I pitched upon her that I had given my Neckcloth and Handkerchief to, and immediately all the reſt were diſmiſſed; and my Bride and I (for it was even ſo) were conducted to a Hut, where there were ſeveral old *Indians* waiting for me to compleat the Ceremony. When my Bride and I came before them, we were ordered to ſit down, then both our Feet were waſhed with Water; After that they brought us a Piece of their *Indian* Cake, of Bread, of which I was ordered to break off a Piece, and give to my Bride. She then came and laid her Head on my Breaſt; and then, kneeling, put my right Foot upon her Neck; when that was done, ſhe roſe and went out, but immediately returned, and brought me ſome Fleſh broiled on the Coals, which ſhe tore into Morſels, and put in my Mouth, and ſtood before me all the while I eat. I muſt confeſs I was ſo hungry, that I had a very good Appetite to my Victuals, for I had not eat any Fleſh for four Days: But I had no great Stomach to my Bride, although a young well-featured Woman, yet her Complexion did not pleaſe me. When I had done eating, my Bride and I were put into a Hut, and ſhut cloſe without any Light; but the old Proverb, *Joan's as good as my Lady in the Dark*, had like to have proved no Proverb with me. In the Morning we were awaked with a rude Noiſe round our Tent, which ſtartled me at firſt; but I found afterwards it was a ſort of *Epithalamium.*

When

When they had made their frightful Noife for fome Time, they entered promifcuoufly Men and Women. The Men came and took hold of me, and the Women of my new Spoufe, led us out with Shouts, unpleafing Noifes, and antick Geftures; They continued it till we came to a River, and then we parted; the Men with me, and the Women with my Wife. They put me into the River, and wafhed me all over, and I fuppofe the Women did as much by my tawny Rib. After they had given Notice by their Shouts, that they had made an End of fcouring me, they put on my Shirt and Drawers again, and led me to the Bank where my Spoufe waited for me with her She-attendants, and we returned with the fame Noife as we came out. When we came to the Huts, the old *Indians* met us; the old Men took me, and the old Women my Wife, and gave us an Entertainment feparately, which lafted two Hours, according to my Computation; when they had made an End, they fetched us out of our different Tents, and feated us on a Bank, and then danced, and played fuch mad, rude, Monkey Gambols, that put me in mind of the mad Feafts of the *Bacchii* in *Virgil*, for they would tear their Faces with their Nails, and fcratch one another fo violently, that one would have thought they had been fo many *Bethlemites*, and yet all in Mirth; for they would laugh fuch Horfe-laughs whenever any one of them was hurt, they quite ftunned me. When this Sport was over, the young *Indians* of both Sexes took my Bride and I into one of their

Huts, and gave us an Entertainment of Fish broiled upon the Coals, and a pleasant Liquor in a *Calabash*, that was exceeding strong, which soon got into most of their Noddles; and as fast as they grew a little tipsy, they reeled out one by one, and laid themselves before the Door of the Hut, and went to sleep. My good Wife, among the rest, got her Dose too; but was so monstrously loving withal, that I could not tell what to do with her. When Night came, we retired to our Rest as before, and were waked next Morning by another Kind of Noise that was made, with rude Knocking at our Door, or rather Basket, for it was nothing else, and five or six of the old *Indians* came in with Hatchets, and other Instruments, to enable us to get Food for ourselves, as I understood. My Wife took me out by the Arm, and carried me into the Wood with our Bows and Arrows, and by her Signs gave me to understand that she would bring me where I should kill some Creature. At last we came to the Foot of a Hill, which we ascended with some Difficulty; but when we had gained the Summit, we discovered vast Numbers, or Herds of Goats. My Spouse shot, and killed one the first Time; but I was such a Bungler at it, that I never could do any Execution. But my Spouse was very dexterous, as all the *Indians* are in the Island of *Dominico*. My Wife seemed to have a great Love for me, and would always make much of me, her Way. When we had skinned our Goat, we took out our Implements, and made a Fire to broil some of it. When it was

ready,

ready, I gave my Creator Thanks for providing for us poor infignificant Mortals ; and looking towards Heaven, the Refidence of him that formed us all, my Wife fixed her Eyes upon me, and then looked upwards too, with a Kind of Concern. After we had done, I returned Thanks again in the fame Manner as before, and my Wife did the fame ; that is, fhe ftared upwards again as if fhe had a Mind to fee fomething as fhe thought I looked at : And when fhe found fhe could not fee any Thing, fhe came to me, and put her Arms tenderly about my Neck, and with a Sort of begging Tone, feem- ed to afk me, by Signs and Words, which I could not underftand, what I meant by looking upwards. I was really grieved to know that I could not make her underftand, for I could not learn any of their Speech, but here and there a common Word ; nei- ther did I ever perceive they had any Manner of Worfhip to any Thing ; otherwife, if I could have made her comprehend what I meant, I might have found it no hard Matter to have converted her from their abominable Heathenifm ; for fhe was of a mighty mild Nature, very loving and courteous, and nothing like the reft of the favage Crew, who were prone to all Manner of Wickednefs. Her Voice too, differed from theirs, for moft of the *Indians* pronounced their Words in their Throat, as indeed you could not well fpeak them without a gut- tural Sound ; yet fhe, whatever was the Meaning of it, fpoke her Words a different Way from the reft, and had a pleafing Manner. I really began to love her,

and

and only wifhed fhe had been my Wife in the ufual Forms: She could pronounce any Word in *Englifh* that I would fay to her, but I could never get her to repeat whole Sentences; and all fhe did was like a Parrot. After we had done our Hunting-work, I was for going over the Hill to view the Country, and walked up and down a good Way; but I obferved my Wife was very uneafy, but efpecially when I got to the Brow of the Hill. On the other Side, which was about half a League over, I made an Effay to go down; fhe laid hold of my Arm, and pulled me back with all her Force, and with many fupplicating Actions feemed to beg of me not to go; and when fhe found I was offering at it again, fhe fcreamed out fo difmally, that it affrighted me from making any more Attempts. I endeavoured to know what fhe meant, but could gather nothing from her Words or Actions, that could let me into any Thing: But fhe would often handle her Bow and Arrows, and with menacing Actions let me know there was fome Danger. As we went homeward, this odd Accident Han very much in my Head, and I was mighty defirous to find out the Meaning of it, and every Time I went to hunt there with my Wife, I wanted fadly to get down the Hill on the other Side. This Hill was of a vaft Length, and extended from Eaft to South-weft, almoft acrofs the Ifland. I did not know how to contrive it, but after hunting I made believe I was very much tired, and laid myfelf down in order to fleep; and my Wife, with her ufual good Humour, accompanied

me,

me, and in a very little Time I found she was in a sound Sleep. I immediately arose, and stole away softly upon my intended Journey. I got away from my Wife without her awaking, and came to the Brow of the Hill, which I surveyed, and found no Difficulty in the descending. When I had got to the Bottom of the Hill, I was mightily pleased with the Evenness of the Ground, and the Prospect round me, which I could compare to nothing but the Vale of *Elham* in *Worcestershire*, bating the Houses and Towns in it. I had walked up and down the Vale for near an Hour, and was preparing to go back the same Way I came, when looking back to take my last Survey, I saw a Smoke at a Distance, and it ran in my Mind it was the very Place that our Men used to go to, from on Board, to truck with the Inhabitants. The Thought took up some of my Time; and I believe, if it had not been for a tender Regard for my Wife, I had certainly directed my Course to the Smoke I saw there. But I must confess, I could not think of leaving her behind me; but Curiosity put it into my Head to go a little nearer the Smoke I had discovered. But just as I was moving that Way, I heard a dreadful screaming behind me, and turning about, I saw my Wife upon the Brow of the Hill, making the most pitiful Lamentation imaginable. The tender Regard I now began to have for my Wife made me make all the Haste I could to her Relief, as thinking some Mischance might have befel her. When I came to the Bottom of the Hill, I saw several of the *Indians*

of

of our Neighbourhood waiting for me above, and
some were coming down. As soon as I had got to
the Top of the Hill, I was immediately seized by
the *Indians* above, and dragged along as if I had
been the greatest Criminal imaginable, and my
poor Wife hanging upon my Arm all drowned in
Tears. I could not imagine what was the Matter,
and what could be the Reason of their using me in
that Manner. I found it must be something extraordinary by the Grief of my Wife, whose Sorrow
increased the further I went towards our Huts; but
ere we could get there, it rained and thundered so
violently, that we were all well washed before we
came to our Journey's End : When we were within
Ken of our Huts, the whole Tribe came near us,
some skipping and dancing, as mightily rejoiced ;
others with the Face of Concern, and hanging their
Heads in Sign of Sorrow, and mightily lamented
over my Wife. After the old *Indians* had consulted
some Time, they tied me to a withered Tree that
stood at the Mouth of the Huts; then I began to
understand what they meant, for I could perceive
they were bringing Boughs of green Wood, in order to burn me. This Sight made my Courage fail
me, and it was impossible to express my Despair
and Horror. I found now that the last Day of my
Life was come, (for it was impossible to foresee any
Thing to the contrary). My last Recourse was to
the Maker and Giver of all good Things, for I had
tried all other Means in vain ; as also had my poor
Wife, whose Rage and Despair overcame her; and

she

she was carried away by the Women in the utmost Agony. After my Wife was gone, they set Fire to the Wood which enclosed me ; which being green and wet with the late Rain, was a great while in burning ; all the while it was a kindling, some of the *Indians* jumped round me, and danced after their barbarous Manner, while others stood ready with their Bows and Arrows to shoot at me (as I supposed) if the Fire should burn the Bands that tied me, and I should offer to run away. The Wood being green (as I said before) was very stubborn in kindling, which made the Apprehension more dreadful : I made several Essays to break the Bands that held me, but all my Efforts were but in vain ; and I observed every Time I made my fruitless Endeavours, the barbarous Crew shouted and laughed for Joy. The Fire increasing, I prayed to Almighty God to give me Strength to bear the horrid Pain I was going to suffer ; and, if it was possible, to go out of the World with the Patience and Fortitude of a good Christian, who was only going to change this troublesome Life for a better. I compared myself to a wounded Person, that must bear probing of his Hurts, in order to cure them.

I now had given myself up entirely to my Thoughts of the other World ; and this seemed to me like abandoning a barren Island, in order to go to one where was Plenty of every Thing. But before the Fire reached me, there fell such a prodigious Shower of Rain, mixed with Thunder and Lightning, that extinguished it. The Storm lasted for several Hours with the utmost Violence, and I remained still tied to a Tree. When the Storm was over, they began to renew their Fire, and brought the Wood nearer than before, it being at first half a Yard from my Body all round, but now they piled it close to me, that the Fire might the sooner be my Executioner, which I wished for, as knowing it would put me to a speedier Death. But before they had well placed the Wood, they heard Shouts, and Noises in the adjacent Woods; upon which the *Indians* immediately ran away from me, and took to their Arms in an Instant, old and young. The Noise came nearer, and nearer still, till at last I could perceive several *Indians* bolt out of the Wood, who were met by our *Indians*, and a bloody Fight ensued. The Enemy *Indians* seemed to have the best on it, by Reason of some Fire Arms that they had, with which they made strange Havock with our *Indians*; the Battle continued for some Hours with a great deal of Heat, and many of our *Indians* fell. At last the Enemy *Indians* drove ours, even beyond the Huts, and I could only hear the Noise they made, for I was still fastened to the Tree. The Fight continued out of Sight about half an Hour, when my Wife came running with all the Transports of Joy imaginable; and after having put her Head under my Feet she untied me, and fell upon me with all the Signs of a sincere Love. I must confess I was mightily rejoiced to see myself at Liberty, and let what would happen, my Condition could not be worse than it was some

Hours

Hours ago. I could not forbear expreſſing my Love to my Wife by Kiſſes and Embraces. We went to our Hut, and I took my Sword that had been laid up from my firſt being amongſt them. I was going out of my Tent in order to go with my Wife to ſome other Part of the Iſland, that was not known to theſe *Indians:* But juſt as we came among the Tents, three *Indians* met us that had run away from the Fight (as I conjectured). As ſoon as they ſaw me and my Wife, they came up with a great deal of ill Nature in their Countenances; and after ſome Talk with my Wife, one of them with his wooden Sword, went to make a Blow at me; but my Wife interpoſing, received the Blow upon her Head, which ſtruck her to the Ground, bloody and ſenſeleſs. My Rage roſe ſo high upon this, that I could not contain myſelf; but I drew my Sword, and thruſt it up to the Hilt in the Wretch's Body; the other two ſeeing their Companion's Death, ran upon me with the Rage of Lions, but I ſlipping on one Side, avoided the Strokes intended me: They turned immediately upon me, and let drive at me ſeveral Blows, which had the good Fortune not to hit me; but I run one of them into the Throat with my Sword; upon which he ſet up ſuch a Cry that frightned me, and ran away, and was immediately followed by the other. I then ran to the Aſſiſtance of my Wife, who lay almoſt ſtrangled in her own Blood. I raiſed her from the Earth, and ſeated her under the Tree where I was tied,

and

and brought her to herfelf a little ; but I found her
Skull was cracked with the Blow the *Indian* gave
her, and to my great Grief perceived fhe was juft
expiring.   But the Sorrow and Tendernefs to part
with me, (as I judged by her Actions) ftruck me
to the Soul.   She laid one Arm about my Waift,
and her Head in my Lap, but with fuch piteous
Looks with her Eyes that almoft diftracted me.
She made Signs to me to look upwards (as I fancied) to pray for her, though I could not tell for
certain what fhe meant ; but fhe pronounced feveral
Words with Earneftnefs and Paffion ; and I really
fancied, if we could have underftood one another,
I fhould have found fhe would have had fome
Notions of a fupreme Being.   Before fhe expired,
the Enemy *Indians* returned with all of our *Indians*
Prifoners, I mean all that they had not killed ; for
out of two hundred *Indians* of our Party, there was
not above twenty-two left.   They were mightily
furprifed to find me, for many of the Enemy *Indians*
knew me ; and when I came to examine their Faces,
I remembered they were the *Indians* that inhabited
about the Bay where our Ship lay.   One or two of
them could fpeak a little *Englifh*, which they learned
by conve fing with the *Englifh* that ufually anchored in the Bay.   One of them knew my Name,
that he had gathered from our Sailors enquiring for
me, when fent by the Captain before the Ship
failed.   Mafter *Falconer*, faid he, me be glad to fee
you ; white Men belong to great Ships come look
for you very great, and not look you here go away
much forry.   My Wife took up all my Thoughts,
who

who was juſt dying; and though her Strength and
Speech failed her, yet ſhe endeavoured to pull
down my Face to hers, which ſhe kiſſed; and then
ſunk her Head into my Boſom and expired. I was
really as much concerned as if I had married one of
my own Complexion and Country; for I had great
Hopes, if ever I could have made my Eſcape with
her, and could but have taught her *Engliſh*, to have
made her a good Chriſtian. With the Aſſiſtance of
my now friendly *Indians*, I laid her in the Earth:
They told me ſhe was Daughter to one of the
Chief of their Enemy-Tribe. From theſe *Indians* I
learned, that thoſe I had fell among were a Tribe
of *Indians* that had lived on this Side the Ridge of
Mountains for many Years, and declared open War
with thoſe of the other Side for holding Correſpon-
dence with *Whites*; and where ſo ſtrict, that they
put all *Indians* to Death that ever attempted ſingly
to go over the Mountains, which was the Reaſon
of my Danger of burning. The Women that they
took, (all that were with Child) were ſhot to
Death, and the Men in general ran the ſame Fate;
for they were reſolved not to have any one of the
Breed alive. When they plundered the Huts, they
went through the Woods, and over the Mountains
again, and ſo to their own Huts, which I knew.
The old Men and Women met them, ſkipping and
dancing for Joy of their Succeſs, and ſome mourn-
ing for a Huſband, Brother, or Father, that was
ſlain in Battle. Theſe friendly *Indians* were often
plagued with their ſudden ruſhing upon them, and
deſtroying

deſtroying many of them, till at laſt they took up a Reſolution to aſſault them, and if poſſible to extirpate the whole Race; and they had often made Inroads upon them, which leſſened their Number till this laſt ended them, as I ſaid before. The Women and female Children dwelt contentedly among them, being they had no where to go. I began to live contentedly among theſe *Indians,* and uſed to partake of their Diverſion and Labour; as, Hunting and Fiſhing, *&c.* Theſe *Indians* were ſo expert in ſhooting with their Bows and Arrows, that I have ſeen them hit the Mark three hundred Yards, within the Compaſs of a half Crown.

This Iſland of *Dominico* took its Name from its being diſcovered on a *Sunday.* It is computed to be in Length about thirty Leagues, and about twenty eight in Breadth. It is very mountainous, eſpecially to the North-Eaſt. I have heard there are ſome *French* Settlements upon the Iſland; but I enquired of the above mentioned *Indian,* who aſſured me there were not any Inhabitants but Natives, and of thoſe not above an hundred Families, who were moſtly ſeated near that Part that compoſed the Harbour. Said the *Indian* that I uſed to talk with, there be ſome indeed a great Way off in de Iſland, dat are our Fathers and Mothers; and ſome of our Wives, that when dey die we throw into the Sea, and dey ſwim to dat place; and when we die we ſwim dere too. By this we might perceive they had ſome Notion of the Immortality of the Soul. I did my Endeavour to make him ſenſi-

ble

ble of the Joys of Heaven, and Pains of Hell, but
to no Purpose. I told him of a superior Being that
commanded all Things below, and that righteous
People dwelt with him after this Life. He asked,
where my God did live? His Throne is in Heaven,
answered I, pointing upward, where he sits to
judge the Quick and Dead. He live up dare,
high; how you get up high, no Steps reach dare?
It is our immortal Part, added I, that ascends, our
Soul, which is cloathed with the Grace of our
Divine Creator, and enjoys an Eternity of Blessings.
You be de *White Man*, you have Soul; we be no
White, we have no Soul; when we die, we fling in
Water, big Fish come carry us to an oder Place, den
we live dare and die again, and Fish bring us upon
Back to an oder Place. How are you assured of
this (said I?) Have you ever seen any that have
been transported in the Manner you tell me of? No
(answered he); but me be sure it be so. But when
we were carried by Fish to that oder Place, we eat
de Leaf of Tree, dat we can no remember what
we do in toter Place, dat we be bring from. All
the Arguments I could use were of no Effect; for
Heathenism was so rooted in him, and all the *Indians*, that it will be the greatest Difficulty imaginable to bring them to embrace Christianity.
Their Understandings are so infirm, that without a
Miracle there will be no curing them. The *Indians*
would have had me married into one of their Tribe;
and I, fearful to deny them, brought myself off by
saying no *White* could marry under twelve Moons
after

after their Wife's Death; with which they seemed satisfied, but made me promise when that Time was expired to change my Condition of Widower to that of Married Man. I might have been accommodated with a She-Companion if I had found any Inclination, but I evaded it as well as I could.

The Soil of the Island is very fruitful, and there's Plenty of every Thing.

I could not perceive that these *Indians* worshipped any Thing except the Moon : Which when at full, they would all gather together, and looking upwards, stand gazing a confiderable time, and then with one Confent pronounce a Word which founded like *Hiu!* This Word they generally repeated three Times. When they had done *Star-gazing* they would fall to Jumping and Capering like fo many mad Things. When that was over, they would retire to their feveral Huts, and not ftir out till Morning upon any Account.

I afked *Will* (for that was the Name of him that could fpeak *English*, who was mighty proud to be called fo) what Ceremony was it they performed after they were retired into their Huts ? But he anfwered, *Me no tell dat, Wife make much Noife, she no care for dat ; when you have new Wife, you know what we do, but me no tell till den.* What gave me a Curiofity to know, was, *Will* told me, that after the Ceremony was over, I muft not offer to come out of my Hut, nor come nigh any of theirs; for if I did they would kill me. The Hut that was built for me was ordered in another Manner than their own,

with

with a high Door made of Wickets, their's being
so low, that an ordinary sized Man must have
stooped to go in or out.

I used to go to fish in their *Canoes* with them,
where they would catch good Store ; and let it be
what it would, the Cargo was divided among the
whole Tribe, only he that caught them chose first.

I told *Will*, that as soon as ever a Ship arrived
there, I did design to embark in her, in order to
pursue my Voyage : But he told me I must take
care not to let any other of the *Indians* know it, for
they would never suffer any one to go from them,
after they had been once settled among them.
How do you know that, said I ? Have you had
any Talk with them concerning me ? He told me
he had not, but it was their Way : For he gave me
to understand, that about six Years ago there were
four Men left on Shore upon their Island, by
Reason of their Vessel driving out to Sea by a
Hurricane ; and these four Men settled among them,
and married *Indian* Wives, and had Children by
them. But at any Time when a Ship came into
the Bay, they were hurried a great Way up in the
Country, and detained there till the Ships were
gone, and then lived with them as before. But a
small Vessel putting in there by Night, the *Englishmen* spied it, before any of the *Indians*, and
were got to the Shore-side, conversing with the
Crew of the Vessel before the *Indians* found them
out ; but when they saw them talking together, they
were mightily enraged. The four Men went on
Board the Vessel to make merry with their Coun-

N

trymen

trymen, and afterwards came on Shore again and made it no Secret that they defigned to go on Board that Veffel in order to go to their own Country. The *Indians* took no Notice for the prefent: But the Day they defigned to embark, they fet upon the Veffel with their *Canoes*, and killed every Perfon on Board it. When they had done that, they took as many Things out of her as they had Occafion for, and fet her adrift. He told me that the four *Englifhmen* were the firft that taught them to ufe Fire-Arms, and in the Ship they took, they had feveral Mufkets and Quantities of Powder and Shot. But carrying the Powder to their Huts, a Boy met them fmoaking in a Cane, they call a fmoaking Cane, and by fome Accident the Fire caught hold of the Powder and blew it up, with the Death of eight *Indians*, and wounding feveral others. After they had brought every Thing up to their Huts, they took the Wives of the four Sailors, (the *Indians* with their Children) and fhot them to Death with Arrows. This is the Senfe of the Story *Indian Will* told me, which was pretty hard to pick out too, confidering his Manner of telling it. The Relation made me very uneafy, yet put me upon thinking to make my Efcape the firft Opportunity. I waited a full Month before I could fee any Veffel, but at laft one came into the Harbour. I perceived they came in order to get Wood by hoifting out their Long Boat; but as I was obfervin; them I was feized by feveral *Indians*, and carried at leaft fix Miles up in the Country, in order to be fecured

till

till the Ship was gone. I began to defpair now of ever getting away, being it was natural to fuppofe, that they would be more watchful over me for the future. Befides, I did not know but they would ufe me after another manner, and not let me have fo much Liberty as I had before. I wanted for nothing in my Confinement, and was only guarded by four *Indians* that went to fleep when I did. I once thought I might make my Efcape whilft they flept; but afterwards repented that Thought, in knowing if they fhould chance to wake, I was certainly a dead Man; for *Indian Will* told me, as I was carrying away, that the *Indians* had Orders to fhoot me if I offered to make my Efcape: Befides, I fhould have found it difficult enough to have known my Way, efpecially in the Dark; for they carried me a Place that I had never been at before. I had been here four Days, and had given over all Hopes of my Liberty, and began to call together my fcattered Thoughts, that were fluttered upon that Occafion; when, on the fourth Day about Noon, I was agreeably furprized, and wifhed they might come to the Place where I was. I was not long in expecting them; for one of them fpying the Hut, where I was, called out to the others to come along; for here's an *Indian's* Hut, faid he; we'll go in it, and fee what they'll give us. With that they immediately came in before two of my *Indians* could hide me, (the other two being gone in the Morning to the Village): as foon as ever I faw them, though Strangers, I could not forbear fhowing my

N 2

Tranfports

Tranſports at the Sight of my Countrymen. They
were mightily ſurpriſed to ſee me; and when I told
them my Condition, they ſaid they would have me
along with them in Spite of their Teeth: But I told
them that was very dangerous; for if theſe *Indians*
ſhould raiſe the Village (that lay within a Mile of
the Shore) we ſhould all loſe our Lives. Some adviſed to knock them on the Head; but I could not
agree to that, for theſe were *Indians* that had never
injured me. Two of my Countrymen had got a
Couple of Spaw-Water Flaſks filled with Rum,
upon the Sight of which a Thought came into my
Head, that ſeemed the moſt likely to compaſs my
Deſign. I told my Countrymen, if we could make
the *Indians* drunk there might be ſome Hopes of
getting off without either hurting them or endan-
gering ourſelves. We drank to one another, and
the *Indians* did us Juſtice in pledging us; for I
believe out of the two Flaſks they drank one and
three quarters. It ſoon began to work with them,
and they got up and fell a dancing moſt madly,
and a while after dropt down drunk; we reſolved
to tie them Hands and Feet, that if they awaked,
they might not follow us, and raiſe the whole Body
of *Indians* upon us. With the Help of our Garters
we tied them faſt enough without waking them,
and made the beſt of our Way towards the Sea-ſide.
All the Danger we ran was in meeting with any of
the other *Indians*, but we happily avoided them,
and came to the Place where the Boat lay. The
Ship was ready to ſail, having got their Wood and

Water

Water aboard; and thefe eight Men were thofe
that had been labouring hard in cutting Wood, &c.
and fo were refolved to go up the Country to view
it, never having been farther than the Place where
they felled the Trees, and happily for me came to
give me my Liberty under Providence. As we
were getting into the Boat to go on Board (the Ship
having made a Waft in her Ancient) *Indian Will*
came running down almoft out of Breath, and
cried, get quick in Ship, they come down prefently
kill all, me go wid you, dey kill me elfe for tell
you. We hurried away, and *Indian Will* with us,
and got on Board in very good Time; for before we
were well under Sail, we could perceive at leaft two
hundred *Indians* bringing their *Canoes* with them.
We had a brifk Gale, fo that they could not well
overtake us; for they never go above two Leagues
from Shore. Neverthelefs they put their *Canoes*
into the Water, and began to paddle after us.
The Captain was for firing at them with our great
Guns, but I perfuaded him againft it, by telling
him it might be worfe for other *Englijh* Veffels, that
fhould come after us; and as they could not overtake us to do us any Damage, it was beft not to
take any Notice of them. When we had loft Sight
of *Dominico*, I afked *Indian Will* the Reafon of their
endeavouring to detain all *Whites* in that clandeftine
Manner; and he gave me to know, that they
feared if the *Whites* fhould know the Smallnefs of
their Number, that they would put them all to
Death, and feize upon the whole Ifland. The

N 3

Ship

Ship that took us up was called the *Twins* from *Carolina*, Captain *Fuller* Commander; she came then from *Barbadoes*, and was bound for *Jamaica*. I took *Indian Will* as my Servant, and did design to give him some Cloaths, as soon as we arrived at *Jamaica*; but for the present I had none for myself, and made but an odd Sort of a Figure. My Beard was pretty long, and being something inclining to red, looked but oddly: My Linnen was all gone, so that my whole Dress consisted of a Hat, a Waistcoat, a Pair of Breeches, and a Pair of Shoes, the Captain was so kind as to lend me a Shirt and a Pair of Stockings, and I got my Beard off, and once more looked like a Christian. We made *Jamaica* without meeting with any Thing material, and found the Fleet at Anchor. I went on Board the Admiral, and paid my Respects to him, which he took very kindly. I there once more met with my Friend Mr. *Musgrave*, and the rest of my Companions who had given me over for lost; for Captain *Walton* told the Admiral and my Comrades, that I was certainly murdered by the *Indians*. I had all my Things restored me, that were brought in the *Albion* Frigate, that arrived about a Week before me with the Stores of the Fleet, after she had been in the Dock at *Plymouth* and well mended. She also brought News of War being declared between *England* and *France*, and the Death of his Sacred Majesty King *William* the *Third*, of Glorious Memory, and the Coronation of her Majesty Queen *Anne*. *July* the 11th 1702, the whole Fleet set out from *Jamaica*, in order for a Descent upon St. *Dominico*, as was supposed; but

Things

Things not anſwering, the Admiral, in the *Breda*, Captain *Fog*, with ſix other Men of War, *viz.* *Defiance*, Captain *Kirby*; *Greenwich*, Captain *Wade*; *Windſor*, Captain *Conſtable*; *Ruby*, Captain *Walton*; *Falmouth*, Captain *Vincent*; and *Pendennis*, Captain *Hudſon*, went in Queſt of Monſieur *Du Caſſe*, the *French* Commodore, that was deſigned for *America* with Ammunition, Forces, Proviſion, and Money to pay the Garriſon, beſides ſeveral Governors to be put in the Room of others that were called back. We directed our Courſe to Port *Longoan*, where *Du Caſſe* was expected every Day : But when we came there we were informed that *Du Caſſe* was ſailed for *Carthagena*, upon which we directed our Courſe for that Place, after having taken three Ships, one of ſixteen, another of thirty, called *Reine de Angelos*, or the Queen of Angels, and another of ſix Guns richly laden, beſides three Barks taken by Captain *Conſtable*, in the *Windſor*, and a fourth ſunk; likewiſe a *French* Man of War of forty Guns burnt.

On the 19*th* of *Auguſt*, O. S. about ten in the Morning, we diſcovered ten Sail to the Eaſtward of us, which we bore up to, and found them to be the Fleet we were in Queſt of; though there were ten Sail, yet there were but ſix fighting Ships, the reſt were Store-Ships which made the beſt of their Way; ſo when the Admiral came up with them we had but ſix to engage. The Line of Battle was formed about Three in the Afternoon, the *Defiance* led the Van, the *Windſor* the ſecond, and *Bembow* in the *Breda* the third. Theſe three kept pretty cloſe together, but

N 4

the

the other four were a League behind. At four in
the Afternoon we began the Engagement, but the
Defiance after firing three Guns bore away to Leeward, and lay there out of Gun-shot all the Evening,
so that the whole Strength of the *French* Fleet lay
upon the Admiral and the *Windsor* till it was dark.
In the Night the *Windsor* fell foul of our Ship, which
startled a great many, that were not upon Deck, as
believing it might be a *French* Fireship, though
we knew they had not one in the Fleet; but Fear,
as well as Passion blinds our Reason. The Wind
chopped about in the Night, so that we had the
Weather-gage of them; upon which we bore down
upon them, and engaged for three Hours; but the
Ruby, Captain *Walton*, was disabled, and ordered
by the Admiral to make for *Port-Royal*. My Man
Indian Will, who was on Board, dressed like an *Eu-*
ropean, was terribly frighted with the Noise of our
Guns; and every Time he saw the Flash of our Enemy's Cannon, he would squat down upon the Deck,
and lye flat upon his Belly for some Time; one of
our Men that was shot in the Guts lay expiring, and
Indian Will was getting away out of Danger, he said,
but unfortunately stumbled over the dying Man,
who in the Pangs of Death grasped *Will* so fast,
that he cried out lustily for Help; but it was more
than I could do to unclench his Hand till he was
quite dead, and then we released poor *Will*, frighted out of his Wits, who could not be prevailed
upon to come upon Deck any more till we told him
we had done Fighting. We took one Ship from

the

the *French*, that they had taken from the *English* in their Voyage. The Fight lasted six Days, on and off; but the Admiral being wounded in the Thigh, and finding that *Wade, Kirby,* and *Hudson,* did not care for fighting, we left them, after disabling two of their Ships, and directed our Course back to *Port-Royal.* As soon as we arrived there, the Admiral sent Orders to confine Captain *Constable, Wade, Kirby,* and *Hudson,* and summoned a Court Marshal, tried them, and found them guilty of Cowardice, excluding *Constable;* and accordingly the other three were sent to *England* to receive Sentence of Death, which was executed upon two of them. The third, Captain *Hudson,* died in the Voyage, and so prevented an ignominious Death. How easy it had been for the *English* to have taken the *French,* if they had been unanimous; but such an Instance of Pusil-lanimity is not to be found in the Records of the Navy.

December the 14th, 1702, we were all concerned at the News of Admiral *Bembow*'s Death, who died of the Wound in his Thigh that he received in the Engagement with Monsieur *Du Casse,* lamented by all. I obseved there was a perfect Groan in every Ship in the Fleet, when the Admiral Flag was lowered with a Whiff, which is the Custom at Sea. He was buried at *Kingstown,* where he died. He had several rich Plantations in *Jamaica,* and many Slaves. He had made five successful Voyages to *Jamaica,* and returned home laden with Wealth and Honour; but the sixth proved fatal to him. He had a perfect

N 5

Knowledge

Knowledge in the Navigation of *America*, having been feveral Years Captain of a Privateer there. He was a Man beloved of both Officers and common Sailors; a Perfon of true Courage, and Fortitude: for when he was wounded in the Engagement, he ordered the Carpenters to make him a Cradle, that he might be upon Deck to give Orders. Nothing went more near his Heart than this unfortunate Expedition; and the Surgeons reported, that the Grief he conceived from it, hindered the Healing of his Wound, which was given with a Mufket-Ball, and not a Chain Shot, as has been reported in our Publick Papers. Admiral *Martin*, as being the eldeft Officer, fupplied his Place till Admiral *Whetftone* arrived in the *Boyne*. My very good Friend Captain *Hercules Mitchell*, Captain of the *Strombolo* Firefhip, was made Captain of the *Windfor*; and Admiral *Benbow* being dead, I removed myfelf, with Capt. *Fog*'s Leave into his Ship. The Fleet fet Sail with the Merchant Ships for *England*, *March* the 8*th*, 1703, and met with nothing worthy of Note.

On *May* the 5*th*, we entered *St. John*'s Harbour in *Newfoundland*, and ftayed there till *May* the 12*th*, then fet Sail for the *Bay of Bulls*, a convenient Harbour for Wood and Water in the fame Ifland. After we had provided every Thing we wanted there, we weighed Anchor in order to fail for *England*. In weighing our beft *Bower* (an Anchor fo called) the Nippers giving Way, the Capftorn-Bars killed us three Men and broke the Back of a fourth, who died in a Week after.

November

November the 1ft, we were feparated from the Fleet by a dreadful Storm, that threw all our Mafts by the Board, and our Boltfprit was alfo fprung, but we fifhed that which preferved it. We were in a very pitiful Condition, and I am fure in great Danger, for I really heard fome of the Sailors at their Prayers. We loft two of our Men, who fell with the Main-maft over Board. The Storm lafted for two Days, and the Weather continued fo hazy we could not take our Obfervations. We put up our Jury-Mafts, but could make but little Way. We had Captain *Titchburn's* Company of *Marines*, and Major *Bowls*, Major of the Regiment that did belong to Colonel *Jones*, who died in the Voyage; fo that having above our Complement, our Provifion began to be at an Ebb, which obliged us all to come to half Allowance, and half a Pint of Water a Day to each Man, for we did not know how long we fhould be out at Sea; but we made *Ireland* beyond all our Hopes *November* the 20th, and got fafe into *Galloway* Harbour on the 23d, and it was a great Providence we did fo; for on the 25th there arofe fuch a violent Storm, that muft have inevitably deftroyed us. This was that fatal Hurricane that did fo much Damage in *England, &c.* There were two Ships in *Galloway* Harbour that were ftranded, and it was allowed by every Body that we fhould have run the fame Fate, if our Mafts had been ftanding; but having none but Jury-Mafts, which we took down when the Storm began to be pretty high, fo that the Wind could not have the fame Power over us, neither do I think

N. 6

that

that the Storm was so violent in *Ireland*, by all Description, as it was in *England*, *Holland*, and *France*. We stayed at *Gallway* four Months, and in that Time we had got Masts up and repaired our other Damages. While the Ship was fitting up, I lay on Shore in the Town. *Gallway* is a neat well fortified Town, as big as *Salisbury*, yet has but one Church. Every Thing is very cheap there. I had my Board in a private House for four Shillings *per* Week, and seldom dined without two or three Dishes at Table: We bought the best *French* Wine for Fourteen Pence *per* Quart, and sometimes under. We set Sail from *Gallway*, *February* the 27th, 1704, and arrived safely at *Plymouth*. Thus after many Misfortunes and Hazards I once more set my Feet upon my dear native Country (accompanied with *Indian Will*, who still lives with me, and proves an honest faithful Servant; and I have taken Pains to have him instructed in the Christian Religion, and likewise to have him christned by the Name of *William Dominico*, from the Island that he came from;) and though warned by many Dangers I had run, I could not forbear making three Voyages more, but yet in a Station different from what I went before. But as they were but common Voyages, that is, nothing extraordinarily happening, I shall conclude with my Prayers and Thanks to Heaven for the many Mercies I have received; wishing long Life and Happiness to my King, Prosperity, Peace and Riches to my Country, and a hearty Union among my Fellow Subjects.

F I N I S.

INDEX.

A.

Bark

INDEX.

A

NARRATIVE

OF A

GREAT DELIVERANCE

AT

SEA.

WITH

The Name of the MASTER, SHIP, and
thofe that fuffered.

By *WILLIAM JOHNSON*, D. D.
Late Chaplain and Sub-Almoner to his SACRED
MAJESTY.

Quod durum eft pati,
Meminiſſe, dulce eft.   Sen.

The SIXTH EDITION, Corrected.

LONDON:

Printed for G. KEITH, in Grace-Church-Street,
and F. BLYTH, No. 87, Cornhill.
—————————————
MDCCLXIX.

To the Honourable Society of the *East-Country* Merchants refident in *England*, *Dantzick*, *Koninfberg*, and elfewhere.

Worthy Friends,

I AM led to honour your Society, not by the haſty Choice and Election of the Will, which oftentimes is tranſported with Paſſion, and loveth without any Merit; but by the rational and underſtanding Part, which hath a long Time perfectly known and underſtood your many Excellencies, that I cannot chuſe but love and honour the Society. Neither are you beholden to any for the Reſpect they give, or rather pay you, but to your own Merit, to which it is due. You are not like Solomon's Merchants, thoſe I mean that brought over Apes and Peacocks; but you furniſh this Iſland with ſuch ſtaple Commodities, that ye have made London as famous as that City of Tyre, that crowned City, whoſe Merchants are *Princes*, and whoſe Traffickers are the Honourable of the Earth. There is as much Difference between the Trade of thoſe worthy Merchants that furniſh us with Spices, Plumbs, and Taffaties, and our Eaſt-Country Trade that bringeth us in Maſts, Materials for Cordage, and Neceſſaries for Shipping, as there is in Religion, between Ceremonies and Fundamentals. Spices and ſuch Things are pretty Ornaments, and ceremonial Supplements to our Well-being: But our Eaſt-Country Commodities are thoſe which do conſtitute the Being, and lay the Foundation of a rich and flouriſhing Commonwealth: And without them, if not the Art, yet the Practice of Navigation would be left among us. For we cannot ſail to the Indies in a Nutmeg, embark ourſelves in Cinnamon, make a

Maſt·

Maſt of a Race of Ginger, and rowing our Ships with Taffaty. No, it is our Eaſt-Country *Trade that doth furniſh us with theſe above our Neceſſaries for Navigation, and is indeed the very Principle and Foundation of all Merchandize, and like a Maſter-wheel in a Watch, ſetteth all other on Work. So that what Goods are brought into this Nation, may be ſaid principally and primarily to be imported by your Aid and Aſſiſtance, though fetched hither by the Hands of others.*

This is a general Good, obligeth every one to honour you: But I have an Argument of an higher Nature, which doth diſpute and convince my Affections into an high Eſteem and Reputation of your Society.

Your Company in Pruſſia *were the firſt that called me to the Exerciſe of my miniſterial Function, being the firſt Charge that ever I undertook to preach to: And had I not been forced to come into* England *by an Obligation which I could not in Conſcience break, I had rather have parted with my* Life *than them, for they were, as the Apoſtle writeth to* the Philippians, my Hope, my Joy, and Crown of rejoicing in the Lord Jeſus.

That I had a Deſire again to come unto them, witneſs thoſe many Sufferings, Loſſes, Shipwrecks, Fears, Straights, Dangers, Deaths that I did undergo in that ſecond Adventure; and for the Love I bear them, am willing to repeat them over again, not in Words only, but in real Sufferings, ſo I might be any Way ſerviceable for the Good and Salvation of their Souls.

But ſome will ſay to me, Why would you venture to Sea again, ſeeing you have ſo often found the Ship unſafe, the Mariners fearful, the Winds treacherous, and the Waves rebellious?

I an-

I anfwer, if God call me to it, I fhall not fear the Frowns of Neptune, *nor the crooked Face of an angry Tempeft.* It *was a brave Spirit of that* Roman, *who being to undergo a dangerous Voyage at Sea for the Service of his Country, being diffuaded from it, made this Anfwer,* πλειν αναγκη, ζην εκ αναγκη : It is neceffary *for me* to fail, *but* it is not neceffary *for me* to live. *And it was a noble and virtuous Refolution in another, who faid, if he were commanded to put forth to Sea in a Ship that neither had Mafts nor Tackling, he would do it; and being afked, what Wifdom that was? replied,* The Wifdom muft be in him that hath Power to command, not in him whofe Confcience bindeth to obey. *When the Service of God calleth us to hazard our Lives, why fhould we not be willing to facrifice them?* Quid revolvis? Deus præcipit, *faith* Tertullian. *If Chrift fhould call me to Sea again, why fhould I be more afraid to go aboard a ftately Ship, than* St. Peter *was to walk upon the very Waves, when Chrift called him to come to him?*

But feeing God would not let me go to Tarfus, *but fent me back in an angry and furious Tempeft, and made me a Preacher of Repentance in this Place, I fhall ferve you in my Devotions, and, as the Apoftle faith,* make Mention always of you in my Prayers, *that ye may be like that wife Merchant in the Gofpel,* who when he had found one Pearl of great Value, fold all and bought that Pearl, which was the Kingdom of Heaven.

The firft that fought after Chrift, and (when they had found him) prefented him with Gifts, were the Wife Men that came from the Eaft: They prefented to him Gold,

Frankincenfe,

Frankincenfe, and Myrrh: I fhould be glad it might be faid fo of you, that go to and from the Eaft. I wifh, with all my Heart, that ye would firft feek after Chrift Jefus, and w en ye have found him out, being guided to him by the Star of your Faith, that then ye offer up to him the Sacrifice of a cheerful Obedience, in a true and faithful Service of him; and that will be as fweet and acceptable to our Saviour, as the Gifts of thofe Chaldean *or* Arabian *Aftronomers, their Gold, Frankincenfe, and Myrrh, or all the Riches of the* Eaft.

So prayeth, Sirs,

Your poor Orator,

and Humble Servant,

WILL. JOHNSON.

To

To the Right Worshipful the Governor, Assistants, and Fellowship of the *East-Land* Merchants in *London*.

Right Worshipful,

IN Ours of the 28th of August, we gave you Notice, that in our destitute Condition, it pleased God by his singular Providence to supply our spiritual Wants by the Ministry of Mr. William Johnson, an able and pious Divine. But he being now called Home, by a Charge fallen unto him, We cannot suffer him to pass without this deserved Testimony: That, for his Person, he hath been amongst us, Grave, Retired, Learned; in his Life, without Blame, and Scandal; in his Studies, Laborious; in his Preaching, both Orthodox and Powerful: so that truly, in Regard of the singular Fruition of his Labours past, and considering our desolate ensuing Condition, We cannot but mourn at his Departure. Yet hath he left us this Comfort behind him, That the present Distractions at Home may be a Motive to dispose of his Living there, and to return to us again in the Spring, if it please God that he be thereunto lawfully chosen and called. Unto us he is a Man without Exception, which we testify by this our general Subscription. It may please you therefore and it is our serious and earnest Request, that, if his Occasion will suit with our Desires, you will hear him Preach, and by an undoubted

Election

(vii)

*Election return him back again with all Speed. And this
will be an actual Prayer to implore Divine Mercy, and
to turn Curses into Blessings. We say no more, but the
Lord be your Protector and Director.*

Your Worships, in full

Dantzick,
Jan. 1.

Assurance to Command,

Will. Gore.	Ambrose Griggs.
Richard Jenks.	Geo. Hackett.
Sam. Travell.	Fran. Sanderson.
Robert Searles.	Amb. Medcalfe.
Ed. Westcomb.	And. Taylor.
Sam. Short.	Ed. Daniel.
John Collins.	Jof. Oley.
Rich. Wallis.	Nich. Mitchel.
Will. Williamson.	Tho. Clench.
Will. Shires.	Tho. Dawson.
Ja. Hutchinson.	Will. Lockwood.
Jo. Coozin.	Jo. Whitehall.
Rich. Waynde.	Jo. Pearce.

The Name of the Ship, The *William* and *John* of
Ipswich.

The chief Owners, were *William Blithe,* and *John
Smytheir,* both Merchants in *Ipswich,* from whom the
Ship had the Name; the latter of these my worthy
Friend.

O   The

The Names of thofe that fuffered in the Ship-wrecks, were, *Daniel Morgan*, Màſter; *Edmund Morgan*, Mate; *Robert Lakeland*, Mate; *Matthew Bird*, Boatſwain; ———— *Taylor*, Carpenter; *John Holmes*, *Rob. Laurence*, *Will. Engliſh*, *Tho. Crofferd*, Mariners; and others, whoſe Names I cannot remember.

A
NARRATIVE
OF A
GREAT DELIVERANCE
AT SEA.

W E went aboard from *Harwich* on *Michael-mas* Day, the 29th of *September*. I confess, a dull Kind of Sadnefs (as a Cloud) fat upon my Spirits, fo that I could not look out cheerfully upon my departing Friends : But I took my Farewell of them, as if I had been going not only out of England, but out of the World. I can give no Reafon for this *Deliquium*, for I was fent on a good Meffage, to preach the Gofpel of Jefus Chrift ; I was embarked in a ftout Ship with a fair Wind, and a fkilful Pilot ; fo that the underftanding and rational Part of my Soul could not forefee any, nor fufpect the leaft Danger : But (fure) Nature (whofe *Apocrypha* we fhall never underftand)

was

was fenfible of fome approaching Storm ; for I was no fooner at Sea, but I was in a ftrange Anguifh and Prepoffeffion, fo that I fuffered Shipwreck in my Mind, and all the Terrors thereof before it came. I prefently fell fick (as I ufually do at Sea) for Water has always been an unkind Element to me : Yet that Sicknefs hath no fpecifical Name ; we neither call it Fever nor Ague, Palfy nor Gout ; but I think it is all thefe, with the reft of human Infirmities, or at leaft an *Index* where we may find them ; for I was fo really fick, that to be drowned had been a Punifhment indeed, but in my Thoughts no Affliction to me. This Sicknefs was neither Tertian nor Quartan, but Quotidian ; for I was as fick the next Day as before. About four of the Clock in the Afternoon, the Mafter of the Ship came into our Cabin with more Hafte than he was wont, for he was quickened with the Senfe and Apprehenfion of fome fudden and enfuing Danger ; which though he concealed from me, I faw it in his very Countenance, written plainly in pale Characters of Fear and Amazement, which made me afk him, *Whether all was well?* And like a loving, a tenderhearted Man, who is loth to tell his dying Friend that he is fo near his End, he anfwered me, *All is well.*

But when I faw him fhift himfelf, and make Hafte out again in great Speed, but greater Paffion, I rofe from my Bed, and crawled upon the Deck, where I faw a fad Spectacle · The Ship having fprung a Leak, or rather a Plank, was ready to fink.

fink. I do not wonder now I was fo fick before, feeing Death was fo near. Oh how the Face of every Man was changed by this Affrightment, fo that we could not know almoft one another, having loft our natural Complexions through the Extremity of Paffion ! One was at his Prayers, another wringing his Hands, a third his Eyes fhedding of Tears, when we had no need of more falt Water. But after this Fit, they fell to Work, and (as it is ufual in fuch Extreams) we were all bufy about doing of nothing, and we did we knew not what. We began one Thing——*fed fazi pænitet*, but we prefently fell to another, and perfected nothing to our Safety. The Mafter's Mate and Brother, whom we fent down to fearch out the Leak, quickly returned to us with a fad Countenance; though naturally his Face was red, yet Fear had fnowed it into a pale Complexion. This Man with trembling Hands, Gnafhing of Teeth, a quivering Tongue, and Words half fpoken, fignified to us that the Wound was incurable, that the Leak could not be ftopped; and the Water came in fo faft upon us, that we muft perifh in this Moment. I never heard a Death's Head fpeak before; for he did look not like a Meffenger, but Death itfelf; had he faid nothing, we might have read our Fate, and Ruin in his Countenance.

Here was now no Room for Counfel, neither had we Time to afk one another, what was beft to be done ? But we prefently caft out our Long-boat, and

O 3

fhot

ſhot off ſome eight or nine Guns, which ſeemed to me to be ſo many Tolls of a Paſſing-bell before our Death. But it was to give Notice to one *Bartholo-mew Cook*, who was Maſter of that Ship that came out with us, and was but a little before us, that he ſhould come to our Relief. In theſe fair Hopes we leaped into the Boat; but it was my ſad Chance to leap ſhort, one Leg in the Boat, *alterum in Charontis cymba :* but not without ſome Danger, I ſcrambled out of the Sea into the Boat; but was no ſooner there, but one of the Mariners leapt out of the Ship upon me, and beat me down with his Weight; which I took kindly enough, being willing to have carried them all upon my Back to have ſaved their Lives. But there was one, and but one, left in our ſinking Ship, who made ſuch lamentable Moan, that his Tears prevailed againſt the Fears of our preſent Danger, and we took him into the Boat, when we expeᴄted our Ship (whoſe Sails lay now flat upon the Water) ſhould ſink immediately, which muſt neceſſarily have drawn our ſmall Boat after it, as the greater Fiſhes ſwallow up the leſs.

But (God be thanked) we all came clear off the Ship, but now were rowing we knew not whither : For Mr. *Cook* came not to our Relief, and we began to be ſevere in Language againſt him, as if he had not been kind enough to us; when all that knew him will ſay, he was a Man of a ſoft, tender Nature, and a Friend to others rather than to himſelf. But all Men are ſuſpicious in Adverſity, and com-

monly

monly take all Things in the worſt Part, and ſo did
we, not conſidering at all how it
might fare with this honeſt Maſter, *Omnes quibus*
who, poor Man, was in greater *res ſunt minus*
Diſtreſs than themſelves, and drank *ſunt neſcio quo-*
a deeper Draught of Affliction : *modo ſuſpicioſi*
for both he and his Ship, and all *ſe ſemper cre-*
his Men, periſhed in that Hour, *dunt negligi.*
not a Man eſcaped to tell us the Teren. Adelp.
Cauſe, Manner, and Method of his Fate.

Now were all our Hopes daſhed, as well as ourſelves, being in Deſpair of human Help ; for we
were left in the North Seas, which ſeldom wear a
ſmooth Brow, but at this Time contending with the
Wind, ſwelled into prodigious Mountains, which
threatened every Moment to fall upon us.

'To ſpeak plainly, it blew half a Storm, and we
were now in a ſmall Veſſel : what Credit could we
give to our Safety in a ſmall and open Shallop, when
ſo ſtately a Caſtle of Wood, which we but now loſt,
could not defend itſelf againſt the Inſolency of the
Waves ; we were many Leagues from any Shore,
having no Compaſs to guide us, no Proviſion to ſuſ-
tain us, being ſtarved with Cold, as well as for
Want of Victuals ; and the Night grew black upon
us, having nothing in our Boat but
a ſmall * Kettle, and three Bags of * Which ſerv-
Pieces of Eight, to the Value of ed us as a
300*l. Sterling.* But alas ! what Scoop to caſt
Good can Money do where there the Water out
is no Exchange ? we could not eat of the Boat.

nor drink our Silver; neither could our Pieces of Eight keep us warm. Money, in its own Nature, is but an impotent Creature, a very Cripple, *inutile pondus, a Burthen of no Value.*

Good God! into what a fad Condition haft thou now brought us! for which of our Sins doft thou thus punifh us? Teach us, O Lord, that we may know it, and firft drown ourfelves in Tears of Repentance, before the Sea fwallow us up; that though our Bodies be caft away, we may fave our Souls. Such Language my troubled Thoughts fpake within me; for it was with us now as it was with St. *Paul*; *All Hopes that we fhould be faved were taken away*, Acts xxvii. Nothing could preferve us but a Miracle, being out of the Reach of human Help; we were finful Creatures, and could not expect that God fhould go out of his ordinary Way to fave us. Though the Waves carried us up to Heaven, yet we could not hope or believe that God fhould put his Hand out of the Clouds, and take us miferable Caitiffs unto himfelf from the Top of the rifing Wave; we had nothing to help us but our Prayers. I am forry that Word flipped from my hafty Pen. Prayer is a Multitude, a Troop of Succours, and many enough to deliver us out of the Depth, though we were intombed in the Belly of a Whale, as it did *Jonah*. Prayer, if it be well qualified, is that Rod of *Mofes*, that can *turn the Sea into a Wildernefs, and make us pafs through upon dry Land*, Pfal. cvii. Upon this only Staff did we all lean; and I fuppofe it was with us, as in the Cafe

of

of *Jonah:* *The Mariners were afraid, and every Man called upon his God,* Jonah ii. And truly, I think I may with Modesty confess, I thought on those Words of *David*, though after a more imperfect Manner: *Out of the Depth have I cried unto thee: Lord, hear my Voice, and let thine Ears be attentive to my Supplication. I sink in the deep Mire, where there is no standing. Let not the Water-flood overflow me, neither let the Deep swallow me up,* Psal. lxix.

But beside our personal Devotion, I am persuaded the Extremity of our Condition pleaded for us, and our Misery cried aloud in the Ears of God, for Pity and Compassion. It is an usual Expression, when we see any Man extremely poor and miserable, to say *his Poverty, or his Misery speaks for him.* And commonly we are not so much moved with a clamorous Beggar, who hunts after our Alms with open Mouth, and makes Hue and Cry after our Charity, as if we had stolen something from him who begs of us. I say, we are not so much moved with such loud Impudence, as with the Silence of those diseased Cripples, and infirm *Lazaro's*, that lie at our Doors, in the Streets, and say nothing, but shew only their Wounds and Sores to those that pass by. These Beggars speak loudest to our Affections; their very Condition is eloquent; *quot Vulnera, tot Ora; so many Wounds, so many Mouths,* that cry aloud for Pity, and cannot chuse but melt us into a charitable Compassion. This was our Case; our Misery was louder than our Prayers, and our deplorable Condition cer-

O 5

tainly

tainly was more prevalent with Almighty God, than our imperfect Devotions; for we may fay with the People of *Ifrael, He heard our Cry, and had Compaf-fion on us,* Exod. ii. It is the ufual Way of God to help in Extremities; when we are in abfolute De-fpair of all outward Means, he loves to fave us, that we may fay, *It is his doing alone.*

For in this Moment of Death, when we were without the leaft Expectation of any Deliverance, he fent a Ship to us, which we muft needs confefs to be *Digitus Dei, the Finger of God,* that pointed and directed that Ship to our Deliverance : For though many Ships come from the fame Place, and are bound for the fame Haven, yet they feldom meet in the vaft Ocean, and fail in the fame Line : for there are no beaten Paths in the Floods, no Highways and common Roads in the Sea. But fuch was the Good-nefs of God, this Ship made towards us, and we what we could towards it ; but we had but two Oars, and the Seamen counted that a great Difadvantage both to their Speed and breaking of the Waves : Befides, it blew hard, and the Sea, that knows no Pity, rofe high upon us, fo that we were forced to fit clofe to one another, to keep out the Sea with our Backs; a poor Shelter againft a raging Enemy, who finding himfelf checked, through Indignation flew over our Heads into the Boat, and fell upon us in angry Showers; fo that had we not had that Kettle, to caft the Water out as faft as it came in, we might have been drowned from above with Rain of our own making. It was my Lot to fit on the

Weather-

Weather-fide, (and there is no Compliment, or changing of Places in a Storm) and the Waves beat on me fo faft, that I had almoft faid with the Prophet *David*, *The Waters had even entered into my Soul*, Pfal. vi. 9.

And now we grew into another Defpair; for with all our Endeavours we could not reach the Ship, nor the Ship us: Yet that good Man the Skipper, hung on the Lee, and did what he could to retard the Courfe of his Ship; and we, on the other Side, did what we could to fpeed our own. His Ship rode on furioufly before the Wind, like the Chariot of *Aminadab*; and ours flowly, like the Chariots of *Pharaoh*; and how could we expect, that our Snail fhould overtake this Dromedary! Thus our pregnant Hopes brought forth nothing but Wind and Water; and we that before flattered ourfelves with an Affurance of Safety, are now as much confounded with a Certainty of Perifhing. It had been better, I think, and lefs Affliction to us, to have had no Hopes at all of a Deliverance, than prefently to fall from it. It did redouble the Punifhment of *Tantalus* to kifs thofe Apples with his Lips, which he muft not tafte with his Tongue: to have Happinefs near us in our Eye, and not to enjoy it, is the Extremity of Unhappinefs. Many Mariners, in a Storm and Tempeft, when they fee a fatal Neceffity upon them, are contented to die; but thefe Men would murmur, *Portu perire, to perifh in an Haven.*

O 6

This

This was our Condition; we had a Ship hard by, but could not board her by Reaſon of the Weather; ſo that we were ready to periſh, whilſt we looked Safety in the Face. And that which, in all Probability, increaſed our Danger, and made our Fate inevitable, it grew dark Night, ſo that we did not know which Way to row.

But this, though it was an Evil in its own Nature, by Accident became a Benefit to us; for now, not ſeeing our Danger, we underſtood it not, and ſo grew bolder, and applied two to an Oar, and ſo broke through the Waves in a moſt deſperate Condition towards the Ship, as we conceived; and that good Chriſtian, the Maſter of the Veſſel, hung out a Light to us, which was as a Star to guide us to him; and ſo, by Degrees, we grew nearer and nearer.

But leſt the *Howzoner* (for the Maſter was one of *Howzon*) ſhould think we were loſt, and ſo hoiſt up his Sails and be gone, (for he could not ſee us by Reaſon of the Night, though we ſaw him by Virtue of the Light he lent us) Order was given, that when a Wave took us up, we ſhould give a great Shout, which we did ſo loud, that I believe our Cry was heard to Heaven; for by God's miraculous Aſſiſtance we grew very near the Ship, and our own Safety.

Now were we in Diſpute which Side of the Ship we ſhould go aboard, which was concluded on the Lee-ſide; and Promiſe was made we ſhould go up by Order as we ſat, leſt by a haſty Riſing we ſhould

endanger

endanger ourfelves, and by making too much Hafte to fave our Lives, lofe them. But we had no fconer come to the Ship, but they all ftrove to run up at once; and the Seamen being dextrous in the Art of climbing, got up in a Moment, and left me alone in the Boat: Neither do I blame them, for Life is fweet, and when that is in Jeopardy, we care only for ourfelves.

And now was I the third Time loft, and in the greateft Danger of drowning; for befides the natural Weaknefs I had in my Hands, they were fo benumbed with Cold and Wet, and made ufelefs, that I could not climb up a Rope though it was to fave my Life. But I held the Rope which was flung to me out of the Ship faft in my Hands, that our Boat might not ftave off; but it ftruck three Times againft our rowling Ship, or rather our Ship againft it, and as often ftruck me down in the Boat, which was half full of Water; fo that I was afraid I fhould have been drowned in that Epitome of the Sea. It would have grieved a Man, but now to have efcaped the vaft Champain of the Sea, and to be drowned in its Enclofure; And it was God's Providence, the Boat, being fo often ftruck, did not break in Pieces, as it did prefently afterwards, when it had done its laft Office to my Deliverance. But having ufed feveral Ways to get up in vain, there came at laft, two Seamen down to me on the Side of the Ship, and would have heaved me up by the Arms: But being fo often wet, my Cloaths, together with my own Weight, were too heavy a Burthen to be trufted in their
Arms;

Arms; and in this Strait and Exigency, I really knew
not what to do.   I began to have fad Thoughts of
myfelf, and to think, that I alone was the Offender,
and muſt now be facrificed to the Fury of the Sea, to
appeafe and calm the Tempeſt.   But whilſt I was thus
wounding my Breaſt with thefe Thoughts, one of the
Seamen gave me down a Rope with a Nooze, and bid
me put it about my Middle: But as foon as I got it on
one Shoulder, he began to pull, and had like to have
forced me into the Sea; but defiring him to ſtay a-
while, I then got it over both Shoulders, and ordered
him to pull, but the Boat waving up and down, caſt
me off at fome Diſtance, to that he firſt drew me into the Sea, and my own Weight drew the Rope fo
faſt through his Hands, that had there not been a
Knot at the End of the Rope by meer Chance, (for
he tied it not, as he afterwards told me in *England)*
I had gone down into the Deep in a Moment; fo that
I may truly fay, there was not an Inch between me
and Death.   Then at the next Pull, he ſtruck me a-
gainſt the Side of the Ship, which I ſhall always look
upon as a Courtefy, being the kindeſt Blow that ever
I received; it was like a Dofe of *Opium* to a Man that
hath the Extremity of the Stone, which maketh him
forget himfelf as well as his Sorrow; and fo it ferved
me, for I remembered no more either Good or Evil.
But certainly the Maſter was a good Chriſtian, and
was indulgent to me; for I found myfelf in his own
Cabin the next Morning, where I ſlept all Night
very well, though in wet Cloaths: But I found myfelf fore and lame all over.   I thought of the Man
                                        in

in the Almanack, wounded in every Part and Member; only I really was what he seemed to be, and had some Signs likewise of it on my bruised Body.

But I rose from my Cabin, very desirous to know how it fared with my Fellow-Sufferers; and truly I found them, contrary to my Expectation, heavy, not with Sleep, but with Sorrow. I thought I should have seen Joy ride in Triumph in their chearful Countenances; but their Looks were dejected, and they murmured within themselves, suffering (I suppose) over their Shipwreck again in their sad Thoughts, and every Man telling himself of his own Misfortune: But the Truth was, they having saved their Lives, were now at Leisure to think of the Loss of their Goods: And I know it was a heavy Loss to some, who lost much; and yet a greater Loss to others, who lost less. For they having but a little, lost a great Deal, that little being all they had. For my own Part, I lost more than I had, (for it cast me in a Debt, which I have not yet waded through:) But the Quantity of my Loss doth not so much trouble me as the Quality; for (besides my Goods and whole Library) I lost all my Sermons, Notes and Observations of some Years Travel abroad, Things in themselves of no Value, nor much in my Esteem, yet they were the Fruits of my (many Years) Labour and Study, and might have been useful to me, both in my ministerial Function, and likewise in the secular and Lay-Part of my Life. But it were a Shame to name any Loss, when God so graciously gave us our Lives; and a Sin to murmur at any Damage,

when

when God so often and so miraculously snatched us
out of the very Jaws of Death. It seems to me like
calling *Lazarus* out of the Grave, and do we
think *Lazarus*, when he was restored unto Life,
complained that his Winding-Sheet, and Napkin,
were spoiled by lying four Days in the Grave? Or
that he murmured that the Ointments and Spices
were spent in vain at his Funeral? For sure *Mary*,
that had a Box of Ointment for the Burial of our
Saviour, would be at some Cost at the Funeral of her
beloved Brother *Lazarus*. But these Things are not
to be thought upon, when our Life is given us: But
we are so enamoured of the World, that we cannot
but look back upon Things we love and lose; and
we would fain be comforted after our Losses, as *Job*
was, with twice as much as we had before: But then
we must remember, it was at the latter End of *Job*;
and before that Time God may redouble these temporal Blessings upon us.

The next Day, being *Tuesday*, it blew very fair
for *Norway*, thither our Ship was bound; and about
Twelve o'Clock at Noon we came in the View of it:
But *Norway* being a ragged Coast, full of Rocks, and
seeing we could not reach it whilst it was Day, and
afraid to come upon it in the Dark, we turned our
Sails, and thought to have kept off the Coast till the
Morning, that the Sun might shew us the Way thither. Which done, we sat down to Meat, some of
us having taken no Sustenance since we first came to
Sea; and truly I eat an hearty Meal, being the only
Meal, I made in five Days: And so we were all very
well refreshed and comforted. And now God thought

it

it fit we fhould fuffer again; had it pleafed the Lord before this Refrefhment to have brought us in fome new Diftrefs, we certainly, being weak, had perifh-ed under the Weight of it, and the very Conceit of it would have killed us, and a little more Sorrow have drown'd us without a Wave. But God will lay no more upon his Children than they are able to bear.

About Ten o'Clock at Night, when we had fet our Watch, and prayed, with fafe and fecure Thoughts we laid ourfelves to reft, fome of us upon our Beds; but God had appointed an harder Lodg-ing for us, fuch as he provided for *Jacob* in his Jour-ney to *Padan-Aram,* when *he took of the Stones of the Place, and made himfelf a Pillow, and lay down in that Place to fleep.* For this our fecond Ship with full Sails ran upon a Rock, and gave fo great a Crack, that it was able to awake the moft dead afleep among us: I wondered, I confefs, what the Matter was; but the Mariners, knowing the Danger better than myfelf, cried out, *Mercy, Mercy, Mercy,* with fo dole-ful a Tone and Accent, that, together with that hi-deous Noife which both the Wind and Waves made in this pitched Battle one againft the other, it feem-ed to me to be the very Image and Reprefentation of the Day of Judgment. I made what Hafte I could out of my Cabin, but was the laft that came upon the Deck; where meeting with our own Mafter, with both his Hands upon his Eyes, which yet could not ftop that Current of Tears, which ran down his Cheeks, he bade me *pray for them, pray for them, for we fhall certainly perifh.* I could believe no otherwife, being taught that Leffon by our Mafter; and there-

fore

fore I fell prefently upon my Knees, and was juft
in the Condition of a condemned Perfon that expected the Stroke of the Executioner, the Night having
put a Blind before mine Eyes; and having prayed
awhile, I wondered the Waves did not come to do
their Office; for I forgave them with all my Heart,
having wholly refigned up myfelf to Death.

But fo it pleafed God, that the Ship with full
Sails ftruck itfelf fo faft into the Cleft of the Rock,
or rather, as the Seamen fay, between two Sledges
of Rocks, with her Bow over the main Rock, fo
that it ftood as firm, for the prefent, I mean the
former Part of the Ship, as the Rock itfelf. So I
prefently rofe, and pulled off my Coat, with an
Intention to caft myfelf into the Sea, and fwim
thither; but was advifed to the contrary by a
prefent enfuing Danger: For prefently there arofe
a high and mighty Wave, one of the chief Giants
of the Sea, which firft knocked againft our Ship,
as if it would have called me forth, and then with
greater Violence dafhed againft the Rock, and
brake itfelf in Pieces; which did plainly reprefent
unto me my future Condition, and foretel my Fortune, had I ventured to ftride that great Leviathan,
and endeavoured to fwim to the Rock.

But prefently our Ship, like St. *Paul*'s Ship,
brake in the hinder Parts, and we were taught to
efcape our Danger, by our Danger; for our Ship
breaking in the Stern, we were for-
Matthew Bird ced to fly to the former Part; and one
of *Ipfwich*. of the Seamen (the fame that pulled
me up by the Rope) leaped from the
Bow

Bow of the Ship upon the Rock with a Rope in his Hand, which was faftened to one of our Mafts, and held it with fo ftiff an Hand, that another flipt down by it, and fo all our Company, and fome of the *Danes*, (Eight and Twenty in Number) came fafe to the Rock that Way.

All this while, being left alone upon Deck, I began to wonder what became of my Company, not then knowing that they had found any Means of Deliverance; but perceiving that they all crowded to the Head of the Ship, I went to fee (God knows that was all my Intention) what they did there, and fo I came to the Knowledge of their Efcape, and an Opportunity of my own. For I found a *Dane* endeavouring to flide down himfelf and a fmall Leather Trunk by that Rope, who like a loving Man took Pity on me, and prefently whipt away his Trunk, and bid me flide down there: But I returned him his Kindnefs, and defired him to go down firft; not fo much out of Compliment, but that I might know how to flide down; for I faw none of them go before me, and I did not know whether I fhould go with my Head or Heels foremoft. I had no Time to afk Counfel, or make Experiment, but prefently I got upon the Rope, with my Heels foremoft, and Back uppermoft; But the Waves beat upon me, and the Wind (which was high) blew me round, and had almoft made me let go my Hold; but, I praife God, I came fafely to the Side of the Rock, and they cried, *Off*, *off*; not out of Unkindnefs to me, (whom they knew

not

not in the Dark) but that I might make fpeedy
Way for another, which I quickly did : For having
laid one Hand upon the Rock, I came off the Rope,
and fo on all four, climbed up to the reft of the
Company.

I was the laft that came down the Ship that Way,
for in that very Moment the Ship began to decline
from us, and give Way, which the Mafter perceiving, (who was ftill aboard) made lamentable
Moan to us to help him, which we did with our
utmoft Endeavours; But the Ship brake, and funk
immediately; there was this good Man, and four
of the Mariners drowned. I faw the Mafter, with
a Light in his Hand, fall into the Sea; the faddeft
Sight that I ever yet beheld in this World, and
that which pierced my very Soul, to fee him that
faved our Lives, lofe his own. There was nothing
fo bitter to me in all my Suffering at Sea, as the
Lofs of this Man; it raifed fuch a Storm and
Tempeft again in my Affections, that I am not yet
calm within. I never think of him, but I am caft
in a troubled Sea of Sorrow, and fuffer Shipwreck
daily in my Mind; for as he was a Man of a meek
and charitable Difpofition unto all, fo I found him
kind unto myfelf after a more fpecial Manner.
How folicitous was he for us in our Diftrefs, and
ufed all Means, though it was to his own Hindrance to fave us! and in all Probability, had he
not ftaid for us, he might have arrived at his own
Harbour in Safety. What fhall we fay! fhall we
plead with the Almighty, with the Prophet, *Jeremy?*
Jer. xii.

Jer. xii. No; it is better to cry out with St. *Paul,
Oh the Depth of the Riches, and Wifdom, and Knowledge
of God! How unfearchable are his Judgments, and his
Ways paft finding out! For who hath known the Mind
of the Lord, or who hath been his Ccunfellor?* Rom. xi.
33, 34, 35. All that we can fay, is, that God
fometimes thus dealeth with his own Children:
Thofe whom by his Grace he hath made Inftruments of great Good upon Earth, he taketh unto
himfelf, to make them highly bleffed in Heaven.
Certainly the Spirit of God moved upon thefe
Waters, and called this good Man, as Chrift did
St. *Peter* on the Sea of *Galilee*, Mat. xiv, to come
to him, that for this high Act of Charity he might
receive him, and prefently crown him with Glory.

Now were we upon the Rock, but knew not
where; and fome of the Company, before I came
to them, had meafured it round with their Feet,
and had found it both a Rock and an Ifle, and,
contrary to our Hopes, inhabitable; fo that we
waited for the Morning Star to draw the Curtain
of the Night, and difcover us firft to ourfelves,
(for as yet, in the Dark, we were as ignorant of
ourfelves, as of our fad Condition) and then, to
fhew and difcover fome Coaft or Land to us. which
we hoped we were near to. It was a long and fad
Night with me: A Rock is an hard Pillow to fleep
on; befide, I was thinly clad, having caft off my
Coat, when I intended to fwim, and had no Leifure
to put it on again, for I thought it beft to leave
that behind me, rather than myfelf. We went
from

from Place to Place, up and down, I may truly ſay, for I had many a Fall upon the ſlimy Rock; ſometimes we were up to the Ankles in Water, I cannot ſay over Shoes, for I had none, ſo that my Feet were cut with the ſharp Stones, as my Body with the cold Wind; ſo that I felt the very Teeth of Winter bite quite through me: for Winter in that Country, is an old Man with a grey Head, when it is but a Child with us. At length we lighted on a Hole of the Rock, which was a warm Shelter to us againſt the Wind. And now the long expected Morning drew near, and we fain would have ſeen before we could. In that Twilight, every black Cloud we diſcerned, we flattered ourſelves was Land; and here it was, we ſaid, and there it was: But when the Sun aroſe, we ſaw it no where, only we had a Glimpſe of the Coaſt of *Norway*; but it was at that Diſtance, that we were not in any Capacity to reach it, but with our Deſires.

Truly, when I roſe up and took a View of the Sea, and the Place where I was, I was ſtruck down again with Amazement to ſee many Hundreds of Rocks round about us, lying for the moſt Part under Water, which the Seamen call *Breakers*, becauſe they break the Sea, and turn it into Feathers. It was a great Providence of God, that we ſhould in the Night, with full Sails, paſs by all theſe Rocks, (the leaſt Touch againſt them had been as mortal to us as our Sins) and then to come to the great Rock, which was as a Church above Water. I am

ſure

fure it was an *Afylum* to us. The Country People deſervedly call it *Arn-Scare*. It was the ſame Hand again of God's Providence, that our Ship ſhould be carried with a full ſtrong Wind into the Cleft and open Part of the Rock, which was as a Boſom to receive us; had we touched upon any other Part, we had been utterly loſt in the Twinkling of an Eye. *They that go down to the Sea in Ships, and occupy their Buſineſs in great Waters, theſe ſee the Works of the Lord, and his Wonders in the Deep*, Pſal. cvii. The Wonders of his Deliverances, as well as the Miracles of his Creation: Neither are the Creatures more to be admired than his Mercies. There is as much Wonder and Variety in theſe as in the other. *Oh that we would therefore praiſe God for his Goodneſs, and the Wonders he doth for the Children of Men*, Pſal. cvii. 8.

But now again were we loſt in the Eye of Man, all our Hope was, that a Ship might paſs by to relieve us, which in my Judgment was Vanity of Thoughts. For if a Ship ſhould by Accident come by us in the Day-time, they ſeeing the Rocks, would be afraid to come at us; had it come in the Night, it had certainly periſhed, as ours did. And yet we did *hope* even *againſt Hope*. But having ſpent all that Day, with ſore Eyes, in Expectation of an imaginary Deliverance, in looking for a Ship (or rather Caſtle in the Air) and ſeeing nothing come towards us, we began to deſpair, having now no Kind of Suſtenance to feed on, nor ſcarce Cloaths to keep us warm; ſo

we

we again crept into an Hole of the Rock, and lodged there, rather than refted, the fecond Night.

In the Morning we arofe before the Sun, and ftill we were looking for that which came not : And now we began to be an hungry ; and fome of our Company went fearching about the Rock, wifhing (I fuppofe) thofe Stones were turned into Bread. One of the Sea-Boys brought me a Leaf of Scurvy-Grafs, which I told him was *Sauce rather than Meat.* Some of us went a fifhing, but with no other Angle than a long Arm, nor no other Hook then a bent Finger. They put their Arms into the Sea as far as they could, and drew up fome fmall Mufcles, which they eat heartily. I began to be very fick in a feverifh Diftemper, and fo had no Stomach, which I think is a Benefit when we have no Meat to eat : But I did burn with Thirft, fo that I would have given all that I had for a Draught of frefh Water. God oftentimes makes us know the Worth of his Creatures by the Want of them : Nothing fo mean in our Efteem as a little Water, we fpill it every where upon the Ground, and we look not after it any more ; yet at this Time a Drop of cold Water had been more welcome to me than the Gold of *Ophir*, and in my Efteem, a better Creature. I went into the higheft Place of the Rock, thinking the Water (that ftood every where in Holes) might be frefher there ; but I found it falt ; fo I perceive in fome Storm it bounded thither from the Sea. Though it was falt, yet it was Water ; and therefore (like one of thofe that were chofen to fight againft *Midian*,) I lapped it with my Hand to my Mouth, till it

quenched

quenched my Thirſt : But it came up again as faſt as it went down, and brought a great Drought with it; and this I did very often, which I am perſuaded was both my preſent Cure, and future Preſervation of my Health, as a learned Phyſician told me ſince, Dr. *H.*

And now between Ten and Eleven o'Clock we ſaw a Ship coming towards us with full Sails, which lifted up all our Hearts with Joy, gilded over our Hearts with Cheerfulneſs, and ſo painted our Faces with Gladneſs, that we ſeemed to be new Creatures. The Ship came nearer and nearer, and then we went all of us to the Top of the Rock, and waved our Hats to ſhew ourſelves to the Men of the Ship. But I know not the Cauſe, for they never came at us ; neither did they ſend out their Boat to know what we were, or our Condition. Whether this Unkindneſs proceeded from the Fear of our dangerous Rocks, or from their own more ſtony Hearts, harder than the Rock we lay upon, I cannot ſay; but it put us out of Charity with them, as they ſeemed to be with us. He was a *Dane,* of the ſame Country with our former kind loving Maſter; ſo that I perceive there may be ſeveral Diſpoſitions under the ſame Climate, and one Womb may bring forth Twins of ſeveral Natures ; one was as ſmooth to us as *Jacob,* the other rough as *Eſau.* When we ſaw the Ship paſs quite from us, our Hearts began to fail, and our Countenances changed into their former Paleneſs. How ſoon was our fair Morning clouded over, and our beautiful Hopes turned into Deformity and black Deſpair? To teach us that Man's Happineſs is but for a Moment,

P

and

and the Joy of this World but a Span long. And
now we were all loſt, even in our own Eyes; our
Condition, being ready to famiſh, would not give
us Time to expect another Ship, neither had we
now Faith enough to believe, ſhould there come one
by Chance, that the Mariners would venture their
own Lives to ſave ou .

So we betook ourſelves to our old Remedy, φάρ-
μακον καθολικον, *our Prayers.* The *Danes* (I confeſs)
firſt began their Devotions, having ſung one of *Luther's*
Pſalms, fell to their Prayers, and then we ſung one of
our own Pſalms, and as long as I was able to ſpeak, I
prayed with the Company; and after ſome Exhorta-
tion to my Fellow-Sufferers, being very weak, I laid
myſelf down upon the Rock, thinking I ſhould riſe
no more in this World.

But I overheard one of the Seamen, *M. B.* (the
ſame that firſt leapt upon the Rock) ſay *Let us make
a Raft, and venture to Sea, I had rather be drowned, than
lie here and be ſtarved.* They all preſently concluded
to follow that Deſign, though it was full of Danger.
But, you know, a ſinking Man will take hold of a
Bull-ruſh, and one that is ready to periſh will catch
at a Feather. All Things fell out to further this Deſign: For the Water had now fallen from the Rock,
and left on the Side of it the Bottom of the Ship, the
Anchors, the Maſt, the Sails lying on the Rock
like Linen upon an Hedge. In a ſhort Time they
brake a Maſt in Pieces, untwiſted a Cable, made
ſmall Cords, tied four or five Boards to the broken
Maſt, put up the ſmall End of the Mizen-Maſt, cut
out a ſmall Sail, with ſome ſlight Stern they had
                                        made,

made, and so ventured to Sea on these Ruins. God oftentimes saves by weak Means, and preserves us by Improbabilities. There were four on this Raft, two *Danes*, and two *English*; I do not remember whether it was by Lot, or voluntary Election.

It was now a great Calm, such a Calm I conceive as was upon the Sea of Gallilee when our Saviour rebuked the Sea and the Winds, *Mat.* viii. It blew only a small Breath, which was our Advantage, for it directly carried them toward that Place we conceived the Coast lay. It was the miraculous Goodness of God, that after the Loss of two great Ships, he should save us by a swimming Plank: For this Raft past through, and got clear of all the Breakers; had it touched only on one of them, they would have rent the Raft in Pieces, as *Sampson* did the Wreath when the *Philistines* were upon him: But they passed by them all, and we that were upon the Rock followed them with our Eyes as long as we could see, or rather as long as they could be seen; for our Life was wrapt up in theirs, and the Hope of our Deliverance had no other Foundation but their Safety.

And now I may say, God stretched forth his Hand, as Christ did to Saint *Peter* when he was ready to sink, and saved these Men, and brought them to Shore; which yet we were ignorant of, and so pulled in Pieces between two several Passions, Hope and Fear, and both of them equally troublesome; as we see in an Ague, which hath two several Operations, contrary in themselves, as hot and cold, yet both of them alike afflictive. Our Hope being with that

Violence

Violence of Paſſion, was as wounding to our Affections as our Fear.

But theſe Fits were ſoon over, for before Night
we ſpied ſeveral Shawls rowing towards us, which
gave us a certain Knowledge of the Safety of our
Men, and a Promiſe of our own Deliverance: They
brought with them Proviſion; but we were more
greedy of the Shore than our Meat, and therefore we
made Haſte into the Boats, and by God's Goodneſs
unto us, we came all of us once more to Land.

The Place that we arrived at was an Iſland in
Norway, called by the People *Waller Iſland*; ſo mean
and inconſiderable, that *Ortelius* takes no Notice of it in
                                his Maps, for I have ſearched with
My Lord of *E*. better Eyes than my own, I mean
Dr. *H*.   more knowing in Geography, and
                    could not find it. A Place it ſeems
not worthy to be remembered, but I am ſure never
to be forgotten by us. Though it was a Wilderneſs
in its own Nature, yet it was a Paradiſe to us.

There was but one Houſe where we landed, and
that was the Parſon's, an honeſt *Lutheran*, who had
many in his Family. *They ſhewed us*, as Saint *Paul*
ſays, *no little Kindneſs:* Acts xxviii. 2. The Language
they ſpake was *Neſs*; but I think it was not much
unlike *Dutch*, for we that ſpake *Dutch*, did partly
underſtand them, and they us, and yet two ſeveral
Kinds of Speech. I ſuppoſe there is the ſame Difference between theſe two Languages, as there is between a Lobſter and a Cray-Fiſh, (which both are in
                                Plenty

Plenty there) for though they both are alike, yet they
are two feveral *Species.*

We made a Shift to tell the fad Iliads of our Mif-
fortune to the People of the Houfe, and they made
a Shift to underftand us, for they wept moft bitterly at
our Relation; fo that one would have thought that they
had fuffered Shipwreck, and not we. Which fhewed the
Goodnefs and Tendernefs of their Nature, which are
principia gratiæ, the very *Beginnings of Grace,* or elfe I
may fafely fay, they are *the firft Difpofitions,* or at leaft,
Capacities of Grace.

They fet before us what Meat they had; and the
Mariners fell to it fo heartily, as if they would have
repaired all they loft before by their long Fafting, at
one Meal. Their ordinary Bread was Rye-Pancakes,
but their Beer very ftrong. I thought of that *Englifh*
Proverb, *A Cup of good Beer is Meat, Drink and Cloathing.* Sure thefe People thought fo; for though at
that cold Seafon fome of the People had no Stockings
nor Shoes to their Feet, yet they kept their Under-
ftandings warm, and their Mouths well lined with
Lubeck Beer.

I loft my Stomach not with eating, but long fafting, and fo went fick to Bed: in the Morning I found
myfelf well, I praife God. And we began now to
examine ourfelves, and one another, what Monies
our double Shipwreck had left us: all that we had
we freely laid down; but there was an *Ananias* a-
mongft us, who, we fufpected, would conceal fome
Part; and therefore we fearched him, and found no
lefs than four and twenty Pieces of Eight, which

P 3

certainly

certainly this Man ſtole out of our Bags when we were in the Boat, after our firſt Shipwreck, at that preſent Time when we expected every Moment we ſhould be call away.   Did this Man think that Saint *Peter* would not let him into Heaven without his *Peter's* Pence? Or that he ſhould go the other Way, and muſt pay *Charon naulum ſuum?* It was a ſad Thing for a Man to ſteal *in articulo mortis, at the Point of Death.* But it was well for us, for we loſt all our Monies in the ſecond Shipwreck, but what this Man ſtole from us.   There are ſome Divines that ſay, Sin is committed *ordinante Deo*; but the Ancients are wont to ſay *Deo permittente,* which is a more modeſt and civil Expreſſion.   I will not diſpute the Queſtion here : But I believe, if God did ever ordain Sin, it was in this Man's ſtealing; for this Money was our Relief in our neceſſitous Condition.

We ſtaid in this Iſland till Sunday : In the Morning we went to hear our Landlord preach ; after Sermon he gave us *Cœna dubia,* a *doubtful Meal,* full of Variety in one Diſh, as Beef, Mutton, Lard, Goat, Roots, and ſo many of God's Creatures, that it ſeemed to me to be the firſt Chapter of *Geneſis* in a Diſh ; but ſo confounded, that the beſt Palate could not read what he eat, nor by his Taſte know and diſtinguiſh the Creatures. Though God hath given all his Creatures for the Uſe of Man, ſo that we may do what we pleaſe with them ; yet I think it not handſome with our grand *Meſſe's* and *Olla podrida's* to confound and undo the Creation, cook it into a new Chaos, and

ſauce

fauce God's Creatures out of our Knowledge. I love
to know what I eat, that I may praife God for the
Variety of his Bleffings; but truly I do not blame
the People of this Place; for I think it is not Curiofity here, but Cuftom, and good Hufbandry, rather
than Luxurioufnefs, who boil all together to fave
Charges.

After much Thanks, and a little Money, we
parted with this good old Prieft; and I having
purchafed an old Pair of Shoes, at the Price of a
new, we travelled on Foot to *Frederickftat* a City in
Norway by the Coaft Side, and were very kindly
entertained by the Burgo-Mafter. The chief of his
Difcourfe to me, was in Commendation of the late
Archbifhop of *Canterbury*, whom he called *Excellen-
tiffimum Dominum.* I wonder how he came to know
him. But fure, thought I, if he be thus charitable
to fpeak well of the Dead, who could not hear
him, he will be bountiful to the Living, who are
ready to thank him even beforehand. And truly
he was very kind to us, for he commanded fome of
the City to entertain us civilly, and provided us
Ships both for *Holland* and *England*, with the
Promife of fome Provifion at his own Charge.

I remember how the People ran after us in the
Streets, and what their compaffionate Eye faw we
wanted, their charitable Hand was ready to give
without afking. A good old Man beftowed on me
an excellent Pair of Mittens, which I brought into
England. We found much Civility every where:
though the Country is all rocky, yet the People's

P 4

Hearts

Hearts are tender; God made them *è meliore luto, out of a better Soil* than their own Country.

But to make hafte out of my Story, as well as out of *Norway:* We went away from *Frederickftet* three or four Miles to *Ofterfound,* the Haven where our Ships lay, having laid into the Ship, that was bound for *England,* fome fmall Provifion, as much as our Stock could pay for, yet not fo much as our Neceffity required; for had not God bleffed us with a favourable Wind, we certainly had wanted much. But we, with all that was left us, which was now nothing, but ourfelves, entered into the Ship in the Evening. In the Morning, before we went out, there came a Ship from *Lynn* in *Norfolk,* that ftruck againft our Harbour, which was naturally walled about with Rocks, and fo perifhed immediately. This was a fad Omen, and it feemed to me as a Prologue to a new Tragedy. We had not been above two or three Hours at Sea, but there was a fad Diftraction amongft us in the Ship, and the Mariners crying again for *Mercy, Mercy;* for we had almoft fell foul on a Rock, which lay fo cunningly in the Water, that we did not fpy it till we were upon it; but by the Goodnefs of God we failed clofe by it, and efcaped it; the leaft Touch of it had been our Ruin. Thus God oftentimes doth bring his Children as near the Mouth of Danger, as may be, but he lets them not fall therein, that they may both fear and praife his Name.

About

About Noon we came clear off all the Rocks on the Coaft of *Norway,* and were failing for *England* with a fair Gale of Wind. But in this Profperity another fad Accident befel us; this third Ship fprang a Leak, a new one I cannot fay, but rather repeated an old one, and fo our Ship began to fwim within as well as without; and we had no Way to relieve ourfelves, (for the Leak could not be found) but by Pumping; which we did Day and Night, and fo took Revenge of the Sea, by fpitting that Water back again in its Face, as faft as it came into our Ship. But now again we were in a fad and deplorable Condition, being in Danger to be drowned from the Spring that rofe within us, and to fuffer an inteftine Shipwreck, which, like a Civil War, is moft dangerous. We had our Life now at our Fingers Ends; and if we had not lifted up our Hands to pump, as *Mofes* did to pray, thefe *Amalekites* had prevailed; I mean thefe mercilefs Waves had overcome us. Good God! in what, and how many Streights haft thou brought us? Our Sins are many, as the Waves of the Sea; and fo haft thou, O Lord, made our Funifhments.

For now we were, as I conceive, in a worfe Condition than ever before; for though our Dangers were great, or rather greater, yet they came upon us fo on a fudden, that we underftood them not. That Danger is lefs afflictive which we lefs underftand; and that Mifery we apprehend not, is none at all, or at leaft none of

P 5   our

our own. But now we fee Death before our Eyes, and are in Expectation to perifh every Moment; fo that we may fay, with Saint *Paul, We die daily.* 1 Cor. xv. We were in the Condition of him that feeth himfelf bleed to Death. In our former Dangers we had like to perifh fuddenly, which had been lefs penal to our Affections: We were now to die at Leifure, and to be drowned with Premeditation; which is more afflictive to our Thoughts, though a lefs Punifhment for our Sins. *Melius eft perire femel, quam timere femper*: the Fear of Death is more dreadful than Death itfelf; and it is better once to die, than to be always dying.

With thefe Fears about us, and black Apprehenfions, we failed on ftill with a fair Wind; and after four or five Days and Nights fail, fo it pleafed God, we came in the View of the *English* Coaft on *Norfolk* Side, near *Winterton*; where we faw the Ruins of a Shipwreck, and the Country People enriching themfelves with the Loffes of other Men; the worft way of getting in the World. This was the Epilogue to our Tragedy, yet we had one Scene of Sorrow more · For when we came near *Yarmouth* Road, on our left Hand lay the Shingles, on our right, the Shore; and we could not agree amongft ourfelves on which Side we fhould go. Our two Mafters, and two Pilots, (for fo many we had in one Ship,) like four Winds, blew contrary Ways. In this Conteft they made a fearful Noife and Quarrel; their Language was as foul as the Weather, and as high as the Wind, and brought us in as

great

great Danger (as our own Master told me), as ever.

I think Monarchy is the best Government in a Ship, as well as in the State. Many Pilots with their Overwisdomness, are oftentimes the Ruin both of themselves and their Vessel.

At length we did agree, and ordered one of our own Company (a *Shotley* Man, who best knew the Coast,) to sit at Stern; but this crazy and ill-built Ship, though she was steered one Way, flew another, as if all Things had conspired to our Ruin. We resolved to sail by the Shore-Side, that in Case our Ship should miscary, we might swim to Land. These were but sad Hopes; but it pleased God, we came safe into *Yarmouth* Road; and having cast our Anchor, thought ourselves secure. But our Anchor came Home to us again; and the Wind, which was very high, had like to have driven us on a *Scotchman:* They cried out, and so did we; for they could not be more afraid of us, than we were of ourselves; for had we boarded them, we certainly had endangered both our Ships : but that God that had begun and gone along with us in such visible Characters of his extraordinary Mercy, would not now leave us at the last, but did perfect our Deliverance; for our Anchor held, and we rode very secure that Night. The next Morning we hung out a Whiff, and there came four Men in a Shallop from *Yarmouth*, and demanded no less than thirty Shillings to carry me, a single Person, to Shore, when our whole Stock was but two Pieces of Eight. Though I did long for Land, yet I could not purchase it at such a

Rate : But at length they were content to take lefs, becaufe they could not get any more ; and took fomething, rather than to turn back with nothing.

But they no fooner had got me into the Boat, but they rowed me up and down, to weigh Anchors ; for there had been a great Storm the Night before, and many Ships had broke their Cables, and were driven away by the Tempeft. They tried at feveral Anchors not without great Danger, as I conceived ; but finding themfelves not ftrong enough, they at length brought me to the Shore, which was no landing Place ; but four Men, which ftood waiting for us on the Shore, ran into the Sea up to their Middles, laid Hands on our Boat, and fo ran it on the Sands, and tumbled us over and over ; fo that I cannot fay, whether I fet my Head or Feet firft on the Shore. After this Manner fure *Jonah* was caft upon the dry Land, when the Whale vomited him up ; I fuppofe that great *Leviathan* did not caft him upon his Legs : But a Man that had made fuch a Trade of fuffering at Sea as we did, and after fo long a Succeffion of Evils, would be glad to be caft on dry Land in any Pofture.

From the Shore I went into *Yarmouth* Town, with a Company of People following at my Heels, wondering at me, as if I had been fome ftrange Creature come out of *America*, though they knew none of my Sufferings, but faw me in a fad ragged, weather-beaten Condition. I prefently got into an Inn, to hide myfelf from the Wonder of the People,

and

and from the Trouble of their impertinent Queſ-
tions; but chiefly, that I might praiſe God in
private for his great and many Deliverances. I
cannot chuſe but tell you ſo much, leſt I ſhould
ſeem ungrateful to my gracious God: But I will
ſay no more, leſt I may ſeem vain-glorious to my
Friend. Therefore I will conceal from you my
particular Devotions: *Non eſt Religio ubi omnia
patent*; I learned it from the Door of a Capuchin's
Convent.

The Sign of the Inn was the Arms of *Yarmouth*,
the Man, I ſuppoſe the Hoſt of the Houſe, was as
kind to me as Saint *Paul*'s Hoſt *Gaius* was to him.
And here I muſt not forget the Kind-
neſs of a true Friend indeed, a good   * *Thomas Le-*
Samaritan, * who had Compaſſion on *man*, Eſq. of
me, bound up my Wounds, pouring *Wenbeſton* in
in Oil and Wine, and ſet me on his *Suffolk*.
own Beaſt, brought me to his own
Houſe, and had a Care of me; and, which I took
moſt kindly, he beſtowed on my Sufferings *Nazi-
anzen*'s Charity, a Tear of Compaſſion, [Orat 6.
Si nihil habes, da lacrumulam]. God I hope, will turn
this Kindneſs to me, in Bleſſings upon him, and
his dear Wife and Children. By the Kindneſs of
this Gentleman, I was recruited with all Manner of
Comforts; and now behold another Shipwreck,
not of my Goods but good Name. Some there
were, when they heard of the Monſter of my Sufferings, were affrighted out of their Wits, I
ſuppoſe, as well as out of their Charity, and concluded

cluded I was a Malignant. Thus God is pleafed to affimulate my Sufferings to Saint *Paul*'s in fome Meafure (the Latchet of whofe Shoe I am not worthy to untie) who, when he had efcaped the Danger of the Sea, was ftung by a Viper as foon as he came to Shore. *Acts* xxviii. Suppofe I fhould fay, I do ferve my God that Way which the World calls Malignancy. Am I fuch an one, becaufe the People fay it ? Or was Saint *Paul* an Heretick, becaufe the World thought him fo ? I do not care what the Many fay of me, *Bellua multorum Capitum, a Beaft of many Heads, fed nullius Ingenii, but of no Underftanding.* Thus the People cenfured *John the Baptift,* the Morning Star of the Gofpel; and likewife our Bleffed Saviour himfelf, that glorious Sun of Righteoufnefs, or as St. *Luke* calls him, Luke ii. *the Day that fprings from on high;* although their Deportment in the World was different, walking under feveral Schemes, and living after feveral and contrary Fafhions. For, *John the Baptift came neither eating Bread nor drinking Wine, and ye fay he hath a Devil, the Son of Man is come eating and drinking, and ye fay behold a gluttonous Man, and a Wine-bibber, and a Friend of Publicans and Sinners.* Luke vii. 33, 34. Thus the People are never pleafed, neither full nor fafting. Neither the Aufterity of St. *John*'s Life, nor the Sweetnefs and Familiarity of our Saviour's Converfation could content the People.

But you are a knowing Perfon, and one whofe good Opinion I efteem ; I have therefore, here enclofed, fent you better Words of me drawn by the Company of *Dantzick*, and fent to the *Eaftland* Com-

pany

pany here in *London*, for whose Sake I have suffered these adverse Things, and am content to run them over again to do them Service ; such an Affection I do and shall ever bear to their Society.

Thus I have given, at your earnest Request, the sad Story of my Sufferings in my *Eastland* Voyage. What I have related, my unhappy Evidence hath found it too true ; yet I cannot tell you all, for there were many Dangers which I understood not. It was my Chance, a Year after our Arrival in *England*, to meet with one of my Fellow Sufferers, (*M. B.* the same Man that drew me out of the Sea) : he presently began to repeat our Shipwrecks, (for Men that have suffered together, love to talk of their Dangers past, and bemoan one another) ; he made Mention of several Streights, Extremities, Dangers, Deaths that we were in, which I do not remember; so that from his Mouth this Story seemed to be so prodigious a Romance, that few but those that felt it would believe. But I have not told you in this Relation, what others say, but what I myself have suffered; and though I was loth to begin, I am now as unwilling to make an End— *Omnibus hoc Vitium*—And therefore I shall tell you what further Adversity I have suffered by this barbarous Element of Water.

I will not tell you of my Venture over the Ears in foul Weather to the *Min* at *Dantzick* in the *Baltick* Seas, for that it may be was our Fear, and not Danger ; neither will I speak of my Passage from

Groningen to *Amsterdam*, when our Ship struck against the Sands; for there was Danger and no Fear; for the Ship got off as soon as we knew it was on: But I will acquaint you with what happened to me upon the River *Loire* in *France*, at *Orleans*.

I was advised by a *French* Gentleman, that had formerly travelled with my noble Lord the present Earl of *Westmorland*, * not to shoot the Bridge at *Bogency*, for the Bridge is made, not with a direct Line

* Whose Brother, Mr. *Robert Fane*, was in our Company.

over the River, but something obliquely, and so oftentimes dangerous to Passengers. When we came near the Bridge, I would have bribed the Batelier with a *Quart d'Escu*, to have set myself and two of my Company ashore on this Side the Bridge, and to have taken us in on the other Side. But the rest of the Company were unwilling to be hindered in their Passage, and we were almost as contented to venture. But this thin Deal Boat (which Boats are made on purpose to swim down the River to *Nants*, and return no more), came with a swift Stream towards a Corner of one of the Arches of the Bridge, which the Batelier seeing, cried *Nous sommes perdu, We are all lost.* He did strive, by putting his Rudder against the Bridge, to keep off the Blow, but brought it upon himself; for it beat him all along, and struck off one Board of our Boat, that we swam almost equal with the Stream, and the Water looked in upon us: One Touch more would have dashed

our

our Boat in Pieces, and so we had been all drowned in wholesale ; for there was no swimming out of a Crowd, when our Arms were pinioned together with sitting close to one another.   But by the Goodness of God we got through the Arch, and came safe to Shore.

There came presently to me two *Cordelier* Friars which were our Fellow Passengers ; the one bade me *thank him, for he made the biggest Cross* ; the other told me, *I must thank him, for he prayed unto the Blessed Virgin for us.*   I do remember, indeed, when we were in our greatest Danger, these Friars being struck with Fear, (which oftentimes killeth before Death), fell down in the Midst of the Boat ; one of them measured himself with his Finger, or, as he saith, crossed himself ; the other pulled out a small Image, I suppose of Wood, about the Bigness of my great Toe, and it seemed to me not much unlike ; to this he whispered something, which I believe it did not hear, no more than we. I thanked them both, one for his civil Ignorance, the other for his religious Folly.   I confess, in so sad and serious a Matter as drowning, I do not love such Puppet Piety, such mechanic and handicraft Devotion ; my Thanks must be addressed to God, the Author and Fountain of our Deliverance, after a more spiritual Manner.

After this, the same Year, it was my Business to return into *England.*   I came to *Calais* the Day after the Packet-boat was gone. Being weary of a charge-
able

able Town, and burning with a Desire of seeing my own Country again; having taken Advice by a Merchant, I ventured to Sea in a Shallop, which the Tide before came from *Dover*, and brought three *Almains* safe to *Calais*, without any Danger. The Example of their safe Arrival, was a sufficient Argument to persuade me to venture from thence to *Dover*. So at four of the Clock in the Morning with the Tide we went to Sea; but had not gone half a League, but there arose a great and mighty Wind, which did blow not only our Candle, but our Lanthorn out, I mean out of the Boat, so that we were fain to let our Boat drive till it was Day-light.

I offered the Seamen their Fare to carry us back again to *Calais*, which they did endeavour, but could not, the Wind was so strong; yet as fair a Wind as could blow out of the Sky to carry us to *Dover*; but we had too much of it. The Surfeit of good Things is as great an Evil as the Want of them, and a Man may be too well sometimes. How did *Neptune* play at Tennis with us poor Mortals, and how like Balls were we banded up and down by his furious Waves? Sometimes, as the Psalmist saith, *they mounted us up to Heaven*, as if they would have shewn us *Lazarus* in the Bosom of *Abraham*. Sometimes they carried us *down in the Deep*, as if we had been sent with more than a Drop of Water to cool the Tongue of *Dives*. By and by there arose a great Wind, which with the first Blast split our Sail in Pieces; so that we were forced to use our great Sail, which was too big for the Wind, as the

Win

Wind was for it, and therefore we made Ufe but of one half: the other lying on the Side of the Boat, made it run fo much on that Side, that I expected every Moment it fhould topple over. We could not go backward, and we were afraid to go forward. I laid myfelf down in the Boat from the View of thefe threatening Waves (as a dying Man is not willing to look the Executioner in the Face), expecting every Moment to be fwallowed by thofe roaring Lions of the Sea, who came upon us with open Mouths, ready to devour us. But God ftopped the Mouths of thofe Lions that they fhould not hurt us; and our fmall Veffel rode in Safety and Triumph upon the Head of the proudeft Wave. We could not fay to the Pilot, as the Emperor did, *Cæfarem vehis, &c.*—but there was in our Boat a noble Gentleman, both by Birth and Virtue, (the beft and trueft Nobility), and likewife another civil Perfon. Thefe Gentlemen had fo much Worth and Merit in them, that they fhould not need fear the Threatening of an infolent Wave, but might boldly fay unto the Sea, *Sea, do thy worft.* But I'll rather impute all to the Goodnefs of God, in whofe Hands we were, and therefore could not mifcarry.

By and by a Wave took us up, and fhewed us *England:* But it was with us as it was with *Mofes,* we might from this watry *Pifgah,* and Mountain of the Sea, behold the Land with our Eyes, which yet we muft not reach with our Feet. One of thefe Gentlemen called to me to rife, faying, I might fee *Dover* Caftle: But I thought it of no Concernment to me, and therefore lay ftill, but wifhing that we we were all Prifoners there, and fo I faid, little thinking that within a few Days after I fhould be apprehended and accufed for taking *Dover* Caftle, and kept fome Months Prifoner in *Kent*. God knows I would have taken it with all my Heart, but for a Refuge only; not as a Soldier taketh the Fort of his Enemy, but as a poor Weather-beaten Traveller taketh the Houfe of a Friend, as a Shelter.

At Weftonhangar, *my Lord* Strangford's *Houfe, which was then made a Prifon to fecure the honeft Gentlemen of that County.*

The Storm continued ftill, and the Wind blew very high, which though it put us in great Danger, yet being fair for us, blew us the fooner out of it.

For now we came near *Dover*, and therefore I defired my Friend to lie off my Legs, for now I thought I fhould have fome Ufe of them myfelf; which he did, and I rofe up and faw a World of People ftanding upon the Pier at *Dover*, holding up their Hands, not only in Admiration of our Dangers, but in Zeal and Devotion for our Deliverance. They directed us with their Hands which Way we had beft enter into *Dover*, and fo with a frefh Gale of God's Mercy, as well as with a fair Blaft of Wind, with full Sails, we, not without fome Danger in hitting the Pier, ran afhore.

I muft not omit one Mercy more, (which I forgot in my laft) becaufe it is fo near of Kin, and allied to my Deliverances at Sea, a Pre-deliverance, a Deliverance before-hand, an antidated Mercy.

For

For after I had spent some Time in *Pruffia*, and had seen *Elbing, Koninfberg*, which is the Univerfity; the *Pillow*, which is both the Key to the Country, and to the chief Revenue of the Marquis of *Brandenburg* in *Pruffia*, I returned to *Dartzick*, with a Refolution for *England*, having met with a fair Opportunity as well as a Wind; for there was one Captain *Sharper* of *New-Caftle*, a King's Man, (as they call thofe that love the King in that Country); this was Argument enough both to confirm and haften my Refolution.

This honeft Captain being ready fraught and bound for *England*, I prefently went to him to fpeak for my Paffage; he, like a kind Man, as well as a King's Man, promifed me a Paffage *gratis*. The *Englifh* Company at *Dantzick* underftanding fo much, the greater Part of them came to me, and importuned me to ftay with them, and continue my preaching with a Promife to anfwer my Pains with more than I could defire or deferve. This unexpected Kindnefs and Love, which is above the Price of any Reward upon Earth, foon melted me into a Compliance with their Defires, and fo without any Contract, I freely, as fuddenly, without farther Counfel, promifed to ftay with them.

But God was in it, who inclineth our Hearts to thofe Ways which lead to our Safety and Felicity, though we do not for the prefent fee the Secrets of his Love and Wifdom; for this good Man, Captain

tain *Skarper*, with all his Company *, fome few Days after they went to Sea, were caft away near the *Scund*, not a Man efcaped. Thus God fometimes preventeth his Children from falling into Evil, as well as to deliver them when fallen, that they may enjoy the Comforts of his Mercy without the Sorrow of fuffering.

To deliver his Children when they are fallen into any Calamity and Trouble, is an high and broad Expreffion of his Love and Kindnefs to them ; yet there is fome Bitternefs in the Evil, though there be Sweetnefs in the Deliverance: but now, by his Grace and Goodnefs, to efcape before we are taken, and to be delivered before we fuffer, is a Mercy we cannot hope for, a Bleffing we could not expect, and I am fure cannot exprefs.

---

* Amongft them were my two loving Friends, Mr. *Randolph Price*, eldeft Son to Mr. *Price* of *Efher*, a Gentleman of great Hopes, taken away in the Flower of his Youth and Virtue. I gave him the Holy and bleffed Sacrament before he went to Sea, which he received with much Devotion, which no Doubt was a prefent and heavenly Cordial to himfelf; fo I mention it as a dwelling and perpetual Comfort to his ftill weeping Friends. Captain *Vaughan*, who accompanied me in my firft Voyage into the *Eaft* Country.

It

It is like pure Wine without the Allay of Water;
a lively Picture, and true Portraiture of the State
of the Blessed in Heaven, who possess Fulness of
Joy without any Mixture of Sorrow, and Life
without the Shadow of Death. I hope I shall never forget this great Mercy; and it is the greater,
because it was bestowed upon one that had no
Title to it, but the free Grace and Goodness of
God.

After these great and many Dangers at Sea,
and as many and great Deliverances, I had
thought once to tell you what happened to me on
the Shore.

Pius habet infesta Terra timoris Aqua.

But I will conceal them from my Friends; for in
this sad Age every Man hath Sorrow enough of his
own, and is not at Leisure to consider the sad Condition of another from bemoaning and pitying
himself: I will therefore conclude, giving Glory to
God for his many Mercies, and my Thanks to
you for giving me an Opportunity to remember
them.

I hope you will pardon my plain Language; Sorrow is dull and black, and sad Stories ought not to
be presented in painted Words, and gaudy Expressions of Rhetorick. No Man mourneth in coloured
Taffety. What is wanting in Allegories, you have

in

in Reality : Truth needeth no Metaphors. You have
a true Relation of many fad Accidents and Afflic-
tions at Sea, by him who did undergo them, who
is,

       Sir,

        Your moſt affectionate

          Friend to ſerve you,

            Will. Johnson.

       F I N I S.